MW00340353

Grover E. Murray Studies in the American Southwest

BRUJERÍAS

Brujerías

STORIES OF WITCHCRAFT AND THE SUPERNATURAL IN THE AMERICAN SOUTHWEST AND BEYOND

English/Spanish

COLLECTED AND TRANSLATED BY
Nasario García

Texas Tech University Press

This book is typeset in Adobe Caslon, Rockwell Extra Condensed, and Monet. The paper used in this book meets the minimum requirements of ANSI/NISO Z39.48-1992 (R1997). ∞

Designed by David Timmons

Library of Congress Cataloging-in-Publication Data

Brujerías : stories of witchcraft and the supernatural in the American Southwest and beyond / collected and translated by Nasario García.
    p. cm. — (Grover E. Murray studies in the American Southwest)
   English and Spanish.
   Summary: "A collection of bilingual oral stories (Spanish/English) of witchcraft and the supernatural (including tales of sorcerers; witches; La Llorona, the vanishing hitchhiker; and apparitions) from old-timers and young people whose ages range from ninety-eight to seventeen and who live in Latin America and the American Southwest"—From the publisher.
   Includes bibliographical references and index.
   ISBN-13: 978-0-89672-607-9 (hardcover : alk. paper)
   ISBN-10: 0-89672-607-X (hardcover : alk. paper)
   1. Witchcraft—Southwestern States. 2. Supernatural. I. García, Nasario.
   BF1577.S68B78 2007
   398.20979'01—dc22
                              2006038872
Printed in the United States of America
07 08 09 10 11 12 13 14 15 / 9 8 7 6 5 4 3 2 1

Texas Tech University Press
Box 41037
Lubbock, Texas 79409-1037 USA
800.832.4042
ttup@ttu.edu
www.ttup.ttu.edu

A
Mi Amigo
John Nichols.

Por cuyas venas
Corre un sincero y profundo
Aprecio
De nuestra cultura hispana
Del Norte de Nuevo México.

To
My Friend
John Nichols.

Through whose veins
Flows a sincere and profound
Appreciation
For our Hispanic culture
Of Northern New Mexico.

"Stories have to be told or they die, and when they die, we can't remember who we are or why we're here."

Sue Monk Kidd, *The Secret Life of Bees*

Contents

TWO
Witches Disguised as Animals 51

Dos Brujas disfrazadas de animales 68

THREE
Lights, Sparks, and Balls of Fire 80

Tres *Luces, brasas, y bolas de lumbre*   *96*

FOUR
Bewitched and Bewildered   107

Cuatro *Embrujado y enyerbado*   *121*

FIVE
Superstitions, Mysteries, and the Bizarre   130

Cinco   *Supersticiones, misterios, y lo paranormal* *179*

SIX
Handsome, with Hoofs and Tail   219

Seis   Guapo, con pezuñas y cola   237

NINE
The Wailing Woman's Agony

Nueve   La agonía de La Llorona

Preface

As I look back at my formative years in the hinterland of New Mexico, I gain increased appreciation for the wealth of traditional folklore that I inherited from family members. Besides riddles, folk sayings, songs, religious hymns (*alaba[d]os*), and a host of other folkloric gems, there were wonderful stories. Little did I envision that the stories I learned from my grandparents and my parents, particularly the tales related to witchcraft, would one day serve as the inspiration for the present work, *Brujerías: Stories of Witchcraft and the Supernatural in the American Southwest and Beyond.*

Like other rural children I did not enjoy the luxury of a radio, a phonograph, or even books to read, and television was unheard of. Yet we had something richer, more endearing and enduring—the stories of our parents and grandparents. Storytelling at the dinner table in summertime or as families huddled around the potbelly stove in the cold winter months engaged children and grandchildren in an atmosphere of warmth and intimacy that today is etched only in memory.

Sharing stories about witchcraft and venturing into the world of magic and the supernatural provided entertainment at its best and prompted us youngsters to use our imagination in the world of make-believe. Some of us found the stories credible; others shrugged them off as far-fetched. Yet we were all spell-bound.

I was the eldest of eight siblings, four boys and four girls. During the summer months when I was between five and eight years old, my parents "farmed me out" to my maternal grandmother in Bernalillo, north of Albuquerque, where I was born. Her name was Lucinda, but I called her Cinda, a term of endearment we grandchildren used.

I look back at those wonderful summers with reverence. No aspect of my childhood looms brighter or more charged with joy than my grandmother's repertoire of riddles. Trying to guess the clue that would unlock the secret of the riddle was sometimes daunting. Yet, with broad hints and a little coaxing, I sometimes hit upon the key. The right response, coupled with what must have been an astonished look on my face, brought a sparkle to my grandmother's eyes that remains inscribed in my mind to this day.

But it was her stories, on a wide range of themes, that mesmerized me. Perhaps it was because my role was more passive. All I had to do was listen, anticipating the next line of suspense or the possible denouement. It was a different kind of guessing game, to be sure, and one that I delighted in. If I erred in predicting the ending I kept the "wrong" answer to myself, but I gleefully shared a correct one with Grandma Cinda. Of course, she was wise, like many grandmas in the small Latino communities of New Mexico, and though she never let me know, she undoubtedly guessed what I was up to.

Of all her tales, I most enjoyed the uncanny and the bizarre—despite the nightmares they sometimes caused. The most suspenseful and captivating were the stories about witches, witches disguised as owls, the devil, ghosts, enchanted places, bewitchment, and hidden treasure.

A favorite was "The Buried Treasure." Like so many tales I heard as a child, it contained a moral. The story concerned an enchanted place. A certain man in a nameless village defied repeated warnings from elders in the community and proceeded to display his bravado by climbing to the top of a long-dormant volcano whose "bottomless" pit purportedly was filled with gold. Many brave souls had tried before him, but they failed to reach the summit, driven away by deafening noises that rose from the volcano's abyss. Nevertheless, one night when the moon lit up the sky—it was taboo to attempt the climb during daylight—this man decided to undertake his quest. But the higher he climbed, the louder the horrific noises became. Shortly after the man returned from the volcano, he went insane. According to my grandma, his greed and curiosity had overcome his capacity for rational thinking. Part of the story's anticlimax rests on whether he was driven to madness by the horrendous noises or by his disappointment at discovering not a pit of gold, but hundreds, if not thousands, of rattlesnakes, which were the source of the endless clamor coming from the pit.

My paternal grandmother's stories about the supernatural in Ojo del Padre, where I was raised, were equally exciting. How can I forget the story about my grandparents heading home from a village dance in their horse-drawn wagon when a young colt kept tugging at the mare that formed part of the team of horses? The mystery arose, as my grandmother explained, because the mare did not have a colt, nor was there any newborn colt at the ranch or anywhere nearby.

Many such incidents related to supernatural phenomena occurred within my immediate family. My discovery of the lantern that burned

Movie set (foreground) for *The Hired Hand*, constructed among already-existing buildings in Cabezón, New Mexico, now a ghost town. Photo by Isabel A. Rodríguez, 1984.

brightly in my paternal grandfather's kitchen while he was visiting my grandmother at their second home in Albuquerque is another case in point. The noise in the middle of the night that came from the *nicho* (an indentation in the adobe wall where a *santo* is kept) where my parents kept their meager savings reveals yet another side of the supernatural to which I can personally attest.

And there are the narratives my father shared with me over the years. Some are based on his own personal encounters, such as the black-garbed lady who walked toward him over the lake in the dead of night as he watered his thirsty horse. Another was his run-in with a ghostly apparition in the middle of the road near the enchanted mesa in the village of San Luis, New Mexico, following a dance.

Some of my father's recollections of the eerie world of the supernatural appear in this collection. These are stories his grandparents passed on to his parents, and they to him. He in turn shared them with me. If we include my daughters in this chain of story sharing, some of the tales have now been in the family for at least five generations.

I hope that the preceding remarks serve as an inducement to the reader

Mission San Luis Rey de Francia, founded 1798 by Father Fermín Francisco de Lasuén, Oceanside, California. Photo by Nasario García, 2004.

to delve into the varied and complex world of the supernatural. Readers, regardless of age, gender, or cultural background, will likely be fascinated by *Brujerías*—and some will be spooked!

Santa Fe, New Mexico
2007

Acknowledgments

We authors look upon the publication of our work as a major accomplishment. From beginning to end, the substantial energy that is exerted in the process is also part of the enjoyment. But I am particularly mindful that the production of a book does not rest solely on the author's shoulders. On the contrary, seeing the fruits of one's labor in print is truly a team effort. The present work is no exception.

As I tip my hat to some special people, I do so with reverence and profound appreciation for the helping hand they have extended to me. Everyone gave not only of themselves but also of their valuable time.

What can I say about the informants? Without their stories, their interest, wisdom, and acute sense of humor, this volume would be nothing more than a skeleton. They have provided the flesh, fiber, and muscle that bind *Brujerías* together. From that standpoint, I am extremely happy, but in the same breath I must confess to a certain sadness knowing that many of them passed on before their contributions became public.

Personal contacts are very important in oral history projects as well, but when a project stretches across several states, these relationships are special. In California, Texas, and Arizona, I am indebted to several colleagues, friends, and new acquaintances for their generous support. They include: Mary Ellen García, University of Texas at San Antonio; Manny Griego, Glendale Community College, Phoenix; Richard Griswold del Castillo, San Diego State University; Gilberta Herguera Turner, Wincrest, Texas; Rolando Hinojosa Smith, University of Texas at Austin; César G. López, Scripps College, Claremont, California; Dori Miras-López, Upland, California; Rita Sánchez, Mesa City College at San Diego; Victoria J. Sánchez, Oceanside, California; Chuck Tatum, University of Arizona; and Richard V. Teschner, University of Texas at El Paso.

I also want to thank José Galarza and his wife, Eugenia Bello, for taking time to share pieces of the culture of their Mexican homeland. Closer to home, I wish to express my profound appreciation to Julia García-Jaramillo, whose assistance in the transcription of a number of the tape recordings was invaluable.

No book, however big or small, escapes the critical eye of competent professionals in the publishing industry. I am especially indebted to Judith Keeling, editor-in-chief at Texas Tech University Press, whose interest in my work says more than any words I could ever offer in return for her support.

BRUJERÍAS

Introduction

Today, with the increasing number of new arrivals from Mexico and other countries of Latin America, the American Southwest is replacing its old cultural face with a new one that is multifaceted, fascinating, and invigorating. We can no longer simply talk about a one- or three-dimensional cultural venue, namely, Spanish, Mexican, and Chicano, lodged in events of the past. Rather, the southwestern United States is spreading its geographic and cultural wings from Pueblo, Colorado, to San Juan, Argentina, and over all the countries in between.

Given the cultural transformation that is occurring in the Southwest, several factors were taken into account in putting together *Brujerías: Stories of Witchcraft and the Supernatural in the American Southwest and Beyond.* Of primary importance was to show, by virtue of the magical world of the supernatural, the long-standing richness of Latino culture and language in northern New Mexico and southern Colorado, even as the passage of time is silencing the voices of our old-timers. Sharing stories of witchcraft and the supernatural from informants of all ages across the Southwest with people of this region and the rest of the United States was of paramount importance. Equally central to this work was opening new doors—and widening older ones—of cultural awareness and understanding to all citizens, Latinos and non-Latinos alike, as newcomers from throughout the Hispanic world, including Spain, settle in the Southwest. And finally, it was essential to dramatize that we are experiencing a cultural and linguistic infusion that is destined to expand our knowledge of Latino culture beyond the geographic boundaries of the American Southwest.

An implicit if not underlying goal was also to reach out to monolingual parents and their children whose principal language is Spanish. Many of these young people already figure in the American educational system and are struggling to make the transition from their cultural world to a new one. The psychological and emotional impact that stems from switching cultural worlds can be lessened considerably through books like *Brujerías,* whose folkloric and linguistic elements relate to these individuals' own language and culture.

Even though my ancestry reaches across more than two hundred years in New Mexico, I know what it is like to have one foot in one world and the other in a new and seemingly strange world. Stating it differently, I am a product of bilingual-bicultural education, these two mutually inclusive worlds whose terminology was not in vogue nor perhaps even heard of when I started school in rural New Mexico. I see both the strengths and the drawbacks of this dichotomy; but in terms of a smooth cross-cultural transition, the positives far outweigh the negatives.

In some respects *Brujerías* is a microcosm of the current cultural metamorphosis taking place in the American Southwest and elsewhere. The idea of compiling a book of stories on witchcraft and the supernatural was born while I was working on *Old Las Vegas: Hispanic Memories from the New Mexico Meadowlands.* Initially, the focus fell only on northern New Mexico and southern Colorado, due to their deeply embedded Spanish-Mexican historical roots. But as the project took form, the geographical scope was broadened to include the other states in the traditional Southwest, that is to say, California, Texas, and Arizona.

Whether we discuss ghosts in the Clawson House in Bisbee, Arizona, ghostly apparitions in Anza-Borrego Desert State Park in California, the haunted house at Rapids Lodge in Grand Lake, Colorado, Juan Oso (half-man, half-bear) in Texas, or the goat-sucker (*chupacabra*) in Las Vegas, New Mexico, what emerges is an alluring puzzle of witchery and the supernatural.

I never envisaged collecting stories whose roots were fixed in the Iberian Peninsula and Latin America other than Mexico. Gathering tales in the Southwest that take place abroad but connect to similar stories in the Southwest occurred more by accident than by design. Like the contacts I established with old-timers in my native New Mexico, which came about by word of mouth, here, too, one informant led to another. Before long, I had a network of sorts that stretched from Santa Fe, New Mexico, westward to San Diego, California, and eastward to San Antonio, Texas. The people with whom I came in contact included friends, acquaintances, and colleagues at colleges, universities, and public schools. The end result was a core of informants whose birthplaces happened to be in Argentina, Colombia, Costa Rica, Spain, and Mexico, but who are now residents and citizens of the United States.

Some informants are common laborers; others are professionals. Most have kept their language and culture alive; a few—the younger ones born in this country—have let their mother tongue slip away, though they have maintained a semblance of cultural traits and practices within their families and communities. As I have commented elsewhere, language and culture go hand in hand, and once one goes—and language is usually the first casualty—then the loss of culture is not far behind.

Spanish is the umbilical cord that binds the Latino world together irrespective of national, regional, or local influences and nuances, which in most cases strengthen, not weaken, the language. Estimates of the number of Latinos who currently reside in this country range from 40 to 45 million. The overwhelming majority live in the American Southwest, mostly in Texas and California, but they can also be found in places like Yakima, Washington; DeKalb, Illinois; and Saginaw, Michigan.

The world of ghosts, magic, witches, and superstitions is just as fluid and far-reaching, as demonstrated by the stories collected in this volume. There is no segment of the population—rich or poor, educated or illiterate—that is not attracted to the mysteries of witchcraft. Its universal appeal binds neighborhoods, villages, and countries to one another, even when they are separated by thousands of miles. For example, hearing the story of the "Crying Baby" once popular in my native village (now a ghost town), and then listening to the same story recounted by María A. Mongalo, a Nicaraguan now living in Riverside, California, was absolutely remarkable. This type of connection proves that, through folklore, the past can merge with the present and present-day populations can connect with one another.

There are sixty-five contributors to *Brujerías*. Slightly more than half (thirty-six) are from New Mexico. Of the remaining states, California has the largest number (twelve), followed by Colorado with eight and Texas with six (two of the six from Texas are currently working in New Mexico). Arizona has the fewest informants (three); although a number of people in Tucson were contacted upon recommendation of then-existing informants, none responded.

With rare exception, I myself conducted the interviews, which began more than thirty years ago. Besides my paternal grandparents, with whom I spoke in 1968, other informants, including my father, were tape-recorded in the 1970s and thereafter. The most recent interviews took place during 2005 in Arizona, California, and Texas. Some stories were submitted in writing as recently as January and February of 2006.

Gilberta Herguera Turner, from Wincrest, Texas, conducted the interviews in San Antonio, guided by instructions as to the areas to be covered regarding witchcraft and the supernatural. The stories from San Diego, submitted in writing, came to me through personal contacts. The same is true of a handful of informants' stories that were sent to me via e-mail; these, for the most part, were from Albuquerque and Santa Fe.

The narrators range in age from ninety-eight—Isabel Romero—to the youngest, Eliel Germán Soriano, who was seventeen years old at the time of the interview. Although every age group from ninety to the teens is represented, the majority of informants are people who, early in my oral history projects, were selected because of their advanced age. The younger contributors are those who were interviewed in 2005 or whose stories were sent to me without consideration for the age of the storyteller.

The submissions by younger people prove, once again, that interest in witchcraft and the supernatural is alive and well among Latinos of all ages. This is true not only of those living in the Southwest, but also those in cities like Chicago, Atlanta, Miami, and Stillwater, Oklahoma.

With only a few exceptions, I personally transcribed the interviews. Similarly, I did any editing I deemed necessary and appropriate for readability and coherence. All but one of the storytellers are lay people and not professional raconteurs (the exception is Rolando Hinojosa Smith). Thus, it stands to reason that a certain of amount of editing, common in oral history or folklore projects, was essential. However, the spirit of the stories and the use of language were never compromised nor was the intent altered to the detriment of the overall story and its cultural impact.

The book is thematically divided into nine chapters, from "Witches, Spooks, and Ghostly Apparitions" to "The Wailing Woman's Agony." Each chapter begins with an introduction on its subject matter. The narrators appear in alphabetical order, followed by their place of residence at the time of the interview and their respective stories. Brief biographical sketches on the informants can be found at the end of the book.

Included as well are black-and-white photographs of some informants, who were either photographed years ago or whose photographs were donated recently. Other informants' reluctance or shyness kept them from providing photos.

More than thirty years have elapsed since I conducted my first interviews with old-timers. A neophyte in oral history back then, at times I found myself so captivated by their voice, diction, or conversation that, alas, I did not have the presence of mind to take their pictures. The interview with my paternal grandparents in 1968 is a case in point. Nevertheless, an image of their aging and wise faces at that moment in their cozy kitchen remains firmly embedded in my mind to this day, as is true of countless interviews with subsequent informants.

I have come to recognize that photographs complement oral history as well as give it life in the here and now. Therefore, a few pictures depicting historical context round out the book.

A glossary on the regional dialect of northern New Mexico and southern Colorado, and a comparison of these regional terms with modern or

Nuestra Señora de los Dolores Church. Four-foot-thick adobe walls, completed in 1857, Bernalillo, New Mexico. Photo by Nasario García, 2002.

Castañeda Hotel, famed Fred Harvey railroad hotel. Built in 1898, Las Vegas, New Mexico. Photo by Nasario García, 2001.

La Morada de Nuestra Señora de Dolores del Alto de Abiquiú, Abiquiú, New Mexico. Photo by Nasario García, 2002.

standard Spanish usage, is included to show some of the contrasts between these two linguistic areas. But it is especially intended to demonstrate how the lexicon of the old-timers, whose words and expressions have long formed part of the cultural and linguistic world of the Southwest, is fast disappearing from our midst.

As I reflect upon that afternoon in 1968 that I spent with my grandparents in Martíneztown in Albuquerque, where they owned a second home, I recall it as one of the most awe-inspiring and memorable experiences of my life. For an hour or so, they opened unsuspected doors to my heritage and enthralled me with cultural insights that are generally not heard in the classroom or gleaned from textbooks. While eminently praiseworthy, classroom learning cannot compare with the cultural nuts and bolts that my grandparents and my parents, as well as other old-timers, passed on to me. What I learned in my village and the similarities I later observed in Spanish villages while I was a student at the University of Granada could be added for good measure.

Brujerías: Stories of Witchcraft and the Supernatural in the American Southwest and Beyond demonstrates, too, how the magical world of witchcraft and the supernatural connects Spain and Latin America with North America in this magnificent historical geographic region called the Southwest. It is here that stories of sorcerers, fiendish witches, the Wailing Woman, evil spirits, and balls of fire come alive as the twenty-first century unfolds.

One

Witches, Spooks, and Ghostly Apparitions

Behind every dark shadow, a ghost is hiding.

INTRODUCTION

Witches and ghostly apparitions (*bultos/espantos*), whether real or imagined, have been part of Latino culture in the Southwest since the sixteenth century. When one compares neighboring hamlets within a prescribed region—New Mexico, for example—local stories regarding ghosts and witches are, curiously enough, very similar. Because of their magical power, these stories reach out and appear to be transcendental as they travel by word of mouth throughout the southwestern United States.

The narratives in this chapter not only show the fluid nature of the mystery and magic of witchcraft, but they also demonstrate a clear connection with other genres pertaining to sorcery in Western Europe. We know, for instance, that stories about the vanishing hitchhiker or the invisible man—personages who appear and disappear—are found in Europe and therefore are not exclusive to the Latino world. Accounts of the same story made their way across the Atlantic to places like Oceanside, California, and San Luis, New Mexico, as we learn from Francisco Argüelles and Damiano Romero, respectively. Other stories, like Sofía Durán's folktale of "Jujiyana," were also popular in Europe and became well known among old-timers in New Mexico and southern Colorado, though today they have been forgotten by more recent generations.

A tale with a different slant, which was collected in Upland, California, takes place on the outskirts of Bogotá, Colombia. According to Luis Esteban Reyes in "A Soul on the Plains," two men have words at a dance and kill each other, and a beautiful young woman dies as a result of an errant gunshot. The two men reappear like phantoms every year on the Plains with the girl peering over their shoulders, perhaps a rueful reminder of men's machismo and tendency toward senseless acts of violence.

Ghosts can appear in various shapes and colors—black and white are the most common, although yellow is sometimes mentioned also. Like some witches, ghosts may be lanky, and they often disguise their faces, which further adds to their mystery. But regardless of their form, color, or whatever disguise they may wear, if you come in contact with one of these wraithlike creatures, the experience with linger with you for years.

I can vividly recall one particularly scary episode from my childhood in rural New Mexico. I was about five or six years old at the time. Going home one late summer night from a village dance in a horse wagon with my parents, we came to a place called El Coruco, renowned among old-timers for its alleged enchantment (it seems people would occasionally hear rattling chains thereabouts). I was lying in the bed of the wagon half asleep when I suddenly heard my father say to my mother, *¡Mira, mira, un bulto en medio del camino!* (Look, look, a ghost in the middle of the road!). *¡Que bulto ni bulto! Son los tragos que tomates* (What ghosts! You had one drink too many).

Under normal circumstances, my mother would have invoked words like *¡Póngote las cruces!* (May God have mercy on you!), a protection against the apparition. That night, however, my mother was evidently angry because my father had spent all night drinking with his compadres instead of dancing with her. Once again I heard my father say, *Mira, de veras. Ahi está un bulto* (No, really. There's a ghost). I stood up and peeked between them. And sure enough! I saw a stark, thin, dark object, short in stature, that kept stepping backwards as the horses became frisky. They trotted forward until the *bulto* stepped to the side of the road and disappeared mysteriously into the dark, and we headed home. That night I could not sleep, thinking about what had happened. This was something real—not a figment of my imagination—because, after all, I had seen the apparition with my own eyes.

From that day forward, young as I was, I began to listen more attentively whenever the old folks talked about ghosts and witches. There are countless theories on witchcraft and perhaps many more stories regarding witches, purveyors of evil (see Chapter 4), commonly referred to as *malefica* because of their evil deeds.

In the stories told in my village of Guadalupe (Ojo del Padre) in the Río Puerco Valley of New Mexico, witches possessed many of the same attributes used to describe sorcerers everywhere, above all in Latino environments, both rural and urban. The fundamental trait of witches was, of course, their ability to punish an "enemy" by virtue of their supernatural or magical powers, which they exercised through herbal concoctions or fetishes.

But witches have also been known to appear inauspiciously at night to cause mischief or to deliver an emotional jolt to their victims (see Chapter 5). Seeing kerosene lamps or candles light up on their own, hearing dishes rattling in the kitchen cupboard, or a field mouse getting caught in a trap where there was no trap—these mysterious things occurred in people's houses after everyone had gone to bed.

In the past, witchery was a kind of double-edged threat, involving both the victims of witchcraft and the individuals suspected of being witches. Adults, both men and women, were the primary victims in the games witches played. If witches were believed to be active, the key questions asked centered on who would be the next victim and why. But if sorcery had become pervasive, the answers eluded them, feeding a kind of paranoia within a given village or region. The drama intensified further if a specific person was suspected of being a witch.

How did someone become a witch in a Latino community? In all the stories I have collected on witchcraft, there is only a passing reference to male witches. Virtually all witches have been female. As to how a woman became known as a witch, a simple description of certain events can further our understanding, though the process of becoming a witch, like anything in folklore, should not be considered firm and precise.

Traditionally, Latinas in enclaves of the Southwest, like those in Spain and Latin America, tended to marry at a young age and to marry men much older than themselves. For that reason many of them became widows early in their lives. Following Catholic tradition, widows remained in mourning for a full year. They dressed in black, especially in public, and attended church several days a week to pray for their departed husbands. Few of these young widows remarried, so they spent the rest of their lives in perpetual bereavement and clothed in black.

The older a woman got, the more idiosyncrasies she developed along the way. These could range from adopting a peculiar gait, growing a mustache, and being ill tempered, especially with children, to chewing snuff or smoking cigarettes, and developing yellow fingers as a result of the nicotine habit. Maybe she even talked to herself as she walked the streets alone and, in consequence, gave the impression of being feeble-minded. For better or worse—mostly the latter—once these features became part of her persona, she led a very solitary existence until she died.

In the meantime, she was subjected to scrutiny and ridicule because of suspicions that she engaged in sorcery. Prime examples are women like the one in "Dancing Up a Storm!" who could seemingly be in two places at once, as told by Juan Bautista Chacón, or the woman named Nieves, the

Shaffer Hotel with Pueblo art deco. Built in 1923 by Clem Shaffer in Mountainair, New Mexico. Photo by Nasario García, 1998.

Catholic church in Montezuma, New Mexico (north of Las Vegas). Photo by Nasario García, 1997.

Sangre de Cristo Catholic Church, built in 1886, San Luis, Colorado. Photo by Nasario García, 2003.

nanny in Marcos C. Durán's narrative of the same name who could make a broom dance. On the surface they appeared to be normal human beings, but in fact they were sorcerers who led normal lives by day and paranormal ones by night.

But people were not obsessed with witchcraft. In fact, some even made light of it, as in the humorous account by Samuel Córdova, in which Franque Márez plays the role of a jumping witch, and in the tale by Isabel Romero, in which Paulín, in "Head of the Witches," was shot down from a tree at night. Unfortunately for him, he had pretended to be an owl (see Chapter 2).

Whether we label these night creatures spooks, witches, or ghostly apparitions is of secondary importance. It is the fascination among people of all ages that has kept their legacy alive, and it will continue to survive so long as people are enthralled with the mystery of magic.

Francisco Argüelles

OCEANSIDE, CALIFORNIA

An Old Man

Francisco, his wife Isela, and some friends were parked in his truck about two or three o'clock in the morning across the street from an old cemetery on Mitchell Street in Oceanside, California. Suddenly an old man carrying a tool over his shoulder appeared out of nowhere. He was walking in the street. He then passed the truck on the passenger's side. He appeared to be very old. Francisco thought, "What is this old man doing here at this late hour?" As Francisco turned his head to keep an eye on the man as he passed the truck's window, the figure of the man was gone!

Francisco, Isela, and their friends got out of the truck to look for the man, but he was gone. All of the truck's occupants immediately left the area and went home. Scared!

Juan Bautista Chacón

PUEBLO, COLORADO

Dancing Up a Storm!

One time this little old man told me a story; well, not so much to me as to my mother. He was already quite elderly. This man also lived in the same direction where I used to travel back when he had this lady friend way up there in the sierra. He was very fond of going to dances and things like that, and like me, he liked liquor a lot. I believe this man headed for the plaza from there in the sierra around evening time, but it got dark on him. Well, as he headed for the plaza, it was already dark when he reached the first house. By the river or thereabouts a woman shouted at him. She said to him, "Guillermo, I'll wait for you at the dance."

Well, he didn't pay much attention. He spurred his horse and took off. Then he went to the bar and stayed there drinking there till way into the night. When he was on his way back, a popular dance was going on at a local schoolhouse, and this man was never afraid. He never got scared. He hitched up his horse and headed for the dust-raising dance being held there at the schoolhouse. He peered through one of the windows. There were lots of women he knew, including the woman he had left caring for his mother where he and his mother lived. When he got home, there was the woman with his mother.

Well, in a jiffy, in no time at all, she was at his home and she didn't even have a car or a horse or anything. The people never found out how she got home. But he saw her through the window at the dance. She was dancing up a storm! It was a whale of a dance!

That's what Mom used to say. I was very young, but she told me that story.

José D. Chávez

BERNALILLO, NEW MEXICO

A Flock of Women

The late Basilio Aragón arrived on horseback. He was short and used a long rope. He found a flock of women on top of a small mountain. They had a mountain that they used for a school and their tricks. They were all there; they had their little bonfire which was very, very dim. That's where they were having their party, all of the witches together, because they all belonged to the same group, to the same gathering.

Basilio got there and first thing he did was to throw the rope. He had it treated with *oshá* [a medicinal root to ward off witches]. He had his roping rope and he tossed it around the women, and they weren't able to escape because the oshá supposedly is one of the most powerful things around. If you grab a tiny root, chew it, and put it inside the corner of a handkerchief and tie a knot and toss it at a rattlesnake, you can put it to sleep. Then you go and grab it with your hands.

The same thing happens with witches. That's where the witches got the idea for all that herbal stuff. That's where you find it. If a weed is bad [toxic] and an animal eats it and dies or because of bad luck goes crazy, that's what the witches use to get their concoctions to work against people.

Many witches even had an altar because on [which] they put many things that they use against us. But they don't believe in that altar at all. Yes, it appears that they're sincere, but not so.

They're far removed from God, because they already sold their soul to the Devil. They no longer belong to God.

Samuel Córdova

ALBUQUERQUE (SAN JOSÉ), NEW MEXICO

A Witch Jumping Around

I was a witch once—me and another fellow. Look! Just to show you what lies are like. Whenever you're scared, you can see just about anything.

There was a young guy, Franque Márez, and we were great friends. And there was a religious wake up around a placed called Santa Clara. It was the Narciso Zamora family, and they were having a wake. The wake was on this side of the Río Puerco and on the other side, up on top of a hill, was an old house, nothing left but some walls. Well, that night while everyone was at the wake, Franque, who was quite a cutup, said to me, "You know what? I'm going to head that way, and I'm going to run on across the river on my horse while I carry the lantern. Keep an eye on me," he said to me, "so you can tell everybody."

There were a lot of cottonwood trees. Sure enough! He went over there, and here he is, riding his horse with the lantern, and when he'd go behind the cottonwood trees, it looked like a witch was jumping around. He kept it up until he got to that "old house." Then he'd go inside and come out and move the lantern back and forth. Then he'd go back in the house again.

Then I yelled to everybody, "Look!"

Everyone was scared out of their wits. "Wow! More witches!" And sure enough, they never figured out who it was.

So He Was a Witch!

Close to where I used to live, there lived a man, Mariano Aragón. And there was a very high mesa. There were lots of owls. You could hear those owls hooting. People claimed that it was old man Mariano! Word had it that he was a witch!

Well, this Franque Márez took the bait. "Let's go!" he said. "Now we'll scare the dickens out of these people."

And he lit a lantern. Well, this Franque Márez grabbed the lantern and we'd go up the hill, up the mesa; it was very steep. We'd go running up the hill with the lantern. From over in El Coruco, across the Río Puerco, people could see and hear the witch flying. "There goes old man Mariano, the witch, jumping up and down! Wow! What's going on? Look at that!"

So he was a witch! And then we'd run down the hill with the lantern all over again.

Marcos C. Durán

PUEBLO, COLORADO

This Woman Named Nieves

I had a sister and she had two boys, and she would leave them with this woman who took them for a stroll. This woman named Nieves. Story has it that the little boys finally told her that they no longer wanted to go for a walk because they were now a little older. That woman had a good time with them and she wanted my sister to leave them with her all the time, but my sister was very religious and she didn't want the boys to see the things the lady had in her home. They would tell my sister that this lady had lots of small rag dolls on the wall. She would say to the little boys, "No, don't worry, kids. I'm going to entertain you. Do you want me to dance?" And I understand she would sing and dance and all that sort of junk.

Then she could make the broom dance in the kitchen or anywhere because a long time ago we had mud huts. A lot of poor people had their small mud huts. That's what I've heard about this woman named Nieves.

Teodorita

I had a brother-in-law and I used to go to my sister's house, and one morning I went to their house. They had this lady. Her name was Teodorita, very fat and ugly. I was very much afraid of her. I was only a little boy, and no sooner I'd see her and I'd go around her. I don't know why I avoided her. I guess it's because people said she was a witch. In any case, one time I went inside my sister's house and she says to me, "Do you know what, dear brother?"

"What?," I said to her.

"Do you believe in witches?"

"Well, I don't know. I've never seen one."

"Well, I have. I have, dear brother."

"What happened?"

"Listen. Our Teodorita, I'm already tired of having her here. She sleeps here, eats breakfast and dinner here, and all of a sudden she disappears. And at night, well, she's nowhere in sight. She's just nowhere around. People say that that woman's a witch. But my husband told me that he's going to catch her because she's a witch. And we caught her!"

"How did you do that, dear sister? Are you lying to me so that I don't run around at night or what? You're not going to scare me with that sort of stuff."

"Not at all! If you want to believe me, fine. If not, that's okay, but it's the truth."

Then my brother-in-law said to me, "Yes. Don't be a skeptic. We already caught her."

"How did you do that?"

"Last night, as soon as she went to bed, I put pins in the shape of a cross, like so [makes a cross], above the door, on this door, that she used for going out, and I also put pins on the window. This morning she got up angry. Then they said to her, "Come, Doña Teodorita. Come eat breakfast, come eat breakfast. Well, what's wrong with you? Well, what's wrong with you? Are you mad?" because they figured something was wrong. "We treat you well."

"You treat me so well," she said, "that you have me tied down."

"But where? Are you tied to a rope or what? When did I ever tie you up?" said my brother-in-law.

"I don't need your breakfast. Nor do I ever want to come here again. If you wish for me to return, remove that junk that you have above the door."

"What junk are you talking about?" said he.

"Those pins that you have above the door to my bedroom, and remove the ones outside and I'll leave," and she took off like a boom, as if a bird had flown off.

I Used to Live with Witches!

I used to live with witches! Because as I say, I resided this side of the river, and the hordes of witches lived on the other side. And there were lots of witches, lots of them. Back then, well, I was quite a character. I used to drink lots of liquor; at that time, when I was young, there was still a lot of moonshine.

A cousin of mine and I were in a jolly old mood, and this woman sold moonshine, so we went to buy some from her. She had a husband. She treated us very well but she was a very ugly woman. Well, she wasn't so ugly, you see, but perhaps since the old witch was so mistreated. . . . You should have seen her flabby arms; why, they drooped down to the ground.

They looked like wings from all her sorcery, to be sure, huh? And that cousin of mine was also quite a cutup just like me and he said to me, "Listen here"—he was older than me—"now we'll go to this lady's house and we'll ask her to sell us some liquor."

And I said to him, "Man, that woman's a witch! You know very well that that woman's a witch."

"It doesn't matter. We'll pay her so she'll take us from here"—we were at Los Pinos, there where the witches' village is—"and we'll pay her to take us in the pumpkin that she has. She'll put you inside the pumpkin and away you go if that's what you want. We'll pay her to take us for a ride and we'll see if what people say is true."

My cousin had some sheep over at a wooded area called Tres Piedras and he wanted to go see them. Then I said to him, "Very well, I'm not afraid either. Let's go!"

Well, we took off, he and I did, but we were also very drunk, eager to cause mischief. We went there. Oh, we were very much the gentlemen with her, and then he goes and tells her, "Auntie, why don't you do us a favor?"

"What is it?"

"Look. It's been a long time, it's been a month since I've seen my flock, my sheep, and I and Machinto, well, we're cousins and we get along quite well. I'll pay you whatever you want just so you can put us in your pumpkin and take us over there," and she didn't get angry or anything.

"Well, I'll tell you what. Now's not the time for doing that, but if you wish, don't come on Fridays. Come some other day and I can take you, but I don't want you to say anything. And when I take you there, I also don't want you to say how you got there or anything like that because otherwise I won't bring you back. I'll disappear."

Well, my cousin and I went back to work at the ranch. After we got over our drunken spree and all, we started fielding alfalfa and the day got away from us so we didn't go. But that woman, as nearly as I can figure out, was a witch because her husband was very young for her. He was very young.

My cousin and I always ran around together so we used to get stone drunk and we'd say to her husband, "But Mr. Mejía, why are you so much younger? Why do you hang around with such demons? And she's so old!"

And he'd say, "Listen. You think she's ugly and all, but when I wish to go to a dance with her. She's the most beautiful woman you'll ever want to see. She's a woman who turns into the most beautiful . . ."

"But isn't she a witch?"

"I don't know. I hardly see her because she makes me sleep at night and during the day, and from then on I don't know. In other words—in any case we're already grown men—when I go to bed with her, she's the most beautiful woman I'll ever find. A beautiful girl!"

And he had cousins himself with very beautiful wives, and whenever they held dances on top of a hill near a pretty lagoon (we lived in a small valley below the hill, like in a canyon), that's where any number of people saw the witches holding their dances. I understand the dances were like those held at the plaza. By the time the dance ended, people claimed that sparks galore flew every which way the witches flew.

Sofía L. Durán

PUEBLO, COLORADO

Jujiyana

Many, many years ago there was a little old man and a little old lady who lived in a very dense forest. These old folks had a granddaughter whose name was Jujiyana, and the scuttlebutt has it that the grandparents were witches and they didn't wish for Jujiyana to know. But she would spy on them because very strange things went on in the house.

Well, time went on, and when Jujiyana was much older, a prince came to that forest. The Monte Negro was very, very dark, and for that reason it was called the Black Forest.

Then the prince ran into Jujiyana. She was out and about near the grandparents' house, and he ran into her. He fell madly in love with her and she with him. He told her that she had to go with him to his palace. She didn't want to go. She was afraid of the old folks, but finally, finally, he convinced her.

She knew something about witchcraft and so she knew that the old folks were going to follow her. At night when they went to bed, she already had a piece of wood ready and she put it in her bed, covered it, and along with it she placed a thimble. That's something she knew the old folks did. They would use a thimble full of water and by using a special kind of witchery they could make it talk.

When they fell asleep, Jujiyana took off, and the old lady, the grandmother, dreamt that she had been stolen. She woke up very frightened and said to her husband, "Old man, old man, they've stolen Jujiyana."

"Not so, you dumb old lady. Jujiyana is asleep," and the little old man said, "Jujiyana!"

And the thimble responded, "Sir, sir."

The old lady woke up about three times dreaming that someone had stolen Jujiyana, and by the third time the water in the thimble was getting low and the thimble said, "Sir, sir," in a very, very low voice. It seemed as if it (the thimble) was falling asleep. Then the old man said to his wife, "You dumb old woman! There you are shouting and shouting and won't let Jujiyana sleep. Let her sleep."

The old lady dreamt once again that someone had stolen Jujiyana. She got up and when she went to Jujiyana's bed, she found that the thimble was already dried up. It could no longer talk and the only thing left was a neatly wrapped piece of wood lying down. Then she grabbed the old man and pinched him a few times.

"Listen here, you stupid old fool. They've stolen Jujiyana. I told you so and you didn't pay any attention." But by her footprints they were able to follow her trail.

They followed her. Since they were witches they walked very fast, and one time they almost, almost caught up with her. Jujiyana went and created such a very thick forest that the old folks couldn't walk through. The trees were so close to one another that they couldn't find a path to cross. But since they were witches, they hopped on their broom, up they went, and they were able to get out of the forest.

One other time, they were almost about to catch Jujiyana. Then she went and tossed a brush at them. And this brush turned into a kind of weed with cobwebs on it. When the old folks started walking, it looked as though the weeds scared them. But finally, finally, because of their witchery, they grabbed their broom and they were able to fly off.

Once again, the third time, they were about to catch Jujiyana. This time she went and tossed a mirror at them. This mirror created a huge lake. She turned the prince into a swan and herself into another swan. When the old folks reached the lake, well, they didn't see either the prince or Jujiyana, but they saw the swans. The old lady was a lot wiser than the old man. She said to him, "Look! That swan is Jujiyana and that other one is the one who stole her. Now we'll catch them."

Just about the time that the old folks were about to catch them, they submerged under water. Then after getting tired of being under water, they stuck out their little necks. Then they went under water again. There the old folks waited, saying to Jujiyana, "Look, Jujiyana. We love you very much. Don't be ungrateful. Come with us."

But no, Jujiyana didn't answer them. All she did was to show her little neck. The old folks waited until they got tired. Then the old man said, "Very well. If Jujiyana doesn't love us, then we'll just leave."

They took off. Then she and the prince emerged from the lake and went to a tiny place. There were few people there. They came to a small house where they saw a light, and there was a lady alone there with her small son. The prince asked her whether, if he gave them wood, he could leave Jujiyana there until he came back for her, because she didn't have clothing to dress like a princess, and he wanted to bring her clothes to show them that she was a princess. He didn't want to take her on horseback. He wanted to bring a wagon. Well, he left her there.

Ah, I forgot. When the old folks got tired of waiting because Jujiyana refused to go with them, the old lady supposedly said to her, "Listen here, Jujiyana. I don't wish you any bad luck except that the prince is going to forget all about you."

Okay, as it turned out, the prince left and he got to his home and told the king and the queen that he had found a very beautiful girl. He informed them that she was going to be the princess and that he was going to bring her home so as to get married, with all the dignity worthy of a princess. He told his father and mother to get the carriages ready and for them to take along many servants and for his carriage to be decorated as beautifully as possible. Well, his parents did as he requested.

Next day they woke up the prince and told him that they were ready, because the prince wanted his father and mother to go with him to get Jujiyana. They told him once again that they were ready, and he responded this way, "What for?"

"Well, didn't you tell us that you had found a very pretty girl and that you were going to get married?"

"No. I never said such a thing. I haven't said any such thing. I haven't found a girl. I don't know any girl."

Why, he couldn't remember! He said that he hadn't said anything and that he didn't know any beautiful girl or anything. All he wanted to do was to sleep.

Jujiyana then got tired of waiting for the prince, and at the house where she was, the lady had a young heifer and a young mule. Jujiyana taught them to do a few tricks so people would come and pay to see them, to help the woman because she was a very nice lady. Well, Jujiyana taught them how to do many things: to dance, to do tricks, and that way they entertained the people very nicely.

Well, finally the servants told the prince, his attendants, about this beautiful girl who was in the lady's house who had the young heifer and a young mule, and that they performed lots of tricks. And they said to him, "Let's go, let's go so you can see how cute those young animals are."

And boy could they dance! Jujiyana would clap her hands and they danced. Finally, finally the prince was convinced to go. Jujiyana already knew that the prince was going to come and advised the young mule and heifer that whenever she said something to them, for them not to do anything on that night. Nothing, not a thing. She told the heifer to only raise an ear and she advised the mule to only raise a leg. Okay, nighttime came and lots of people went to see the heifer, Jujiyana, and the mule.

When the show started, Jujiyana would tell them what to do. She would clap her hands for them to dance, but they didn't do anything. All the heifer would do was to lower one of her ears and the mule raised one of her legs. Then the prince said to them, "¡*Halagos!* (Flattering words). Why don't you want to do anything? How come you say you do so many nice tricks? Now all the heifer does is to raise an ear and the mule lifts up a leg. Did Jujiyana tell you what to do?"

The same thing that happened to the prince, happened to Jujiyana—she couldn't remember anything. Then the prince opened his eyes. He woke up because he was always like in a daze. He was wide awake and saw her and said, "Jujiyana, it's you!"

"Yes, and you forgot all about me."

"No, I was ill," but it's because the little old lady had made him be that way.

"You stay here. Tomorrow for sure. I'll be back tomorrow, and my father and mother will come with me to welcome you," said the prince.

Next day very early in the morning the prince got up, woke up his servants, got the carriage ready, they fixed it up real nice, and the king and queen went with him to get Jujiyana and they took her to the palace. That's where they got married. Jujiyana became a princess and they lived happily thereafter . . . and that's the end of the story.

Juvenal A. Fuentes

OCEANSIDE, CALIFORNIA

A Truck Driver

A truck driver traveling at night, before reaching a bridge, saw a very beautiful girl who was in need of help. She told him that her car had broken down. He picked her up, gave her a ride, and they engaged in chit-chatting. He took her to her house and there dropped her off. The truck driver had liked the girl very much.

Time elapsed, and one day when he was traveling on that same road, he decided to go see her, but he was in for a big surprise. He asked her mother for her, and her mother told him that two years had gone by since her daughter died in an automobile accident. She had died on the exact spot where the truck driver had picked her up. That's where she died in an automobile accident while driving her car.

She told the truck driver that her car had broken down, but she was already dead.

Bencés Gabaldón

BERNALILLO, NEW MEXICO

A Witch Pumpkin

My mom used to tell us. . . . They [she and her husband] lived, I think, there in Algodones. What do they call that place? El Yeso. She used to say that El Yeso was the hub for those kinds of goings-on—male witches.

Once upon a time the people were clearing out the ditch. There where they were clearing out the ditch, they found a pumpkin. This pumpkin had some holes carved out. Those who were more knowledgeable, among them the old-timers, wanted to break up the pumpkin, but the male witches who were among them advocated just the opposite. "Leave it there," so they said. "That one was left there when the time came, that is, dawn," so said one of the witches. "They couldn't travel anymore because it was already daybreak," he continued. "They can only travel at night, so they left it here."

Well, they did not break up the pumpkin. They left it there. Next day when they went to look for the pumpkin, it was no longer there. The pumpkin was long gone. The witches had taken it with them.

See? The witches were capable of hopping on the pumpkin to get around. [Laughter] See there! You never know!

A Little Old Lady

I remember one other time, a brother and a cousin of mine were coming from Cabezón. And there was a little old lady; she had a little shack next to the road. That's where she lived. When they were headed home to San Luis from Cabezón, well, it must have been about ten o'clock at night, somewhere around there, twelve o'clock, something like that. When they were going by the little old lady's house, she was digging up the ashes where the trash was dumped. God knows what she was doing!

Then she disappeared, but they saw her for sure. That I know because they told me so.

Nasario P. García

LOS RANCHOS DE ALBURQUERQUE, NEW MEXICO

A Dark Ghost

One time in San Luis, well, I was on my way. It was already late, like three o'clock in the morning. I was on my way home, on foot, when we were working for the WPA [Works Progress Administration]. That night there had been one of those political meetings and everyone left, and so I took off walking.

By the time I reached the village of San Luis—that I went by it—I saw a dark object coming toward me, right down the middle of the road. Then I said to myself, "I guess some-one's coming." Before it got to where I was, like from here to the door, about four or five feet, I started to talk to it, but this, this ghost wouldn't answer. It was a black ghost and it crossed the road and went right into the sagebrush After it headed to the left in the direction of the sagebrush toward the mesa, then I got scared. Then that dark ghost took off that way, in the direction of the mesa, and I headed down the road for the campsite.

I spoke to it, but God knows who or what it was. And the only thing I saw, from head to toe, was a dark ghost, as nearly as I can recollect. It was already three o'clock in the morning!

23

Teodorita García-Ruelas

LOS RANCHOS DE ALBURQUERQUE, NEW MEXICO

That Woman Is a Witch

Well, I understand there were lights, falling lights. That sort of thing was seen and heard of more than anything in San Luis. And in Cabezón. More recently also in Salazar. But I was small at the time.

There where the Jaramillos lived, my *primo* [cousin] Celso's family, there in that nook a woman reputedly would come out and yell all the time. That's what people used to say, but I never got to see her.

In Salazar there was a woman; her name was Rita. She was very dark, quite dark, and she had eyes just like a cat. Green, green! That woman liked me a lot. I was already big, and she would grab me in her arms. And she was always going around saying that she liked me, that she liked me very much.

Mom would say to me: "That woman, that woman is a witch. I wish that woman wouldn't hold my little daughter." [Laughter]

But she was a woman who caught one's eye. She lived in Salazar.

Phoebe Martínez Struck

PUEBLO, COLORADO

She Wasn't a Pretty Woman

I remember when I was a little girl, about ten or eleven years old; I believe that's how old I was. My siblings were older, my sister and my brother, and what follows is about this woman who used to go clean house for Mom, because she was always in very delicate health. She was very sickly, and my dad brought this lady to clean house. This woman was even a cousin of ours—long ago everybody was a cousin—and she wasn't pretty.

She was quite a dark-complexioned woman. She wasn't a pretty woman, but she was very tidy. You could even eat off her floor. I maintain that it's because of being ugly that people claimed she was a witch.

But since children must be children, my brother and sister said, "Let's put a cross for her to see," because they had heard that by putting a cross, she would not be able to leave the house. They put two needles in the form of a cross. I recall that they placed the cross in a corner of the door. Anyway, it was already late when she came to the house, and then every once in a while after cleaning the house, she would say, "Well, I guess it's time for me to go." Then she'd start talking about something else. Then a bit later she would repeat again, "Well, I guess it's time for me to go," until my mom figured out what was happening and then signaled my brother and sister [with her eyes] to go to the kitchen.

"Remove those needles!" she says to them, and they did.

A little while later the woman said, "Very well. I'm leaving now, for sure. It's getting late. I have to go fix supper."

I maintain that perhaps it's because she was not pretty—since she was ugly—that I felt she was a witch.

Filimón Montoya

LAS VEGAS, NEW MEXICO

He Didn't See Its Face

Why, I remember one time when my son Rogelio was over where the old folks [Rogelio's grandparents] had like a pantry and it was during harvest time, and they had harvested lots of corn. They stored the corn without husking it, you see? So they either sent the boy off to husk the corn, or he was going on his own. He was no longer a young boy. It was nighttime, not very late though, but it was already dark. There was talk that someone had appeared before him, because he had told them that a person or a ghost had suddenly sprung upon him. But he didn't see its face because it was covered. He got so scared that he took off running and, at about the time he opened the door to the house, he failed to open it enough, and, whammo!—he hit himself on the sharp edge of the door as he was running. That's what he told the old folks.

They went outside to see what they could find, but they didn't see anything. And they had one of those kerosene lanterns that they used to hang from the ceiling a long time ago. That's the one story I can recall.

Why, of course people talked about witches this, witches that. I don't

know, but word has it that they would get together and leave in a horse carriage, and then it would turn out that the carriage and the horses would be found tied to a pine tree, but there were no people in the carriage. But nobody recalls having seen the witches fly off from the buggy, and they'd take off in different directions, to other places. People always said that they would head for Mora. I don't know why, but Mora was a kind of place where they fulfilled their wishes. Stories floated constantly about the fact that there were many witches in Mora.

Luis Esteban Reyes

UPLAND, CALIFORNIA

A Soul on the Plains

This story is about the legend of Santa Elena. There was a very beautiful girl who lived with her family. During the summer they would celebrate her birthday—the beautiful and precious *catira* [a redhead with bright eyes].

When friends and relatives arrived, they all began to join in the festivities. The father brought a musical group who played music from Los Llanos, the Plains, with the harp. Everybody was dancing and, as always, everyone was drinking, because drinking is a way of life on the Plains. A lot of liquor is consumed. They might have a fiesta that goes on for three, four, five days of any given week. And they celebrate the festivities by slaughtering an animal [such as a hog].

What happened at this fiesta is very common on the Plains, that is, for the musicians to begin with a song from the Plains, which consists of two people, two Plains people, who start improvising a song featuring a particular theme, and they started singing *versos* to the girl. Let's take the girl as an example. "I love you very much, dah, dah, dah, dah" [singing].

No sooner said than done, two men arrived on horseback as though they were the Devil. Right away they got down with their revolvers hoisted, but they took off their spurs and came in as if to fight. At a given moment they started arguing with some of the men from the Plains. There's a moment during which they insult each other, and continue to do so, but they were still bearing arms. And all of a sudden shots started going off and one of them hits the fifteen-year-old girl and kills her, and they die as well.

Thereafter the girl was buried, and everyone in her family died. Her grandparents died, and so did her parents. Everyone died from sadness after all that transpired.

I don't know for sure if it's in December or some other time during the year, but it is said that two men on horseback can always be seen on the Plains at that time, and the girl is right behind them, keeping them at bay.

Damiano Romero

LOS RANCHOS DE ALBURQUERQUE, NEW MEXICO

The Man Who Hitched a Ride

One time I was coming to Albuquerque, about eleven o'clock in the morning. I wasn't drunk or anything, and close to San Luis there was a man who asked me for a ride. I picked him up in my truck and I drove about one hundred yards, and then I asked him where he was headed and he didn't answer me. I saw him sitting right next to me. He didn't answer me. A little farther on I said to him, "Where do you want me to drop you off? Which home in San Luis?" because we were almost in San Luis.

He didn't answer me. All he did was look at me. That's all. When I came to the church, the back of the church, and the oratory, because the road is behind them, I turned around to say something to him, but he was no longer riding with me. He got off, but I don't know where. Without having stopped the

27

truck, without having opened the door! I don't know what it was! A spirit or what have you. And I've told many individuals about this, but they don't believe me.

Many things happened at one time or another to people over in the Río Puerco Valley, but since they were alone, nobody ever believed them. Or if individuals liked liquor a little, they'd say, "Why, he was drunk when he saw those things and all." But no, things that were a bit strange, which can't be proven, used to occur. Those things just happened.

Isabel Romero

LAS VEGAS, NEW MEXICO

A White Ghost

I remember once upon a time there was a place on the way to Las Vegas called Laguna de Piedra. There was always water in it, and many travelers who were headed this way to Las Vegas stopped at Laguna de Piedra. That's where they camped and slept. There was a very, very old house. It didn't have a roof or any doors. All that was standing were the walls. Some people used to say that right there in that old house a ghost would appear

and people took off running. Whenever there was a moon is when the ghost appeared in the house.

One time I was on my way from here in Las Vegas to Laguna de Piedra. I had heard stories about the house and a ghost appearing—a white ghost. I was on horseback, and yes, something was moving. "Now I'll go and find out for myself," I said to myself. "Let's see if a ghost appears in that house. I'll go see." And I dismounted. I had a pistol tied to the saddle horn. And I said to myself, "No. I better get on my horse because if I go on foot and I fire at the ghost, the horse will get startled and he'll leave me on foot. No. I'd better ride." I got on the horse and I took off. I took off.

28

As it turned out, it was a Hereford that was inside the old house. Whenever the cow moved, the moon would shine on it. But I said to myself, "No. I'll talk to the ghost and if it doesn't answer me, I'll shoot it." It's a good thing that it moved, which is when I saw that it was a cow. If not, I would have killed it. [Laughter]

Fright. Fright begets many, many things.

Andrés Sánchez Rojas

PHOENIX, ARIZONA

Peeing on the Father's Feet

It was approximately twelve o'clock at night. Back then I was interested in this one girl. Right next to my house she and some other girls had just returned from a large city where they were studying. The place where we lived was a small town. It's called Camalote, because it's a kind of plant that was plentiful around there. That's why it's called Camalote. So as it is, these girls came home to see their parents and I liked one of them.

Well, I fell asleep in a hammock that was parallel to the corral. From their house long about twelve o'clock midnight I heard a noise coming from the side of the house where the girls were. Among the persons who were there, as I said before, was the girl that I was interested in courting, another sister of hers, a younger girl, and the mother and father. I was curious as to what was going on in that home because there was a fence made of these palms.

Afterwards I went and took a peek, and I saw the father standing and the daughters circled around him. Beginning with the youngest girl, they formed a circle around the father. He was in the middle. I don't know what all they were saying, but they had something in their hands. I don't know exactly what, because you couldn't see. It was nighttime and dark, but also circled around the father was the mother. There were the daughters all peeing on the father's feet.

As to why they were doing that, I just don't know, because I never asked them. But I never again got close to the girl that I was interested in courting.

A Brother-in-Law's Brother

Many years ago my family lived in a place called Redundadero. Then the brother of a brother-in-law of mine came to where we were. It was a place all by itself. He was afraid to get back to the village because he had to walk quite a distance. He had to pass by a peak and he asked me if I would accompany him. "Why don't I go with you to the road and then you can take off from there? Take the rifle in case you run into an animal or something."

Well, I took off. I got to the road and left him there. Then he headed down the road. He was on horseback. I heard the horse galloping like mad, without doubt practically exhausting the horse because of how scared he was. I had to walk back to where we were at our little ranch.

I returned to where I was staying with my brother. I heard an animal. I don't know what kind of an animal it was because I didn't see it—why lie?—but it sounded like a bark and a growl, both at the same time. It was very dark. I frankly didn't see it, but my brother and my brother-in-law also heard it. When I got to where they were, I couldn't talk. I had grown up around that place of ours and I had never heard any such thing, but it was blood curdling. We never saw it, whatever it was. If we had seen it, we wouldn't have been able to speak at all.

Ernesto Struck

PUEBLO, COLORADO

Don't Run!

There was a woman who was a witch. One time during Holy Week this boy and I went to nose around. When we were on our way back home, after we passed by the small school, there was this woman sitting in the middle of the road. What I did was to go around one side and the boy who was with me went round the other. When we had passed by her, the woman said to me, "Don't run! I'm Ssshh."

Well, we flew out of there! That boy lost his shoes. How he was able to get home is beyond me. That guy took off without any shoes. When he got home, he told his father, and he got up and they came back but didn't find the woman. They just didn't find her.

That's the only thing, the only personal experience I've had with ghosts. The woman was dressed in black and was sitting down in the middle of the road, so when we went past her, she said, "Don't run! I'm Ssshh." [Laughter]

Eileen Dolores Treviño Villarreal

SAN ANTONIO, TEXAS

A Redheaded Boy

One other time my mother told me about a boy—this happened before I was born—that would come out from the garage to the yard of my house around three o'clock, a redheaded boy about six or seven years old. He would come out from the garage, and the first time they saw him they thought that he was one of my brothers. But no, they were all inside the house. My mother saw him, one of mother's sisters-in-law saw him, as well as one of my mother's cousins. He would appear on top of a pecan tree that we had in the yard, but then he would disappear. They saw him come out of the garage three different times, and he would walk and then stop to look at our house and then disappear. They never found out who the boy was.

The house is on Harbor Street and Brazos, in downtown San Antonio, not even two miles from here, the Navarro House, right in the center of San Antonio.

My feeling is that it wasn't so much the house as it was the land. That house was constructed in 1938, and so my thinking is that before that house was built, there was something else there, or a battle had taken place there. There's a lot, a lot of history in San Antonio; that is why there's lots of places about ghosts and scary things.

Alfredo Ulibarrí

LAS VEGAS, NEW MEXICO

A White Ghost

One time, I was already married and living here in Las Vegas, I was going after my wife, because she worked over at the sanatorium. I left the kids here at home because they were small. I was going after her about eleven-thirty at night. You know where the tortilla factory is, right there is where I was driving my truck. Then you know the road down below the tortilla factory, a little ways beyond, there are some houses down the hill. That's

where I saw a real white ghost moving, like a
white bed sheet. I had a spotlight on my truck,
and I shined it right in its face, and it went up
the hill one more time where the tortilla factory is located. Where the tortilla factory used
to be, there was a bar right at the corner that
cuts into another short street farther on up.
That's where it stopped, behind a telephone
post, and it waved at me to come on while I
kept shining the spotlight on it to see what it
was.

That's the only ghost I've ever seen.

Brujas, espantos, y bultos

···

Detrás de cada sombra oscura, hay un
bulto oculto.

Francisco Argüelles

OCEANSIDE, CALIFORNIA

Un viejo

Francisco, su esposa Isela, and unos amigos, estaban estacionados en su camioneta como a las dos o tres de la mañana al otro lado de la calle de un cementerio viejo en la Calle Mitchell en Oceanside, California. De repente un viejo que cargaba una herramienta al hombro saltó quién sabe de dónde. Iba andando por la calle. Luego pasó por la camioneta al lado del pasajero. Se veía muy viejo el hombre. Francisco pensó, "¿Qué andará haciendo este hombre por aquí a estas horas?" Al voltear la cabeza Francisco para ver a dónde iba el hombre después de pasar al lado de la ventana de la camioneta, ¡la figura del hombre había desaparecido!

Francisco, Isela, and sus amigos se bajaron de la camioneta para buscar al hombre, pero se había ido. Todos se marcharon en seguida y se fueron a casa. ¡Espantados todos!

Juan Bautista Chacón

PUEBLO, COLORADO

¡Un bailazo ahí!

Una vez me platicó a mí un viejito, pos no a mí, a mamá. Era ya algo viejo. Este hombre vivía tamién en el mismo rumbo donde iba yo en ese tiempo cuando tenía él esta señora tan arriba pallá. Él era muy amante de andar en los bailes y cosas semejantes y tamién a él, como a mí, le gustaba muncho el licor. Creo que este hombre salió pa la plaza de ahi como ya de la tarde y se le hizo oscuro. Güeno, cuando iba pal rumbo de la plaza, pos iba oscuro ya pa llegar a la primera casa. Por ahi en el río le gritó una mujer. Es que le dijo,

—Guillermo, allá te espero en el baile.

Pos él no puso atención. Le dio al caballo y se jue. Logo se jue pallá pa la cantina y estuvo quién sabe hasta qué horas de la noche tomando él. Cuando ya venía patrás, en una escuela estaba un baile muy mentao, y este hombre nunca tenía miedo. Nunca le daba horror. Vino y amarró el caballo y se jue ahi onde estaba el bailazo ese. Por una ventana empezó a mirar pa dentro. Ahi andaban munchas mujeres que conocía él, y la mujer esta de que platicaba él, ésa la había dejao allá con su mamá donde vivían ellos. Cuando llegó a la casa, ahi estaba la mujer.

Pos uno por otro, en dos por tres, se jue ella a la plaza y no tenía ni carro ni caballo ni nada. No supo la gente cómo se jue a casa. Pero él la vio por la ventana en el baile. Es que andaba bailando como parlamentario. ¡Un bailazo ahí!

Eso es lo que platicaba mamá. Güeno, yo estaba muy joven, pero ella platicó esa historia.

José D. Chávez

BERNALILLO, NEW MEXICO

Un rebaño de mujeres

El dijunto Basilio Aragón llegó a caballo. Era chiquito él y usaba un cabestro muy largo. Halló a todo un rebaño de mujeres arriba de un montecito. Tenían un monte ellas como su escuela y sus triques. Estaban todas ahi; tenían una lumbrita muy, muy opaca. Ahi estaban teniendo su *party* ellas, todas las brujas juntas porque todas pertenecían al mismo grupo, a la misma unión.

Llegó Basilio y lo que hizo jue que tiró el cabestro primero. Él lo traiba curado con agua de oshá. Llevaba el cabestro de lazar y lo tiró en redondo de ellas y no se pudieron salir porque la oshá reclaman que es una de las cosas más fuertes que hay. Si usté agarra una raicita chiquita, la masca y la pone en la esquina de un paño y la amarra y se la pone a una vívora, la hace dormirse. Luego va uno y la 'garra con la mano.

Es la misma cosa que las brujas. De ahi sacaban las brujas los materiales de cosas de hierbas. Ahi es onde está la cosa de las hierbas. Si una hierba es mala y se la come un animal y se muere o de mala suerte agarra un enojo, eso es lo que usan ellas, las brujas, pa poner sus materiales a trabajar en la gente.

Munchas brujas tenían hasta un altar porque ellas ahi en su altar pueden tener munchas cosas que ellas están usando en contra de nosotros porque ellas no creyen y en ese altar del todo. Sí parece que están muy de veras, pero no.

Están muy lejos de Dios porque ya ellas le vendieron su alma al Diablo. Ya ellas no pertenecen a Dios.

Samuel Córdova

ALBUQUERQUE (SAN JOSÉ), NEW MEXICO

Una bruja brincando

¡Yo jui brujo una vez! Yo y otro muchacho. ¡Mira! Pa que veigas como son las mentiras. Uno se espanta y mira cualesquier cosa espantao.

Había un muchacho, Franque Márez, y éranos muy amigos. Y había un velorio aá arriba, onde le dicen Santa Clara. Esa gente se llamaba Narciso Zamora, y tenían velorio. Estaba el velorio de este lao del Río Puerco y pal otro, aá en una loma, estaba una casa vieja, unas paderes nomás. Pues en la noche estaban aá en el velorio y dijo este Franque, era muy atroz,

—¿Sabes qué? Voy ir por allá, a correr en el caballo por de aquel lao del río con el farol. Me cuidas tú—me dijo—, pa que le avises a la gente.

Y había munchos álamos. ¡Pues sí! Se jue pallá y ahi viene él corriendo con el farol, y, cuando pasaba los álamos, parecía que venía brincando una bruja. Pues ahi se jue, hasta que llegó a la casa esa "vieja." Y loo se metió aá dentro y loo salía ajuera y hacía con el farol asina, par un lao y par otro. Loo se metía otra vez.

Y loo le avisé yo a la gente,

—¡Miren!

Todos espantaos. "¡Uh! ¡Más brujos!" Y no, no se dieron cuenta quién era.

¡Que es que era brujo!

Cerca onde yo vivía, vivía un hombre, Mariano Aragón. Y estaba una mesa muy alta. Ahi había munchos tecolotes. Se oían llorar los tecolotes esos. ¡Que es que era el señor Mariano! ¡Que es que era brujo!

Pues se destajo la puntada este Franque Márez.

—¡Amos!—dijo—. Ora los espantamos más.

Y prendió un farol. Pues, este Franque agarró el farol y subíanos la loma, la mesa. Era muy alta. Subíanos corriendo con el farol. De aá del Coruco, del otro lao del Río Puerco, alcanzaba la gente a ver y a oyer el brujo volar. "¡Aá va el señor Mariano, el brujo, brincando! ¡Hijo! ¿Qué hay? ¡Híjola!"

¡Que es que era brujo! Y loo bajábanos corriendo otra vez con el farol.

Marcos C. Durán

PUEBLO, COLORADO

Esta mujer Nieves

Yo tenía una hermana, y tenía dos muchachos ella, y los dejaba con esta mujer que los llevaba a paseo. Esta mujer Nieves. El cuento es de que al fin le dijieron los muchitos que ya no querían ir a paseo porque ya estaban grandecitos. Tenía güen tiempo con ellos esa mujer y quería que mi hermana los dejara con ella todo el tiempo, pero mi hermana era muy católica y no quería que ellos vieran esas cosas de la mujer. Ellos le dijían a mi hermana que esta mujer tenía munchos monitos en la pader. Ella les dicía a los muchitos,

—No, no tengan cuidao hijitos. Yo los voy a entretener. ¿Quieren que baile?—y es que les cantaba y bailaba y todo ese garrero.

Y luego la escoba la hacía bailar en la cocina o onde estuviera porque ya antes teníanos jacales. Muncha gente muy pobre tenía sus jacalitos. Eso es lo que yo ha [he] oido de esta mujer Nieves.

Teodorita

Tenía un cuñao yo y iba a cas' 'e la hermanita, y una mañana jui a su casa. Tenían ellos una mujer. Ésta se llamaba Teodorita, muy gorda y muy fiera. Le tenía yo muncho miedo. Yo ya estaba mediano y nomás la vía y le rodiaba. No sé por qué le juía. Creo que porque dicían qu'era bruja. El cuento es que una vez entré yo en la casa de mi hermanita y dice ella,

—¿Sabes qué hermanito?

—¿Qué?—le dije.

—¿Crees tú que hay brujas?

—Pos, yo no sé. Yo no ha visto niuna.

—Pos, yo sí sé. Yo sí sé, hermanito.

—¿Qué pasó?

—Mira. Ya nuestra Teodorita, ya estoy cansada de tenela aquí. Ella duerme aquí, almuerza y come aquí, y de repente se desparece. Y de noche, pos, no se sabe d'ella, y nomás no se sabe d'ella. Esa mujer dicen que es bruja. Pero me dijo mi esposo que él la iba 'garrar que es que porque era bruja. ¡Y la 'garramos!

—¿Cómo hermanita? ¿Me estás mintiendo tú tamién a mí pa que yo no ande de noche o qué? A mí no me metes miedo con eso.

—¡No! Si quieres creilo, bien. Si no, déjalo, pero es verdá.

Antonces me dijo mi cuñao,

—Sí. No seigas incrédulo. Ya la 'garramos.

—¿Cómo?

—Anoche. Nomás se acostó y puse alfileres en cruces ansina en la puerta, en la puerta esta, en lo que salía, y tamién en la ventana. Esta mañana amaneció enojada. Antonces ellos le dijían,

—Ande, doña Teodorita. Venga almorzar, venga almorzar. ¿Pos qué tiene? ¿Pos qué tiene? ¿Pos qué está enojada?—pos ellos figuraron algo—. Nosotros la tratamos bien.

—Me tratan tan bien—dijo ella—, que me tienen amarrada.

—¿Pos ónde? ¿Tiene cabresto o qué? ¿Cuándo la'marré yo?—dijo mi cuñao.

—No quiero su almuerzo. Ni quiero volver aquí. Si quieren que vuelva, quítenme esas mugres que tienen ahi en la puerta.

—¿Qué mugres tenemos?—le dijo él.

—Esos alfileres que tienen ahi en la puerta de mi cuarto donde duermo, y quiten los de ajuera y yo me salgo—, y es que salió como un pum, como si hubiera salido un pájaro.

¡Yo vivía entre las brujas!

¡Yo vivía entre las brujas! Porque ya le digo, yo vivía d' este lao del río y el brujerío vivía de aquel lao. Y había munchas, munchas brujas. En ese tiempo, pos, yo era horroroso. Yo tomaba muncho licor, pero en ese tiempo había mula tavía cuando yo estaba más joven.

Andábanos yo y un primo mío poco alegres, y esta mujer vendía mula, y juimos a comprale mula a ella. Tenía un esposo ella. Ella nos trató muy bien pero era una mujer muy fea. Pos, no era tan fea, ves, pero quizás como era tan maltratada la bruja . . . ya tenía los brazos que le colgaban al suelo, oiga. Parecían alas de lo que andaba en brujerías, seguro, ¿eh? Y aquel primo mío era muy atroz tamién como yo, y me dijo,

—Mira—era mayor que yo—, ora vamos a case de la señora esta y le dijemos que nos venda licor.

Y le dije yo,

—¡Pos esa mujer es bruja, hombre! Tú sabes muy bien que esa mujer es bruja.

—No importa. Le pagamos porque nos lleve de aquí—estábanos en Los Pinos, ahi en la placita esa de las brujas—, y le pagamos que nos lleve aquí en su calabaza que tiene. Lo echan a uno ahi en la calabaza y lo llevan si quiere uno. Le pagamos porque nos lleve de paseo y vamos a ver si es cierto lo que dice la gente.

Mi primo tenía borregas y quería irlas a ver allá en el monte en Tres Piedras. Luego le dije yo,

—Bueno, pues, yo no tengo miedo tampoco. ¡Vamos!

Pues, nos juimos yo y él, pero nojotros íbanos tamién muy envolaos, calientes de hacer mal. Juimos allá. O muy gente nojotros con ella, y logo va él y le dijo,

—Tía, ¿por qué no nos hace un favor con nojotros?

—¿Qué?

—Mire. Ya hace muncho, ya tengo un mes que no voy a ver mi ganao, mis borregas, y yo y Machinto, pos, semos primos y nos queremos muy bien. Yo le pago lo que usté quiera porque nos ponga en su calabaza y nos lleve allá—y ella no se 'nojó ni nada.

—Pos, yo les diré. Hora no es el día que puedo hacelo, pero si ustedes quieren, no vengan los viernes. Vengan otro día y yo puedo llevalos, pero no quiero yo que vayan a mentar nada. Y allá onde los lleve yo, tampoco no quiero que vayan a decir cómo jueron ni nada d'eso, porque no los traigo. Me desparezco.

No, pos nos juimos a trabajar en el rancho nojotros. Ya después que se nos quitó todo el pensamiento eso de borrachada y borrachera, nos pusimos alzar alfalfa y se nos pasó el día y ya no juimos. Pero esa señora sí, me figuro yo, era bruja porque tamién su marido era muy joven par' ella. Era muy joven.

Yo y mi primo siempre andábanos muy juntos y nos poníanos parrandas y le dijíanos,

—Pero señor Mejía, ¿por qué usté está tan joven? ¿Por qué anda con mal demonios, hombre? ¡Ella tan vieja!

Y dicía él,

—Miren. Ustedes creen que la ven fiera y todo, esa mujer, pero cuando yo quiero salir con ella a un baile qu' esté, es la muchacha más linda que ustedes pueden ver. Es una mujer que se hace tan bonita . . .

—¿Pos qué no es ella bruja?

—No sé. Yo no la veigo, pero me hace dormir en la noche y el día y ahi allá no sé. En otras palabras—al cabo que ya semos hombres—cuando me acuesto con ella, es la mujer más linda que yo puedo encontrar. ¡Bonita muchacha!

Y tenía primos él muy ricos con sus mujeres muy bonitas, y cuando ellos hacían bailes en una loma onde había una lagunita muy bonita (nojotros vivíanos en un vallecito abajo de una loma, como en un cañón), ahi hallaban varios a las brujas en esos bailes. Que es que eran unos bailes como los que hacían en la plaza. Cuando ya se acababa el baile, decía la gente que era un braserío que por ondequiera volaban las brujas.

Sofía L. Durán

PUEBLO, COLORADO

Jujiyana

Pues hace munchos, muchos años que estaban un viejito y una viejita que vivían en un monte muy espeso. Estos viejitos tenían una nieta que se llamaba Jujiyana, y ellos se decía que eran brujos y no querían que Jujiyana supiera. Pero ella los ispiaba porque vía que pasaban cosas muy extrañas en la casa. Logo ella se escondía y ispiaba a los viejitos y vía sus triques que ellos hacían de brujerías.

Pues, con el tiempo, ahi cuando Jujiyana estaba muy grande, llegó un príncipe a ese monte. El Monte Negro era muy oscuro, muy oscuro, y por eso le decían el Monte Negro.

Luego se topó el príncipe con Jujiyana. Andaba ella en los alrededores donde estaba la casita de los abuelitos y se encontró él con ella. La quería muncho él y también ella lo quería a él. Le dijo él que se tenía que ir con él al palacio. Ella no quería irse. Les tenía miedo a los viejitos, pero al fin, al fin, la consiguió.

Ella sabía algo de brujerías y sabía que los viejitos la iban a seguir. En la noche cuando se acostaron los viejitos, ya ella tenía un leño listo y lo puso en la cama y lo cubrió y puso un dedal. Eso sabía que hacían los viejitos. Ponían un dedal con agua y era cierta clas de brujería que lo hacían hablar.

Güeno, pues, cuando se durmieron ellos, se jue Jujiyana, y la viejita soñó que se la habían robao. Recordó muy asustaa y le dijo a su marido,

—Viejo, viejo, se llevaron a la Jujiyana.

—No, vieja tonta. La Jujiyana está dormida—, y es que decía el viejito,

—¡Jujiyana!—y el dedal respondía.

—Señor. Señor.

Como tres veces recordó la viejita que soñaba que se habían robao a la Jujiyana y a la tercer vez se estaba acabando l'agua del dedal y decía el dedal,

—Señor, señor—ya muy, muy bajita la voz. Parecía que se estaba durmiendo. Logo le dijo el viejo a su esposa,

—¡Oh vieja tonta! Tú estás grito y grito y no dejas durmir a la Jujiyana. Déjala que duerma.

Güeno, pues, volvió a soñar la viejita que se habían robao a Jujiyana. Se levantó y cuando jue a la cama de la Jujiyana halló ya el dedal seco. Ya no hablaba y no estaba más de un leño acostao muy envuelto y cobijao. Logo ya lo agarró al viejo y le dio sus pellizcos.

—Mira viejo tonto. Se robaron a la Jujiyana. Yo te lo dicía y no hicites aprecio,—pero por los rastros la siguieron.

Fueron y la siguieron. Como eran brujos caminaron muy aprisa, y una de las veces ya, ya la alcanzaban. Vino Jujiyana y formó un monte muy espeso que no podían caminar los viejitos. Los álamos estaban tan cerca uno de otro que casi no hallaban por ónde pasar ellos. Pero como eran brujos, se subían en su escoba, se subían parriba, y se salían del monte.

Ya otra vez ya, ya la alcanzaban a la Jujiyana. Antonces vino y les tiró un cepillo ella. Y este cepillo formó una clas de yerba como con telarañas. Cuando los viejitos caminaban parecía que los asustaban las yerbas. Pero al fin, al fin otra vez con sus brujerías volvieron agarrar su escoba y hasta que al fin subieron.

Ya otra vez, la tercer vez, ya mero la alcanzaban a la Jujiyana. Ya esta vez vino ella y les tiró un espejo. Este espejo formó una laguna muy grandota. Ella volvió al príncipe una ansara y ella mesma otra ansara. Cuando llegaron los viejitos a la laguna, pues, no vieron ni al príncipe ni a la Jujiyana, pero vieron las ansaras. La viejita era más sabia que el viejito. Es que le dijo ella,

—¡Mira! Ésa es la Jujiyana y esa otra es el que se la llevó. Ora los pescamos.

Nomás era que los viejitos los iban a pescar se zambulleron pa l'agua. Logo cuando ya se cansaron d'estar bajo l'agua, asomaron el pescuecito. Logo se volvían a zambullir. Ahi se estuvieron los viejitos y le dicían a Jujiyana,

—Mira, Jujiyana. Nosotros te queremos muncho. No seas ingrata. Vámonos con nosotros.

Pero no, la Jujiyana no les respondió. Nomás asomaba el pescuecito. Ahi estuvieron los pobres viejitos hasta que se cansaron. Logo dijo el viejito, —Güeno. Si la Jujiyana no nos quiere, pues nos iremos.

Se jueron ellos. Antonces salieron ella y el príncipe de la laguna y se jueron a un lugarcito muy pequeño. Había poquita gente. Llegaron a una casita que vieron luz y estaba una mujer solita con su hijito. Les pregunta el príncipe que si les daba leña les dejaba a la Jujiyana hasta que viniera por ella porque la Jujiyana no traiba ropa para vestirse como princesa, y él quería traile ropa pa enseñarles que era la princesa. No quería llevarla a caballo. Quería traer un carruaje. Pues la dejó ahi.

Ah, se me había olvidao. Cuando los viejitos ya se cansaron que no quiso la Jujiyana irse con ellos, es que le dijo la viejita,

—Mira, Jujiyana. No te deseo más mal ni te echo más maldición que el príncipe te va olvidar.

Güeno, pues se jue el príncipe y llegó allá a su casa y le platicó al rey y a la reina que había hallao una muchacha muy hermosa. Que ella iba ser la princesa y que la iba llevar pa casarse con toda la dignidad de una princesa. Les dijo a su papá y a su mamá que alistaran carruajes y que llevaran munchos mozos y que el carruaje de él lo adornaran lo más bonito que pudieran. Pues, hicieron sus padres lo que él mandó.

Otro día de mañana lo recordaron al príncipe y le dijieron que ya estaban listos porque el príncipe quería que jueran su papá y su mamá con él por la Jujiyana. Le dijieron otra vez que ya estaban listos y es que les dijo él,

—¿Pa qué?

—¿Pues que no nos dijites que habías hallao una muchacha muy linda y que te ibas a casar?

—No. Yo no he dicho nada. Yo no he dicho nada. No he hallao una muchacha. Yo no conozco una muchacha.

¡Pues no se acordó! Dijo que no había dicho nada y que no sabía de ninguna muchacha hermosa ni nada. No quería más de estar durmiendo.

Luego esta Jujiyana ya se cansó de esperar al príncipe, y en la casa onde ella estaba, la mujer tenía una becerrita y tenía una mulita. Las enseñó Jujiyana hacer algunas gracias pa llamar gente que les pagaran pa que le ayudaran a la mujer onde ella estaba porque era muy güena mujer. Pues, Jujiyana las enseñó hacer munchas cosas: a bailar, a hacer gracias y así divertían muy bonito a la gente.

Güeno, al fin le contaron los mozos al príncipe, sus atendientes, de la muchacha esta tan linda que estaba ahi en esa casita de la mujer que tenía la becerrita y la mulita, y que hacían tantos triques. Y le dijieron,

—Vamos, vamos pa que veas que curioso esos animalitos.

¡Y qué si sabían bailar! Les craquiaban Jujiyana las manos y ellos bailaban. Al fin, al fin lo consiguieron al príncipe que juera. Ya ella sabía que el príncipe iba ir y aconsejó a la mulita y a la becerrita que cuando ella les dijiera algo que no hicieran ellos nada esa noche. Que nada, nada. A la becerrita le dijo que nomás agachara una orejita y a la mulita le aconsejó que nomás alzara una patita. Güeno, se llegó la noche y jue muncha gente a ver a la becerrita, a la Jujiyana, y a la mulita.

Cuando comenzó la función, les dicía la Jujiyana qué hicieran. Les craquiaba pa que bailaran, pero no hacían nada. Nomás la becerrita agachaba una orejita y la mulita nomás alzaba una patita. Logo es que les dijo el príncipe a la becerrilla y a la mula,

—¡Halagos! ¿Por qué no quieren hacer nada? ¿Pos cómo dicen ustedes que hacen tanto triques, que tan bonitos? Hora nomás agacha la oreja la becerra y la mula alza el piecito. ¿Pos qué les dijo la Jujiyana ya?

Lo mismo que al príncipe, se le olvidó a la Jujiyana. Antonces abrió los ojos el príncipe. Que recordó porque siempre estaba como durmido. Recordó bien y la vio y dijo,

—Jujiyana, ¡tú eres!

—Sí, y tú me has olvidao.

—No, estaba enfermo—, pero era que la viejita lo tenía así, la abuela. — Aquí te estás. Mañana sí. Mañana vengo y vienen mi padre y mi madre a recibirte—dijo el príncipe.

Otro día sí muy de mañana se levantó el príncipe, recordó a sus criados, alistaron el carruaje, lo compusieron muy hermoso, jueron el rey y la reina con él por la Jujiyana y la llevaron allá al palacio. Pues allá se casaron. La Jujiyana jue la princesa y vivieron muy contentos . . . y ahi se acabó.

Juvenal A. Fuentes

OCEANSIDE, CALIFORNIA

Un troquero

Un troquero manejando en la noche, antes de llegar a un puente, se le apareció una muchacha muy bonita que necesitaba ayuda. Le dijo ella que su carro se le había descompuesto. Él la levantó, o le dio un *ride*, y fueron platicando. Él la llevó a su casa de ella y la dejó allí. Al troquero le había gustado la muchacha mucho.

Pasó el tiempo, y un día que iba él por ese mesmo camino, decidió ir a verla, pero se llevó una sorpresa. Le preguntó a su mamá por ella, y su mamá le dijo que habían pasado dos años que su hija había muerto en un acidente. Ella había muerto en el mesmo lugar que la levantó el troquero. Allí se murió en un acidente en su carro.

La muchacha le dijo al troquero que su carro estaba descompuesto, pero ya ella estaba muerta.

Bencés Gabaldón

BERNALILLO, NEW MEXICO

Una calabaza bruja

Mamá nos platicaba . . . porque ellos [ella y su esposo] vivían pienso que en los Algodones, ahi. ¿Cómo le dicen? El Yeso. Platicaba ella que ahi era la mapa d' esa clase de negocios—de brujos.

En una vez es que estaban sacando la 'cequia la gente. Güeno. Ahi onde estaban sacando la 'cequia jallaron una calabaza. Esta calabaza tenía unos ajueros. Güeno. Los que sabían más, quizás de los viejitos que sabían más, querían quebrar la calabaza, y los brujitos que andaban entre ellos, es que dijieron que no. "Déjenla ahi," es que dijieron. "Ésa la dejaron ahi cuando ya se llegó el tiempo, la madrugada," es que dijo uno. "No pudieron caminar más porque ya estaba la madrugada," continuó. "Solamente en la noche pueden caminar, y la dejaron ahi la calabaza."

Pues, no la quebraron. La dejaron ahi. Otro día que jueron ya no estaba la calabaza, Ya no amaneció la calabaza ahi. Se la habían llevao los brujos.

¿Ves? Los brujos se subían en la calabaza pa andar [Risas]. ¡Pa que veigas tú! ¡Si no sabe uno!

Una viejita

Una vez me acuerdo yo y un hermano y un primo mío venían de Cabezón. Y había una viejita; tenía un cuartito en un lao del camino. Ahi vivía. Cuando venían ellos de allá del Cabezón pacá pa San Luis, pus ya serían como las diez de la noche, por ahi una cosa asina, las doce, una cosa asina. Cuando iban pasando, ahi estaba aquella viejita nomás escarbando la ceniza onde tiraba la basura uno. ¡Sepa Dios!

Loo de ahi ya no se vido, pero la vieron ellos. Eso sí lo sé yo porque ellos me platicaron.

Nasario P. García

LOS RANCHOS DE ALBURQUERQUE,
NEW MEXICO

Un bulto

Una vez en San Luis, pus, yo iba ya tarde, como a las tres de la mañana. Yo iba a casa a pie, cuando estábanos trabajando ahi en el WPA. Esa noche había una de estas juntas de políticos y se jueron todos, y de ahi me jui yo a pie.

Cuando yo ya llegué, que pasé la plaza de San Luis, vide venir un bulto negro. Aquí viene todo el camino. Antonces yo dije, "¿Quizás viene alguien?" Antes de llegar a donde estaba yo, como de aquí allá a la puerta, a unos cuatro, cinco pies, empecé a hablale, pero este, este bulto no contestaba nada. Era un bulto negro y cruzó el camino y entró asina a un chamisal. Después que ya se dirigió asina a la izquierda, al chamisal, pal rumbo de la mesa, pues antonces me dio miedo a mí. Luego se apartó pallá el bulto ese, pal rumbo de la mesa, y yo me jui todo el camino pal campo.

Yo le hablé, pero sabrás Dios quién, quién sería. Y todo lo que vide jue nomás un bulto negro de arriba hasta 'bajo, que me acuerdo yo. ¡Ya eran las tres de la mañana!

Teodorita García-Ruelas

LOS RANCHOS DE ALBURQUERQUE, NEW MEXICO

Esa mujer es bruja

Pues, es que había luces, que caían luces. Eso se vido y se anunciaba más lo que era en San Luis. Y el Cabezón. Ora en un tiempo en Salazar tamién. Pero yo estaba mediana.

En onde vivían los Jaramillos, la familia d' en primo Celso, ahi en ese rincón es que salía y llamaba una mujer too el tiempo. Platicaban, pero yo no la llegué a ver.

En Salazar estaba una mujer; se llamaba Rita. Era muy trigueña, bien trigueña, y tenía los ojos bien como un gato. ¡Verdes, verdes! Esa señora me quería muncho. Yo ya estaba grande, y me agarraba en brazos a mí. Y siempre andaba ella que me quería a mí, muy bien esta mujer.

Me decía mamá: "No, esa mujer, esa mujer es bruja. Esa mujer no quisiera que agarrara a mi hijita." [Risas]

Pero sí era una mujer que llamaba la atención a ti en vela. Vivía en Salazar.

Phoebe Martínez Struck

PUEBLO, COLORADO

No era mujer bonita

Yo me acuerdo cuando estaba muchacha, como diez o once años yo creo que tenía. Mis hermanos eran mayores, mi hermana y mi hermano, y lo que sigue esque esta mujer iba a limpiale la casa a mi mamá, porque ella siempre fue muy débil. Era muy enferma, y mi papá la trujo pa que limpiara la casa. Esta mujer era hasta prima de nosotros—más antes todos se decían primos—y no era mujer bonita.

Era una mujer algo trigueña. No era mujer bonita, pero era muy limpia. Podía uno hasta comer del suelo d'ella. Digo yo que es acaso que porque sería fea, que dicían que era bruja.

Pero como los muchachos son muchachos, mi hermano y mi hermana dijieron, "Vamos a ponele una cruz," porque habían oido ellos decir que poniéndole una cruz que no podía salir la bruja de la casa. Le pusieron dos abujas en una cruz. Me acuerdo yo que le pusieron la cruz en la esquina de la puerta. De todos modos, ya estaba tarde cuando vino a la casa, y loo cada rato, después de limpiar la casa, dicía,

—Pos, yo creo que ya me voy—luego se ponía a platicar otra cosa.

Luego al rato dicía otra vez,

—Pos, yo creo que ya me voy—hasta que mi mamá supo qué estaba pasando y les hizo un genio antonces a mis hermanos, que se jueran a la cocina.

—¡Quiten esas abujas!—les dice, y jueron y las quitaron.

Al rato dijo la mujer,

—Güeno. Es cierto que ahora sí me voy. Ya está tarde. Tengo que ir hacer de cenar.

Yo digo que falta que porque no era bonita, como era fea, yo sintía que era bruja.

Filimón Montoya

LAS VEGAS, NEW MEXICO

No le vido el rostro

Pues una vez estaa mi hijo Rogelio allá onde tenían los viejitos [los abuelos de Rogelio] como una dispensa, y era durante el tiempo de la cosecha, y habían cosechao muncho maíz. Lo metieron, sin deshojalo, ¿ve? Despacharon al muchacho a deshojar el maíz, o iba el muchacho a deshojar el maíz. Ya no estaa muy joven. Era en la nochi, no tan nochi, pero ya escuro. Luego dicían que se le había aparecido alguien allá, que él les había dicho que se le había aparecido un individuo o un bulto. Pero no le vido el rostro porque traiba el rostro tapao. Le metió tanto miedo, que salió juyendo y, al tiempo que abrió la puerta, no la abrió suficiente, y pégase en la cabeza con el filo de la puerta onde iba juyendo. Eso jue lo que les platicó a los viejitos.

Jueron allá fuera a ver qué había, pero no vieron naa. Y tenían un farol d'esos de aceite que usaban en esos tiempos colgao en el techo. Eso es lo único que me recuerdo yo.

Oh, sí platicaban de brujas pallá y brujas pacá. Yo no sé, isque se juntaban y salían en un bogue, y loo resultaba el bogue, los caballos amarraos en un árbol, en un pino, y no había gente en el bogue. Pero naiden se acuerda de habelas visto que volaban del bogue y iban a otras partes, a otros lugares. Siempre platicaban que vinían pacá pa Mora. Yo no sé, Mora era su desquite. Siempre estaan con el cuento que en Mora había munchas brujas.

Luis Esteban Reyes
UPLAND, CALIFORNIA

El ánima llanera

Esta historia es de la leyenda de Santa Elena. Había una muchacha muy linda que vivía con su familia. En la época de verano ellos celebraban el cumpleaños de ella—esa linda y preciosa catira [mujer rubia con ojos claros].

Cuando llegaron los amigos y los familiares todos empezaron a celebrar la fiesta. El papá trajo un conjunto de música llanera, con su arpa. Estaban todos bailando y siempre estaban todos tomando, porque se toma mucho en Los Llanos. Se consume mucho licor. Se hace fiesta tres, cuatro, cinco días de la semana. Y celebran las fiestas matando ganado.

Entonces lo que pasó en esta fiesta es muy común en el Llano, es que comiencen los músicos con la copla llanera, que son dos personas, dos llaneros, que empiezan a improvisar coplas sobre un tema, y empezaron a cantarle a la muchacha versos llaneros. "Yo te quiero mucho, da, da, da, da" [cantando].

Pronto llegaron dos hombres a caballo como si fueran el diablo. De pronto se bajaron con los revólveres, pero se quitaron las espuelas, y entraron como a pelear. En cierto momento comenzaron a disputar con los llaneros. Hay un momento en que se ofenden, y siguen ofendiéndose uno con el otro, pero los dos hombres todavía tenían sus armas. Y cuando de repente empiezan a pegar tiros y le pegan un tiro a la muchacha de quince años y la matan, y también se matan ellos dos.

Después de esto enterraron a la muchacha, y se murió todo el mundo de su familia. Se murieron los abuelitos, y se murieron los papás también. Se murió todo el mundo de tristeza de que eso pasara.

No sé exacto si es en diciembre o en alguna otra época del año, pero dicen que siempre se ven por el Llano a dos jinetes cabalgando y a la niña que va detrás ahuyentándolos.

Damiano Romero

LOS RANCHOS DE ALBURQUERQUE, NEW MEXICO

El hombre que pidió pasaje

En una vez venía pacá pa Alburquerque, y venía yo como las once del día. No venía tomao ni nada, y ahi cerca de San Luis estaba un hombre y me pidió pasaje. Lo subí en la troca y caminé como unas cien yardas y loo le pregunté que si par ónde iba y no me respondió. Lo vide yo que iba juntra mí. No me respondió. Poquito más aá le dije,

—¿Ónde quiere llegar? ¿A qué casa en San Luis?—porque ya estaba San Luis.

No me respondió. Nomás me vía, era todo. Cuando enfrenté la iglesia, lo de atrás de la iglesia y el oratorio, voltié a hablale y ya no iba conmigo. Se apeó pero no sé ónde se apearía. Sin haber parao la troca yo; sin abrir la puerta. ¡No sé qué sería! Un espíritu o qué sería. Y hay munchos que les he platicao pero no me creyen.

Munchas cosas llegaron a pasar a gente aá en el Río Puerco; como eran solos pues no les creiban. O ya si eran medio borrachos, "el señor, pues no, andaba borracho cuando las vido y too." Pero no, pasaban algunas cosas poco extrañas que no puede uno probar pero pasaban. Pasaban las cosas.

Isabel Romero

LAS VEGAS, NEW MEXICO

Un bulto blanco

Yo me acuerdo una vez que había un lugar que iba pacá pa Las Vegas que le dicen la Laguna de Piedra. Había agua siempre ahi, y munchos pasajeros que vinían pacá paraban en la Laguna de Piedra. Ahi campaban y dormían. Pus había una casa, muy, muy vieja. No tenía techo ni puertas. Estaan las paderes. Algunas personas dicían que ahi en esa casa vieja, que se aparecía un bulto y salían juyendo [la gente]. Cuando había luna es que se aparecía un bulto en la casa.

Una vez iba yo de aquí de Las Vegas paá pa la Laguna de Piedra. Yo oía el cuento de la casa, que se aparecía un bulto, un bulto blanco. Yo iba de a caballo, y sí, se vía moverse allá. "Ora voy y me desengaño," dije yo. "A ver si se aparece un bulto ahi en esa casa. Voy a ver." Y me apié del caballo. Llevaa la pistola en la cabeza de la silla amarraa alderedor. Y yo dije, "No. Vale más subirme en el caballo porque si voy a pie y le tiro al bulto, se espanta el caballo y me deja a pie. No. Vale más subirme." Me subí en el caballo y me jui. Me jui.

Pus era una vaca bole que estaba adentro la casa vieja. Cuando se movía, pues, le pegaba la luna. Pero yo dije,

—No. Le hablo al bulto y si no me responde, le doy un balazo.

De güena suerte que se movió, y vide qu'era una vaca, que si no la mato. [Risas]

El miedo. El miedo hace munchas, munchas cosas.

Andrés Sánchez Rojas

PHOENIX, ARIZONA

Urinando los pies del papá

Eran aproximadamente como las doce de la noche. Entonces yo andaba en pues de una muchachilla. En seguida de mi casa, ella y otras muchachas acababan de llegar de donde estaban estudiando en una ciudad grande. Donde nosotros vivíamos era un pueblo chiquito. Se llama Camalote, porque es un tipo de planta o mata que hay muncho. Por eso se llama Camalote. Entonces estas muchachas llegaron a visitar a sus papás, y a mí me gustaba una de ellas.

Pues, yo me quedé dormido en una hamaca. De la casa de ellas como a las doce de la noche escuché ruido yo, del lado donde estaban las muchachas. Entre las personas que estaban allí, como dije antes, estaba la muchacha que yo pretendía, otra hermana de ella, una niña más chica, la mamá y el papá. A mí me llamó la curiosidad de qué era lo que estaba pasando en aquella casa porque había una cerca de palapa.

Después fui y me asomé y miré al papá parado y a las hijas alrededor de él. De la más chiquita empezaron el círculo, circulando al papá, y el papá estaba en medio. No sé qué tanto decían, con algo en las manos. No sé exactamente qué era porque no se miraba. Estaba oscuro y era de noche, pero alrededor del papá también estaba la mamá. Allí estaban las hijas urinando los pies del papá.

Por qué estaban haciendo eso, yo no sé, porque yo nunca les pregunté. Pero yo nunca más me le acerqué a la muchacha que yo pretendía.

El hermano de un cuñado

Hace muchos años mi familia vivía en un lugar que se llama el Redundadero. Luego un hermano de un cuñado mío llegó allá donde estábamos nosotros. Era un lugar solo. Él tenía miedo regresarse al pueblo solo porque era bastante lo que tenía que caminar. Tenía que caminar por un cerro y me dijo a mí que si por qué no lo acompañaba. "¿Por qué no te dejo hasta la carretera? ya de donde te puedes ir. Llévate la escopeta por si te encuentras un animal o algo."

Pues ya fui yo. Ya llegué a la carretera y lo dejé a él allí. Luego él agarró la carretera. Él iba a caballo. Yo oí el galope del caballo donde él se fue seguramente que prácticamente matándolo al pobre animal del miedo que llevaba. Yo me tuve que regresar caminando patrás allá donde estábamos en el ranchito.

Ya me regresé patrás donde estaba yo con mi hermano. Escuché un animal. No sé qué tipo de animal sería porque no lo miré, para qué le voy a echar mentiras, pero era entre un oído como que ladraba y como que gruñía a la vez. Estaba muy escuro. Prácticamente yo no lo miré, pero mi hermano y mi cuñado, ellos también lo oyeron. Cuando yo llegué donde estaban ellos, no pude ya hablar. Yo tenía mucho tiempo allá en ese lugar nuestro y nunca había escuchao eso, pero era algo escalofriante. Nosotros no lo miramos. Si lo hubiéramos mirao, hubiéramos estado todos mudos.

Ernesto Struck

PUEBLO, COLORADO

¡No juygan!

Había una señora que era bruja. Una vez andáanos pa tiempo santo y juimos yo y este muchacho a novelar. Cuando veníamos de allá pa casa, que pasamos la escuelita, estaba una señora sentada en medio del camino. Lo que hice yo jue traspasar por acá por un lao y el muchacho que andaa conmigo por este otro lao. Cuando ya pasamos, me dijo la señora,

—¡No juygan! Yo soy Ssshh.

¡Pos a volar! Ese muchacho perdió las chinelas. Cómo, cómo se iría pa la casa, *I don't know*. Siguió ese muchacho sin chinelas. Cuando llegó a la casa, le dijo a su papá, y se levantó su papá y vinieron y no hallaron a la señora. No la hallaron.

Ésa es la única cosa que a mí me pasó d' esperencia con bultos. Estaba vestida la señora de negro y estaba sentada en el mero camino, y cuando pasamos por el lao, dijo,

—¡No juygan! Yo soy Ssshh. [Risas]

Eileen Dolores Treviño Villarreal

SAN ANTONIO, TEXAS

Un niño pelirrojo

Me platicó mamá otra vez de un niño—esto también ocurrió antes de que yo naciera—que salía del garaje al solar de mi casa a eso de las 3 de la tarde, un niño pelirrojo de unos 6 o 7 años. Salía del garaje y cuando la primera vez que lo vieron pensaban que era uno de mis hermanos pero no, todos estaban adentro. Lo vio mi mamá, lo vio una cuñada de mi mamá, y una prima de mi madre. Se aparecía en un árbol de nuez que teníamos en el solar pero se desaparecía. Lo vieron tres diferentes veces que salía del garaje y caminaba y se paraba viendo así a la casa de nosotros y se desaparecía. Nunca supieron quién era el niño.

La casa está por la Calle Harbor y Brazos, en el centro de San Antonio, ni a dos millas de aquí, la Casa Navarro, que está en el mismito centro de San Antonio.

Mi pensamiento es que no era tanto la casa sino que era el terreno. Esa casa se construyó el 1938, y entonces mi pensamiento es de que antes de que construyeran esa casa era otro sitio, o había habido una batalla. Hay mucha, mucha historia en San Antonio, por eso aquí hay muchos lugares de fantasmas y espanto.

Alfredo Ulibarrí

LAS VEGAS, NEW MEXICO

Un bulto blanco

Una vez, ya estaa casao y vivía aquí [en Las Vegas], y iba por la mujer mía, porque ea trabajaa aá en l'asilo. Dejé a mi plebe aquí, pus estaan chicos. Yo iba como a las once y media por ea una vez de la noche. Tú sabes aquí onde estaa el *tortilla factory, right there*, ahi mero iba yo en la troca. Loo tú sabes el camino ese abajo del *tortilla factory*, poquito pa unas casas que estaan abajo, abajan pa bajo, ahi iba un bulto blanco, blanco, como una sábana blanca. Yo traiba una *spotlight* en mi troca, y se lo puse asina en la cara, y se subió parriba el bordo otra vez. Onde estaa el *tortilla factory*, estaa una cantinita *right* en el *corner* paá pa una callecita que entra pallá. Ahi se paró atrás de un telefón, y me hacía asina con la mano [Vente. Vente.], y yo poniéndole el *spotlight* pa ver si podía ver yo qué era.

Ése es el único bulto que me ha salido.

Two

Witches Disguised as Animals

If it's not an animal, then what is it?

INTRODUCTION

From antiquity to the present we find humans and animals forming partnerships. This relationship constitutes an unequivocal human–animal legacy that has continued through the centuries, spread around the globe into different cultures and practices, whether in literature, art, or religion.

As Christianity came to dominate Western Europe, certain animals assumed—and in fact were relegated to—different roles, including in the bizarre world of the occult. As witches aligned with the Devil, for example, in the battle of good versus evil, the Devil presumably presented them with an array of animals with which to disguise their true identity while they participated in their nighttime activities. These animals in the world of sorcery varied from country to country and across the religious spectrum, not only in Western Europe, including Spain and Portugal, but also in Africa (where the owl is common) and the New World as well, including Mexico and the American Southwest.

Today, witches disguised as animals continue to form part of the fascinating lore of the supernatural in California, Arizona, Texas, Colorado, and my native state of New Mexico. The discussion of witches masquerading as animals was also part of the folklore in my family when I was a child.

My paternal grandmother once told me a true but chilling story about a grandson she was raising who was attacked by a small dog. As he passed by a cemetery one darkish night on his way home, something kept nipping at his ankles. As he looked around, he found that it was a small black and white dog. He kicked it (the dog did not even bark), and almost instantaneously the little dog jumped up and scratched one side of his face. A bleeding grandson was proof enough for my grandmother that his encounter with the little creature was no lie.

Although she was genuinely concerned and sympathetic, she reminded him that the dog might have been a roving spirit from the nearby cemetery, or possibly a witch in disguise out to wreak havoc in the dead of night. Regardless, she cautioned him, it was a lesson (*un escarmiento*) to him, a punishment for having disobeyed when he left home against her wishes to go play with his cousins.

Stories like my grandmother's of witches transforming themselves into animals once abounded in New Mexico and elsewhere in the Southwest. Day or night, a woman (rarely a man) can transform into a cat or an owl to hassle people or inflict harm. Besides the cat and the owl, the creatures most commonly mentioned in stories I have collected over the years, particularly those by old-timers, are the dog, donkey, horse, goat, coyote, milk snake, and lizard. These animals, according to most informants, are magical creatures endowed with mystical and destructive powers. (Lucius Apuleius, Roman satirist, AD 125?, author of *The Golden Ass*, turned into a donkey; a witch, in the same work, turns into an owl.)

The narrators of the following tales hail from New Mexico and Colorado, but also from Spain, Nicaragua, and Mexico. Encounters with the supernatural, we learn from Samuel Córdova and Marcos C. Durán, do not always take place at night. Moreover, Latino sorcery tales also spill over into the indigenous world, combining elements from both cultures. This can be seen in stories like Benny Lucero's "A Coyote Turned Navajo" or Bencés Gabaldón's "An Indian."

The wide variety of animals that transform into witches is also quite intriguing. The reader will enjoy a story by Marcos C. Durán from Colorado about a beautiful black mare—a witch in disguise and leader of a herd of horses, all witches—and Yolanda del Villar's tale about a mystery beast on the Texas–Mexico border.

In a story by María A. Mongalo, a Nicaraguan now living in Riverside, California, the black sheep and the white one that mysteriously appear alongside an oxcart on a country road in the backlands of Nicaragua may well depict good and evil. Ernesto Struck, a former New Mexican who moved to Colorado years ago, talks about the appearance of a white dog, but nothing happens, thus adding to the mystery.

The hateful mother-in-law who secretly changes into a cat to victimize her daughter-in-law in a story by Tomás Lozano, a Spaniard who until recently resided in Albuquerque, takes us way back to the Pyrenees in Catalonia, Spain. The mother-in-law ultimately is the victim of her own shenanigans.

Cowboy boots worn by New Mexico ranchers and wranglers. Photo by Nasario García, 2001.

However, the most enduring and perhaps charismatic of all the animals mentioned is the owl, with its universal appeal in the world of the occult. There are countless stories about the owl, but they all basically take us through the same scenario, with equally disastrous results for the owl or the witch-turned-owl.

A woman-witch in the community may well anoint herself with certain oils or concoctions that enable her to leave her house transformed into an owl and roam here and there at night, even landing on someone's rooftop. The owl's mysterious appearances may vary from a premonition of death, as we see in María A. Mongalo's "The Owl," to a humorous confrontation between a man and a talking owl that utters "chickenshit" to its challenger. Parents at times have used the owl as a kind of bogeyman to scare their children; such is the case in Eileen Dolores Treviño Villarreal's story about the blood-sucking night creature. (*Lechuza* is very common in New Mexico, but it usually refers to a burrowing owl, also known as a prairie-dog owl because it lives in or hovers over a burrow once occupied by a colony of prairie dogs.)

No matter who comes out the winner in a duel with an owl, in the majority of cases the owl is either permanently injured or killed. One certain way to ensure that the owl does not escape unscathed is for someone, usually a man, to fetch a rifle, make a cross in the tip of a bullet, insert the bullet in the chamber, and fire! The owl is doomed. And the next day, the lady-witch is found either dead or hobbling about, thus confirming everyone's suspicions about a witch in the community.

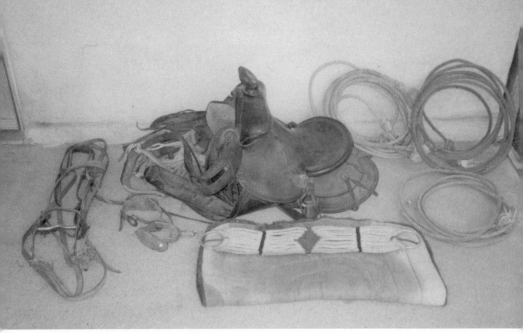

New Mexico rancher's saddle, saddle blanket, bridles, and ropes. Photo by Nasario García, 2001.

Whether tales of animals disguised as sorcerers in the world of witch-craft are believed or rejected depends on the circumstances and whether they are based on personal experience or second-hand information. In either case, stories of a person who can transform into an animal and back again, along with everything that transpires in between to both the perpe-trator and the victim of malice, are engaging reading.

Yolanda del Villar

SAN ANTONIO, TEXAS

The Monster

The following story occurred in a small place called Nava, situated on the Texas border with Coahuila, Mexico. In this place around twenty years ago certain events transpired that were a bit strange. At that time my father was the chief of police. Therefore, he was acquainted with the resi-dents of the place, since at that time the population was only about two thousand inhabitants.

It all began as a rumor about people being pursued by a strange being who, according to witnesses, had the shape of a dog but walked on two legs. This strange entity especially went after persons who had to cross the railroad tracks in the dark, late at night. The railroad ran along the outer edge of the town, which means that it was not a well-traveled place. The neighbors in the area, who for whatever reason had to go out at night, were in constant fear of being followed by this strange being.

Everything would have been treated as nothing more than hearsay or drunken stories, according to my father, had it not been for the body of a young boy that was found torn to pieces by the wheels of a train. This young boy was very well liked in the community and had the reputation of being very congenial, so the idea of a crime stemming from hatred was rejected. He also had not drunk any liquor, so the theory that he perhaps had fallen asleep on the rails was also rejected.

The rumors regarding the strange entity that went after night owls in the area close to the railroad tracks intensified, so much so that the police patrol had to be reinforced. My father himself decided to be part of the patrol in the respective area. He says that during one of those frigid and dark nights, when all you think about is a hot cup of coffee and a good stove to warm up, is when his encounter with the Monster took place.

It was after midnight and nothing strange was going on; the stillness of the night made the vigil even more difficult. All of a sudden the patrol and my father saw the figure of a staggering drunkard who was headed home. Happy and oblivious to the danger that hovered over him, the drunkard was humming a melody. He had not even advanced a half block from where the half-hidden patrol was when a menacing shadow stood in his path.

As my father saw this, he quickly climbed down from the vehicle with pistol in hand and he hollered at the drunk, "Watch out!" The beast, that is, the Monster, forgetting momentarily about his intended victim, launched itself at my father. My father pulled the trigger, but it did not discharge. The pistol had jammed! The beast proceeded toward my father. Smelling its sickening breath, he (my father) moved backward. Nevertheless, the beast managed to scratch him, and at the very moment that the strange being was about to go at him again, the light from a backup patrol shined on the unexpected scene.

The beast turned halfway around to take off, but my father, with adrenaline coursing through his veins, fired once again at the beast, this time with more luck than the previous time. Although the bullet didn't stop the Monster in his tracks, traces of blood were found at the site, whereby it is presumed that the beast was wounded or killed.

In spite of the fact that Nava was a small town, no evidence came to light in the days following the incident that anyone had been wounded or shot dead. Nevertheless, the Monster never again tormented the neighbors in the community.

Marcos C. Durán

PUEBLO, COLORADO

A Black Mare

This woman, a good friend of my wife, had a husband who was a very good friend of mine. He was a very wise man and quite good at telling stories. The only thing is that I already forgot most of those things. This man claims that there were these wealthy men who had large herds of horses and, you know, haciendas. Alberto was his name.

And he talks about looking for his horses. . . . They were called magical—magical, you understand? Mustangs, on the plains. Well, that's where he found a bunch of horses, mares and all. And he says that he tried to catch the first horse he spotted, a black mare, claiming that he could tame the herd because there are many different herds of horses. That I know because I was a cowboy myself. And there's always a horse, a mare, at the head of the pack that leads the herd.

As it turned out, this man liked one of the horses for himself, so he took off after the herd to catch him. He had a very fast horse. Among the herd was a black mare and he ran a lot after her on the plains, but he couldn't round up the herd because it was quite spread out. But he was able to cut the mare. He separated the black mare from the pack; it was beautiful and he liked it a lot. And yes, he took off after it on his horse, a good horse, and he tried and tried but couldn't catch up with the mare.

About that time, the men were almost to the village where they lived. There was like a forest, and he turned his horse around and the mare headed toward a cottonwood tree. The mare was very quick, and when it headed toward the cottonwood tree the mare disappeared. It was a woman! And he referred to her by name, but I just don't recall what it was. The woman said to him, "Alberto, I'm what you're looking for, but I'm not an animal. I'm not a mare."

She was from the men's village. He then responded to her, "Listen, I always took you for a woman of high standards, but are you a witch?"

"Yes. Yes, I'm a witch, and all that herd of horses you were trying to round up, they're my friends. They're both my female and male friends. But we were having a dance, and so we took off as soon as we saw you rather than having you find us at the dance."

And I can vouch that that woman was a witch. She turned into a mare. The mare appeared before Alberto's eyes in the form of a woman. He was a man already up in years, but he was a very wise man. He lived in Antoñito, Colorado. I also lived in Antoñito.

Bencés Gabaldón

BERNALILLO, NEW MEXICO

The Cat Lost an Eye

My mom used to tell us that once upon a time this woman . . . well, ah, they were in somebody's home. Back in those days the people got together, I understand, I don't know, in someone's home to fix snacks at night. To eat and that sort of thing. And one of the ladies went into the pantry to fetch—I don't know what she went after. She was going to get something from the pantry, when all of a sudden a cat leaped at her and she hit it. I don't know what she hit the cat with, but she put out one of his eyes. The cat leaped and took off and they didn't catch him.

On the following day people found out that it wasn't a cat; it was a woman. It was a woman who was snooping around. Then people went about saying that she had lost her eye on a door's lock, but it was from the blow that she received instead.

See what things are like. Those things used to happen!

An Indian

My father used to tell us that the Indians did many things there in our part of the country, but he didn't know in quite what way. The Indians performed very intelligent feats!

They had a huge room and that's where they gathered around to smoke and all that sort of thing. They sang. Wherever they were singing, you understand, according to my father, they'd put a buffalo hide, cover it, and put some corn underneath. The Indians were singing and shortly after-wards, when they lifted up the buffalo hide, a bunch of chickens would run out.

Then my father talked about this Indian who rode a billy goat like on a mountain ridge. And there was a precipice on either side. I understand that it was on that ridge that the billy goat walked gingerly, first to one end and then to the other, with the Indian on its back. Oh, another thing, what the billy goat did not succeed in doing, because there was a snake to one side, was to allow the snake to strike the Indian. The reason it did not happen was that whenever he came close to the snake, due to his petition to God, it did not strike him, you see. I understand the snake would raise itself so high, about two or three feet in the air and hissed, but it failed in its attempt to strike. That's the only thing the snake was unable to do—to bite him.

My father said that it was really something, what the Indians could do. He simply didn't know how they did it. That was his story to us.

Nasario P. García

LOS RANCHOS DE ALBURQUERQUE,
NEW MEXICO

A Horse Popped Out

One time I understand there were about two or three men and they were riding their best horses and all. For sure they were drunk! Anyhow, my dad told me that when these men were crossing El Alto, named after the Jaramillos, it was nighttime, a horse popped out of nowhere in front of them. Then one of them I guess said, "And where in the world did this horse come from?"

No sooner said than done, he took out his rope, tied it to the saddle's horn, and hollered, "I'll rope it." And he took off after it, but the horse took off running. Well, he caught up with him and roped it.

When his friends got there, he was thrown to one side of the rope and his horse to the other, and the rope down the middle on the ground, but the horse he had roped was nowhere in sight.

That's what my dad used to tell me about the Moras. That was their name, the Moras.

Tomás Lozano

ALBUQUERQUE, NEW MEXICO

Daughter-in-Law and Mother-in-Law

In a small village made up of small stone houses in the Pyrenees in Catalonia a young couple who was in love got married and made their home with the groom's mother. They had exchanged vows without the mother's consent. For this and other reasons the mother-in-law and daughter-in-law got along like cats and dogs.

The young wife had the habit of going near the fireplace every night after supper. That's where she spent long whiles on a wooden bench looking at the flames with a pensive look on her face. This intrigued the mother-in-law a lot, who herself had the habit of leaving the house as soon as she finished supper. And every night while the young girl contemplated the fire, a black cat would come near to keep her company. This cat stared and stared at her from top to bottom.

The young girl became very distrustful of the strange cat that sympathized with her every night next to the fire. So this one time when the cat made its presence, she grabbed a frying pan with olive oil and set it on the fire. The cat observed attentively all of her moves with hungry eyes, thinking that the girl was going to cook something delicious in that frying pan. When the olive oil began boiling, the young girl skillfully grabbed the frying pan and poured the boiling oil on the head of the cat that had not stopped looking at her with snooping eyes. The cat took off flying like a bolt of lightning and disappeared.

Next day the mother-in-law wouldn't get out of bed, and the young girl went to find out what was going on and asked her why she wouldn't get up. As the mother-in-law answered her, she said, "You know very well what's wrong with me. Woe is me! Last night you poured the boiling oil on my head."

"So the black cat that cuddled up to me every night next to the fire was you?"

"Oh dear! Yes, that was me."

Benjamín "Benny" Lucero

ALBUQUERQUE, NEW MEXICO

A Coyote Turned Woman

There was a gringo with whom we traded goats for cows, who migrated to the Río Puerco Valley in the last few years, and he was checking up on the cows that he had there. And this gringo took off after a coyote, but the latter chickened out. The coyote jumped to the bottom of the arroyo and the gringo took off on a trail to one side, and there at the bottom he spotted a Navajo woman, up against a riverbank, covered with a shawl. When the coyote went down, it turned into . . . it was a Navajo woman.

As I say, that's what this gringo said who was in the local grocery store, because my compadre Emilio, who understood English *very* well, overheard him.

A Coyote Turned Navajo

But then again, my compadre Emilio used to tell me about another simi-

lar case. It seems this Navajo took off after a coyote, but he did have a rifle. As he circled this juniper, about to step on the coyote that he thought was doing damage to his sheep, there was a Navajo.

He turned into a Navajo. The coyote turned into a Navajo. You see, he must have gotten tired of running. The coyote-turned-Navajo kept saying to the Navajo, "Man, don't kill me. Don't kill me," when the witch himself, the coyote-turned-Navajo, suddenly let go with an arrow. The only thing is that the arrow hit the lower part of the sad-

dle. But there was the arrow, stuck.

There he was, the coyote-turned-Navajo, pleading, "Don't kill me. Don't kill me," begging because the Navajo had a rifle. The Navajo kept asking him why he did those things and the witch would merely respond, "No. Don't kill me. Don't kill me," when suddenly the shrilling sound of an arrow struck the mount. The arrow missed the Navajo with the rifle.

That's one more story my compadre Emilio used to tell me.

Navajo Witchcraft

Emilio, this compadre of mine, used to tell me that the Navajos inflict evil on one another. He'd tell me stories, like what happened to a particular Navajo whose father was still living and was a witch.

From Torreón to El Pueblo del Alto is quite a ways, but for witches distance is a relative thing when it comes to a party. They grab a horse, ride it, and go. Back in those days they rode on horseback, and the father supposedly said to the son, "Oh, I'll take you to that party in a little bit, but we'll have to return before midnight." When the two arrived, it was in the form of two coyotes. That's what this fellow, the Navajo's son, used to tell my compadre. My compadre is one hundred years old now.

He took me into his confidence, see? And he told me that the boy had confided in him that he and his father got there having turned into two coyotes, he one and his father the other. This happened before midnight because after twelve o'clock midnight the witches can't be roaming around. When midnight came, because they had already been at the party, "I went back," so said the son to my compadre.

That's when he told his father that he didn't want anything to do with him. No more! His father was a witch, and I overheard that a lot among the Navajos, that is, the son knew that they suspected his father of being a witch.

Manuel de Jesús Manzanares

PUEBLO, COLORADO

The Hooting Owl

My mom used to talk about my dad when he was young. He was living there in Crestones, in Redwood, as it's called now. I believe Dad was working for some ranchers in the vicinity called Los Doches. He used to pass through a small canyon, and one time, in the evening or in the morning, I believe it was in the evening, he went through there, and there was an owl in a pine tree. The wooded area was populated with pine-nut trees. There was that owl hooting and hooting, and Dad shouted at him, "Tomorrow you shall come for salt and urine specimen because of that rotten hooting of yours."

Well, the owl answered, but I don't know what he said to him. Next day in the evening there was the owl again, and he challenged Dad to be at a certain place at a certain hour, and Dad said that he would be there.

Dad then strapped on his pistol and took off, but he couldn't get the horse to go to the designated place. It was an empty house, according to what Mom used to say. That's where the owl was. I understand Dad grabbed his pistol and kept trying to shoot, but the pistol wouldn't go off. Dad then was afraid to continue because, as I said, he couldn't get the horse to come closer. The horse was afraid. As a consequence, Dad turned around and left the owl behind. Next day in the evening the owl confronted him again. The owl kept repeating to Dad, "Chickenshit! Chickenshit. I made you mad."

The owl got the best of him. Mom also used to say that, according to Dad, when this owl flew it looked as though it was wearing a slip. Dad became so frightened that you couldn't get him out of the house after dark. You couldn't get him out of the house for anything.

At night, because it was a large family and the beds were spread out on the floor, my grandma would put my father in between everyone else because of the fear that he had. Dad continued being scared and so my grandpa started thinking of what to do.

Someone told him about an herb healer in New Mexico who treated certain illnesses, whereupon my grandpa, as I understand it, went and brought this man so he could treat my father. He cured him with the understanding that my father was not to reveal the name of the person who had inflicted evil on him. Because the herb healer said to him, "The day you mention the person's name, you're right back where you started," and Mom said that Dad never mentioned who the person was. I understand it was a woman, but he never gave her name.

The owl was a woman, and Dad got over his fright. He escaped that fear. That was the only evil he suffered from that woman. She didn't cause any damage to him physically, as was the case with witches. The only thing is that she frightened him so much that he couldn't go out after dark.

But that herb healer cured him with that understanding; he was not to mention the lady's name. She didn't inflict any physical illness. Only fear. She got him frightened, scared.

María A. Mongalo

RIVERSIDE, CALIFORNIA

They Looked Like Sheep

This is a story my father told me. He had a big farm and a very big home. I was about eight years old. I remember my father owned an oxcart, but he was riding on horseback. Two farmhands were in charge of the oxcart, in addition to one more who was going to help load the sacks of corn.

He said that he was in the middle of the road. There was no moon and you could barely see anything, but there they were moving right along because the trip was very long. Hours and hours! They were carrying water and food for the animals as well as for themselves. Since he was on horseback, he went up ahead so he could go faster and left the oxcart behind.

My father said that suddenly he saw clear as day some animals that looked like sheep. One was white and the other one was black. He was a very strong man and for that reason he was not afraid. He said there was no reason why these animals should be there.

He started to pray because he began getting scared. Fact is that all of a sudden the animals appeared alongside him. Then the black one disappeared, and the white followed right alongside him, as if to keep him and the oxcart company. Then it disappeared. He doesn't know which direction the animal took off.

The Owl

This is the story about a woman who was dying. This woman had not been very nice in her lifetime. A daughter of hers even worked here at one of the colleges. The mother was very cruel and wreaked lots of havoc in her life. People say that she was dying of cancer, but that she found herself unexpectedly in a coma when an owl then appeared quite close to the window of her room. The owl made very ugly sounds and it didn't leave until the woman died.

Filimón Montoya

LAS VEGAS, NEW MEXICO

He Killed the Owl

Oh, yes! Let me tell you this story. There was this little old lady who lived alone. She was already old. We kids thought she was quite old because we were young. She was a very tall and lanky woman who was always dressed in black, and she wore very long dresses that came down to the floor. People claimed she was a witch, a real witch. Everybody accused her of being a witch. I don't know whether she was a witch or not.

But anyhow, one night, this came much later, you see. I believe I was even married when this happened. There was this neighbor of ours who lived, oh, quite a ways from us. And I understand an owl would show up every night to sing or whatever owls do, there on a post close to his house, but the owl was on the road, and the neighbor's house was right close to the road. In any case, one night he got tired of listening to it hoot, and he took out his rifle and he wounded it. He killed the owl, in fact. A few days later, or a day or two afterwards, they found the little old lady dead in her house. She was totally nude, and she had an injury like when you shoot somebody in the head. People claimed, I didn't see it, but people claimed and believed that it was the owl.

But I just don't know. It was all based on what we heard.

José Nataleo Montoya

LAS VEGAS, NEW MEXICO

The Milk Snake

One time, well, we were just kids. We were about eight years old, I believe, and we used to look after the cows. There was a cow that had a *very*, very large teat. It was always very large. That one didn't give any milk. The story people told was that a milk snake had sucked it, and that's the reason that teat was that way. The cow had very twisted horns. Well, we used to go into the corral, we'd turn it around and grab it by the horns. What if it had tossed us up in the air or something like that? And the cow didn't defend itself. But those were dangerous things we did as a matter of monkeying around.

Isabel Romero

LAS VEGAS, NEW MEXICO

Head of the Witches

This took place over in Sabinoso. There was a very bushy walnut tree, large, with shade in front of the house. And there was a man whose name was Paulín. He was a sorcerer. He was half witch. Okay, there was also a man named Celso Martínez, and he was married to a cousin of mine. He liked to run around a lot. It was well into the evening when he was making the rounds over in Sabinoso. It was late. On his way back, he saw the owls' roosting place on top of this tree and on the ground the small owls moving about. He was a real cutup and he always carried a pistol. When he saw them, he took out his pistol and started to fire. Here were the owls scurrying about, some on the ground while others on top of the tree. He was shooting at them.

Very well, next day, "Well, what happened, Celso? What were you firing so many shots at?"

"Why, nothing!" he said. "Would you believe that even my aunt was playing the role of an owl?"

Well, next day, there you are. "The word's going around that Paulín is very ill."

"How could that be?"

"Celso Martínez went and shot him. [Laughter] Paulín is very ill."

As it turned out, Don Paulín had a broken leg [he fell from the tree after being shot]. He was one of those who practiced sorcery.

Mother was very sick at that time. I understand she was very sick. Who knows what was wrong with her. Well, when Paulín was shot, mother got well. Yes, she was cured.

She used to spend most of her time crying. She went from bad to worse. That man Paulín would say that he could cure her, but he never did anything. As it turned out, he was the head of the witches. When that man died, mother got well. Mother was cured once and for all.

Ophelia Ipolita María de Gracia Sandoval de Rinaldi

BERNALILLO, NEW MEXICO

The Old Hag Disappeared

I remember this old woman who lived there in Taos, near Los Ranchitos. This old woman had so much power that if you went to her house or if she went to yours and she asked you for something, you could not deny her because you just had to give it to her. Nobody liked her, but she would always ask for things. And people claimed that she was a witch. You know very well that in Taos, like other places, there were witches that roamed

the mountains like balls of fire, jumping about in the hills. You could see them at night.

This one time there were two hunters and they saw a coyote that was running, really running, and they shot at him and killed him. After they went to see him, they saw that he was wearing a multi-colored kerchief around the neck the same color kerchief as the one the old lady had.

65

After that, the old woman disappeared. She was never ever seen again. She never reappeared again, but the scuttlebutt was that this old hag had the power of turning into other animals.

An Owl

A story that's related to witches is the one concerning the women who would go out at night and turn into owls. Every time you heard an owl outside, well, you just didn't go out. It was a good excuse not to go outside. My grandpa told us about all that sort of thing.

His name was Martiniano de los Reyes; he was a playboy and a drinker. He always entertained us with his little anecdotes. But one time when he was already quite old, we were at the kitchen table making little dolls with modeling clay, and he got really mad at us. He said that was witchery and we were not to do that.

But I recollect that the old folks talked a lot about witches that roamed the mountains. And children weren't supposed to be outside at night. And we simply didn't go outside at night! I don't know how true it was about the witches, but I think that they [the old folks] did believe that stuff. It wasn't just hearsay; it was serious stuff they believed in.

Ernesto Struck

PUEBLO, COLORADO

A White Dog Popped Out

One time the Rancho de Taos fiestas were going on, and I, being interested in making money, said to Dad, "Don't go. I'll go for wood in the morning. I'll go alone."

We used to go after wood that was still green. Very well. Dad got up, and we hitched up the horses. When I left the house, I went around this orchard. That's where the road was and a creek. I had to cross the bridge. When I went down this small hill a white dog popped out.

I didn't have a white dog. Nobody did. And we were accustomed to using long reins and a whip, but the dog was still able to back me up against the wagon. I would crack and show him the whip to see if I could drive him back, but nothing doing. By the time I crossed the bridge he stepped to the side of the bridge. He didn't do anything to me, but there he was as he tagged alongside the wagon.

Eileen Dolores Treviño Villarreal

SAN ANTONIO, TEXAS

The Owl

My mother used to say to me, "Be good, because if you're not, the owl is going to come and get you. If it comes to the rooftop it's not going to like it if you're not behaving. Then the owl will come and suck your blood all up. That's why you still have those bruises."

In the morning, since I was a little girl and went around playing and would fall down, I would wake up with bruises and I would cry because I knew the owl had come to suck up my blood. I thought that the owl was a . . . , well, I had never seen photographs of it; I had not seen anything at that time. But now as an adult, yes. There's a photograph of an owl, but I always imagined it like a huge bird, like a monster. That's the image of the owl that I had.

I believe that you can find the owl in Mexican folklore and I believe that it's aligned with vampires, but yes, all these stories that we have in our culture came from someone, and they probably happened. Who knows? But those stories have been passed on from generation to generation. I believe the Spaniards brought this folklore, "The Hairy Hand," et cetera, and then they were mixed with the indigenous element.

Brujas disfrazadas
de animales

....

Si animal no es, ¿entonces qué es?

Yolanda del Villar

SAN ANTONIO, TEXAS

El Nahual

La siguiente historia ocurrió en un poblado pequeño, Nava, situado en la frontera de Texas y Coahuila. En esta población hace alrededor de veinte años pasaron hechos por demás extraños. Mi padre era comandante del cuerpo policíaco del lugar. Por lo tanto tenía conocimiento de los pobladores del mismo lugar, ya que en ese entonces la población sólo tenía dos mil habitantes, aproximadamente.

Todo empezó como un rumor de gente siendo perseguida por un ser extraño, que según los testigos tenía forma de perro, pero caminaba en dos patas. Este extraño ente perseguía especialmente a las personas que debían cruzar las líneas ferroviarias a entradas horas de la noche. Los ferrocarriles pasaban por la orilla del pueblo, por lo que no era un lugar muy transitado. Sin embargo, los vecinos del lugar que por algún motivo tenían que salir de noche vivían atemorizados ante las continuas persecuciones de este extraño ser.

Todo habría pasado a ser cuentos de la gente o invenciones de borrachos según palabras de mi padre si no hubiera aparecido el cuerpo de un jovencito destrozado por las ruedas del tren. Dicho jovencito era muy apreciado por la comunidad y tenía fama de ser muy amable por lo que se descartó la posibilidad de un crimen por odio. Tampoco había ingerido alcohol por lo que la teoría de que se había quedado dormido en los rieles se descartó también.

Los rumores del extraño ente que perseguía a los trasnochadores en la zona del riel se intensificaron, por lo que la vigilancia policíaca debió ser reforzada y mi padre en persona decidió montar guardia en la zona señalada. Cuenta mi padre que en una de esas noches gélidas y oscuras, cuando en lo único en que se piensa es en una taza de café caliente y un buen fogón para calentarse, es que tuvo lugar su encuentro con el Nahual.

Pasaba de la medianoche y nada extraño sucedía; la quietud de la noche hacía más difícil soportar la vigilia. De pronto vieron mi padre y la patrulla la figura de un borrachín tambaleante que se dirigía a su hogar. Alegre, ajeno al peligro que sobre él se cernía, el borrachín tatareaba una melodía. No había avanzado ni media cuadra desde el lugar donde se encontraba la patrulla semi-escondida cuando una sombra amenazante le salió al paso.

Al mirar esto mi padre, rápidamente con pistola en mano descendió del vehículo y le gritó al borrachín. "¡Cuidado!" La bestia, o sea, el Nahual, olvidándose momentáneamente de su supuesta víctima se avalanzó hacia mi padre. Jaló él el gatillo de su pistola, pero la bala no salió ¡La pistola se había encasquillado! La bestia siguió avanzando hacia mi padre, y él sintió su nauseabundo aliento y retrocedió. Sin embargo, la bestia alcanzó a arañarlo, y en el momento en que el ser extraño se disponía a arremeter de nuevo sobre él, la luz de una patrulla de refuerzo alumbró la insólita escena.

El ente se dio la media vuelta para retirarse, pero mi padre con la adrenalina corriendo por sus venas disparó de nuevo hacia el ser, esta vez con mejor suerte que la anterior. Aunque el balazo no detuvo al Nahual, en el lugar se encontraron rastros de sangre por lo que se presume que el ser fue herido o muerto.

A pesar de que Nava era un pueblo pequeño, nunca se dio constancia de un herido de bala o de un difunto en los días consecutivos al hecho. Sin embargo, nunca más los vecinos del lugar fueron molestados por el Nahual.

Marcos C. Durán

PUEBLO, COLORADO

Una yegua prieta

Una señora muy amiga de mi esposa, tenía marido que era muy amigo mío. Era un hombre muy estudiao y muy güeno pa 'cer cuentos. Nomás que ya se me olvidaron munchas cosas d' ésas. Este hombre cuenta que había unos hombres muy ricos y tenían caballadas y, usté sabe, haciendas. Se llamaba Alberto el hombre.

Él cuenta de que andaba buscando sus caballos—usté sabe que les dicían mágicas, mágicas, ¿no? Mesteños, en el llano. Pues ahi halló él un bonche de caballos, de yeguas y todo eso. Y dice que hizo lucha de agarrar la primer bestia que vido—una yegua prieta—y que él amanzaba a la caballada porque hay munchas caballadas. Eso sé yo porque yo jui vaquero y todo eso. Y siempre hay un caballo, una yegua, que va delante, que manija la caballada.

De modo que a este hombre le gustó uno de los caballos pa 'garralo pa él y le rompió a la caballada. Muy ligero el caballo que traiba. Pos ahi que iba la yegua prieta y corrió muncho en el llano y no podía juntar la caballada porque se estendía muncho. Pero pudo cortar la yegua. Cortó la yegua prieta; era muy linda y le gustó muncho. Y sí, le rompió en su caballo—buen caballo—pero no la podía alcanzar y no la podía alcanzar a la yegua.

En esto, ya iban llegando a la placita donde ellos vivían. Hacía como un bosque, y le dio güelta a su caballo él tamién y la yegua voltió hacia un álamo. Muy liviana la yegua, y cuando voltió al álamo se desapareció la yegua. ¡Era una señora! Y la mentaba él pero ya no me acuerdo cómo se llamaba. Es que le dijo la señora,

—Alberto, yo soy lo que tú andas buscando, pero no soy animal. No soy yegua.

Era de la placita d'ellos. Antonces es que le dijo él,

—Oiga, pos yo la tenía a usté por una señora de lo mejor, pero, ¿usté es bruja?

—Sí. Sí soy bruja, y toda esa caballada que andabas queriendo agarrar, son mis amigas. Ésas son mis amigas y mis amigos. Pero nosotros teníanos un baile y salimos ansina logo que te vimos a ti en lugar de que nos hallaras en el baile.

Y eso le puedo contar yo que esa señora era bruja. Se volvió yegua. A Alberto se le apareció la yegua hecha mujer. Él era ya hombre muy anciano, pero él era un hombre muy estudiao. Vivía en Antoñito, Colorao. Yo tamién vivía en Antoñito.

Bencés Gabaldón

BERNALILLO, NEW MEXICO

Le sacó un ojo al gato

Nos platicaba mamá a nosotros que una vez esta mujer . . . pues, eh, estaban en una casa. En esos tiempos la gente se juntaba, quizás, yo no sé, se juntaba la gente en una casa y se ponían a hacer lonche en la noche. A comer y eso. Y entró una de las mujeres, es que entró, pa la dispensa pa sacar . . . no sé qué iría a trae. Iba a trae alguna cosa de la dispensa, y cuando menos pensó se le vino un gato encima a ella y le pegó ella. No sé con qué le dio y le sacó un ojo al gato. Y el gato voló y se jue y no lo agarraron.

Otro día no era el gato; era una mujer. Era una mujer la que andaba. Loo decían que se había sacao el ojo en un' armella, de la puerta, pero jue el garrotazo del gato.

Pa que veiga usté lo que son las cosas. ¡Esas cosas pasaban!

Un indio

Mi papá nos platicaba a nosotros que hacían munchas cosas los indios ahi en nuestro país, pero no sabía en qué manera podían hacelas. Unas cosas tan inteligentes que hacían estos indios.

Tenían un salón grande, y ahi se rodeaban ellos a chupar y todo. Cantando. Onde estaban cantando, pues ahi dicía él, mi papá, que ponían un cuero de cíbolo y lo tapaban y le ponían maiz abajo. Estaban cantando los indios y al rato que levantaban el cuero salían puros pollos, de abajo el cuero.

Loo platicaba mi papá que se había subido este indio en un chivato, como en un filo de una sierra. Y estaba un voladero par un lao y el otro. Ahi es que iba poniendo el chivato las piernas entremedio y pasaba con él [el indio] pal otro lao, y loo de allá pacá. Ah, y otra cosa, lo que no pudo hacer jue que la víbora, porque estaba una víbora par un lao, le metiera la lengua a él, porque cuando se arrimaba a onde estaba la víbora, en el pedimento de él, le pedía a Dios, ves, y no se arrimaba la víbora. Que se alzaba tan alta asina (dos o tres pies). No pudo. Nomás eso no pudo hacer la víbora, metele la lengua.

Mi papá platicaba que era una barbaridá lo que hacían los indios; y él no sabía cómo. Eso nos platicó él a nosotros.

Nasario P. García

LOS RANCHOS DE ALBURQUERQUE, NEW MEXICO

Apareció un caballo

Otra vez tamién es que venían como dos o tres hombres, y éstos traiban sus güenos caballos y todo. ¡Seguro que venían embolaos! De todos modos, me platicaba en papá que cuando iban por El Alto de los Jaramillos, es que ahi se les apareció un caballo adelante d'ellos. Loo es que dijo uno d'ellos, "¿Y este caballo de diónde resultó?" Pronto sacó su cabresto, lo amarró en la cabeza de la silla, y gritó, "Yo lo lazo," y le partió pero salió a juir el caballo. Pos lo alcanzó y lo lazó.

Cuando los compañeros llegaron, él estaba caido par un lao y su caballo pal otro y el cabresto en el suelo par un lao, pero el caballo que había lazao no estaba.

Eso me platicaba en papá de los Moras. Asina se llamaban ellos; eran los Moras.

Tomás Lozano

ALBUQUERQUE, NEW MEXICO

La nuera y la suegra

En un pueblecito de casitas de piedra en las montañas del Pirineo catalán una pareja de jóvenes enamorados se casaron quedándose a vivir con la madre del novio. Éstos habían contraído matrimonio sin el consentimiento de la madre. Por estas y otras razones la suegra y la nuera se llevaban como el gato y el perro.

La joven esposa tenía por costumbre arrimarse al fuego de la chimenea todas las noches después de la cena. Allí pasaba largos ratos sentada en un banquito de madera mirando las llamas del fuego con rostro pensativo. Esto intrigaba mucho a la suegra quien tenía la costumbre de salir de casa en cuanto acababa de cenar. Y todas las noches mientras la joven contemplaba el fuego un gato negro se le arrimaba a hacerle compañía. Éste se la remiraba y remiraba de arriba a bajo.

La joven desconfiaba mucho de aquel extraño gato que todas las noches compadecía junto al fuego con ella. Así que en una ocasión, cuando llegó el gato, cogió una sartén con aceite y la puso al fuego. El gato observaba atentamente todos sus movimientos con ojos golosos, pensando que alguna cosa deliciosa iba a guisar la joven en aquella sartén. Cuando el aceite empezó a hervir la joven cogió con destreza la sartén y le echó el aceite hirviendo al gato por la cabeza que no había dejado de mirarla con curiosidad. El gato salió corriendo como un rayo y desapareció.

Al día siguiente la suegra no se levantaba de la cama y la joven fue a ver qué pasaba y le preguntó que por qué no se levantaba. Respondiéndole la suegra le dijo,

—Bien sabes tú lo que me pasa. ¡Ay de mí! Pues anoche me echaste el aceite hirviendo por la cabeza.

—¿Así que el gato negro que se me arrimaba cada noche junto al fuego eras tú?

—¡Ay! Sí, era yo.

Benjamín "Benny" Lucero
ALBUQUERQUE, NEW MEXICO

El coyote se cambió a navajosa

Había un gringo que vino en estos últimos años, que nosotros le cambiamos las cabras por vacas, y este gringo le andaba dando güelta a las vacas que estaban ahi. Y este gringo le partió a un coyote, pero éste si se acobardó. Brincó el coyote pa bajo del arroyo y el gringo agarró una vereda asina par un lao y vido que estaba una navajosa atrincada contra el barranco, cobijada con un tápalo. Cuando bajó abajo el coyote se cambió . . . y es que era navajosa.

Eso es que platicó este gringo que estaba en la tienda del lugar, como te digo, porque mi compadre Emilio, que tenía *muy* güen inglés, lo escuchó.

Se golvió navajó

Pero también me platicaba asina otro caso semejante mi compadre Emilio. Es que un navajó le partió a un coyote, pero este navajó sí traiba rifle. A la güelta de un sabino, que ya iba pa pisotear el coyote, que pensaba que andaba haciendo mal a las borregas, estaba un navajó.

Se golvió un navajó. De coyote se golvió a navajó. Se cansó de correr, seguro, ¿ves? Es que le dicía el navajó, "No me mates, hombre. No me mates," cuando el mesmo brujo, el navajó, se soltó con una flecha, nomás que pegó en la silla abajo, la flecha. Pero la flecha estaba clavada.

Es que estaba el navajó con un tápalo rogando, "No me mates. No me mates," es que le dicía, porque traiba rifle el navajó. Que le estaba diciendo el navajó que si pa qué hacía esas cosas, y el brujo es que le dicía, "No. No me mates. No me mates," cuando el chillido de la flecha pegó abajo en la montura. Le jerró al navajó del rifle.

Ésa es una historia que me platicaba mi compadre Emilio.

Brujerías navajosas

Este compadre mío, Emilio, me platicaba a mí que entre los navajoses hacen males. Me platicaba historias, lo que pasó en un individuo navajó, que tenía a su papá, y su papá de él era brujo.

De Torreón al Pueblo del Alto es muy lejos, y estos brujos no importa que tan lejos esté una fiesta, agarran un caballo, lo caminan, y van. Iban en aquellos años de a caballo, y es que le dijo, "Oh!," es que le dijo el papá al hijo, "orita te llevo a esa fiesta, pero nos vamos a tener que venir antes de medianoche."

Cuando llegaron a la fiesta, es que llegaron en forma de dos coyotes. Esto le platicaba el muchacho este, el hijo, a mi compadre Emilio. Cien años tiene ora él.

Salió esa confianza, ¿ves? Y me dijo que es que le había platicao el muchacho que habían llegao hechos dos coyotes: uno jue el papá y el otro jue él mesmo. Antes de medianoche, porque después de medianoche no pueden andar los brujos, estuvieron en la fiesta. Cuando ya se llegó la medianoche, me arrendé patrás, es que le dijo el hijo a mi compadre.

Ahi le dijo a su papá que no quería nada con él. ¡No más! Su papá era brujo. Oí yo mentar mucho eso entre los navajoses, que sabía el hijo que dijían que su papá es que era brujo.

Manuel de Jesús Manzanares

PUEBLO, COLORADO

El tecolote llorando

Mi mamá platicaba tocante a mi papá cuando era joven él. Vivía ahi en Crestones, en Redwood, que le dicen ora. Creo que papá trabajaba por unos rancheros en la vecindá que se llamaba Los Doches. Él pasaba por un cañoncito, y en una de las veces, una tarde o en la mañana, pienso que en la tarde, pasó por allí. Estaba un tecolote en un pino. Había muncho monte de piñón. Estaba el tecolote llorando como un animal. Y es que le dice papá,

—Mañana vendrás por sal y orines por podridos gritos que das.

Pus le respondió el tecolote, pero no sé qué le dijo. Otro día en la tarde andaba otra vez el tecolote, y desafió a en papá hasta cierto lugar, a cierta hora que juera allá, y le dijo papá que sí iba.

Antonces se fajó en papá la pistola y se jue, pero no pudo hacer llegar el caballo al lugar. Era una casa despoblada según platicaba mamá, ahi estaba el tecolote. Es que agarró en papá la pistola y le tiraba tiros, pero la pistola no dio fuego. Tuvo logo miedo en papá seguir a pie porque el caballo, como dije, no lo pudo hacer arrimar. Por donde se vino en papá y dejó el tecolote. Otro día en la tarde le salió otra vez el tecolote. Es que le decía a en papá,

—Cagao, cago. Te hice enojar.

Ganó el tecolote. Tamién platicaba mamá que decía en papá que cuando volaba este tecolote, que parecía que llevaba 'naguas colgando. Se atemorizó tanto en papá que no lo hacían salir de casa después que se oscurecía. No lo hacían salir ajuera de casa por nada.

En la noche, pues era muncha la familia, y tendían camas en el suelo, y a en papá lo acostaba mi agüelita en medio de todos del temor que tenía. En papá seguía temeroso y mi agüelito empezó a buscar a ver qué podía hacer.

Alguien le dio razón de que en Nuevo México había un arbolario y él curaba, por donde jue me agüelito y entiendo que trujo al hombre pa que curara a en papá. Lo curó con el compromiso de qu' en papá no tenía que mencionar el nombre de la persona que le hizo mal. Porque le dijo el arbolario, "El día que tú menciones el nombre de la persona, tú vuelves otra vez a la mesma," y dicía mamá que nunca había mencionao en papá quién era la persona. Que es que dicía que era una mujer, pero nombre nunca mencionó.

El tecolote era una mujer, y se le quitó el terror. Se erró d'ese miedo. Ése jue el único mal que le hizo la mujer. No le hizo daño en su cuerpo como logo dicían que enfermaban las brujas. Nada más que lo atemorizó que no podía salir después de oscuro.

Pero ese arbolario lo curó con ese entendido, que no tenía que mencionar el nombre. No le puso enfermedá ninguna. Nada más que temor.

María A. Mongalo

RIVERSIDE, CALIFORNIA

Eran como ovejas

Ésta es una historia de mi padre. Él tenía una gran finca de agricultura y una casa muy grande. Tenía yo unos ocho años y recuerdo que mi padre tenía una carreta con dos bueyes, pero él iba en su caballo. Dos peones iban manejando la carreta, y otro que iba ayudar a cargar los sacos de productos de maíz.

Él decía que iba en el medio del camino. No había nada luna y se miraba muy poco, pero ahi iban porque el viaje era muy lejos. ¡Horas y horas! Llevaban agua y comida para los animales y para ellos. Como él iba a caballo, dejó la carreta detrás para caminar más rápido.

Decía mi papá que de repente vio clarito unos animales que eran como ovejas. Uno era blanco y uno negro. Sin miedo porque él era un hombre muy fuerte. Dijo que no había razón para que hubiera estos animales.

Empezó a rezar porque ya así le dio miedo. El caso es que de repente se aparecieron al lado de él. Luego se desapareció el negro y el animal blanco siguió con él, como acompañándolo a la carreta. Luego se desapareció. No sabe para dónde agarró el animal. Eso es algo que él vivió.

La lechuza

Ésta es una historia de una señora que se estaba muriendo. Esta señora no había sido muy buena en vida. Hasta una hija de ella trabajaba aquí en los colegios. La mamá fue bien dura y hizo mucho daño en vida. Dicen que ella se estaba muriendo de cáncer, pero que de repente había estado en coma cuando se le apareció una lechuza cerquita de la ventana de su cuarto. La lechuza hacía un ruido muy feo y no se fue hasta que la señora falleció.

Filimón Montoya

LAS VEGAS, NEW MEXICO

Mató el tecolote

¡Oh sí! Déjeme contale este cuento. Estaa una viejita que vivía sola. Ya estaa viejita. A nojotros se nos parecía porque nojotros estáanos muy jóvenes. Era una mujer larga y siempre andaba vestida de negro y usaa vestidos largotes hasta que le arrastraan al suelo. Dicían qu' era bruja, qu' era bruja. Toos le echaban qu' era bruja. Yo no sé si sería bruja o no.

Pero, güeno, una nochi, esto era, o ya muncho después, ¿no? Yo pienso que ya estaba hasta casao yo cuando sucedió esto. Estaa un vecino de nojotros que vivía, oh, poco retirao. Y isque vinía un tecolote toas las noches a cantar o lo que hagan los tecolotes, ahi cerca de su casa en un poste, pero estaa en el camino, y su casa estaa junto el camino. Güeno, una nochi se aburrió de estalo oyindo, y sacó el rifle y lo balió. Mató el tecolote. Pocos días después, o un día o dos después, jallaron a la viejita esta muerta en su casa. Estaa bien desnuda, y tenía un' herida en la cabeza como cuando le dan un tiro. Dijían, yo no la vi, pero dijían y creían qu' era el tecolote.

Pero no sé. No era más de lo que oíamos decir.

José Nataleo Montoya

LAS VEGAS, NEW MEXICO

La culebra mamona

Una vez, güeno estáanos medianos. Teníanos como unos ocho años, yo creo, y cuidáanos vacas. Había una vaca que tenía una teta *muy*, muy grande. Muy gresa siempre. Ésa no daba leche. Dijían que ésa la había mamao la culebra mamona. Qu'esa era lo que la había mamao y por eso tenía la chiche asina. Tenía la vaca los cuernos bien doblaos. Pus veníanos nojotros y nos metíanos en el corral. Voltiábanos y la agarrábanos de los cuernos. ¿Qué tal si los [nos] levanta parriba el animal ese o algo? Y no se defendía. Pero que eran unas cosas peligrosas y que hacía uno de chiste.

Isabel Romero

LAS VEGAS, NEW MEXICO

Capitán de los brujos

Esto jue aá en el Sabinoso. Había un árbol nogal muy coposo, muy grande con sombra pa delante la casa. Y había un hombre que se llamaa Paulín. Él era hechicero. Era la mitá brujo. Güeno, pues que había un hombre Celso Martínez, y estaa casao con una prima hermana mía. Era muy pasiador. Andaa pallá pasiándose, en la tarde ya. Muy tarde. Cuando vinía, vido la tecolotera arriba el árbol, y aquí en el suelo andaan pasiándose allí los tecolotes. Él era muy atroz y siempre traiba pistola. Cuando vido, sacó la pistola y enpezó a tirar balazos. Andaan unos en el suelo y otros arriba. Les tiraba balazos.

Güeno, pues, que otro día,

—¿Pues qué pasa, Celso? ¿A qué le estaas tirando tanto balazo?

—No—es que dijo—. Pus ahi andaa de tecolotera hasta mi tía.

Pues, otro día,

—Isque don Paulín está muy malo.

—¿Cómo?

—Pues ahi le pegó [Celso Martínez] un balazo. [Risas] Isque don Paulín está muy malo.

Resultó con una pierna quebraa don Paulín. Él era d'esos de la brujería.

Mamá en ese tiempo estaa muy mala. Muy mala que estaa. Que sabe qué. Pus cuando baliaron al brujo ese sanó mamá. Sei, sanó.

Too el tiempo se la pasaba llorando. Tan mal y tan mal. Ese hombre Paulín, dijía que él la curaba, pero no le curaba nada. Pus él era el capitán de los brujos. Pus cuando se murió el hombre ese, mamá sanó. Mamá sanó.

Ophelia Ipolita María de Gracia Sandoval de Rinaldi

BERNALILLO, NEW MEXICO

Despareció la vieja

Me acuerdo que estaba esta vieja que vivía allí en Taos, junto a Los Ranchitos. Esta vieja tenía un poder que si tú ibas ahi pa su casa, o si ella iba pa tu casa y ella te pedía algo, no le podías negar porque tenías que dárselo. Nadie la quería, pero ella siempre se arrimaba a pedir cosas. Y la gente dicía que era bruja. Tú sabes que en Taos había, como en otros lugares, brujas que andaban en las montañas como bolas de lumbre, que brincaban en las lomas. Sí las veía uno en la noche.

Esta vez iban dos cazadores y vieron a un coyote que iba corriendo, corriendo, y le tiraron y lo mataron. Después que fueron a verlo, vieron que traiba colgado en el pescuezo un paño de colores así del mesmo color del paño que tenía la vieja esta. Después despareció la vieja. Nunca se volvió a ver más. Nunca se apareció, pero dicían que esta vieja tenía el poder de cambiarse a otros animales.

Una lechuza

Otro cuento que está relacionado con brujas es una historia de una lechuza, de las mujeres que salen en la noche que tamién se vuelven lechuzas. Cada vez que se oía una lechuza allá fuera, pus, ya no salía uno. Era buena excusa para no salir. Todo eso nos contaba tamién mi abuelito.

Él se llamaba Martiniano de los Reyes y era jugador y tomador. Siempre nos tenía entretenidos con sus cuentitos. Pero una vez cuando estaba ya viejito, estábanos ahi en la mesa de la cocina haciendo monitos de *clay,* de barro, *modeling cla*y. Se nos nojó muncho. Él dijo que eso era brujería y que no debíanos de hacer eso.

Pero yo me acuerdo que hablaban los viejitos muncho de las brujas que andaban allá en las montañas. Que los niños no debían andar aá juera en la noche. ¡Y no salíanos en la noche! No sé qué tanto verdá sería que había brujas, pero yo creo que ellos [los viejitos] sí lo creían. No era nomás historia; era cosa seria que la creían ellos.

Ernesto Struck

PUEBLO, COLORADO

Saltó un perro blanco

Una vez eran las fiestas de Ranchos de Taos, y yo por enteresao de dinero, le dije a en papá,

—No vaya usté. Yo voy en la mañana por leña. Voy ir solo,

Íbanos por leña allá que tavía estaba verde. Güeno. Se levantó en papá y pusimos los caballos. Cuando salí de casa, di la güelta por allá por una arbolera. Por ahi iba el camino y un riito. Tenía que pasar el puente del riito ese. Cuando bajé la lomita saltó un perro blanco.

Yo no tenía perro blanco. Naiden. Y usabábanos las riendas muy largas y un chicote, pero me baquiaba patrás del carro el perro y le pegaba y le enseñaba el chicote a ver si lo hacía patrás pero nada. Cuando ya pasé el puente se embocó pa fuera del puente. No me hizo nada, pero ahi iba nomás cerca del carro.

Eileen Dolores Treviño Villarreal

SAN ANTONIO, TEXAS

La lechuza

Mi mamá me decía siempre, "Pórtate bien porque si no va a venir la lechuza. Si viene al techo de la casa no le va a gustar si no te estás portando bien. Entonces viene la lechuza y te chupa. Por eso te quedan los moretones."

En la mañana, pues como yo era niña y andaba jugando y me caía, amanecía yo con moretones y lloraba porque sabía que la lechuza me había venido a chupar. Yo pensaba que la lechuza era un . . . , bueno yo nunca había visto fotografías de ella; no había visto nada en ese tiempo. Pero ahora de adulta, sí. Hay una fotografía de una lechuza, pero yo siempre me la imaginaba como un pájaro enorme, como monstruo. Ésa era la imaginación de la lechuza que yo tenía.

Pienso que el folklore mejicano utiliza la lechuza y pienso que esto está alineado con los vampiros, pero sí, todos estos cuentos que tenemos en la cultura nuestra tuvieron que venir de alguien, y probablemente sucedieron, ¿quién sabe? Pero esos cuentos se han dado de generación en generación. Pienso que trajeron los españoles este folklore, por ejemplo, "La mano pachona," et cetera, y luego se mezclaron con la cultura indígena.

Three

Lights, Sparks, and Balls of Fire

··

People claim that Mary the bitch, is a witch.

INTRODUCTION

Since time immemorial, natural phenomena such as lights, sparks, and balls of fire have been an integral part of witchcraft lore among Latinos in the Southwest (balls of fire are also associated with witches in Nigeria). This is especially true in northern New Mexico and southern Colorado, where traditions have held their ground for centuries. Whether actually seen or only imagined, these natural occurrences are reputed to represent witches, and one makes light of these phenomena at one's peril, as the accounts in this chapter attest.

People I have interviewed over the years contend that lights in an abandoned house—some would label it a haunted dwelling—or traversing the clear or cloudy night skies are nothing other than witches in disguise. These nocturnal creatures are destined to inflict harm on their enemies, wreak havoc with anyone they encounter, or join other witches in a ritualistic rendezvous away from home.

Car lights descending a mesa where there is no road or balls of fire cascading down a hill or bouncing down a dirt road much like a tumbleweed on a windy day—these are testimonies to the natural phenomena that add to the allure of sorcery. Even more unusual are candles flickering of their own accord in a dark room or glowing creatures crawling up a wall, neither one leaving any physical evidence for us to determine how the illumination is created.

Some people are able to see or envision these things, while others cannot explain why they lack the *don* or gift to experience them. Such is the case with Marcos C. Durán in "Balls of Fire." Whatever balls of fire his family was able to observe coming from an old house were not visible to him—precisely the kind of circumstance that oftentimes breeds skepticism. In this case he was outnumbered; hence a window of opportunity for disputation was rendered moot since it is inconceivable that his family would conjure up something on the spot simply to play a trick on him.

The antithesis of Marcos C. Durán's episode, recounted with undisputed veracity, is "A Terrible Ball of Fire," by Bencés Gabaldón. He tells how a ball of fire almost literally hobbled a mule team as the fire swirled around the beasts' legs. He punctuates his story by saying, "I saw it! And that's no lie."

A certain aura surrounds natural phenomena that most people find both intriguing and mystifying. Benny Lucero's story of a light that looked like a post hanging in the sky, as well as Manuel de Jesús Manzanares's experience with the light that would come on and go off when he entered the room adjacent to his bedroom, are both mysterious.

Lights seem to play a kind of cat-and-mouse game—first you see them, then you don't—as described by Damiano Romero in "Lights." Still, neither he nor any other informant has ever been able to explain the causes and effects of fleeting lights, balls of fire, or sparks. The indefinable nature of these phenomena is perhaps what has kept interest in them alive through the centuries in the American Southwest. As the folklorist Arthur L. Campa said in *Treasure of the Sangre de Cristos*, "I've been curious about those lights since the first time I saw them, but no one has been able to explain them [to me]." Today they may be referred to as UFOs.

What can be demonstrated beyond question is how, by invoking the magical name of John, a person can bring to earth streaking lights that traverse the skies in the dead of night. Is it mind over matter, or is it a manifestation of how the religious force with which the name John is imbued can countermand the occult, as witnessed in Nasario P. García's narrative "Two Witches and Two Fellows Named John"? Having the two *juanes* turn their T-shirts inside out and place them in a circle to catch the witches may be of secondary importance, but it is an indispensable part of the ritual.

We can be sure of at least one thing: every Latino community, by design or tradition and not by mere happenstance, has had at least one Juan or Juana among its inhabitants because of their avowed power to ward off evil. From time to time a Juan or a Juana would be called upon to "lift" the evil eye from an ailing child (see Chapter 8) before the next Friday passed, thus saving the child from death, a matter much more serious than merely capturing witches.

Tomás Lozano's absorbing tale "And Sunday, Seven" is another example of the important role religion plays in counteracting the bizarre prac-

Stone home in southeastern rural New Mexico. Photo by Nasario García, 2001.

The Plaza Hotel, a majestic landmark built in 1882, Las Vegas, New Mexico. Photo by Nasario García, 2001.

Spanish Mission, Old San Antonio, Texas, eightneeth entury. Photo by Nasario García, 1989.

tices of witches on their Sabbath, when they dance and prance around the bonfire. The two victims, both hunchbacked, suffered surprising and diametrically opposed fates at the hands of these wicked sorceresses. Neither outcome falls within the scope of human understanding, though both lie well within the boundaries of the supernatural.

I well recall how, when I was a small boy, the kitchen at my grandfather's ranch house would light up when he was away in Albuquerque. Upon looking closer—along with my mother, of course—we found that the *farol* or lantern would extinguish itself as we neared the kitchen window. It happened to us more than once. Or there was the mysterious glowing light mentioned in the preface that shone from time to time at night in the bedroom where my parents kept their small life savings (a few dollars, as I recall) in a Mason jar hidden for safekeeping in the mudplastered adobe wall.

One may hear about car lights shining down a mesa (enchanted mesas tended to be associated with automobile lights), phantasmal lights, balls of fire, glowing objects climbing walls, luminous candles, or corner fireplaces that lit up a room, the latter more symbolic of buried treasures. All of these speak to the fascinating world of the supernatural and the active role witches played while people slept.

Marcos C. Durán

PUEBLO, COLORADO

Balls of Fire

Listen, I just don't know. I did my share of running around. I was quite a party man, a rover of sorts. From the time I married my wife, not because she's my wife, but she's been very good to me, so I don't run around anymore.

I used to work in Los Alamos, New Mexico [northeast of Las Vegas], and we had our son here in Pueblo, Colorado. One time we left from over there, it was already quite late, and we passed by that plant in Ojo Caliente. There's a place called Gavilán and there were lots of houses. Our older son was even with us, plus the one that's in the hospital. I was driving. There we were, my wife and I and the two sons, and they said to me, "Look! Look! What is that?," claiming that sparks were coming from an old empty shanty. "Look, look over there!"

Well, I didn't see anything. Why lie? I said to them, "I can't see anything. You're lying."

But the three of them did say that witches came out from there. The balls of fire were presumably witches, since they're like a spark. But God hasn't given me the ability to see. The Lord has not given me permission to witness any of that stuff.

In any case, in chatting with a compadre I had, he used to say to me, "They're not lies, compadre. It's the real truth."

A Whole Bunch of Witches

One time a compadre of mine and some friends were out and about, and I understand they saw a bunch of sparks like fire. One of them was named John, whereupon one of the friends said, "Well, my grandma claimed that fellows named John could catch the witches by taking off their jacket and turning it inside out."

That's where they'd fall, but he must be a John.

"Come, John!" they said to him, and he took off his jacket and tossed it on the ground.

It was a whole bunch of witches. I understand they were really beautiful and pretty girls that you just can't imagine. But the witches asked that particular John to fetch the jacket from the ground, for him to put it on, and to set them free so they could take off.

"It's very far and we have to be at a certain place by such and such time," and they flew off.

So John put on his jacket and the sparks flew off again.

Tiny Candles

I saw this one thing. That I can say for sure, but I can't say if it was a witch or what it was.

At home my dad many times had farmhands, and one time a man from a place over in what is called Chaperito, New Mexico, went to work for him. I became acquainted with Chaperito when I was working in Los Alamos [northeast of Las Vegas]. Mom fixed up a bed for this man. Well, we really didn't have beds or anything like that unless you were rich folks. Right there on the floor is where you fixed the beds for sleeping, and so Mom made up a bed for that man from Chaperito, right there by the door that we used to come in or to go out.

Well, we were sound asleep, and there he was snoring like all get-out and so we woke up. The first one to wake up was Mom, and she in turn woke up Dad.

"Listen," she said to him.

"What?" he answered.

"Listen here! Don't you ever bring a farmhand here again to sleep with us."

"Why?"

"Look at what's happening. Look at those tiny candles climbing there."

The lights were climbing up the door frame headed the other way, and then turning downward and so forth.

"Next time you want to hire farmhands, put them up in the dispensary. I don't want to see those things here. I don't know what they are."

"Oh," said Dad. "He's a good man. Perhaps they're lights that God has sent our way."

"I don't know if it's God who has sent them, but I don't want to see them here."

That's one thing I remember seeing. I was already a grown boy. We were all sleeping in the same room when all of that happened.

An Animal That Radiates Light

One time my dear wife and I were alone, so I'll tell you about it. She was no longer teaching and she had a card game and she said to me, "Why don't you come and play cards with me tonight?"

We were already married. When it comes to cards . . . as for that sort of thing, I was never very good at it. I can't play cards or anything like that. I don't recall what she called the game. I believe it was Black Cat and Cat. I don't know what it was, but we started playing cards, she and I did.

Well, do you know what happened when I dropped a card under the table and I stooped down to get it? I grabbed the card when all of a sudden there goes a small flame, the same thing like when you light a candle, and I said to my wife, "Good gracious! Look what's moving there!"

"What is it?" she said.

I thought it was . . . I don't know what you call it. It's like an animal that radiates light at night. I told her it was something like that.

That's the only thing my wife and I have ever seen. But I didn't get scared. She got scared, yes. Not me.

Bencés Gabaldón

BERNALILLO, NEW MEXICO

A Terrible Ball of Fire

Well, listen, I got to see sorcerers. One time, a long time ago, a family who lived very close to us in San Luis moved to a place where they were going to farm. That's all they were going to do, cultivate it. They moved from San Luis northward, about a mile or two, thereabouts. They took all of their junk. In fact, no one stayed back; the house was left empty. The house that these people left behind was nearby. It must have been about, at the very most, about one hundred yards from our house.

Well, in the evening, thereabouts, into the night, while already dark, the boy who had moved all of the family's junk came back to return the horse wagon to an uncle of mine. About the time he was passing by his house, which had been left vacant, a terrible ball of fire started coming from the house and got in between the mules' legs. They took off running with him, headed down range, and that ball of fire persisted in getting entangled in the mules' legs. The place was really lit up! The fire really traveled fast, to the point where it seemed like everything was illuminated with lanterns.

And then, then we took off from our house because, as I said, it was close by. It wasn't more than one hundred yards away. We went to see. Nothing! There was nothing. Not even a straw could be seen moving. No matter how hard we tried! And then when we headed back, the house was lit up again, but there was no one home. The empty house was all alone. All alone! The sparks of fire could be seen coming out the chimney, but when we went there, there wasn't anybody. I saw everything! I saw it! And that's no lie.

Sparks That Flew

And something else too! I'm going to tell you something else I saw. I recall a young man named Juan Mora. This fellow was on his way from Albuquerque with a wagon full of cargo headed for San Luis. When he was about to approach the Río Puerco, a huge ball of fire overwhelmed him and he didn't know what it was. He simply didn't know. He just didn't.

Listen, I don't know where in the devil all those sparks came from back in those days. I remember that they could land on top of trees and the trees lit up. I myself got to see it all. That I can attest to. And that's no lie. It's not a lie because I saw it.

Many things like that happened. Many! Yes. There were red sparks that flew the same way airplanes do today. They flew through the sky.

Nasario P. García

LOS RANCHOS DE ALBURQUERQUE, NEW MEXICO

Two Witches and Two Fellows Named John

My paternal grandfather's name was Juan García, and he was blind. He was on his way from Guadalupe to town, to Albuquerque. Besides Dad, I don't know who else was with him, or the purpose of the trip. I don't know if it was to take groceries back to the ranch or what. I just don't know, but there in La Ceja, where he and his buddies were camping—it was during the month of May—they saw two lights coming. The lights came from here in Albuquerque.

Then my grandfather and his other companions started to chat, and among them was another Juan, besides my grandfather. At that point I understand my grandfather asked them which direction the lights were coming from, so they told him. "Well, take me," my grandfather said to my dad, and the two fellows named John took off, far from where their campsite was.

There the Johns made a line pointing in the direction of the two lights. Then they made a circle, one in one place and another in another, one for each light. Then they took off, yes, each took off his undershirt and put one in each circle and went back to their campsite.

All of a sudden here go the lights and they disappeared. A little while later my grandfather and the other fellow named John returned to the circles and there were these two women covered with the two undershirts that my grandfather and the other Juan had left.

I understand that these two women were on their way to La Sierra del Valle, as it's called, where their husbands were shearing sheep. The women evidently were from here in Los Duranes or Los Griegos in Albuquerque. Or I don't know where my dad said they were from. That's what my dad used to tell me.

Well, they were witches! Witches! What else could they have been! These witches were airborne, you see, but those fellows named John, they're capable of catching them, provided they know how. Do you understand? The *juanes* have a lot of power if they know how to catch witches. It so happened that on that occasion there were two *juanes*.

Well, the women told them they were headed for La Sierra del Valle, where their husbands were involved in shearing sheep. Then the witches offered the two *juanes* I don't know how many goats if they would just turn them loose. The *juanes* turned them loose, and they rose and took off, flying.

But many people claim that witches—I don't know how they do it—can go outside and right there they can turn into a bird and fly. That's one thing my dad used to tell me.

Carmelita Gómez

LAS VEGAS, NEW MEXICO

Why, She Was a Witch, Wasn't She?

People claim there was a bogeyman. There was supposedly the Wailing Woman. They used to tell us, "Keep quiet, children. The Wailing Woman is to going to come and get you. If you don't keep quiet, it's going to come." My father would tell us that there was this woman. She had lots of kids and they were terrible. "Keep quiet, kids! The Wailing Woman's going to come." But I understand that where I lived, in Jorupa, that there were lots of witches. Why, we even saw them. We'd see the sparks flying. José Lucero used to say, "Come and sit down here so you can see. From Jorupa on down to Antón Chico you can see lots of lights [witches] flying."

And it was true. You could see them bouncing, and bouncing, and bouncing. But I'm going to tell you something. One time, I was still single, we were at a dance in Los Torres. I was at the dance. My brother Liberato, who was also single, was at the dance as well. There was María, Franque Tapia, and Vitoriano. When we left the dance, we saw a light moving like so [bouncing] on top of the mountain. It was bouncing on top of the mountain, and I said to them, "Adolfo Martínez's sheep [witches] are on the loose," because it seemed like they were headed from down below [where Martínez lived], and that's where the light came down.

From time to time we'd come down from Los Torres through San José, cross the river, and the witch, the light, would pass by behind us. Then there she'd be in front of us. This witch took off in the direction of Los Torres. She headed right up the small canyon, and we never saw her again. Why, she was a witch, don't you think?

Reynaldo Gonzales
LAS VEGAS, NEW MEXICO

Two Lights Flying

Who knows whether it's true or lies, but they used to tell me stories. I was already a big boy. I was a little grown-up. This other boy and I used to go to this school at night to kill some time. It had a huge door. That's where we sat down to chat when the weather was nice. We were sitting down one time when we saw in the distance—there was a mesa—two lights [sparks] flying in the sky, headed our way. They'd go up and down. They descended close to where we were. They whizzed by over the roof of the house. The humming was just like when the wind is blowing. They took off down range. Who knows? Surely they were witches. That's what they were, witches! When it comes to witches, that's what I saw.

Edumenio "Ed" Lovato
ALBUQUERQUE (LOS GRIEGOS), NEW MEXICO

A Light Flashed By

My daddy and some other men one time were at a religious wake. A young girl died there in San Luis. They were outside, and a light flashed by. A light raced on by. It crossed the river; it went across the river. It

wasn't a car, but it did go down into the river. Then it went up, close to where the men were. They were about a quarter of a mile from the light.

And from there it took off, and my daddy saw it headed our way, moving, and then it disappeared. From the time it went down into the river, they went to see, my daddy and four other men. When they got to where the light disappeared into the river, it was already going up the mesa. There was no indication that it was a car. The mesa is very steep, and the light went straight up. It disappeared from sight.

The men never could learn what it was. It could have been one of those fireflies or something like that, you know. It could have been that.

Tomás Lozano

ALBUQUERQUE, NEW MEXICO

And Sunday, Seven

There once lived a hunchbacked farmer who walked several kilometers every day to his fields where he spent the entire day doing his work. It so happened that one day he stayed longer than usual and the sun was setting when he finished his farm chores. He gathered his tools and headed home by way of the mountain paths.

As he went behind a few rocks on the side of the road he thought he heard several chants followed by laughs and bursts of laughter. The farmer stopped to listen more attentively, strayed from his path, and then went where he thought the chants and strange laughs were coming from. As he came near the forest's underbrush, the chants and laughs could be heard more clearly and he was able to make out the flames of a huge bonfire. He got as close as he could to observe the spectacle—his eyes could hardly believe what he saw. Circled around the huge bonfire were many witches dancing and making all kinds of gestures amid laughs, screams, and bursts of laughter as they sang all together.

> *Monday, Tuesday, Wednesday, three,*
> *Thursday, Friday, Saturday, six.*

The hunchbacked peasant for a long while was absorbed in listening and contemplating what he saw before his eyes. The song that the witches were repeating time after time began to stick in his head. First he started singing it softly, and little by little, as if he were hypnotized, he began to raise the tone of his voice until he felt totally seduced by the melody and continued singing with the witches.

Monday, Tuesday, Wednesday, three,
Thursday, Friday, Saturday, six.

Such was his enthusiasm that at a decided moment he stood up from his hiding place and hollered loudly, responding to the witches' chorus,

And Sunday, Seven!

The witches' Sabbath stopped immediately and in the blink of an eye he found himself surrounded by witches. The poor hunchbacked peasant thought that his hour of reckoning had come. The witches grabbed him and carried him off in flight to the bonfire.

"How dare you insult us with that miserable and wicked day!" said the witches.

He didn't say anything since fear had numbed his tongue, but he understood his blunder. Sunday is the Lord's sacred day. The witches then huddled among themselves. "This man deserves a punishment. What can we do to him?" And they decided that because he intruded, they would all at once give him a good whack on his hunched back, whereupon the latter disappeared instantly. This was followed by getting rid of him.

The peasant couldn't believe his good fortune and got home at dawn, proud as a peacock. He changed clothes and went to town on the other side of this hill. He headed for the home of a friend who was also hunch-backed and told him everything that had occurred the night before.

From that day forward the only thing his friend could do was to roam those parts in search of the witches' Sabbath. Finally one day at dusk he was able to hear in the distance the witches' laughs and voices. He got close and saw the same scene that his friend had described to him earlier. He waited there for the opportune moment to interrupt the noisy celebra-tion, just as his friend had told him.

This time around, a second major flight took place and he felt himself being transported through the skies until he reached the bonfire sur-rounded by witches. They responded in the same fashion. "This man deserves to be punished. What can we do to him?" But this time they decided to give him a good whack on his chest as punishment, a sentence that resulted in a second hump on the back of the poor peasant, whom they got rid of immediately.

Benjamín "Benny" Lucero

ALBUQUERQUE, NEW MEXICO

Something Is Headed Our Way

One time I was on my way home with a cow that I wanted to sell. And this cow took off all the way up the river. As I turned it around, it fell into a backwater. You know what it's like when the river's running. You know, why tell you about the Río Puerco, you grew up over there. This cow fell into a stagnant pond, and I said to myself, "I've had it. This cow's stuck."

Well, I came back with a set of pulleys and some ropes, to see how I could pull her out. And we [he and his wife] went down to the riverbed. The sun was about to set. It was already very late, and so we left the truck above the riverbank and we went down on foot. You know well how you can't get down to the river just anywhere. Well, I didn't want to risk getting the truck stuck, so I unloaded the ropes and everything. Say no more. I don't know how the cow managed to get out. "Let's go!" I said to my wife. "Let's go! The cow's out! What luck!" The cow was close by, close to where she had lain down. There she was. "Oh, I hit it lucky!" I said to my wife. "We don't have to pull her out."

I thought I was going to take a beating, having to get into the water, or having to thrash from one end to the other. But the first thing I was going to do was to try the pulleys, to see if I could get the cow out. I said to myself, "I'll tie them to this bush for support."

Well, all of a sudden something is headed our way from the direction of the sun. Shaped like a post, you see. The only thing is that the sun blinded us from seeing it very well. And what with the good feeling of the cow having gotten unstuck, since I wasn't going to have to work to get it out, especially after spending so much time on horseback, tired and all, I almost didn't pay attention to that thing.

By the time I saw it for the last time, the sun had already shifted more to the west. The thing, shaped like a post, was moving as though it were hanging like a post, but it disappeared. It was headed for La Sierra, toward the ranch where I live in Cabezón. But I can't tell you what it was since I couldn't make it out because of the sun. The sun screwed me up. When the object appeared close by, I still can't tell you what it was, what color it was, or what it was like. But I was watching and it looked like a post. And it went off. It went off. What it was, I don't know. I can't tell you.

Manuel de Jesús Manzanares

PUEBLO, COLORADO

A Light Came On

One time, it was at night also, and a light came on over in the corner of the house. There was a fireplace over here in this other corner, and another one inside another room in the corner. The wife had a small table, and from there a light would come on as though you were pointing a flashlight. It lit up the children's room. I saw it and I got up tippy-toe and I went in the other rooms to see where the light was coming from or to see if a reflection or something was coming in from outside. And nothing! I couldn't see anything. Then I was getting ready to go back to bed when my wife heard me.

"What are you doing?"

"Nothing," I said. "Look up above the window to see if you spot anything."

At that very moment that I was talking to her the light came on again, and so she was able to see it herself. By and large, whenever anything like that happens, you get like shook up or scared or something.

After we moved there to the house, some men went looking for treasures. They dug where the corner fireplace was and where another one was in the other room in the corner where the light came on, but they never found anything.

I Didn't Hear Any Noise

Over at this small ranch that I bought, I rounded up some cattle that Mom had at her ranch and I took them to that place of mine. It wasn't long as it turned out before a younger sister of mine was going to get married, and Mom wanted to slaughter a calf so as to have meat for the wedding. She didn't have a young calf; she had heifers. So I said to Mom, "If you want, I have a young steer over at my ranch. It's very fat. If you wish, I can exchange it for a heifer."

"Yes," said Mom.

Why, yes. We took off one afternoon when I was working at the Turner Mine at the time, and so we took off, my "brother-in-law" and I, to slaughter the calf. We went there and killed it, loaded the meat in the wagon, this and that, and then started picking up the knives and ropes and everything that we had used. At the very last moment I had left the ropes in the corral, and we had gone inside the house to put up what we

93

had used. I then said to my brother-in-law, "I'm going after the ropes."

I took off for the corral, grabbed the ropes and brought them with me. When I was on my way back, I saw my brother-in-law who was already on the wagon and I said to myself, "I guess Fidel is anxious to leave."

Well, I went inside the house, threw the ropes down, closed the door, climbed on the wagon, and we took off. He didn't say anything. Later on he told my wife, "And you're going to live in that house? That house is noisy."

Later on as time went on I got hurt at the mine and couldn't work. I went to the rancho to do whatever little chores I could. I said, "Rather than work at the mine I'm going to do any little thing at the ranch."

Well, the wife fixed me my lunch and I headed for the ranch to do my small chores. All I took with me was a bedroll, but I didn't hear any noise. I didn't hear noises. I was over there alone, and the only noise came from the rats. That's all I heard until I was getting ready to head home for Mom's house. That last night it sounded like someone had tossed a door on top of the roof. I got scared, left the house, and took off.

But afterwards when my wife and I moved to the ranch, before reaching the house, you climbed a small hill, and then you could get a full view of the house. Several times on our way back at night from our neighbor's house down below from us, upon climbing up the hill you could see like a small fire. It seemed as though the flame rose in the atmosphere and then went out two or even more times, but when you reached the house, there was nothing. I don't have any idea what it could have been.

Damiano Romero

LOS RANCHOS DE ALBURQUERQUE, NEW MEXICO

Lights

Yes, there were places where you could see lights and all of that stuff. One could never find anything, but lights were seen in certain places. Even now there's places, locations, in some old, abandoned homes, which can be seen from a distance, and you can pick a night and stand outside and take a look and there's a light in that certain house. And no one's living in it! The place is already abandoned.

I've seen lights myself in those homes. Of course when one gets close to them, they go out, but as soon as you walk away, they light up again. I don't know what it is! People say that there's hidden treasures or something. Perhaps that's true!

But on other occasions I've had the opportunity of having gone in the evening, at dusk, with my two boys. We got to see cars, I mean, car lights on top of the mesa at San Luis. There's no road there or anything, but when they reached the edge of the mesa, the lights pointed downward without there being a road. I don't know what it was! One thing for sure, my two boys were with me. Whenever I talk about this, a few people believe me, but the rest of them don't.

Eileen Dolores Treviño Villarreal

SAN ANTONIO, TEXAS

The House Where I Was Raised

The house where I was raised is not too far from San Antonio, actually quite close to downtown. Mom used to tell me about strange things that happened in that home without knowing how. That's before I was born.

My oldest brother was lying down on the couch and he saw balls of fire and he thought that he was burning. He then went after Mom, and by the time they returned they [the fireballs] were gone. There was nothing. My mother told me that it was in that house where you could hear things and things happened.

Luces, brasas, y bolas de lumbre

Es que María la Maruja, es bruja.

Marcos C. Durán

PUEBLO, COLORADO

Bolas de lumbre

Yo no sé, oiga. Yo anduve muncho. Yo jui muy parrandero, muy andalugo. Ya de que me casé yo con mi esposa, no porque es mi esposa, pero ella ha sido muy güena, y por eso ya no ando de vagamundo.

Yo trabajaba en Los Álamos, Nuevo México [al noreste de Las Vegas], y teníanos aquí a mi hijo, aquí en Pueblo, Colorado. Una vez nos vinimos de allá, ya muy tarde, y pasamos esa planta del Ojo Caliente. Ahi está un lugar que le dicen El Gavilán y había munchas casas. Hasta el muchacho mayor venía conmigo, y el otro que tengo en el hospital. Yo venía arriando. Ahi viníanos yo y mi vieja y los dos hijos y me dicían ellos,

—¡Mira! ¡Mira! ¿Qué es?—es que salían brasas de un chante que estaba ahi desocupao—. ¡Mira, mira allá!

Pues yo no vide nada. ¿Por qué voy a mentir? Les decía yo,

—No estoy mirando nada. Están mintiendo.

Pero los tres dijieron que sí salían de ahi las brujas. Es que eran brujas las bolas de lumbre, que son como una brasa. Pero Dios no me ha dao licencia pa ver. No me ha dao licencia mi Señor pa ver nada d'eso.

De modo es que me platicaba un compadre que tenía yo y me dicía, "No son mentiras, compadre. Es la mera verdá."

Un carajal de brujas

Una vez un compadre mío y unos amigos andaban por ahi y es que vieron venir munchas brasas, como lumbre. Uno d'ellos se llamaba Juan, y dijo uno de los amigos, "Pos, mi abuelita dicía que los juanes podían agarrar las brujas quitándose la leva y tirándola al revés."

Ahi caiban ellas, pero que sea un Juan.

—¡Anda Juan!—es que le dijieron, y se quitó la leva y la tiró en la tierra.

Era un carajal de brujas. Es que eran unas muchachas tan lindas y tan bonitas que no tiene usté idea. Pero le pidieron ellas a ese Juan que quitara esa leva de la tierra, que se la pusiera, y que las hiciera libres pa salir de ahi.

—Está muy lejos y tenemos que estar pallá pa tales horas—y se despidieron.

Ansina se puso Juan la leva y es que salieron las brasas otra vez.

Velitas

Una cosa vide yo. Nomás eso sí puedo decir, pero no puedo decir si era bruja o qué sería.

En casa tenía munchas veces mi papá piones, y una vez jue un hombre d'ese lugar de Nuevo México que le llaman Chaperito. Jue a trabajar por él. Yo conocí ese Chaperito ora que trabajaba en Los Álamos [al noreste de Las Vegas]. A este hombre le puso mamá cama. Güeno, pues no teníanos camaltas ni nada a menos que juera la gente rica. Ahi en el suelo se ponían las camas, y le puso mamá a ése de Chaperito cama en la puerta onde salíanos pa juera.

Pues, estábanos muy bien dormidos y antonces estaba él con unas roncaderas del caramba y recordamos. La primera que recordó jue mamá, y ella recordó a en papá.

—¡Oye!—le dijo.

—¿Qué?—contestó él.

—¡Fíjate! No vuelvas a trae a un pión aquí a dormir.

—¿Por qué?

—Mira lo que está pasando. Mira como están subiendo como velitas.

Las luces subían el marco de la puerta y logo se iban paquel lao y logo pa bajo y ansina estaban.

—Otra vez cuando quieras buscar piones, ponlos allá en la dispensa. Aquí no quiero ver esas cosas. Yo no sé qué serán.

—Oh—dijo en papá—. Ése es buen hombre. Pueda que sean luces que manda Dios.

—Yo no sé si las mandará Dios, pero no quiero velas aquí.

Eso sí me acuerdo yo que vide. Ya estaba yo grandecito. Estábanos todos dormidos en el mesmo cuarto cuando pasó too eso.

Un animal que da luz

Una vez estábanos yo y mi viejita solos, que ora le platicaré. No estaba de mestra ya, y tenía un juego de barajas y me dijo,

—¿Por qué no vienes a jugar a las barajas conmigo esta noche?

Ya estábanos casaos. Yo de barajas . . . yo d'eso sí nunca pude. No sé jugar baraja ni nada. No sé cómo le dicía ella al juego. Creo que Negro Gato y Gato. No sé cómo, pero nos pusimos a jugar a la baraja, yo y ella.

Pos sabe usté lo que me pasó cuando se me cayó una baraja pa bajo 'e la mesa y me abajé yo a'garrala. Agarré yo la baraja cuando iba una llamita, la misma cosa que cuando prende usté una vela, y le dije a mi señora,

—¡Ay caramba! ¡Mira lo que va ahi!

—¿Qué es?—dijo ella.

Yo pensé que era . . . yo no sé cómo les dicen. Es como un animal que da luz en la noche. Le dije que era como uno d'esos.

Eso es lo único que hemos visto yo y mi señora. Pero no me dio miedo a mí. A ella sí le dio miedo. A mí no.

Bencés Gabaldón

BERNALILLO, NEW MEXICO

Un brasero bárbaro

Pues yo llegué a ver brujos, oiga. Una vez, en un tiempo, una gente que vivía ahi cerquita de nosotros en San Luis se cambiaron a un lugar que iban a sembrar. Enteramente lo iban ellos a sembrar. Se cambiaron de ahi de San Luis pa arriba, quizá como una milla o unas dos millas, por ahi. Se llevaron todo el garrero. Güeno, no quedó naiden en la casa; estaba vacía la casa. La casa que dejaron estaba cerquita. Puede que como unas, cuanto más, puede que hubiera cien yardas de la casa de nosotros.

Pues, de ahi en la tarde, en la noche, ya oscuro, vino el muchacho que había llevao el garrero; vino a trae el carro de caballos pa case un tío mío. Pues, que cuando iba pasando por su casa, que había quedao vacía, va saliendo un brasero bárbaro de ahi y se le metió a las mulas aquí abajo entre las patas. Arrancaron a juir con él, pa 'bajo, y aquel brasero metiéndosele a las mulas aquí en las patas. ¡Se alumbraba bien alumbrao! Bien corría la lumbre, que parecía que tenían alumbrao con lámparas.

Y luego, luego juimos nosotros de ahi d'en casa, porque estaba cerquita, como dije. No había ni cien yardas. Juimos a ver, ¡y nada! No había nada. No se movía una paja. ¡Por nada! Y luego cuando nos vinimos ya estaba la casa alumbraa otra vez, pero no había naiden. Estaba nomás la pura casa vacía. ¡Sola! Salía el brasero por la chiminea, y cuando juimos nosotros no había naiden. ¡Yo lo vide! ¡Yo lo vide! Y no es mentira.

Brasas que volaban

¡Y luego verás te tú! Te voy a platicar otra cosa que vide yo tamién. Me acuerdo yo diun muchacho que se llamaba Juan Mora. Este muchacho iba con flete de aquí de La Plaza pallá pa San Luis. Cuando iba aá llegando al Río Puerco, se le prendió un brasero a él, que no sabía qué era. Pues nomás no supo. No supo.

Yo no sé diónde demonio habría tantas brasas en esos tiempos, oye. Yo me acuerdo que se podían parar arriba en los álamos; se alumbraban los álamos. Yo lo llegué a ver yo. Eso sí lo llegué a ver yo. Y no es mentira. No es mentira porque yo lo vide.

Muchas cosas pasaban asina. ¡Munchas cosas! Sí. Eran brasas que volaban lo mesmo que los oroplanos ora. Volaban por el viento.

Nasario P. García

LOS RANCHOS DE ALBURQUERQUE, NEW MEXICO

Dos brujas y dos juanes

Mi agüelo se llamaba Juan García, su papá d' en papá, y estaba cieguito. Él venía de allá de Gualupe pacá pa La Plaza, pa Alburquerque. Amás d'en papá, yo no sé con quiénes vendría él [sus nombres], o a qué vendría. Yo no sé si a llevar provisiones pal rancho o qué. Yo no sé, pero ahi en La Ceja, onde estaban campeando—era en el mes de mayo—vieron, vieron venir dos luces. Iban de aquí de Alburquerque.

Loo empezaron a platicar mi agüelito y sus otros compañeros, y venía otro Juan tamién, amás de mi agüelo. Y loo es que les preguntó mi agüelo que si de qué rumbo venían las luces. Ya le dijieron. "Pues, llévenme," es que le dijo mi agüelo a en papá, y se jueron los dos juanes, lejos de dionde tenían el campo.

Ahi es que hicieron una raya los juanes pal rumbo que venían las dos luces. Loo hicieron una rueda, una aquí y otra allá, una pa cada luz. Loo se quitaron, sí, se quitaron la camiseta y la pusieron en cada rueda y se jueron patrás pal campo.

Cuando de güenas a primeras aquí van las luces y se desaparecieron. Al rato vinieron mi agüelo y el otro Juan a ver y es que ahi estaban cobijadas dos mujeres con las camisetas que dejaron los juanes.

Tengo entendido que éstas eran dos mujeres que iban pa La Sierra del Valle, que le llaman, par onde estaban sus maridos en la borrega tresquilando. Es que las mujeres eran de aquí de Los Duranes o de Los

Griegos en Alburquerque. O no sé diónde dijo en papá. Eso sí me platicaba él.

¡Pues eran brujas! ¡Brujas! ¡Qué pueden haber sido! Estas brujas iban volando, ¿ves? Pero aquéllos, los juanes, pueden agarrar las brujas, si saben. ¿Entiendes? Los juanes tienen muncho poder si saben pa 'garrar las brujas. Tocó que en esa oportunidá había dos juanes.

Pues, es que ellas les dijieron a ellos que iban pa La Sierra del Valle, par onde estaban sus maridos, que estaban en la tresquila. Antonces ellas les ofrecían no sé qué tantas cabras nomás porque las soltaran. Las soltaron, y se levantaron ellas y se jueron volando.

Pero reclaman munchos—yo no sé en qué modo lo harán—que pueden salir pa juera y ahi mesmo pueden volverse como un pájaro y volar. Eso sí me platicaba en papá.

Carmelita Gómez

LAS VEGAS, NEW MEXICO

Pus era bruja, ¿qué no?

Isque había coco. Había La Llorona. Dicían, "Cállense hijitos, va venir La Llorona. Si no se callan va venir La Llorona." Platicaba mi papá que había una mujer. Tenía munchos muchichitos y eran muy atroces. "Cállense hijitos. Orita viene La Llorona." Pero ahi en onde yo vivía, en Jorupa, isque había munchas brujas. Pus nojotros las víanos. Iban las brasas volando. Dicía José Lucero, "Siéntense aquí pa que vean. De aá de Jorupa salen munchas luces [brujas] paá pa Antón Chico."

Y era verdá. Iban saltando y saltando y saltando. Pero le voy a platicar. Una vez, taa yo soltera, andábanos en un baile en los Torres. Andaba yo. Mi hermano Liberato estaa soltero. Él andaba, tamién. Andaba la María, andaba Franque Tapia, y andaba Vitoriano. Cuando salimos del baile, vimos venir una luz asina, saltando, sobre el monte. Venía corriendo sobre el monte, y les dije, "Ya se le salieron las borregas [brujas] a Adolfo Martínez," porque parecía que venían de abajo y ahi bajó [donde vivía Martínez] derecho la brasa, la luz.

Nosotros veníanos en veces de aá de Los Torres por San José y pasáamos el río. Una vez pasó la bruja, la brasa, atrás de nosotros. Loo adelante iba. Esta bruja pescó too ahi en los Torres. Loo pescó too el cañoncito, y no la vimos más. Pus, ésa era bruja, ¿qué no?

Reynaldo Gonzales

LAS VEGAS, NEW MEXICO

Dos brasas volando

Quién sabe si será verdá o será mentira, pero a mí me contaban historias. Yo estaa muchacho grande. Grandecito estaa yo. Yo y otro muchacho íbanos a aquea escuela a estarnos en la noche. Tenía una puerta grande. Ahi nos sentábanos cuando estaa bonito el tiempo, a platicar. Táanos sentaos cuando vimos de aá lejos, taa la mesa, vinían dos brasas volando en l'aire. Bajaban y subían. Bajaron cerca onde estáanos nojotros. Por arriba el techo pasaron. Un zumbío lo mismo que l' aire. Se fueron pa bajo. ¿Quién sabe? Seguro qu'eran brujas. ¡No eran más de brujas! Eso jue too lo que vide de las brujas.

Edumenio "Ed" Lovato

ALBUQUERQUE (LOS GRIEGOS), NEW MEXICO

Pasó una luz

Mi *daddy* y otros hombres una vez estaban en un velorio. Una muchacha se murió ahi en San Luis. Estaban ajuera, y pasó una luz. Pasó una luz. Cruzó el río; pasó el río. No era carro, pero sí bajó el río. Luego subió, cerca dionde estaban ellos. Estaban como un cuarto de milla.

Y de ahi pescó, y la vido mi *daddy* venir, caminando y luego se jue. De allá cuando bajó el río se vinieron ellos a ver. Ahi iba mi *daddy* y otros cuatro hombres a ver. Cuando ellos llegaron onde vieron que bajó, ya ésta iba caminando subiendo la mesa. No había *signs* de que juera carro. La mesa es muy alta, y subió derecho. Se tapó.

The men never could learn what it was. It could have been one of those fireflies or something like that, you know. It could have been that!

Tomás Lozano

ALBUQUERQUE, NEW MEXICO

Domingo siete

Vivía en las montañas un labrador jorobado que todos los días caminaba varios kilómetros hasta donde tenía sus campos en donde pasaba el día en sus labores labriegas. Sucedió que un día se tardó más de la cuenta y el sol se estaba poniendo cuando acabó su labranza. Recogió sus aperos y se encaminó hacia su casa por los senderos de la montaña.

Al pasar tras unas rocas al borde del camino le pareció escuchar unos cantos acompañados de risas y carcajadas. El labrador se paró a escuchar más atentamente y salió de su camino para dirigirse hacia donde creía él que venían esos cantos y risas extraños. A medida que se acercaba entre la maleza del bosque, los cantos y risas se oían más claramente y pudo divisar la luz [las llamas] de una gran fogata. Se acercó tanto como pudo a observar aquel espectáculo al cual no daba crédito a sus ojos. Alrededor de una gran fogata muchas brujas danzaban con grandes gesticulaciones y entre risas, gritos y carcajadas cantaban todas a coro.

Lunes, martes, miércoles, tres,
jueves, viernes, sábado, seis.

El campesino jorobado se quedó un largo rato ensimismado escuchando y contemplando lo que tenía frente a sus ojos. La canción que repetían incesantemente una y otra vez se le fue metiendo en la cabeza. Empezó primero a cantarla en voz baja y poco a poco, como si estuviese hipnotizado, empezó a elevar el tono de su voz hasta que se sintió totalmente transportado por la tonada y siguió cantando con las brujas.

Lunes, martes, miércoles, tres,
jueves, viernes, sábado, seis.

Tal fue su entusiasmo que en un momento determinado se levantó de su escondite y gritó fuertemente respondiendo al coro de brujas,

¡Y Domingo, siete!

El aquelarre se detuvo de inmediato y en un abrir y cerrar de ojos se encontró rodeado de brujas. El pobre campesino jorobado pensó que le había llegado la hora. Las brujas le agarraron y le llevaron volando hasta la hoguera.

—¿Cómo te atreves a injuriarnos con ese día maldito y fatídico para nosotras?— le dijeron las brujas.

Él no dijo nada pues el miedo le había paralizado la lengua, pero comprendió su metedura de pata. El domingo es el día sagrado del Señor. Entonces las brujas discurrieron entre ellas. "Este hombre merece un escarmiento. ¿Qué le podemos hacer?" Y decidieron que por intrometido le darían todas a la vez un fuerte golpe en la joroba y ésta desapareció al instante. Acto seguido lo echaron de allí.

El campesino no podía creer su buena fortuna y llegó más contento que un ocho a su casa cuando rompía el alba. Se cambió de ropas y se fue para el pueblo que se encontraba al otro lado de una colina. Se dirigió a casa de un amigo suyo que también era jorobado y le contó todo lo que le había ocurrido durante la noche.

Desde aquel día el amigo no hacía más que rondar aquellos parajes en busca del aquelarre de brujas. Hasta que por fin un día al anochecer escuchó a lo lejos las risas y las voces de las brujas. Se acercó y contempló la misma escena que su amigo le había descrito antes. Aguardó allí hasta el momento que le pareció oportuno para interrumpir la celebración gritando tal y como su compadre le dijo.

Esta vez se armó un revuelo mayor y se sintió transportado por los aires hasta la hoguera rodeado de brujas. Éstas respondieron de la misma manera, "Este hombre merece un escarmiento. ¿Qué le podemos hacer?" Pero esta vez decidieron darle un fuerte golpe en el pecho como castigo y escarmiento, resultando en otra joroba en la espalda del pobre campesino a quien echaron de allí seguidamente.

Benjamín "Benny" Lucero

ALBUQUERQUE, NEW MEXICO

Ahi viene una cosa

En una vez venía con una vaca yo, que la quería vender. Y esta vaca agarró todo el río parriba. Cuando la golví patrás, se estalló en un remanso. Tú sabes cómo es cuando está el río corriente. Tú sabes. ¡Pa qué te platico del Río Puerco! Tú te has criao allá. Güeno, cayó en un remanso esta vaca, y dije, "Ya la fregué. La vaca la atascué."

Pus, me vine con unas rondanillas y unos cabrestos, a ver cómo la jalaba. Y nos bajamos [él y su esposa] pa 'bajo del río. Estaba el sol en juerza de meterse. Ya era muy tarde, y dejamos la troca arriba del río y nos bajamos pa 'bajo a pie. Tú sabes que uno no puede bajar en munchos lugares. Pus, no quería yo atascar la troca y apié los cabrestos y todo.

¡Nada! No sé cómo la vaca había salido. "¡Vámonos!," le dije a la mujer. "¡Vámonos! Ya salió la vaca. ¡Qué güena suerte!"

Estaba la vaca ahi cerca, ahi onde mesmo se había acostao nomás que había un ancón. Ahi estaba. "¡Oh, ya me armé!," le dije a la mujer. "Ya no la tenemos que sacar."

Yo pensé que iba a llevar una friega, pus meterte al agua, o en fin apalear este fin o el otro. Pero le iba hacerle lucha primero con las rondanillas a ver si la sacaba. Yo dije, "Las amarro de este amarraje."

Güeno, cuando ahi viene una cosa el rumbo del sol. En la forma de un poste, oye. Nomás que no nos dejaba el sol vela bien. Y loo yo con el gusto de que se había salido la vaca, que no iba yo a trabajar, porque tanto que anda uno a caballo y cansao y eso, ya casi ni le puse atención a la cosa esa.

Ya la última vez que la vide, ya el sol había cambiao más pal poniente. Iba la cosa esa como en la forma de un poste, lo mesmo que si se juera colgando asina como un poste, pero despareció. Iba como pal rumbo de la sierra, pal rancho de onde vivo yo en el Cabezón. Pero no te poo decir qué era porque no la podía ver bien a causa del sol. El sol me fregó. Cuando la cosa estaba cerca, no te poo decir qué sería, qué color sería, o cómo sería aquello. Pero la estaba mirando lo mesmo que un poste. Y se jue. Y se jue. ¿Qué cosa sería? No sé. No te poo decir yo.

Manuel de Jesús Manzanares

PUEBLO, COLORADO

Se prendió una luz

Una vez en la noche tamién se prendió una luz allá en el rincón de la casa. Había un jogón mexicano acá y loo pallá estaba la esquina de la casa, adentro. Tenía la vieja una mesita y ahi de la mesita se prendía una luz como si pusiera uno una *flashlight*. Alumbraba la cama de los muchachos. La vi yo y me levanté muy suavecito y anduve por otros cuartos a ver dónde venía esa luz o qué vislumbre había por fuera o algo. ¡Y nada! No pude ver nada. Loo me jui acostar y cuando me estaba acostando de güelta, me sintió la vieja.

—¿Qué andas haciendo?

—Nada—le dije—. Cuida ahi arriba de la ventana a ver qué miras.

En esto que le estaba diciendo se volvió a prender la luz otra vez y ya entonces la vio ella tamién. Pero por lo general cuando pasa una cosa ansina, le da a uno como un terror o miedo o algo.

Ahi en casa después que nos mudamos nosotros, jueron a escarbar allá. Escarbaron donde estaba el jogón mexicano y otro en el rincón ese donde se prendía la luz, pero nunca hallaron nada.

Yo no oí ruido

Allá en el ranchito este que compré yo, junté unas vacas que tenía ahi en el rancho amá y las llevé pal lugar ése. En poco tiempo tocó que se iba casar una hermanita mía, y mi mamá quería matar un becerro pa la carne pal casorio. No tenía ella un becerro novillo; tenía terneras. Yo le dije a mamá,

—Pues si quiere, yo tengo un novillito allá en mi ranchito. Está muy gordo. Si quiere yo le cambio por una ternera.

—Sí—dijo.

Pues, sí. Nos juimos una tarde, trabajaba yo ahi en la mina en Turner, y nos juimos yo y mi concuño a matar el becerro. Juimos allá y lo matamos y loo que lo matamos echamos la carne en el carro y esto y lotro, y loo nos pusimos a recoger los cuchillos y los cabrestos y esto que usamos. Al último había dejao yo los cabrestos en el corral y habíanos entrao a la casa a poner alguna cosa de lo que habíanos usado. Ya le dije a mi concuño,

—Pues voy a trae los cabrestos.

Me jui al corral, agarré los cabrestos y los truje. Cuando venía yo de allá, vide a mi concuño que ya estaba sentao en el carro y dije, "Quizás ya Fidel está apurao pa irse."

Pues, entré yo pa dentro, tiré los cabrestos, cerré la puerta, y me subí en el carro y nos vinimos. No me dijo él nada. Después le dijo a mi esposa,

—¿Pues van a vivir en esa casa? Esa casa es ruidosa.

Después con el tiempo me lastimé en la mina y no podía trabajar. Me jui pal rancho a 'cer trabajito allá. Dije, "Mejor de trabajar en la mina voy hacer alguna cosita allá en el rancho." Pus me alistó mi lonche la vieja y me jui yo pal rancho pa 'cer trabajito. Nomás llevé una mochila pa dormir, pero yo no oí ruido. Yo no oí nada. Allá me estuve yo solo, y no había más ruido que las ratas. Jue todo lo que oí hasta que no estaba pa venirme a case 'e mamá. Esa última noche parecía que habían tirao una puerta sobre la zotea. Me dio miedo y me salí y me jui.

Pero después que nos mudamos yo y la esposa pallá pal rancho, antes de llegar a la casa, subía uno en la lomita, y loo daba vista uno a la casa. Varias veces cuando veníamos de a case'l vecino de aá bajo en la noche, cuando subíamos ahi se vía como una lumbrita fuera. Parecía que se levantaba la llama y loo se apagaba casi dos y otra vez, pero cuando llegaba uno ahi en casa, no había nada. No sé qué podría ser.

Damiano Romero

LOS RANCHOS DE ALBURQUERQUE, NEW MEXICO

Luces

Había lugares que se vían luces y todo, sí. Nunca había nada pero se vían luces en ciertos lugares. Toavía ora mismo hay lugares en algunas casas viejas que están abandonadas, que mira uno de aá lejos, y viene uno una noche y se para y mira y hay luz en aquella casa y no hay naide ahi. Ya está abandonao el lugar.

Yo mismo he visto luces en las casas. Por supuesto que cuando llega uno cerquita, se apagan las luces, pero nomás se retira uno y se güelven a prender. ¡No sé qué será! Dicen que hay tesoros, que hay algo ahi. ¡Puede que haiga!

Pero ha tocao en otras ocasiones que he ido ya en la tarde, pa la luz de la tarde, yo, mi muchacho y mi otro muchacho. Llegamos a ver carros, güeno, luces de carro arriba de la mesa de San Luis. Ahi no hay camino ni nada, y cuando llegaron a la orilla de la mesa, se clavaban las luces abajo derecho pal camino. ¡No sé qué sería! Eso sí, iban dos muchachos conmigo. Cuando platico eso me creyen pocos, pero los demás no me creyen.

Eileen Dolores Treviño Villarreal

SAN ANTONIO, TEXAS

La casa donde yo me crié

La casa donde yo me crié no está muy fuera de la ciudad de San Antonio, muy acercado al centro. Me platicaba mamá que allí en esa casa ocurrieron cosas que no tenían explicación. Esto fue antes de que yo naciera.

Mi hermano mayor estaba acostado en el sofá y vio unas llamaradas de lumbre y él pensaba que se estaba quemando. Entonces fue a traer a mi mamá y para cuando regresaron se habían ya terminado. No estaba nada. Me platicó mi madre que allí en esa casa se oían cosas y que pasaban cosas.

Four

Bewitched and Bewildered

....

One evil deed begets another.

INTRODUCTION

The notion of bewitchment has long existed among Latinos of the Southwest. Some view it as superstition, but others find it to be based on credible evidence. The debate between adherents and skeptics inevitably has focused on who, what, and where.

Stories vary according to the victim of record. The malevolent person suspected of inflicting evil, the reasons for his or her secret incantations, and where the wicked act may have been catalyzed, concocted, or carried out are also important. Oftentimes lost in this context, however, were the victim's family members as they searched to find a cure for the afflicted. The agony of seeing a loved one deteriorate physically and emotionally could prove devastating to them as well as to the victim.

Bewitchment terminology in Latino folklore of the Southwest may include, but is not limited to, *hacer (un) mal* (to inflict evil), *embrujar* (to bewitch), *enyerbar* or *dar chamico* (to poison with toxic herbs), or *hacer maleficio* (to cast a spell). These are the terms I am most familiar with; their connotation may vary according to geographic location, the context within which they are couched, and respective nuances. But in essence all denote bad news and something harmful to the injured party.

Let us examine these terms one by one. *Hacer mal* simply means to cause or inflict harm. However, the individual meting out pain is not necessarily deemed a witch. Causing harm (*haciendo mal*) can come not only in the most subtle and unanticipated way, but also from the least expected person—a family member. We find this surprising revelation in Lucinda Atencio's "Out of Envy They Do Evil Things to You." Yet *hacer mal* still does not pack the wicked jolt that *embrujar* and some of the other terms carry.

In the case of *embrujar*, the perpetrator's cruel practices may be combined with poisonous concoctions and used in a more deliberate and systematic fashion to harm either man or woman. *Enyerbar*, on the other hand, affects men more than women because the instigator in this case is generally a woman, who gives her husband or lover an herbal concoction to ensure that he continues to love her even after he has abandoned her. *Hacer maleficio=maleficium* is more a matter of casting an enchantment or spell; it can come from either gender and affects both men and women.

Except for cases of *hacer mal*, the person responsible for causing both physical and psychological harm is an outright witch or someone heavily endowed with sorcerer-like tendencies. In either instance, the witch remains anonymous until a cure is found, whereupon the true identity of the witch, the purveyor of evil, is divulged. This may be done by the folk healer, but only to the victim and no one else. To reveal the evildoer's name would put both the healer and the healed in jeopardy, especially if the perpetrator later sought revenge.

The ailments discussed here fall into two categories: white magic and black magic. *Hacer mal*, to inflict evil, stands alone under white magic; the remaining ones fall under black magic. Normally, as we see in Lucinda Atencio's account mentioned above, a *curandera/o*—a folk healer, a kind of general practitioner in the community and the quintessence of white magic—would be consulted to determine if the ailing person was suffering from an infliction of evil (*un mal*). Since this kind of illness purportedly does not come from witch-like sources, it requires a folk healer to treat it. Treatment could include herbs, ointments, or home remedies, depending on the symptoms, which might range from disorientation to lack of appetite, physical fatigue, moodiness, or sleepiness. Prayer on the part of the folk healer and the patient is central to the recovery process.

The opposite is true of the other illnesses. They come from the world of witchcraft, where black magic is practiced and prayer is shunned. A cure for these ailments can be found, but hope does not rest with a folk healer. What is needed is an *arbolario/a* or *herbolario/a*, an herb specialist who at some point expanded his or her "practice" by treating people who allegedly were *embrujados/as* or *enyerbados/as*. As a consequence, the *arbolario* (in most cases the herb specialist was male), because of his curative powers, was looked upon as possessing witch-like qualities.

This perception came about in part because of the amazing stories that circulated about the *arbolario*. How often did I hear, even as a child, of patients who vomited balls of hair or experienced similar horrors in the bathroom? If such a patient did not die, he was deemed cured—and thus was proved to have been bewitched. As a result, people, including the victim, became convinced of the *arbolario*'s medical expertise and the efficacy of his treatments.

One-room schoolhouse, 19th century, Red Wing, Colorado. Photo by Nasario García, 2003.

The *médico*, also an herb specialist and not a medical doctor, carried out many of the same functions as the *arbolario* to the extent that he, the *médico*, was also viewed in many communities as a witch doctor capable of curing patients who had been bewitched. This was certainly true in northern New Mexico villages.

Based on what I witnessed in my own extended family many years ago, I believe that the people's misplaced trust was often rooted in ignorance or superstition. I recall that one of my aunts went through a difficult period, but nobody, including the local folk healer, was able to determine what ailed her. Even the priest got involved, but to no avail. In desperation, my uncle concluded that my aunt had been bewitched: *Está embrujada.* Faith in God was vital to the cure, so family members recited the rosary in the evenings to help soothe my aunt's pain. Eventually she recovered. Years later her daughters determined that her so-called bewitchment was nothing more than an acute case of menopausal symptoms.

The stories that follow will take the reader into a world of witchcraft where malevolence, illness, and even death occupy center stage. All of the storytellers hold something in common, yet each also has something unique to share with us. As the stories will bear out, bewitchment was—and perhaps still is—serious business and can sometimes carry bewildering, even dreadful consequences.

Lucinda Atencio

BERNALILLO, NEW MEXICO

Bewitched

I cured Beltrán. Why, when he came, he was half swollen, since he came to me so sick. Well, he wanted me to cure him, and I said to him, "But what am I going to treat you for?"

"One time you treated me and I got well."

"Yes," I said to him. "What I treated you for then, if that's what's wrong, I can do it. But what you've brought with you from over in the Río Puerco, I can't do it."

That's the condition he was in when he came here. And he told me the whole story, what had happened to him over there. Yes, that's what was wrong with Beltrán—he was bewitched.

This last time when I treated him . . . let me tell you. Everyone was outside, sitting down. There was Nasario and Agapita. There at the door facing this way, that's where Beltrán was, standing. He says he doesn't know what hit him, like a shock, and he got frightened. Like he wanted to fall down. But he doesn't know what it was. Well, nothing was done about it, whereupon Nasario said, "Oh, whatever is wrong with him comes from sheer laziness."

They took him to Guadalupe. He stayed there for a month. When they brought him here, Beltrán was almost dead. Then they brought him here to the house [in Bernalillo]. Why, I was having a hard time curing him, since he was suffering from fright. He was really in bad shape. I said to Agapita, "I'm going to try to treat him, but I don't know if I can. Yes, God is very powerful," I said to her, "but Beltrán was neglected too long."

But I cured him, by the will of God, which always comes first with me. God helped me, and Beltrán got well. That's why he wanted me to treat him, but I don't know anything about that sort of thing [witchcraft].

I believe that people do inflict evil on others, but when it comes to that sort of thing, like bewitchment, I don't know how to treat people for it. I just don't.

Out of Envy They Do Evil Things to You

Oh! I have seen some terrible things, which if I started to tell you, you'd be horrified. Where I used to seek treatment [she suffered from rheumatoid arthritis], I saw some very cruel things, very sad.

I recall that. . . . Who was it that was very ill and was being treated and we went with him? I don't remember who it was. Oh! My godmother! It was my godmother! That's just to tell you. Well, you know there was the late . . . her cousin, cleaning her house. I don't know if she [the cousin] got up on the wrong side of the bed or what.

But I guess she knew about that sort of thing, about putting a curse on someone. And she had some trowels on top of that chair, that chair there, because my godmother gave it to me. Well, my godmother sat on the edge of the chair, to chat with her, I guess, I don't know. A little while later my godmother couldn't get up from the chair. Well, she didn't know what hit her. They picked her up from there, because there she was. She started trying to take care of herself, with whatever she could find, but to no avail. It was no use. But she coped as best she could. She *was* able to walk.

Then a folk healer came by. He was a friend of ours. He was from over in Ranchitos, on the other side of Española. And he dropped by my house. Then we got to talking about all that stuff. Then I asked him if he could cure a certain person who was ill.

"Oh, yes! I can. Why not!"

"Well, let's go over there," I said to him.

We took him ourselves, my husband and I, to the late Lonisio. He's dead; he died already. We entered my godmother's house. They greeted him quite cordially, the way they usually do. And then he just looked at her.

"You're ill [bewitched], ma'am," he said.

"It can't be," she said.

"Yes, you are," he said. "You're bewitched."

Well, my godmother just shrugged her shoulders, and then he said to her, "Somebody cast an evil spell on you. Somebody put a curse on you," he said to her just as I'm sitting here telling you, he told it to her.

"You sat down," he said, "where there was a chair that had a couple of trowels on it, the kind they use to plaster with, like brushes. There on that chair somebody put something. And you sat down."

"Yes," said my godmother. "That's true."

"But look. You go where I'm going to be, there in Albuquerque..."

That's where my godmother went. He cured her, he healed her. And he told her who the person was, who had put the curse on her. Look, it was the late... my godmother's cousin.

You see? That's why one musn't be too trusting in this world, because there are very envious people around. And out of envy some people do evil things to you. Well, no, he took care of my godmother and she got well.

José D. Chávez

BERNALILLO, NEW MEXICO

They Performed Evil Things

At one time there were some witches here in Corrales. There were some people who performed enchantments. They inflicted harm on people. But why did that sort of thing come about? Because they were in cahoots with evil spirits, and they had the authority to do whatever they pleased. People were left in an invalid state, in a stupor, but there were some husbands who didn't abandon their wives, because people were more religious than anything else. If it so happened that the wife lost her mind or something like that, they [the husbands] stayed with them until they died. Death is what separated them; that was the only divorce that existed.

Leonila "Linda" Galván de Chávez

CLAREMONT, CALIFORNIA

Witchcraft

I got married in 1944, and it was that year that I had a woman who worked for me taking care of the house and then later, my kids. This woman used to tell me stories about witchcraft. I never believed in them, because I was never prejudgmental, but I liked the stories. She swore that witches did exist.

She claimed that there were medicinal herbs that were used to cure bad as well as good illness [black versus white magic]. She would tell me that many times when a person is disliked, certain herbs can be selected to inflict harm by invoking a slow death. It's like a poison. The only thing I can remember is an herb . . . at this moment I can't recall its name. That herb, according to her, can be given to a person you don't like and little by little she begins to lose her sanity. That's witchcraft.

Reynaldo Gonzales

LAS VEGAS, NEW MEXICO

Malevolent Witches

But long ago there were witches—malevolent witches and folk-healing witches. There were herb specialists and practitioners of black magic. They inflicted evil on people. God only knows why, because there's the father of a brother-in-law of mine. He's already dead. The son took off to California and he lived over there and he left his father here. From San Agustín, farther on down from there, there was another village. They called it Contación. Now people call all that area Lourdes. That's where they inflicted evil on that man. His own wife, of all people!

This man was married twice, my brother-in-law's father. His name was Niceto Tapia. But I knew Don Niceto. I've never known a better musician than him. Boy, could he play the violin! Wow! But what musician doesn't like to drink? He liked to drink a lot. And a long time ago men went looking for work wherever they could find it. Sheep started gaining popularity over in Roswell, in Fort Sumner, and all those places around there. A large group of men got together. There was a dance there in San Agustín, and that man had been playing, the one who was bewitched. People claimed that he said, "Tomorrow, I'm out of here. I'm taking off with these sheepherders. I'm going to go as a sheepherder."

And she wasn't even his first wife; it was the man's second wife. His wife said to him, "You're not going."

"Yes I am. Nobody bosses me around!"

A whole bunch of men took off on horseback, on donkeys, all strung out in a row. Roswell is far. When they got to a resting place, they stopped to rest their animals and to rest themselves. This woman I'm talking about [the man's second wife] sent her son. She told him, "Good gracious! Your father forgot this little package. Will you be able to catch up with them?"

Of course, he loved his father very much. He had his own horse. Next morning he woke up, grabbed his horse, and took off. He caught up with them. They were eating breakfast when he got to where they were. The son headed straight to embrace his father. His son took out a package and presumably uttered these words, "Mom (she was the boy's stepmother) sent you this bottle that you forgot. She asked me to bring it to you. That's why I came, to bring it to you." Well, he grabbed it. Right away he took a drink. As I told you, there isn't a musician who doesn't take a swig. What musician doesn't drink?

By noon, the man was going nuts. He was like crazy. He stripped naked and was uttering nonsense as he followed the rest of his companions. They finally noticed what he was doing. They turned back. They brought him back to San Agustín. By the time they got here, the man was, like, crazy. And I saw that man. You should have seen him. His drool ran down to his chest. Just like a dog that has been poisoned. It was some drooling. There he was, the poor thing. He couldn't eat or anything due to his drooling. That's the way he was until he died.

But it was that second wife of his. She's the one who inflicted evil on him. I believe it was his wife. She inflicted harm on him because she didn't want him to go sheepherding because they weren't going to be able to have a dance here in San Agustín. He was the only musician.

Celia López
SANTA FE, NEW MEXICO

To Inflict Harm

San Juan is a city in the interior of Argentina close to Chile. In general, in all the interior of Argentina the tradition of the folk healer has been, and continues to be, very common. Regarding witchcraft and/or superstitions, I grew up hearing how there were people who inflicted evil on others.

That evil could be obtained by going to a person who was the mediator (whether folk healer or not). If someone wanted to inflict harm on another person because of revenge or something like that, he or she would ask the folk healer or the mediator for help. The mediator, by virtue of a special ritual, would ask (I don't know for sure who) for the victim to receive a certain punishment. I heard this many times, ever since I was a little girl. To get out of that situation, the person who was considered the victim would go to another mediator or folk healer so that with her rituals she could have the opposite effect—that is to say, to extract the evil from the victim.

In general, it is very common for people to say, "things aren't going well for me, the folk healer says it's because someone has inflicted evil on me." That evil does not necessarily refer to the evil eye, but rather to what everybody else calls black magic or something like that, that is, when someone resorts to a special process carried out by a mediator (folk healer or not) to direct the evil deed toward a person (normally this is asked of a folk healer by another person who seeks revenge). This type of belief prevails in Latin America in general, above all in the rural areas or in towns in the interior of these countries (in the capitals and large cosmopolitan cities, these customs no longer exist).

I recall that there were certain things that people said was best not to have around the house because they attracted evil; for example, the plant called the "rubber" or gum tree. In my family home in San Juan we had a huge gum tree. There was a time when my family situation (economic and otherwise) was not very good, so my mother had the gum tree taken out from our garden because she said that the tree brought bad luck.

The theme about evil inflicted by some people onto others continues to be popular among common beliefs in San Juan. A few months ago I was visiting San Juan and I didn't feel well physically or mentally. At that time I went to a medical doctor, but my father insisted that we should go to a "very good" folk healer named Doña Dominga, someone he and some members of my family always go to. More out of curiosity than anything else, I agreed to go. Doña Dominga lives in a modest house on the outskirts of San Juan. During the visit, they left me alone with her; she started to mutter some prayer and put her hands on my head, putting strong pressure on it. Then she rubbed her hand with some "special" oil and ran her hands over my body while she continued muttering a prayer or something like that. She told me that someone was "trying to inflict harm" on me, someone with very negative energies and that that's the reason I didn't feel well. She said for me to buy a pendant to hang around my neck with a glass-like container with a special oil (I believe it was mercury), and if I didn't feel well within a few days, for me to come back. I decided that I wasn't going to buy anything, but my father's wife, Isabel, bought what Doña Dominga asked me to put around the neck. I never used it, but I put it in my purse and carried it with me at all times. I didn't go back to see Doña Dominga. I preferred to go back to the medical doctor for treatment.

People say that when you're dealing with folk healing, especially "inflicting and curing evil," you have to be convinced that it's going to work and you have to believe this in order to make it happen. Meanwhile, it is not just the folk healer's role; rather, one has to help oneself by believing in the healing process. In general, I heard very positive stories regarding how Doña Dominga has helped members of my family, who at times got well in a matter of hours from their physical maladies. At times she prescribes tea made with certain weeds, which are herbs; other times, lemon juice or putting certain "protective" elements around your neck. They truly have faith in her and that's fine. I respect those customs as long as they are intended to heal and not to be harmful. After all, I continue to repeat what I heard as a little girl in San Juan: "I don't believe in witches, but as for them being around, they're around."

Salomón "Sal" Lovato

ALBUQUERQUE, NEW MEXICO

Sujarana

What one really saw a lot of over in San Luis was witchcraft. I only got to see it once. Not sorceries as such. What I saw were lights on the road. That's all. But I don't believe in any of that stuff, because I believe that sorcery is people themselves who inflict harm on other people who are also living. It's not the dead who harm the living. It's the other way around. But there are still many ways—perhaps you've heard—many ways of doing hocus-pocus or whatever. I believe that that's what it was, but people put a lot of stock in witchcraft.

Let us say that a man or a woman became ill. "Someone did something evil to my husband. Did you see him dancing with that woman?" But that wasn't during my time. I heard that from the old-timers.

I once had the opportunity of seeing this man, which still sends chills up and down my spine when I think about it. I came over here to Bernalillo with my grandfather. There was a . . . what do you call her? A *sujarana,* a *sujarana,* that's what they called her, one of those people who treats sorcery. And they brought this man to this lady because someone had done something evil to him or what have you. And I came along. I was just a kid. You see, I did a lot of traveling with my grandfather on my father's side. He liked me a lot. He lived alone; he didn't have a wife. My grandma had died. I didn't even know her. In a way I was his companion. And he was a relative of this man.

We came to Bernalillo from San Luis, and he went and saw this woman. I remember that we entered this house that had a kiva fireplace. And she had a tub full of weeds. And the stench was something else! The smell was terrible! I didn't care. It didn't bother me. The lady had a fire going. There were lots of people. And there she was. I don't know what she was doing, praying or what? It doesn't matter what she was doing. Then all of a sudden when I least expected it, she said, "Look! Here he is. This is the one who's caused you evil. It's an Indian," she said.

Everybody went over there to see (the Indian's image in the bathtub). I didn't see anything. There was nothing.

Benjamín "Benny" Lucero

ALBUQUERQUE, NEW MEXICO

The Peyote Lady

I remember my dad saying that he had a relative, a cousin. All this relative's wife had to do was look at him—because my dad was a very thick-skinned man and, in a way, very temperamental . . . and she'd say to him, "Do you know what?" she'd say to him. "You're a very thick-skinned man. Not even witches can inflict harm on you."

And Dad swore that this cousin was married to a woman who was capable of sorcery. Evil doings! "I am who I am," she'd say to my dad.

He used to say that no sooner she'd see him than she'd take off. She just couldn't stand the sight of him. She was a peyote woman; she was versed in inflicting evil. I understand witches can inflict harm only at certain times.

One time, many years later, my dad arrived on horseback to see his cousin, and his wife said to him, "Come on now! Come!" She tried to say, "I'm no witch. I'm no longer a witch!"

Why, Dad swore that the woman was capable of doing people harm. "But I didn't sit down to eat," he said. "I just stared at her. I just looked at her, and that's the way it happened."

Cesaria Montoya

LAS VEGAS, NEW MEXICO

The Little Old Lady Was Dead in the Morning

My mother was a midwife. I don't know how many babies she delivered in her lifetime. Many, lots of them! I remember hearing about folk healers, about witchcraft. The scuttlebutt was that my grandma had been bewitched. I don't know how or anything, but this other little old lady was a folk healer. They went after her to come and cure my grandmother. The little old lady supposedly said to them, "Why, she's my friend! But I'm going to die if I cure her. But let's go anyway. I'll go with you, but come after me at midnight, so that no one knows that I went with you."

Well, they took the little old lady. I don't know how she cured my grandma or what she did. Fact is that next morning the little old lady who treated her was dead. And my grandma got well, except that she became—what do you call it—hunchbacked. People say that it was all witchcraft.

Rudy Montoya

BERNALILLO, NEW MEXICO

Libe

Well, there was a story about a man who lived in El Llanito. They called him Mano, el Chinito, and he had a son. I believe they called him Libe. This Libe was paralyzed. People said that the Indians from Santa Ana had cast an evil spell on him and that's why he was paralyzed.

The story has it that one day Mano, El Chinito, was watering his small patch of land behind the house. He had a little land; he had an orchard and all. He was watering when an Indian stopped by whose name was Tiny. He was a very fat Indian. He knocked on the door and out came Mano, El Chinito, to tend to the fence that was broken so that Tiny wouldn't damage it more, and about that time José Güero stopped by. José Güero was an Indian from Santa Ana and it wasn't long before Libe died. People always said that he had been bewitched, that it was an evil affliction. Bewitched, let us say.

Damiano Romero

LOS RANCHOS DE ALBURQUERQUE, NEW MEXICO

Witches

I believe there were witches, but I was never able to prove if any existed or not. They flew from one village to another; you could see them. People claimed that witches did exist, and that's possible.

Around Guadalupe and Casa Salazar, I heard a lot of talk about a woman who was a witch, who would get a boy sick just for the heck of it. If it happened to be a serious illness, she'd have him suffering for a long time. And it wasn't until the woman died that the boy died as well. The two of them had to die at the same time. If she put a spell on him, a real humdinger of an evil spell, there he was, suffering. And neither the herbal healers [folk healers who specialized in evil spells] nor anybody else could cure him. It was a grave illness.

Eddie Torres, Jr.

BERNALILLO (EL BOSQUE), NEW MEXICO

The Jurupiana

They used to scare you. "If you don't go to bed and behave, the Jurupiana, Indian Rose, is going to come and get you." The Jurupiana was an Indian. I remember that she was very light complected and had blond hair [probably an albino], but she was Indian. She dressed like an Indian. They mentioned her to scare us. She used to visit my grandma. My grandma at one time lived in the pueblos; she was Indian-Mexican. She had lots of friends who were Indians from the pueblos, and I recall vividly how they scared us

with the Indian Rose, Jurupiana, the Indian, who was a witch with sorcerer's powers.

At work they used to call me El Brujo, the Witch, but I didn't believe in witches and that sort of stuff. But when you're young they try to frighten you. It was all fear that came from the stories about witches inflicting harm and the fact that the old-timers long ago believed in that stuff a lot. I know that my dad believes lots in that sort of thing because he says that he saw it with his own eyes. I can't say that it isn't true. I have never seen it, but it was more the fear they used than anything else.

Embrujado y enyerbado

si haces mal tú, espera otro mal.

Lucinda Atencio

BERNALILLO, NEW MEXICO

Embrujao

Yo lo curé a Beltrán. Pues, cuando que vino, si ya medio se hinchinchó, como vino tan malo. Pus, quería que yo lo curara, y le dije,

—¿Pus qué te voy a curar?

—Una vez usté me curó y yo sané.

—Sí—le dije—. Lo que yo te curé, si tienes eso, yo te curo. Pero de lo que tú traes de allá del Río Puerco ora, yo no te puedo curar.

Porque de allá vino asina. Y él me platicó toda la historia, como le había pasao allá. Sí, Beltrán eso tenía; estaba embrujao.

Esta última vez que lo curé . . . ora verás te tú. Estaban allá ajuera, todos, sentaos. Estaba Nasario, Agapita. Ahi en la puerta que quedaba pacá, ahi estaba Beltrán parao. Que no sabe, dice Beltrán, qué le pegó, como un estrellido y se espantó. Se quiso cae. Pero que no sabe qué cosa sería. Güeno, pus asina se quedó Beltrán. Es que dijo Nasario,

—¡Oh! De güevón está malo éste.

Lo llevaron pa Gualupe. Allá se estuvo un mes. De allá, cuando vino ya no lo contaban a Beltrán. Loo me lo trujieron aquí a la casa [en Bernalillo]. Pus no lo podía curar; aquel muchacho solevao. Tan mal que estaba. Le dije yo a Agapita,

—Yo lo voy a tratar de curar pero no sé. Sí, Dios es muy grande—le dije—pero a Beltrán lo abandonaron muncho.

Pero lo curé, con la voluntá de mi Dios, que es lo que pongo yo primero. Me ayudó mi Dios y sanó Beltrán. Por eso él quería que yo lo curara, pero yo de eso [de brujerías] no sé nada.

Yo creo que sí hacen mal las gentes, pero yo no sé curar d' esas cosas, d' estar embrujao. No sé yo.

Por envidia le hacen mal

¡Oh! Yo he visto unas cosas que si yo me pusiera a platicarles, les daba horrores. Onde yo iba a curarme [padecía de los reúmas] vi cosas muy duras, muy tristes.

Yo me acuerdo de, "¿Quién estaba muy malo que lo curaban, que juimos nosotros?" No me acuerdo quién era. ¡Oh! ¡A madrina! ¡A mi madrina! Es deciles a ustedes. Pues sabes tú que estaba la dijunta . . . , su prima hermana, limpiándole la casa. Yo no sé si ella amaneció de malas o qué.

Pero sabía eso, quizás de hacer mal. Y tenía las cucharas arriba de esa silleta, de esa silleta ahi, porque mi madrina me la dio a mí. Pues se sentó mi madrina allá en la orilla de la silleta, a platicar con ella, quizás, no sé. Al rato ya no se podía levantar mi madrina de allá. Pues que no sabía qué le dio. La levantaron de ahi, porque ahi la tienes. Ahi empezó a curarse ella, ahi con lo que podía y nada. Nada. Pero asina anduvo. Sí *pudo* andar.

Luego vino un curandero. Era amigo de nosotros. Era de allá de Ranchitos, de aquel lao de Española. Y cayó aquí en casa. Loo ya estábanos platicando, el cuento de eso. Loo le dije yo que si podía curar una gente que estaba enferma.

—¡Oh sí! Sí puedo. ¡Por qué no!

—Pues vamos pallá—le dije.

Lo llevamos nosotros, yo y mi esposo, al dijunto Lonisio. Ya es muerto; ya murió él. Entramos a case mi madrina. Lo recibieron muy gente, como son ellos. Y loo se estuvo viéndola nomás.

—Usté está enferma señora—le dijo.

—No puede ser—le dijo ella.

—Sí está—le dijo—. Está enferma.

Pues se torció mi madrina y loo le dijo él,

—A usté le hicieron mal. A usted le hicieron un mal—le dijo, lo mesmo que te lo estoy platicando se lo dijo él.

—Usté se sentó—le dijo—onde había una silleta que tenía unas cucharas d' estas cosas que pintan, como d' estas brochas. Ahi en esa silleta le pusieron una cosa a usté. Y usté se sentó.

—Sí—le dijo mi madrina—. Verdá.

—Pero mire. Van par onde yo voy a estar, ahi en la Plaza . . .

Ahi jue mi madrina. La curó; la sanó. Y le dijo quién era la persona, quién le había hecho el mal. Mira, era la dijunta . . . , su prima hermana.

¿Ves? Por eso no hay en este mundo que tener uno muncha confianza, porque hay gentes muy envidiosas. Y por envidia le hacen mal unas gentes. Pues no, la curó y sanó.

José D. Chávez

BERNALILLO, NEW MEXICO

Hacían malificias

Aquí en Corrales hubo una vez unas brujas. Estaban unas gentes que hacían malificias. Le hacían mal a la gente. ¿Pero por qué venía eso? Porque ellos mismos estaban contratados con el espíritu malo y ellos tenían autoridad pa hacer lo que les daba gana. Dejaban algunas gente inválida, la dejaban sonsa, pero habían unos hombres que no se apartaban de sus mujeres, porque la gente era más religosa que ninguno. Si así tocaba que a la mujer se le iba el mente o alguna cosa, vivían con ella hasta que se morían. La muerte los separaba, era el único divorcio que había.

Leonila "Linda" Galván de Chávez

CLAREMONT, CALIFORNIA

Brujerías

Yo me casé en el año de 1944, y en ese año tuve yo una señora que trabajaba en mi casa cuidándome la casa y luego después cuidando a mis niños. Esta señora me contaba historias de brujerías. Yo nunca creí, porque yo nunca fui prejuzgosa, pero me gustaban los cuentos. Ella decía que sí había brujerías.

Decía que había yerbas medicinales que se usaban tanto para curar cosas buenas como para curar cosas malas. Me decía que muchas veces cuando no se quiere a una gente se recogen ciertas yerbas pa irla matando a la persona poco a poquito. Es como un veneno. Yo lo único que me acuerdo es una yerba que se llamaba. . . . Por el momento no me acuerdo el nombre. Esa yerba decía ella que la toma una persona poco a poquito hasta que la van golviendo loca. Esa es una cosa de brujería.

Reynaldo Gonzales

LAS VEGAS, NEW MEXICO

Brujas hechiceras

Pero había brujas antes: brujas hechiceras. Había arbolarios y había malechores. Le hacían mal a la gente. Pus sepa Dios, porque su papá de mi cuñao mío, ya murió él tamién. Él se jue pa California y vivió aá y dejó a su papá aquí. Ya murió él tamién. De ahi de San Agustín, poco más pa abajo, había otra placita. Le dijían la Contación. Ora le dicen a too el pais, Lourdes. Ahi le hicieron mal a ese hombre. ¡Su misma mujer!

Este hombre jue casao dos veces, su papá de mi cuñao. Se llamaba Niceto Tapia. Pero yo conocí a don Niceto. Yo no he visto otro músico como ése. ¡Cómo tocaba bonito el violín! ¡Qué bárbaro! Pero, ¿pus a cuál músico no le gusta beber? ¿Cuál es el que no le gusta beber? Él le gustaba beber muncho. Y antes se iba la gente a buscar trabajo aá onde jallaban. Comenzaron a entrar con borregas aá a Roswell, a Fort Sumner, y too eso de ahi. Se juntaron un montajo de hombres. Había habido un baile en San Agustín, y estuvo tocando el hombre ese, ése que le hicieron mal. Isque dijo,

—Yo mañana me voy. Me voy con toos estos compañeros a la borrega. Voy a cuidar borregas.

No era ni su primer mujer; era su segunda mujer dél. Isque le dijo,

—No te vas.

—Sí me voy. ¿Quién me manda a mí?

Se jueron un bonche de hombres a caballo, burros, hechos chorro. Roswell está lejos. Cuando llegaron aá en la noche, se pararon a descansar los animales y a descansar eos. Mandó la mujer esta que le digo yo, a su hijo. Isque le dijo,

—¡A qué carajada! Aquí olvidó tu papá un encargadito. ¿Lo alcanzarás?

Pus él quería a su papá. El hijo tenía un caballo. Otro día nomás amaneció y agarró su caballo y se jue. Los alcanzó. Estaan almorzando eos cuando llegó aá. Su hijo seguro se jue abrazar a su papá. Pues su hijo isque le dijo,

—Aquí le mandó mamá—era su madrastra del muchacho—esta botea que olvidó. Mandó que se la trujiera. A eso vine, a traila.

Pues que la agarró. Diuna vez bebió él. Pus, como le digo yo, ¿cuál músico no bebe? ¿Cuál músico no bebe?

Pa mediodía se jue haciendo loco el hombre. Como loco, estaa. Enpelotaba solo, y disparatiando solo en onde iba con compañeros. Hasta que lo notaron los demás compañeros. Isque dijieron,

—No. Vale más volvernos a llevar este hombre patrás pa San Agustín.

Se volvieron. Lo trujieron patrás. Ya cuando vino acá, taa como tonto el hombre. Pero yo vide ese hombre. Le corrían las babas oiga, hasta aquí asina [al pecho]. Como un perro envenenao. Era un babero. Ahi se estaba el probe. Pus no podía ni comer ni naa, por el babero. Se estuvo asina ese hombre hasta que se murió. No podía comer.

Pero era la mujer dél esa. Jue la mujer dél que l'hizo mal. Pues yo digo qu'era su mujer. L'hizo mal nomás porque no quería que se juera porque no iban a tener bailes aquí. Era el único músico.

Celia López

SANTA FE, NEW MEXICO

Hacer el mal

San Juan es una ciudad en el interior de Argentina, junto a Chile. En general, en todo el interior argentino la tradición de la curandera ha sido y sigue siendo muy común. En cuanto a brujerías y/o supersticiones de ese tipo, yo crecí escuchando hablar de cómo había gente que "hacía el mal" a otra gente. Ese "mal" se conseguía yendo a una persona que era la mediadora (curandera o no). Si alguien quería "hacer el mal" a otra persona, por revancha o algo así, pedía a la curandera o mediadora que la ayudara. La mediadora, mediante un ritual especial, pedía (no sé bien a quién) que la víctima recibiera algún castigo. Esto yo lo escuché muchas veces, desde que era pequeña. Para salir de esa situación la persona considerada la "víctima" recurría a otra mediadora o curandera para que con sus rituales hiciera el efecto contrario; es decir, que sacara de la víctima ese mal.

En general, es muy común que la gente diga "no me está yendo bien en la vida, la curandera dice que es que me han hecho mal." Ese "mal" no necesariamente se refiere al mal de ojo sino a lo que mucha gente en el resto del mundo llama "magia negra" o algo así; es decir, cuando alguien recurre a un procedimiento especial llevado a cabo por una mediadora (curandera o no) para ocasionar el "mal" a alguna persona (normalmente esto es pedido a la curandera por otra persona quien quiere revancha o venganza). Este tipo de creencia es muy común en Latinoamérica en general, especialmente en las zonas rurales, o en ciudades del interior de estos países (en las ciudades capitales, más grandes y cosmopolitas, estas costumbres ya no existen).

Recuerdo que hay ciertas cosas que decían era mejor no tener en casa porque atraían el mal; por ejemplo, la planta llamada "gomero." En casa de mi familia en San Juan solíamos tener un gran gomero; en una época en que la situación de mi familia no era buena (económicamente y por otras razones) mi madre sacó del jardín el gomero porque decía que esa planta traía mala suerte.

El tema del "mal" ocasionado por algunas personas a otras sigue siendo común en la creencia popular en San Juan. Hace unos meses yo estaba de visita en San Juan y no me sentía bien física y mentalmente. En esa ocasión fui al médico, pero mi padre también insistió en que fuéramos a una curandera "muy buena," Doña Dominga, a la que él y algunos miembros de mi familia siempre van. Yo, más por curiosidad que por otra razón, acepté ir. Doña Dominga vive en una casa modesta en las afueras de San

Juan. En esa ocasión, me dejaron sola con ella, quien comenzó a murmurar una oración y puso sus manos en mi cabeza presionando muy fuerte. Luego se puso un aceite "especial" en sus manos y frotó sus manos en todo mi cuerpo mientras seguía murmurando un rezo o algo así. Me dijo que alguien estaba tratando de "hacerme mal," alguien con energías muy negativas, y que por esa razón yo no me sentía bien. Me dijo que comprara un colgante para colgarme al cuello que tenía en un recipiente de vidrio un líquido especial (creo que mercurio) y que si en unos días no me sentía bien que volviera. Yo decidí que no iba a comprar nada pero la esposa de mi padre, Isabel, compró lo que doña Dominga me pidió que me colgara al cuello. Yo nunca lo usé pero lo puse en mi bolso de mano y siempre lo llevaba conmigo. No volví a doña Dominga y preferí seguir con el tratamiento del médico.

Dicen que en el tema del curanderismo, sobre todo de "hacer y curar el mal," uno tiene que estar convencido que va a ocurrir y tiene que creer para que ocurra; por lo tanto, no es sólo la acción de la curandera sino uno mismo quien tiene que ayudar creyendo en la curación. En general, escuché historias muy positivas de cómo doña Dominga ha ayudado a los miembros de mi familia, a veces en cuestión de horas se han sanado de sus molestias físicas. A veces les receta tomar el té hecho con ciertos "yuyos," que son hierbas, otras veces el uso de jugo de limón, o colgar en su cuello ciertos elementos "protectores." Ellos creen fervientemente en ella y me parece bien; yo respeto esas costumbres siempre que sean para curar y no para perjudicar. Después de todo, yo sigo repitiendo lo que siempre escuché desde pequeña en San Juan: "Yo no creo en las brujas pero que las hay, las hay."

Salomón "Sal" Lovato

ALBUQUERQUE, NEW MEXICO

Sujarana

Lo que sí se vían más aá [en San Luis] eran brujerías. Yo nomás una vez me tocó ver. No brujerías. Lo que vide jue luces en el camino. Es todo. Pero yo no creibo; no creibo nada en eso. Porque a mí se me hace que la brujería es la gente que está viva que hace mal a la gente que está viva. No es la gente que está muerta que hace mal a la gente que está viva. Es al revés. Pero hay munchos toavía—usté habrá leido—que hay munchos modos de hacer, de hacer *hocus-pocus* y lo que sea. Y yo creo que eso era pero la gente se creiba muncho en brujerías.

Se enfermaba un hombre o una mujer: "Le hicieron mal a mi marido. ¿Vites que andaba bailando con aquélla?" Pero eso no era en mi tiempo. Yo oí eso de los viejitos.

Me tocó ver una vez este cierto hombre, que me da escalofrío toavía cuando me acuerdo. Vine con mi agüelito pacá pa Bernalillo. Estaba una, ¿cómo le decían? *Sujarana, sujarana,* le decían, d'esas gentes que curan brujerías. Y este hombre lo trujieron ahi porque le tenían hecho mal o no sé qué. Y vine yo. Yo estaba mediano. Porque yo anduve muncho con mi agüelo, por lao d'en papá. Me quería muncho. Él estaba solo; no tenía esposa. Mi agüela se murió. Yo no la conocí. De manera que yo era su compañero. Y él era pariente d'este hombre.

Vinimos pa Bernalillo de San Luis y jue y vido esta señora. Yo me acuerdo que entramos a una casa que tenía un fogón de campana. Y loo tenía un cajete con hierbas. ¡Y el apeste! ¡El olor era terrible! Yo no me fijé. No me importaba. La mujer tenía lumbre. Había muncha gente. Y estaba esta señora ahi. Yo no sé qué estaría haciendo, rezando o qué. No importa qué estuviera haciendo. Loo cuando menos acordé, dice,

—¡Miren! ¡Aquí está! Éste es el que le tiene hecho mal a usté. Un indio—dijo ella.

Todos jueron aá a ver (la imagen en el cajete de hierbas). Yo no vide nada. No había nada.

Benjamín "Benny" Lucero
ALBUQUERQUE, NEW MEXICO

La peyotera

Me acuerdo de que dicía en papá que él tenía un pariente, un primo. La mujer de este pariente nomás lo vía—porque en papá era un hombre muy pesao, en un modo, era muy corajudo—y es que le dijía, "¿Sabes tú?," es que le dijía a en papá. "Tú eres un hombre muy pesao. A ti no te pueden hacer mal ni los brujos."

Y dijía en papá qu' este primo estaba casao con una mujer que sabía hacer males. ¡Eran males! "Yo soy quien soy," le dijía a en papá.

Él platicaba que nomás lo vía esa mujer y arrancaba. Nomás no lo podía ver. Era peyotera; sabía hacer males. Es que tienen cierto tiempo los brujos, que hacen mal.

En una vez es que llegó en papá a caballo a ver a su primo, ya cuando pasaron munchos años, y es que le dijo ella, "¡Ándale! ¡Corre!" Quiso decile, "No soy bruja. ¡Ya no soy bruja!"

Asina dicía en papá que la mujer sabía hacer mal. "Pero no me arrimé a comer," dijo. "Me quedé mirándola. Nomás me quedé mirándola, y asina pasó," dijo.

Cesaria Montoya

LAS VEGAS, NEW MEXICO

Amaneció muerta la viejita

Mi mamá era partera. Yo no sé qué tantos niños hizo *deliver* mi mamá en su vida. ¡Munchos, munchos de eos! Me acuerdo de oyer decir de curanderas, de brujerías. Decían que a mi agüelita la habían embrujao una vez. No sé cómo ni naa, pero esta otra viejita era curandera. Jueron a verla que viniera a curarla [a su abuelita]. Isque les dijo,

—¡Pus es mi amiga! Pero yo me voy a morir si la curo. Pero vamos. Yo voy con ustedes, pero vengan a medianoche, que no sepa naiden que me jui con ustedes.

Pus llevaron a la viejita. No sé cómo la curaría [a mi abuelita] o qué haría. Cuento es que otro día en la mañana amaneció muerta la viejita que la curó. Y mi agüelita descansó, nada más que quedó—¿cómo le dicen?— jorobada. Dicían que brujería.

Rudy Montoya

BERNALILLO (EL BOSQUE), NEW MEXICO

El Libe

Pues estaba una historia de un hombre que vivía aquí en El Llanito. Al hombre le dicían Mano, el Chinito, y tenía un hijo. Pienso que le dicían el Libe. Este Libe estaba paralizado. Dijieron que los indios de Santa Ana le habían hecho mal y por eso estaba paralizado.

La historia es que un día estaba Mano, el Chinito, regando su terrenito atrás de la casa. Tenía un poco terreno; tenía huerta y todo. Estaba regando cuando vino un indio que le dicían el Tiny. Era un indio muy gordo. Tocó la puerta y salió Mano, El Chinito, para atender la cerca que estaba quebrada para que no fuera a hacer Tiny más daño, y en ese tiempo habían visto entrar a José Güero que llegó. El José Güero era un indio de Santa Ana y con el tiempo se murió el Libe. Siempre dijieron que le habían hecho mal, una maldición ellos. Embrujao, diremos.

Damiano Romero

LOS RANCHOS DE ALBURQUERQUE, NEW MEXICO

Brujas

Yo creo que sí habría brujas, pero yo nunca pude probar si hubiera o no. Volaban diuna plaza a otra; se vían. Decían que eran brujas y posible que sí.

Por ahi por Gualupe y Casa Salazar oyí yo munchas pláticas onde una señora que era bruja, enfermaba a un muchacho nomás porque quería enfermalo. Si era una enfermedá dura, ahi lo tenía sufriendo. Y hasta que no se muría esa señora, antonces se muría el muchacho tamién. Tenían que murirse los dos. Si le ponía una brujería, una queja dura, ahi lo tenía sufriendo. Y no podían ni los arbularios ni nada curalo. Era una enfermedá dura.

Eddie Torres, Jr.

BERNALILLO (EL BOSQUE), NEW MEXICO

La Jurupiana

Te metían miedo. "Si no te acuestas y eres bueno viene La Jurupiana, la India Rosa." La Jurupiana era una india. Me acuerdo que era muy blanca y tenía los pelos güeros, pero era india. Se vistía de india. Nos metían miedo con ella. La visitaba a mi abuela. Mi abuela vivió en los pueblos; era india-mexicana. Tenía munchos amigos que eran indios de los pueblos, y me acuerdo bien cuando nos metían miedo con la India Rosa, la india jurupiana que era bruja que tenía poderes.

Yo a mí en el trabajo me dijían El Brujo, pero yo en los brujos y eso no creía. Pero cuando está uno chico te meten miedo. Era puro miedo de las historias que hacían mal las brujas y que la gente anciana más antes creía muncho en eso, muncho. Yo sé que mi papá cree muncho en eso porque dice que él lo vido con sus mismos ojos. No puedo dijir que no es verdá. Yo nunca lo ha [he] visto, pero era más el miedo que hacían para metértelo.

Five

Superstitions, Mysteries, and the Bizarre

···

When God's willing, nary a door will close.

INTRODUCTION

In this chapter the reader will travel vicariously to Mexico, Nicaragua, Spain, Texas, California, Colorado, and New Mexico as we explore the tantalizing and paranormal world of superstitions, mysteries, and the bizarre. To mention any one of these components even half-seriously today may well evoke a snicker from cynics who hold that they are based on people's gullibility. Yet the stories that follow hold a sure veracity because, with rare exception, they are based on personal experiences or on events that happened to individuals' family members or friends.

According to *Webster's New World Dictionary*, "bizarre" is "that which is extraordinarily eccentric or strange because of startling incongruities and extreme contrasts." Even a cursory glance at the titles in this chapter readily reveals which stories are imbued with elements that could be construed as far-fetched and unbelievable. But as the reader hears the narrators' voices, a sense of reality comes to life and challenges us to reflect more deeply on what they have to tell us.

If a man wakes up in a pool of blood for which there is no explanation, as we learn in José Nataleo Montoya's "Genoveo Showed Up Crying," and this is followed by news the next morning that his *comadre* passed away that same night, it's undeniably eerie. Even more so is the fact that on her deathbed his comadre spat globs of blood, meaning that the compadre's blood was an omen of her imminent death.

There are also several fantastic stories by Filiberto Esquibel. One is the tale about his wedding ring, which disappeared from his jewelry box only to reappear—along with pornographic materials—in his lock-secured mailbox, even though there had been no mail delivery. Equally incredible is "The Casket Was Lowered Right before My Eyes," in which he wonders aloud how, after his mother was buried wearing her wedding ring, the ring could show up in his jewelry box the day after the interment.

The strange circumstances surrounding the comadre's death and the mysterious appearance of the mother's ring defy logical explanation, but they add to the drama and suspense of extraordinary events that leave the principals in a state of confusion and wonderment. It could also be said that the deceased are capable of communicating through some kind of powerful energy that is transmitted to those they have left behind. This energy connection is yet another mysterious aspect of the supernatural that most of us cannot comprehend or dare explain.

In the case of Filiberto Esquibel, perhaps it was the undying love between mother and son. But even he is at a loss for words. "I can't explain that," he says. "Maybe she wanted me to have something. I still have it [the ring]." At the opposite end of the spectrum, however, perhaps someone, because of jealousy or whatever reason, sought to drive a wedge between him and his wife by placing unsavory materials in the mailbox.

The element of noise and the appearance of benevolent or animate objects in diverse forms are also a source of energy that can be a powerful omen of impending death. What varies from one narrative to another are the forewarning signs. The messenger of death may be a crestfallen little bird whose flight takes him into someone's house to alert those present of impending sad news, a belief not limited to Latinos but which transcends cultural boundaries to other groups, including Anglos. Consuelo Martínez, from Escondido, California, tells the story of "The Mysterious Lady in White" (why not black?) in Baja California, in which the anonymous lady wanders the house at night, a presentiment, as it turned out, of a grandfather's looming death.

While some episodes may well leave the principals scratching their heads, that is not the case with Phoebe Martínez Struck. In her story "Dead People Make Noises," she goes from skeptic to firm believer. This often happens when the individual is affected directly or is privy to empirical evidence, as was the case with her. The pan falling in the kitchen and the stomping noises on the rooftop not only served to foretell deaths in the family, including her own mother's, but also were sufficient proof to convince her that strange noises can indeed forewarn and should be taken seriously.

In addition to stories of the bizarre or the fantastic, there are other equally fascinating tales. One in particular is the story about the talking and crying baby found on the side of the road, which was popular in my native Río Puerco Valley. What is even more amazing is the fact that María A. Mongalo, who is from Nicaragua (she now lives in Riverside, California), shared the same story with me, but with a slightly different ending.

Unlike stories of the evil eye or the vanishing hitchhiker, which command universal appeal, the stories about the crying baby that come from my interviews of the past thirty years are pretty much restricted to New Mexico. So it is fascinating to speculate how such a tale could exist in Nicaragua but, to my knowledge, not elsewhere in the Southwest (I have never come across a similar reference in my readings). I suppose one could rationalize that a coincidence in linking New Mexico with Nicaragua is part of the enchantment within the overall expansive world of witchcraft.

The same could be said of superstitions, both negative and positive, for they transcend cultures and oftentimes connect one country with another. When one talks about broken mirrors and black cats as symbols of bad luck in this country, mention is also made of Friday the 13th. Yet in many Hispanic countries, including Spain, it is not Friday but Tuesday the 13th that is looked upon as a day of potential misfortune.

On a regional or local level, the focus with regard to superstitions may shift for entirely different reasons. I can recall my paternal grandfather, a formal and a no-nonsense person, saying, *Lávense la cara con agua fría en la mañana antes del almuerzo pa que lleguen a viejo* (Wash your face with cold water in the morning before breakfast so that you reach old age). Whether there is any correlation—and I doubt that there is—between cold water and longevity, my grandfather died at age one hundred. I still wash my face in the morning with cold water, but it is not so much a matter of putting stock in my grandfather's pronouncement as it is in not being able to give up a well-entrenched habit.

The same thing could be said with regard to other interviewees. Among them is Gilberta Herguera Turner, whose story about the chicken that crowed after it was roasted is told and retold in different versions throughout the Santo Domingo de la Calzada region in northern Spain. It concerns an innocent man who was convicted of a crime, sent to the gallows, but through some miraculous quirk of fate came back to life.

A rooster and a chicken are now housed in the local church in Santo Domingo de la Calzada as part of local tradition and to bring good fortune. It is said that if the rooster crows during a wedding celebration, the newlyweds will enjoy a long and blissful life together. Many people firmly believe this to be true, including Gilberta Herguera Turner's friend, who told her the story and has been happily married for thirty years.

There is also the widely circulated folktale of the disobedient daughter or son whose punishment from God is harsh and unmistakable. In "Chaveta," Manuel Pérez recounts the story of a son who raised his hand against his mother, and from then on was compelled to roam the streets, physically disabled, until his death.

When, as a child, I spent summers with my maternal grandmother in Bernalillo, north of Albuquerque, I often saw Chaveta. But my recollection of him differs slightly from that of Manuel Pérez. Since Chaveta had no legs, his upper body sat on a wooden platform with roller-skate wheels underneath. To gain traction in the dirt streets, he used two wooden pegs as he struggled to push himself along, and he would sometimes keel over onto the ground. Needless to say, I felt sorry for him. The first time I saw him, I ran to tell my grandmother and asked her about the man on "skates." Though sympathetic about his situation, she was quick to point out that the earth had allegedly swallowed him for striking his mother. Such an assault violated one of the Commandments, she said, and for that reason Chaveta was destined to roam the earth in his condition until he died.

The story of the disobedient son, whether Chaveta or someone else, was popularized in Mexico and has been kept alive in both oral tradition and music (presumably originating in Parras, Coahuila) in many communities in New Mexico and elsewhere in the Southwest. The late Tomás Rivera (Crystal City, Texas), in his classic novel, *. . . y no se lo tragó la tierra/ . . . And the Earth Did Not Devour Him,* treats the same theme but, as the title suggests, with different results. Nothing happened to the son whose mother admonished him not to malign God for the problems plaguing the family.

The popular Mexican ballad of "Rosita Alvírez" originated in Colima, Mexico, according to Vicente T. Mendoza. I remember my mother singing this beautiful but heartbreaking ballad at our ranch when I was small. It is the story of a young woman who went to a dance against her mother's wishes. At the dance a young man became enraged at her refusal to dance with him. A rebuff of this kind was unheard of and an affront to the male's ego. The end result was that the man shot and killed the young woman.

But not all stories in the ensuing chapter deal with the unpleasant aspects of life. In fact, some are cheerful, with quasi-happy endings, especially those with a magical bent. Included among them is the surprise nocturnal visit to Mariel Romero Ocaranza's altar by her deceased grandmother during the Day of the Dead, or Yolanda del Villar's account of the magical children in "The Little Hands," who push cars across the railroad tracks, reminding everyone of the children who perished when a train hit their school bus.

The Benigno Romero House, Territorial style, built 1874, Las Vegas, New Mexico. Photo by Janice M. García, 1989.

Farmers' tools common among Hispanics of New Mexico and southern Colorado. Photo by Nasario García, 2001.

Whether the narrators in this chapter are talking about superstitions, mysteries, the bizarre, or the fantastic, they are obviously sincere and not prone to fanfare or exaggeration. Those are the aspects that make their tales credible, whether we choose to believe them or not.

Enrique Campos

POMONA, CALIFORNIA

You Could Hear Steps

In a town in Oaxaca, Mexico, in a place called San Pedro, I was living with a girl. One night all of a sudden she woke up in the wee hours of the morning. She turned purple and kept pointing to the ceiling, but she wasn't able to talk. At that moment I felt the pressure.

I grabbed some eggs, something I had seen people do to lift the so-called evil spirits. That's what I did in between prayers, and when she was able to talk she said that she had seen various persons reflected on the ceiling. After she finished talking to me, I cleaned her up.

Soon thereafter I began to hear steps outside, like those of an animal near the wall around the house. I was by no means afraid. I was not even intimidated, but you could feel that energy. And since it was a very strong energy with which I was wrestling, you could hear steps like an animal's (knock, knock, knock), all right outside the door. After about five minutes, they disappeared and everything was back to normal.

Connie Chacón

PUEBLO, COLORADO

A Little Bird

People claim that when ailing people are on the verge of saying farewell, a little bird comes in the house. That's what happened to me when we first came to Pueblo. My mother was ill and she died.

In the morning the door was open. It was in the summer, and a little bird came inside. He came in the bedroom with his little wings fallen, and my comadre Rosa's mother said to me, "That little bird is the bearer of bad news. He's from over in El Rito. Who knows what has happened to my family!"

She came and caught the numb little bird with its fallen wings and stuck the bird's tiny crop in the water and turned it loose outside. Well, by evening the news hit home. My mother had passed away.

Whenever your relatives are dying, they come to say goodbye. My mother came to say goodbye to me. That little bird came when Mom died.

A Noise in Their Home

An uncle of mine who lived close to where we lived got married. He had gotten married recently, and every night he and his wife heard a noise in their home and they would go and sleep at our house because they were afraid. Then they went and put paper and pen so that those responsible for the noise could write down why they made the noise, if someone had died or whatever, or perhaps because there was a buried treasure or something in the house. But they didn't write down anything.

The noise persisted on the rooftop, and my uncle and his wife could never figure out why, but they would go sleep at our house because of the terrible noise in their house.

Juan Bautista Chacón

PUEBLO, COLORADO

Three Whistling Sounds

One time I went over to this man's house. He was an herb healer. I went there and I gave him a few pennies to find out if he was a witch. I went with two cousins of mine who came along so I could pay him. Next day I was going to leave for the ranch, you see, because I was married to another woman at the time. I was going to head for the ranch that evening on horseback. I only had so much time before dark, and the herb healer said to me, "I bet you I can foretell something for you."

Very well, but you're not going to believe this. I was there sitting down like so, looking like now, toward the door. He had a little window this way, with small curtains, and the other boys were sitting there. The man was sitting over there on a bed when I glanced at the window. He had like a prune on a cord, and I kept staring at it. The prune kept opening and closing, opening and closing. My hair stood a little bit on end. Then he said to me, "You're scared, aren't you?"

"No," I said to him. "Why?"

"Well, you don't believe in witches, right?"

"Why should I believe in witches? I've never even seen one."

He was an herb healer, you see? And he said to me, "Okay, I'm going to divine something."

"Okay, that's fine," I answered.

I had seen him not too long ago, but I had never been in his house.

"Okay. I'm going to divine one thing. Tomorrow you're headed for the sierra, to your father-in-law's ranch. You'll be on horseback, and you're going to be taking off a little late."

"Yes, yes, late."

"And you don't believe in witches!"

"No, I don't believe in witches."

"And before you leave for the sierra on horseback, you're going to shoe the horse. You're going to put horseshoes on it."

"Yes, that's true. I'm going to put horseshoes on it."

By that time I got suspicious because he was guessing what I was thinking. Then every time he spoke he stared at the prune. The prune kept bothering him. It kept opening and closing.

"You're nervous. I believe you're scared."

"No," I said to him. "Why should I be scared?"

And the other boys, cousins of mine, just looked at me and sort of smiled, because they already knew that he was an herb healer, a witch.

"Well, let me tell you. When you get home this evening, when you're shoeing the horse, an animal's going to let out three whistling sounds, in front of your house."

I lived in the sierra where the *monte* or wooded area begins. My house was at the edge of the sierra, and down below there were pine trees. Lots of pine trees! To the left, to one side, toward the west, it was hilly. There was just a tiny embankment. A very pretty embankment.

"There close to your house you're going to hear three whistling sounds," and I had a good dog around, a German shepherd.

"Yes, that's fine."

"You're going to hear them real clear, but you're not going to be afraid, are you?"

"No," I said to him. "Why should I be afraid?"

"And you'll be going to the sierra, right?"

"Yes, yes I'll be going."

And so I told the wife everything when I got home. She spoke Spanish as well as us [she was Anglo]. I told her what Teodoro had told me—that was the herb healer's name.

"Who knows," she said, "he might try to inflict evil on you."

"No way. He can't inflict evil on me. Why, my name is Juan! I'm not afraid of anything. I'm not afraid of him."

Well, no sooner said than done. I was shoeing the horse and I was about to finish when three whistling sounds blasted. I heard them clear as day! Three of them right in succession from my house up on top of the hill, and I said to myself, "It's true."

Okay, I wasn't afraid. I went in the house and my wife already had supper ready for me before leaving, and I said to her, "Did you hear the whistling sounds coming from the top of the hill?"

"No, I didn't hear anything," she responded, since she was in the house.

"Those three whistling sounds that Teodoro told me about, went off."

"Don't go. Who knows but what something might happen to you on the road."

"Whatever happens, happens; I'm going."

Very well. I ate supper and I looked for my jacket. It was summertime but it was still cold, a little cool. I tied my jacket into a bundle behind the saddle and I fastened the saddlebag for carrying the food, and in it I put what my wife was going to send to my mother-in-law in the sierra. I mounted the horse and took off.

It must have been about a mile or mile and a half, when it turned a little dark on me. Teodoro had mentioned three embankments.

"When you come to the first embankment you're going to hear three whistling sounds. At the second bank you'll hear two sounds. At the last bank you'll hear one whistle."

"And are you sure you're not afraid?" he said to me.

"What do you mean, afraid!"

Before taking off I strapped—I had a '38—I strapped it on, and I said to my wife, "You go stay with Mom," because she lived nearby, and I took off.

I called the dog and he left with me. Well, sure enough! As soon as I got to this small embankment, there were the whistling sounds again. Really, really close, brother! My hair stood on end, but I continued.

Between one thing and another, I had hidden a quart of moonshine, as I used to drink a lot back in those days. Why lie? At that very moment I felt like taking a good swig of liquor. By the time I reached the next embankment, it was already dark. The moon was shining, but it was in a canyon and the corner was in shadow. I was about to reach the other embankment, about eight or nine miles from the house. As soon as I got to the next embankment, two more whistling sounds sounded. I already knew what the herb healer had told me. I said to myself, "Some kind of an animal's going to appear." No wonder, he was an herb healer. I had brought a pouch full of cartridges.

Very well, between one thing and another, I passed through the place (the canyon). When I reached the top, the terrain was barren. There the ground was flat so I spurred the horse into a trot. Well, nothing happened to me. I got home, but I was still pretty shook up.

That's all I can recall about this man Teodoro, the herb healer.

Adrián Chávez

ALBUQUERQUE (ATRISCO), NEW MEXICO

Seeing Things

I knew this gentleman. He could make people see things. For example, he would be riding along on this horse and he'd manage to play tricks on a pal of his who was with him. He'd let drop his quirt and he'd say to him, "I dropped my quirt. Get it for me!"

His friend would get down from his horse and about the time he was going to stoop down to get it, he saw clearly that a snake was about to strike him. The quirt would turn into a snake. In the end he refused to grab it. Eduardo, the one who had the power to make people see things, had to get down off his horse to pick up his quirt and show his riding pal that it was not a snake. I heard people talk about all of this. The two of them were cowboys.

On another occasion when they got to the ranch, Eduardo's pal went inside the house where he slept, whereupon a female bear leaped at him. Well, he grabbed hold of the bear by the ears and here he was wrestling with it, when all of a sudden Eduardo opened the door.

"But what are you doing?" he said to him.

"This animal . . ."

He supposedly had ahold of a pillow.

"One of these days when you play a trick on me and make fun of me, I'm going to put a bullet in you."

The two of them were very rough on each other. One other time Eduardo made him start filling up this room with water. His pal then climbed on top of a chair and, when the water was about to rise above him, he jumped and fell smack on the floor—not in the water.

Many of those silly things took place. How Eduardo managed to do them, I don't have any idea! He used to tell me that as a young man he traveled quite a bit with the circus. That's where he learned lots of those things.

Samuel Córdova

ALBUQUERQUE (SAN JOSÉ), NEW MEXICO

"The Nene"

Years ago there was this man, Benito Lucero, a violinist. He played the violin. And he didn't have, I believe, any means of getting around. He lived in Guadalupe and he came on foot to play for a dance in Salazar.

When he was on his way back from Salazar to Guadalupe, around El Puertecito, where, according to people, "the Baby" had the habit of appearing, there was Don Benito, walking along with his violin tucked under his arm. He was drunk . . . when all of a sudden he came upon a baby on the road, crying, wrapped in rags, and he picked it up in his arms and headed for home. On the way home, it was already early in the morning, the story has it that the baby said to him, "Daddy. I have 'yeeths [teeth]."

He then dropped the baby. He was scared out of his wits! But we never found out what happened to the baby. It disappeared.

The Doll

People used to tell tales about El Puertecito, and I maintain that they would intimidate the young kids with their lies. Many of the kids suspected that it was the old men themselves who made up all of that stuff.

One time they sent me in the evening from Guadalupe to Salazar, to spread the word that someone had died. I don't remember who had died. The fact is that it was well into the evening.

I went. I had a white horse, a very good horse, very gentle and quite fat. When I was on my way back, I had to pass through El Puertecito, but I had to cross El Arroyo de la Tapia first. It was already dark. Oh, I was so happy, I was singing! As I crossed that arroyo, a coyote howled, and it startled me.

Nevertheless, the fact that they talked about The Doll that supposedly came out at you in El Puertecito didn't faze me in the least. I remembered.

They said it climbed on the rump of someone's horse. Boy, I don't know what all! Well, I closed my eyes and I turned the horse loose. Off I went. Nothing happened.

Who Knows What It Is!

There was another place, quite close to my house. We called it La Joyita. The horse was pretty stirred up, wanting to run. It was dark, and I spotted what looked like a man headed my way on the road. I saw clear as day his white shirt and hat. And that restless horse was still anxious to take off. I myself wasn't much better off, with my hair standing on end from being so scared. "That thing is going to climb on my horse's rump! Who knows what it is!" And here's the horse snorting and wanting to take off with me.

Finally, it let out a real loud snort, and guess what, it was a donkey that belonged to a man who had four black and white donkeys. They would stand in the middle of the road to look at you, dumb as they are. No sooner had they moved to the side of the road, than I really took off on my horse. Once I got home, they noticed right away that I had crapped in my pants.

Yolanda del Villar

SAN ANTONIO, TEXAS

The Little Hands

The story about the little hands that are left imprinted on the rear end of cars is common knowledge among the inhabitants of San Antonio, Texas, and it concerns an accident that occurred a long time ago. This accident happened at one of the many railway lines that go through San Antonio.

According to the legend, it was a school bus that was run over by a train and all of the little children riding on the bus died. In spite of the fact that at first sight the railway lines appear to be above the level of the road, when people turn off their car lights and put their cars in neutral, the cars are pushed mysteriously toward the railway line. They stop being pushed once they find themselves across the tracks.

The legend tells us that it's the children's spirits that attempt to prevent another tragedy from happening, because this phenomenon doesn't happen as the train is going by. To be sure, it's all about a legend because railroad accidents have been researched regarding such a place with all the details mentioned before and nothing has been found.

Nevertheless, when we [my family and I] had recently emigrated from Mexico to San Antonio, this was one of our favorite places to visit. Every time a relative of ours came to see us, a visit to the railways was compulsory. It's been approximately fourteen years since this custom disappeared because of something that to this day is difficult to explain.

My brother was in San Antonio one time, and so as to keep the custom alive we went to the railroad tracks so the children could "push" us. The only thing is that on this occasion we put talcum powder on the rear of the vehicle, because we had heard that the imprints of the little hands would be left implanted on the car.

My older daughter was ten years old, and she and her cousin, who was the same age, rode in the back seat of the car looking out the back end of it. As we got to the place I mentioned before, we did what we had done so many times before, except that this time the experience was different and more terrifying. About the time the vehicle started to roll down the road, my daughter and her cousin let out a frightening howl, throwing the adults into a state of confusion. The girls swore that they saw just then the imprints of the little hands on the rear window of the car. However, they didn't see anything else.

After we got home we checked out the place where we had put talcum powder previously and, sure enough, you could see the little hands outlined in the powder. This put an end to our visits to the railroad tracks.

Years later on a radio program a disk jockey talked about his experience with that place. In addition, a national television network came to San Antonio with the idea of filming a report regarding the topic. The disk jockey mentioned that he and his wife accompanied the lady reporter to the designated place.

It was on a Sunday morning and the site is where there are no homes around; in fact, it is an isolated and quiet place. Silence is only interrupted by the curious who go there in search of a novel experience. The radio announcer says that on starting the taped interviews, they heard a lot of noise, but it was children's voices as though coming from recess at school. This caught their attention since it was Sunday, and even so they thought that there must be a park or walkway where the noise was coming from.

Intrigued because of this incident, they decided to drive around several blocks trying to find where the noise was coming from, but their efforts were in vain. There were no schools or parks anywhere around. As they realized this, they felt the hair on their skin stand on end and Oscar, the disk jockey, promised never again to disturb the spirits' peacefulness.

Footsteps

I have not personally verified this story, but my neighbor. . . . Well, I've been living in my present home now for ten, no, twelve years. I had been living approximately one year in that house when this family moved in—the old man, his wife Leonor, and two sons, Willie and Rudy, both bachelors in their forties. Doña Leonor, I believe, is of Mexican-American descent and Don Willie also, and their two sons speak Spanish very well even though they're third- or fourth-generation Mexican American.

When they moved there, well, it's an large old home, and they started to restore it, and behind the main house, right in the corner, they had what we call a garage. Then the boys, the bachelors, they fixed it up like an old bachelor's quarters. That's where they lived, toward the back. They didn't live with their father and mother.

Well, as it turned out, one of them, Willie, would hear footsteps at night that went from the house, footsteps that traveled in the wee hours of the morning to the garage door that now was their living quarters, and stopped at the door. Willie would open the door but couldn't see anything. He would then take a peek to see, because even though the house has a fence, you always have to be on the lookout in case someone comes in to rob you or something, but he would look and no, there was no one.

Intrigued by the footsteps they kept hearing, Doña Leonor took it upon herself to ask people who had lived previously in the neighborhood whether there was something there, what was going on, and why the noises. A neighbor of mine on the same street lived in that house ten years previously, before Doña Leonor and her family came. Her name is also Leonor. When Doña Leonor moved in, she went and asked Leonor [the second Leonor], and the second Leonor tells her, "Why, of course. We also used to hear those footsteps, but we don't know what they were," but she gave her information as to whom she could ask who had actually lived in that house before them. Doña Leonor then took it upon herself to investigate.

As it turned out, this man who was extremely jealous and lived there with his wife and two small children. The boy was ten and the little girl was eight. One day the very jealous man, in one of his fits of jealousy, killed his wife, and the children, frightened as they were, ran and hid in the garage. The father came out and went after them and killed them in the garage. Thereafter he hanged himself in the garage.

We think that the tiny footsteps, the footsteps that go and stop at the doorstep of the garage [the new living quarters]. . . . We don't know if they're those of the children running or whether they belong to the father who's after them. We just don't know. And the noises can still be heard.

The mother was killed inside the house, and nothing can be heard there. The footsteps run from the house to the garage and stop right at the entryway.

This occurs at the corner of San Fernando and Thirty-Fourth Street on the West Side. It has been going on for twenty years and footsteps continue to be heard. Lately, since Willie the husband died of cancer, followed by the death of Willie the son, I haven't asked Doña Leonor anything. Now the grandson lives there with Doña Leonor, but I haven't asked him whether he, too, hears those footsteps or not.

They're not afraid to live there. That's where they live. I guess as long as there's no ghosts that move things around, then they are able to live [coexist] with the ghosts.

Filiberto Esquibel

LAS VEGAS, NEW MEXICO

Don't You Want to Go to the Funeral?

If you want me to tell you about things that we can't explain, I'm going to tell you something, something that happened to me. I had an old car. I had a Chevy, old, and I gave it an overhaul. I had never fixed a car that wouldn't start. From one car to another. Ever since I was small I was overhauling caterpillars, bulldozers, and machinery. I gave the car an overhaul. It was a '36 Chevy. It just didn't want to start. I checked everything, but nothing. There was a funeral going on at that time at the home of some people who lived nearby. I was about done with the car and getting ready to start it. Then my wife said to me, "Don't you want to go to the funeral?"

"Well, I would like to fix this car. I need it for work. You go ahead."

Well, this person, this certain person [the deceased] got angry because I refused to go to his funeral. The day that they were going to bury him, he got mad. He stayed behind to watch me fix the car. I checked the carburetor. I checked the points. I checked everything. Everything was fine. It was supposed to start. It had gasoline. It had everything. I hit the starter until I ran the battery down, and you could crank the '36 Chevys. I cranked it. Nothing. It didn't even hum, and so I left the crank in it. My back was already hurting. About that time some people stopped by the house. And my father-in-law was ahead of them. He said to me, "Haven't you been able to fix the car? Hasn't it started?"

"It doesn't want to start," I said to him. "The battery's even gone down. I'm tired of cranking it. I'm tired. Now I'm going to hitch it up to the back of my uncle's truck and I'm going to give it a good jerk because I'm annoyed."

At that moment there was this person returning from the funeral, one of the mourners. The dead person's anger had subsided, and a woman passed close by.

"What's wrong?" she said. "Can't you start the car?"

"No" I said to her. "It doesn't want to start."

I didn't suspect anything.

"Good gracious!" she said. "I don't understand why it doesn't start and you're such a good mechanic."

And she caressed the fender with her hand, and she went inside the house. My father-in-law and I kept on chatting. And I said to him, "I've tried starting this car in every which way. I've wasted the whole blasted day. I've tried everything and it doesn't want to start."

I put the key in the ignition one more time. No sooner had the engine made noise than the car started. You explain that to me.

There was this certain person [the deceased], and he didn't like me, you see. We had a disagreement.

My Wedding Ring and Some Filthy Stuff

My wife and I went to a dance on a Saturday night. Next day we had to go to Albuquerque. And she said to me, "Put on your ring, your wedding ring."

She was kind of jealous. Fine, it's a very beautiful thing. I put it on and we went to the dance. When we got back I said to her, "I'm going to take off my ring so I don't lose it, because tomorrow we have to go to Albuquerque."

"Okay," she said. "Put it in my chest of drawers."

That's where I had my cufflinks with my wife's brooches and stuff like that, and so I put my ring in the drawer. It had my name on the inside, and I put it in the box. I closed the lid. I closed the drawer. It was about one o'clock in the morning. We slept for a little while. Then we woke the girls up early in order to go to Albuquerque to buy groceries and to visit the aunt who raised my wife. Very well, we went and came back on Monday, very early. We came back very early from Albuquerque. And my wife had the habit of checking the mailbox when we got home.

"Look!" she said when we were going in the house. "Look! There's a letter; there's a letter with a stamp, stamped here in Las Vegas."

It was mailed here in Las Vegas, okay. The letter was a bit bulky. I opened it and it had an obscene picture of a certain person. My wedding ring was inside the envelope, and I looked at it. Inside the ring was my name. "I wonder what we have here?" I went to look for my ring inside the house where I had put it.

That Monday morning we were over in Albuquerque before the mail went out. How can that letter have been mailed on Sunday and delivered on Sunday here in Las Vegas? You explain that to me.

"Look," I said to my wife. "This is my ring. There's the sealed letter. There's the letter with our address. Look at the day it was mailed. How could the ring jump backward in time so that it could have been mailed Thursday, Friday, or Saturday so as to get here?"

There was nothing in the mailbox when we left. I always locked it whenever I went anywhere because the school kids were close by and they would take out the letters. They'd throw them away. They were mischievous.

"Do you have an explanation how my ring was able to go through the mail, for the clock to go backward, and for my ring to come in that letter?"

Had I left my ring somewhere? My wife wondered aloud, "Have you been at some hotel?"

I never went anywhere, but somebody had it in for me. My ring was in that letter and some filthy stuff. But how did it get there?

The Casket Was Lowered Right Before My Eyes

Okay. Another thing happened. And let's see if you can explain it to me. When my mother died, she had a ring that she had bought. She lost the original one. It fell in the sink, and we didn't find it. We couldn't find it. Then later on she bought another one a bit cheaper. When my mother died, I saw when they closed the casket that she had her wedding ring intact. Her hands were crossed. She had her ring on. I made darn sure that she was wearing her ring. They buried her. The casket was lowered right before my eyes. That casket never left my presence. It was never out of my sight. We buried my mother. Next day my wife said to me, "Listen," she said. "Isn't this your mother's ring? It sure looks like it. It also has her name on the inside."

The ring that my mother supposedly was wearing when she was buried was in my box. That I remember. I still got the ring. I can't explain that. Maybe she wanted me to have something. I still have it.

Perhaps we'll never be able to explain in our lives what happened. But things like that happen. I have seen them.

Bencés Gabaldón

BERNALILLO, NEW MEXICO

A Huge Palm-Like Growth

The story goes something like this: an uncle of mine was cutting wheat. Back then there was what you call a fraternity. It was the Fraternity of Our Lord Jesus Christ. Anyway, a man began to whip himself with wheat tassels. I understand that the Brothers admonished him, "Why are you doing that, man?" because he was [feigning to] whip himself like the Penitente Brothers did.

"Look!" interjected another one of the Brothers. "The Good Lord is going to punish you for doing that. He's going to punish you."

Well, so much for that. The man didn't believe it. It wasn't long before this man developed a huge palm-like growth right on his back. He went around making fun of the Penitente Brothers, and that's why he got that huge palm-like growth. His days were numbered, he was dying.

He had to join the brotherhood in order to get rid of that thing which he had brought upon himself, because of what he had done, you see? No sooner he joined the fraternity and the huge palm-like growth disappeared. And that was the last time he messed around with that kind of thing.

You see, these are things that went on. That's no lie. Those things used to go on. And they still do! That's why it's wise not to get involved in those kinds of things, that kind of business, of wanting to mock someone else. It doesn't pay. It just doesn't pay. You only harm yourself. Don't you agree?

That's what I remember about that incident. That's what we were told many times regarding things that one is unaware of, or how they happened or came about.

Nasario P. García

LOS RANCHOS DE ALBURQUERQUE, NEW MEXICO

A Rag Doll

I'm going to relate to you what my dad used to tell me. It's possible that he was still a young man. I wasn't born yet. Anyway, the fact is that my dad used to tell me that he and friends of his would attend dances in Salazar. Back in those days Salazar was well known. They held many dances in that village.

There was a man; he played the violin. And one night he was on his way back from Salazar. I'm not sure whether he was riding a donkey or a mule, but it wasn't a horse. At a place called El Alto de los Jaramillos, this man, the musician, was riding all by himself. When he got to El Alto, someone, like a rag doll, popped out in front of him and climbed on the donkey's rump. The man got terribly frightened. Fact is that when he got home, when he saw the kitchen light, he fainted.

On that Alto de los Jaramillos, according to what my dad talked about, many things would pop out at people. They weren't witches, but like ghosts and things like that.

Adelita Gonzales

ALBUQUERQUE, NEW MEXICO

Chains Rattled

Many persons really believed in witchcraft of yesteryear. They believed in that sort of thing. I never believed in any of that stuff, and still don't. Who knows? Perhaps there is such a thing.

There was this one time—my husband, Salvador, was on his way home and when he went by this place called El Coruco (The Bedbug) chains rattled. So much so that the poor man got home and it was as if he had fainted! I don't know how he made it home! Then I said to him, "What, what's wrong?"

He shouted at us, "Come. Come with me to unsaddle the horse."

It was already night. He was on his way back from Don Teodoro García's house. Then I said to him, "What, what happened?"

"I don't know," he responded. "Come with me. Unsaddle the horse and close the gate," he told the girls.

He claims that when he went by El Coruco, chains rattled and the horse got startled, so I said to him, "I don't know about that."

Perhaps those things do go on. I was never frightened like that. You know Doña Melesia and all of them, perhaps she's told you. A little donkey did pop out at her.

Not me. I never, never in my entire life ever saw such things.

Gilberta Herguera Turner

WINCREST, TEXAS

The Chicken That Crowed after Being Roasted

Santo Domingo de la Calzada is a large town in La Rioja (in northern Spain) whose capital is Logroño. In the past, the province of Logroño, whose capital was the city of Logroño, as is the case at the present time, belonged to Castilla la Vieja (Old Castile).

Santo Domingo has a very peculiar church since inside there is a very beautiful chicken coop, with some ornate wrought-iron railings in which a rooster and his companion, a hen, live. Both are white as snow. Every year these two birds are replaced and a new couple is introduced to the chicken coop. I don't know what happens to the old couple, and I don't think I want to know, nor even think about it, but I suspect that it ends up in some village on the dinner table.

Besides the chicken coop, the church has another peculiarity: its belfry is not set in the church. Instead it is found across the street.

The folk saying "Santo Domingo de la Calzada where the chicken crowed after being roasted" comes from medieval times, toward the twelfth century more or less. Back then there was a feudal lord, and a crime was committed. I don't recall if it was a robbery or a murder. I believe it was a murder, and the feudal lord ordered his soldiers to find the culprit and hang him.

The soldiers found a man and accused him of the crime, and without much ado they hanged him from a tree at the edge of town. The friends of the man who was hanged searched for him and found his body swinging from the tree. Not knowing what to do, they prayed to Santo Domingo since they were certain of their friend's innocence. As the prayer ended, what surprise should they be in for but that the hanged man came alive and they all headed happily for town.

While this was going on, food was being prepared that would be served that night to guests at a fiesta in the feudal lord's house. The chefs were preparing the roasted chickens and the rest of the food that was to be served.

Suppertime came and, as the feudal lord was surrounded by his dinner guests, his servants came to inform him that the townspeople were stirred up because the criminal who had been hanged was seen walking through the town with his friends.

The feudal lord didn't believe it, and so he sent his servants to confirm that the report was true. They returned, bringing news that the man was indeed alive and that they themselves had seen him and his friends walking about the town.

The great lord continued to insist that these were lowly matters of the common folk, and he exclaimed, "I will believe this bunch of lies when the chicken on this dish, ready to be devoured by my guests, gets up and sings." He had hardly finished uttering these words when the chicken rose and walked all around the table, clucking.

That's where the phrase "Santo Domingo de la Calzada where the chicken crowed after being roasted" comes from.

My friend Raquel, a native of this town who told me the story, also said that if the rooster crows and cock-a-doodle-dos during a wedding celebration, it's a good omen and an indication that the newlyweds will be happy and will live many years together.

Well, it must be true, because during her wedding the rooster crowed and crowed and cock-a-doodle-dood and cock-a-doodle-dood to the point of barely being able to hear the bride and groom utter their assents or the priest pronounce them husband and wife. Raquel and her husband have been happily married for more than thirty years. To be sure, the rooster's crowing was a good omen.

César G. López
UPLAND, CALIFORNIA

The Holy Company

Of all the regions in Spain, the one where supernatural traditions most endure is Galicia. Perhaps because of its Celtic past, or because it's a region where mist and the wooded landscape lend themselves more to such things. The fact is that the majority of Galicians, men and women alike, believe in ghosts, supernatural phenomena and, of course, witches, the famous *meigas*. There is not a single story or legend that does not include them, to the point of having people talk of Galicia as the "Land of Meigas," that is, the Land of Witches or the Bewitched Land.

Perhaps of all the legends and traditions, the most enduring and persistent is the one called Santa Compaña or Santa Compañía, The Holy Company. One is assured that in the forests or on the roads of Galicia a person can run into the Holy Company at night. It's a group of grieving spirits or souls that are condemned to roam the roads because of indiscretions they committed on this earth that prevent them from enjoying eternal peace. Generally these spirits form a procession and dress in religious habits or in white sheets or shrouds. As a rule they are headed by a person who carries a wooden cross, a bell, or perhaps a cauldron with holy water. At times this individual is not yet dead but has to carry on as though doing penance for a horrendous crime that he has committed.

If a person comes across the Holy Company on some road, the most common thing is for them to invite him to join the procession, which means that the person is destined to die soon.

The story that I'm about to relate here did not occur to me personally; it was told to me by a seaman who was in the military service with me at the Cartagena Naval Base in Cartagena, Spain, which is in the Mediterranean. I don't recall his first name, only that his surname was Atienza, and he was a commercial fisherman from Huelva. Before his boat was docked at the Cartagena Base, it had been stationed at El Ferrol Base in the Coruña province of Galicia.

The facts as I now recount them occurred to another seaman whose brother told them to Atienza, who in turn shared them with me. This is the story:

One night in November, which is All Souls Month, the boat in which a group of fishermen was fishing got lost in the midst of a storm. The fog was so dense that you couldn't see a single light on the coast, even though they had not gone far. When they thought they were going to die, amid the noise coming from the wind they clearly heard the sound of a bell, and thinking that it was a church bell they headed in the direction where they thought the sound was coming from. Miraculously the boat passed through the coastal reefs without suffering any damage, running aground on a small beach that was totally foreign to them. There were no homes or a church whatsoever, but the bell could be heard faintly toward the interior. At this point the seamen, who were exhausted, decided that one of them would go to find out where the bell was, to ask for some help. The one chosen was the brother of Atienza's friend. He walked among the trees looking for a road, guided the whole time by the sound of the bell. In a little while he found something that changed his life forever. Near a crossroads preceded by an intersection, he saw a procession of Penitentes, made up of two rows. All of them were covered with white sheets and each one was carrying a burning wax candle, except for the first one who was ringing a bell and reciting a litany to which everyone responded in unison.

Scared to death, the seaman knelt down on the dirt and asked them where the closest town was. Then one of the Penitentes, without saying a word, pointed to a road and gave him the burning wax candle that he was carrying in his hand. Following the directions, the seaman was able to reach a village, where they helped him and the other seamen. Next morning no one could understand how the boat had been able to reach the beach in the midst of the storm without smashing into the reefs. It was as though it had flown over them. In fact, they had to put the boat on a handcart and carry it by land until reaching the village, which was not very far. But the most surprising thing is that when the seaman who had asked the Penitentes for help took a look at the burning wax candle that one of them had given him, he was horrified to discover that it wasn't a wax candle but the bone of a person's leg, although it showed signs of having been burnt at one end.

The impression that the seaman was left with was so strong that he went half crazy and for three days went without eating, drinking, or talking to anyone, dying on the fourth day. Everybody who was on the boat was convinced that what had saved them was the spirits, and that only the seaman who saw the Holy Company paid with his life, in exchange for the salvation of his companions' lives.

Following the seaman's burial, attended by all the town, his companions put at the church, at the foot of the Virgin of Carmen, a reproduction of his boat as an ex-voto, a votive offering, for having saved them from the storm, in keeping with the Galician custom.

That's how I heard the story, and that's how I like to tell it myself.

Benjamín "Benny" Lucero
ALBUQUERQUE, NEW MEXICO

Strange-Looking Objects

I have seen some strange things in my day! At first I didn't. It's only been lately, perhaps in the last two or three years. I saw one of the most beautiful things that, even among the family, they thought it was a lie.

It was on a Friday when we left Albuquerque for the ranch in Cabezón, my wife and I. I took Friday off from work and we left, because we felt like slaughtering an animal. It had been a long time since we'd slaughtered one. I was anxious to locate this large steer I had. I didn't find it but found another one instead and locked it up in a corral that Eduardo Valdez has there in La Merced. I said to my wife, "Come morning, we'll go after it in the truck."

It was already dark that Friday when we returned home. I fed the horse and my wife fixed me supper. After she gave me something to eat, I felt like going to the outhouse.

I went out. I almost missed seeing this strange thing I mentioned earlier. While in the outhouse, just as I got up to leave, I started to hear a music-like noise. Then I saw this beautiful object, shaped like a cigarette, but quite huge. It was shaped like a cigarette with a very long tail. The light, coupled with its colors, made that object so beautiful! It was like seeing a helicopter without wings, but with a *much* longer tail. There's an embankment we call El Banco de la Cañada de la Máquina and La Cañada del Camino. We also have, like you folks, a *cañada* (ravine) called Cañada del Camino. That was the old road. Then there's a wheat-threshing machine that was popular years ago, buried there by the water, whence the name El Banco de la Cañada de la Máquina. It was on that embankment where this object landed.

But as I'm telling you, that thing was in the form of a cigarette, like a train, shaped like a train. A very huge and beautiful thing! And the embankment where this object came down is quite high. It descended until it was flat on the *cañada*. As it got to this arroyo, as it landed on the ground, the light on its tail disappeared, and the front end of it spit out fire. From there it vanished completely.

Had it not been for the noise—I was telling my wife—she would have missed it, because she stayed back in the house washing dishes until she came out to toss out the dishwater.

"One of those strange-looking objects just landed," I said to her. "One of those strange things. One of those strange things that people claim can fly."

When I brought a drawing of the object here to Albuquerque, to my foreman, I talked to him about it, and he listened. The other guys said I was lying. My foreman said to me, "That was a UFO. Draw it for me," and then I proceeded to draw the thing for him. We were in a café. I was telling him all about it. I was telling him that not even my family wanted to believe me. The only person who believes me is my wife because she saw it. After I had returned to Albuquerque, my daughter came to see me, and there was my granddaughter. I was talking to my daughter in Spanish, and to my granddaughter in English. And even she, my daughter, said to me, "It was a UFO, Daddy. It was a UFO."

And then my daughter says to the little girl, my granddaughter, "Grandpa saw a UFO! That's what it is," she said to her. "It's a UFO."

And my foreman told me the same thing. He said it was a UFO.

"Okay. Let's go see," said my granddaughter.

Imagine! Even the young squirt was skeptical.

"Come on, grandpa! Come on, grandpa! Don't lie to us!"

Then I said to her, "Listen here. I'm going to tell you one thing, little one. Grandpa's not going to tell the family a lie, and by the same token he's not going to tell you one either," I said to her.

"I want you all to take me next Saturday to see if I can see it," she said.

Why, I have seen strange objects but I didn't know that's what it was (a UFO).

"It's possible I won't see it, but I'm going to take you."

"Look here, Dad. That's between you and your grandchildren," said my daughter, because the grandchildren said they would keep on going to Cabezón until they saw the object.

One time when they were playing in the patio, in the backyard, as it was beginning to get dark, suddenly an object similar to the one I had seen before went by, but farther away, in the direction of San Ysidro. There came the object. The little girl, the granddaughter's the one who saw it. And sure enough! It moved right along. It was headed for San Ysidro, the same thing as what I had seen before, but farther away, not as close as before. We didn't hear a noise or anything like I did; it was too far away, toward San Ysidro. Quickly that thing disappeared! Then all of a sudden another one appeared, in the shape of an egg. Glittering but toward Cuba. There we were in utter amazement. The grandchildren saw it. It, too, disappeared into space.

But this other one I told you about, it was really close, about three-fourths of a mile from Cabezón.

If some day I should show you the spot where it vanished, you'll say, "You weren't far from it!"

Manuel de Jesús Manzanares

PUEBLO, COLORADO

I Saw a Man's Body

One day, I believe it was even on a Sunday, my neighbor and I were working with the horses in the ditch, clearing out the ditch. At noon I came home to eat. When I pulled up to the table, no sooner I sat down—there was a door leading to another small room—I saw a man's body standing at that door. The body was perfect from the shoulders down, but as for a head, nothing. But I didn't say anything to the wife, because if I did, she wasn't about to stay home alone.

After midday I went back to work and I said to her, "When evening begins to set in, take the pitchforks so that as soon as we stop cleaning the ditch, we'll pile up the alfalfa."

Then after we finished piling up the alfalfa, which was already raked, I said to my wife, "Do you know what happened at noon?"

"I suppose the horses took off running," she responded.

"No," I said to her. "I don't know if you noticed when I sat down at the table, that I got up very quickly."

"Yes, I did notice that you got up, but I didn't know why."

I then proceeded to tell her what had happened. At that time there was a brother-in-law of mine in the hospital who was very sick. All of this prepared me for what was to happen because people claimed that sick people would forewarn you that they were going to die. I said to myself, "I wonder about my compadre Antonio?"

And sure enough! Next day they came to inform us that my compadre, my brother-in-law, had passed away.

The Ouija Board

This happened when my wife and I were still over in El Rito del Oso with my mom and dad. We were careless and let a heifer go beyond six months

old without branding it. How this heifer got into the neighbors' ranch—
they were Italians—I don't know, but they went and put on their own
brand. Said Dad, "Well, we can't do anything. We should have branded
the heifer before it was six months."

But the heifer would escape and mingle with our cattle. And Mom,
who was much more determined, said, "No way. I won't let these thieves
have my heifer."

"Oh," said Dad, "let them have it. We can't do anything about it."

And one day Mom says, "Nothing doing. I won't let them have it," and
she finally convinced Dad to do something. He said to us, "Take the cattle
over to the other ranch, to the Indito Ranch," as it's called.

Well, my brother and I took the cattle over there. It was there that we
slaughtered the heifer. We killed it and dressed it, and Dad and Mom
loaded the meat in the horse carriage and headed for Aguilar to take it to
my grandparents where they lived because Mom didn't want the Italians
to profit from the heifer. As for the hide, I can't recall what we did with it.
I believe we buried it somewhere around there. I can't remember, because
we slaughtered the heifer as if it were stolen.

Very well, then. Nobody knew except Dad, Mom, my brother and me.
We were the only ones who knew what had happened to that heifer. Later
on the Italian who had branded the heifer came over to ask about its
whereabouts.

"I have no idea what happened to it. You're the one who branded it,"
said my mom.

None of us admitted anything. No one confessed anything. Nothing!
In the end my grandparents were able to enjoy the heifer the Italians had
stolen from us.

I don't know how many years later, a brother-in-law of mine had one of
those ouija boards, as they're called, a small board that had the alphabet,
the sun, the moon, the stars and so forth. Then it had like a tiny heart that
ran backwards and forwards.

Well, one night we were messing around with the ouija board. There
were my little sister and a young cousin of mine, and they had to place
their hands on this tiny heart. Of those present I don't know how or who
it was that decided to ask the ouija board what had become of the heifer
the Italians had branded. No sooner said than done and the tiny heart
started moving. That darn tiny heart moved that way and this way and so
forth. Then it started to spell. It spelled and read, "Vidal and the old lady
took it to Aguilar."

Of those who were present, nobody knew what had happened except my brother and me and Dad and Mom. How did that darn ouija board know? I can't tell you. I was always, as I told you, very skeptical about all this stuff. That particular time it scared me how that ouija board had spelled out, "Vidal and the old lady took it to Aguilar."

A Throng of Horses

One night my wife and I went outside when suddenly you could hear a throng of horses as if a whole bunch had just gone by, and it seemed as though they had blown away the cornfield. I was left with my mouth wide open. And I said to her, "My compadre's horses have kicked the gate open again."

There was a horse that could open the gate. He would hit the gate wires with his muzzle. Then I took off to check things out. It was very dark, so I grabbed one of those oil lanterns that we had. I walked up and down all over the cornfield. I then turned back home.

"Forget it," I said to her [his wife]. "Let them eat all they want."

In the morning as soon as it got light, I got up to go scare off the horses. The first thing I did was to take a look to see if the gate was open. Nothing! What could all that have been? I don't know.

To this day I don't have any idea what it could have been, but you could hear quite clearly the throng of horses.

The Car Lights On

One time we had just returned home from someplace. Bernice, my daughter, was still very small. Our house was like so—next to that of my parents. The door, the entrance, was toward the front. To one side there was a window and right there is where we had parked the car. When we were about to go inside, my wife with the baby in her arms, and me trying to open the door, we finally made it inside the house. Through the window my wife saw that the car lights were on. She says to me, "Look, did you leave the car lights on?"

"No," I responded. "I didn't leave them on," but I went and turned them off, nonetheless. We were never able to figure out what caused them to come on.

On another occasion we went from here at home to the countryside to check on the cows. When we got there, it was already getting dark, and we went from El Rito farther on up. We went up a small hill. From there I could make out the shapes of animals. My wife stayed in the car, and I got out and took off on foot. I spotted the cows and then walked on up ahead and there were the horses also. Thereafter I returned to the car.

Well, when I was on my way back quite a distance from the car, the lights came on. I followed the lights. When I got close, close to the car, the lights went out. I got to where the car was and I said to the old lady, "Boy, you really know how to do things! When I was a ways from the car the lights didn't do me any good, but you turned them on, and when I got close, you turned them off."

"No," she said. "I didn't turn them off."

"Well, I wonder how they came on?"

To this day we don't know what's what. But that's what happened to us.

Consuelo Martínez

ESCONDIDO, CALIFORNIA

The Mysterious Lady in White

I remember it was just a few months after having my quinceañera, and my *abuelito* Ramón was ill. He was trying to recover from a stroke (he had had several) and he was bedridden for a few months. It was the Fourth of July weekend, and we usually spent our holidays at my parents' home in Rosarito, Baja California, Mexico, where my father built a house for his future retirement. His parents lived in that house in the meantime.

It was a Saturday night, July 2nd, but technically July 3rd since it was about one or two in the morning. I was falling asleep upstairs in one of the bedrooms with the rest of my family and some other family members who were visiting when all of a sudden I heard my youngest sister and my cousin scream and run into their rooms. They were upstairs in the hallway when they noticed a thin lady with long dark hair in a white flowing dress, almost like a nightgown.

At that time, we asked what scared them and they said there was a lady downstairs next to my grandfather's bedside. My grandfather had a bed in a large open area downstairs that you could see from our upstairs hallway.

We told my sister and cousin to go to bed, that it was probably our *tía*, aunt, walking to the bathroom. Later that morning we wondered who was up in a white nightgown. No women in our house had a white nightgown, so we were left to wonder who she was.

Two days later when we left to return home, it was the 4th of July, and about an hour after returning from being at the house in Rosarito, the phone rang. Then came the news that my *abuelito* Ramón had died.

Now the mysterious lady in white who visited my grandfather at his bedside just less than two days before his death all makes sense.

Phoebe Martínez Struck

PUEBLO, COLORADO

Dead People Make Noises

Concerning witchcraft, I never saw any of that stuff. Neither lights nor anything like that that people talked about. Nor ghosts. The only thing I do believe in is that dead people make noises because that's something that happened in my family. At one time I also didn't believe in that kind of stuff.

One time when we were living over at the ranch we were in the kitchen, I believe it was at night, when all of a sudden a pan fell and then Ernesto, my husband, says, "Someone is here making noises, trying to tell us something."

"Oh," I said to him. "Do you believe in witchcraft and nonsense like that? I don't. Well, perhaps the pan was hanging the wrong way and it fell."

"No," he says to me. "Someone made noise, came to tell us something."

Next morning a lady neighbor of ours passed away.

"See there," he said to me. "I told you someone was going to die."

Well, from then on we didn't hear anything about that sort of thing until we came here to Pueblo. We were living in Avondale [east of Pueblo]. At that time my mother was very ill, and one thing for sure, we were in bed. We had barely gone to bed, but we couldn't sleep. We only had that room and the kitchen. There was a large arched door right in front of the stove. We had a gas stove, butane gas, and suddenly the burner on the stove came on, and I says to Ernesto, "Look! The burner on the stove is lit."

He then got up and he says, "Well, wasn't the gas (knob) turned off completely?"

And sure enough! It was shut off, and he then went to where the bottles of gas were. We had bottles outside. And nothing. Everything looked normal. Very well. When he came back in, the burner was shut off and he went back to bed. Once he was back in bed, the burner came back on again. The coffee pot was on top of the burner, and my husband says, "Well, what's going on here?"

I got scared. Then he says, "Oh, someone is making noises (came to tell us something)."

"Oh," I said to him. "There you go again with your noises." [Laughter]

I was afraid, but at the same time I didn't want to believe in what I was seeing. Right at that moment I don't know what made the burner go out, but next morning we got word that Mom had passed away. They telephoned me. At that time she was living in Gallup. They called me at work from over there that she had died. That's why sometimes I'm scared of those noises.

A long time ago, before I married Ernesto, my grandma had told my mother about those noises, and I was wanting to believe in them because Mom, as nearly as I could recollect, never told lies. But before Grandma died she was very ill, and she and my grandpa lived in a small place farther on down from us. In any case, it was nighttime when they heard someone walking on the roof. And my stepfather went outside to see what was going on. It sounded like a horse walking on top, stomping. My mom said to him, "Go. If not, the roof is going to come crumbling down on us."

He went outside, but he couldn't see anything. Then he hollered from the top of the roof, that where was the noise coming from. My mother hit with the broom to pinpoint the spot where the stomping was on the ceiling, but there was nothing up there. Later, next day, my mom found out that my grandma had died.

Whenever Mom told me all that stuff about noises, it seemed like fibbing, but that wasn't the case. When it comes to dead people making noises [warning you that death is imminent], perhaps it's true.

A Tumbleweed

One time Nestor, my husband's brother, came home around two or three o'clock in the morning. Word has it that a whirlwind—the wind was blowing—was coming and he got very scared. One of those huge tumbleweeds was chasing him without him knowing what it was. He headed for the gate to this small fence—they had a small wooden fence. He went inside the gate and the tumbleweed took off down the road.

It is my understanding that he never again went out at night. But he swore that it was a witch.

María A. Mongalo

RIVERSIDE, CALIFORNIA

The Tiny Baby

My dad used to say that a man was driving an oxcart back when. He said that he was pretty sun-beaten from traveling who knows how many kilometers on his oxcart when suddenly he heard a tiny baby crying on the road. He cried tirelessly, famished and cold. There he was abandoned on the side of the road.

Then, according to my father, the man muttered, "That's a small child and I can't just leave him there. I have to get down and go see."

People say that he approached and saw the child and picked him up in his arms. "Look," said the child, "at my little fingernails," and these enormously long nails stuck out.

The man was dumbstruck and overcome with a very high fever for several days until he was able to recount what happened to him.

Cesaria Montoya

LAS VEGAS, NEW MEXICO

Her Compadre Passed Away

My father used to tell us—well, not just my father, my grandma also—that she had an uncle, and they got along really well with each other. They were always kidding around. The little old man used to say to her, "Listen here, comadre! If you don't get used to calling me 'compadre,' and one day I die before you do, I'm going to come back and shake you [grab your feet]."

She didn't call him "compadre," she called him "uncle." Nothing changed. Suddenly the little old man died, and we heard something in the evening. The old lady was alone, my grandma, with my father and his sister, an aunt of mine. They were small; they were playing on top of the bed, and grandma was fixing supper, when all of a sudden my daddy jumped off the bed.

"Mom! Mom! My uncle just came in."

"What uncle?"

I don't recall what the little old man's name was. Ah, his name was Antonio.

"Is it really him?"

"I don't know," he said to her. "He came through that door and it appears that he hid behind the sewing machine."

My grandma had a sewing machine behind the door.

"Oh," she said to him, to my daddy. "You're crazy. Quit your dreaming."

"No, Mom. He did come in."

And my dad told her how he was dressed, that he was wearing a gray suit, and that he was wearing no shoes. Only socks. And he was wearing a white shirt, and one of his cuffs was unbuttoned.

Well, ah, nothing happened. The kids went to bed; they fell asleep. She

[Grandma] stayed up fixing supper for when Grandpa came home. Right about that time she heard a boy whistling on the way back from the store, because there was a store at that time, and it was the grandson of the little old man who had died that was whistling. He was coming to tell her that her compadre had died. When the boy got there, he wouldn't say anything; he just kept whistling. He was sitting at the doorstep. My grandma says to him, "What are you doing at this late hour?"

"Why, nothing," he said. "I'm on my way back from the store and thought I'd drop by here."

"No, no, no," she said to him. "Don't lie to me, don't lie to me. Tell me why you came," because she knew that the little old man had been ill.

"You're right. I came to tell you that your compadre died."

That's all she needed to hear. She wrapped up the kids and picked them up.

"Let's go!" she said to him. "Give me a hand with the girl."

There was a saying back then: "We've gone to the other side," where the old man now found himself, and they went in and found him lying in repose. They already had him laid out on a table. No sooner had my grandma knelt down to pray than my father began pulling at her. And she kept asking him to keep quiet.

"Look, look, look how he's dressed!"

He was wearing gray pants, a white shirt with the cuff unbuttoned, and wasn't wearing shoes. She paid her respects to the deceased. Afterwards, my grandma got up and headed for the kitchen to chat with the wife of the deceased.

"Comadre, perhaps it's true."

When grandma was about through talking, I understand that the little old man kept raising his hand as if in the direction of where my grandma lived.

"Perhaps my husband did go visit you that night to tell you that he had died."

Whether it's true or not I don't know. But why is it that things like that don't happen anymore? Superstitions! I believe it was nothing more than superstitions.

The Crown Had Fallen

My mother had the kitchen, like, sunk down below, and then you climbed three little steps to reach the living room. And a boy that my father and mother raised was sitting up here on the last step. They had a wood stove like in a corner, with a decorative crown on top. Do you remember those wood stoves that had very beautiful crests or crowns on top? Well, all of a sudden, and I was playing on the kitchen floor, we heard the thump. It happened right there in that room. Well, the boy got up right away and flew to the room, and then my father and mother and everybody went there. That crown had fallen off the top of the wood stove, and it was pretty well attached to the stove. It couldn't fall off by itself, but it fell off anyway. So there it was on the floor. And there they were speculating—my father, mother, and everyone, "I wonder what's going on. I wonder what's happening? I wonder what could have happened?" They were in the midst of the discussion when someone came to tell us that a cousin of my mother had passed away. The way they figure it is that the crown falling off the stove was a message from the cousin that she was dead.

I also had an aunt, my father's sister, a very dear aunt. I can't recall what her name was. She lived in Colorado, and I understand that a kestrel flew into the house. Do you know what a kestrel is? It's a small, tiny hawk. It came in the house. They say that it stood right on my aunt's head. No one scared it. The little hawk then just flew off by itself. No sooner said than done, someone came to inform my father and mother that my aunt in Colorado had died.

My parents claimed that it was a warning, a premonition, that God gave to the deceased as a way of informing people of their deaths.

José Nataleo Montoya

LAS VEGAS, NEW MEXICO

Genoveo Showed Up Crying

Whenever somebody died, there was a certain way of letting people know. I still remember this Genoveo. When his mother died, we were living up on top of the mesa, there in San Pablo. There was the kitchen, then a vestibule, followed by a bedroom. That's where my grandma and I were sleeping, and a cousin of my wife and a daughter were in the vestibule. And my uncle Estelito, who had just gotten home from the sierra, he was sleeping in the kitchen. They set up his bed in the kitchen. He was like, from here to that door. Right there!

In the morning this aunt Rafaelita got up. That was her name. When she went to build a fire, she saw a pool of blood at my uncle Estelito's feet, because this uncle was a compadre of Genoveo's mother. Well, she went and told my grandma that her son must have been ill overnight, since he was always getting sick. Then everybody got up. They even woke Estelito up. He was asleep.

"Listen. Were you sick last night?" they asked him.

"No," he responded. "Why?"

"Look here. There's blood there."

"No," he said to them. "Why, I didn't even get up. I didn't spit or anything."

A short time later this Genoveo showed up crying that his mother had died. When she died, I understand that she spat a big glob of blood. That's something I recall seeing. I believe I was about six years old at the time.

Rima Montoya

ALBUQUERQUE, NEW MEXICO

Two Dwarf Events

A long time ago when Costa Rica was a primitive and an agrarian country, it was made up of forests, jungles, country estates, and fields where one could hear the birds' long and serene warble, the gurgling of clear waters cascading between the mountain rocks, the creaking down the road of the oxcarts, and the faraway singing of the women washing. That's when the fields belonged to the oxen and the people were part of the land, when you ground with a stone and the only thing available was corn.

Back then men still conversed with the dead and beckoned the saints so they would bring about a miracle; back when torrential downpours at night shook the heavens that trembled with fearsome thunderbolts and lightning that looked like huge balls of fire that traversed the skies. During those years legends abounded among people, and one heard rumblings about encounters with the Wailing Woman, la Segua, the Cadejos [the Devil] itself, and you couldn't leave out the bothersome dwarfs, irksome like lice and fleas.

It is said that dwarfs like to annoy not only adults but children as well, and they thrive on moving objects from one place to another, putting filthy stuff in your food, and even disturbing chickens' nests. Worst of all, they are famous for luring children away from their homes and getting them lost. The annoying thing is that they appear and disappear in a whimsical way, and more than once they have caused trouble for the innocent victim. Those who have seen them claim they wear green or blue caps like berets and that they have beards and large pointed ears.

This story concerns what happened one day to Mr. Feliciano, a neighbor from Río Segundo. People claim that he left early one morning before the sun came out, to catch the bus that stopped in San Antonio at nine-thirty. He had more than enough time since Río Segundo to San Antonio is only half an hour on foot. When he reached La Ribera he saw that the road was impassable, and so as not to get dirty he took off through a fence to come out in front of the bottleneck. After about ten yards he came out on the same street that he had been headed down. For a good while he continued quick as a flash without reaching San Antonio. He was very surprised not to recognize the road that he was on, since he thought he knew all those environs like the back of his hand. He continued on the road, determined to catch the bus. He walked until he found himself completely disoriented. Up ahead, there was a fence, and behind him he was surrounded by wires. He searched for a way out on one side but found himself entangled in a brushwood; he looked for a way out on the other side and was cut off by a furrow. Downcast and without being able to escape from the entanglement, he sat down on a stump to rest. After a long while he was able to make out where he was. He had almost reached San Francisco!

He quickly stood up to go back. When he was about to reach the bus station, he heard the bus's horn. Relieved, Mr. Feliciano whistled at the man driving, waved at him, and finally hollered at him, and with no explanation in the world the damned driver refused to stop to pick him up. The poor soul had to wait until the following day because of the prankish dwarfs. Mr. Feliciano claims that on that day "nobody else made fun of me but them [the dwarfs]."

But, as I was saying, there is nothing that entertains dwarfs more than getting children lost. Around San Rafael de Escazú, one day among many, a four-year-old child from the Saborio family disappeared. The parents were at a loss as to where to look, so they gathered all the neighbors to search for the lost child. "Who knows where he's hidden," were words they uttered among themselves. They searched the coffee plantations where today Sareto [a large grocery store] and the rest of the businesses are located. Some people even said that a small tiger had come down from the mountains and had taken him away. Others went to the river's edge thinking that perhaps the child had fallen off the embankment, but they didn't find a trace of him.

When suspicion and desperation began to set in, someone heard shouting in the distance along the Río los Anonos. Running, they went to find out what was happening, and to everyone's relief a young boy had finally found the child. But don't you doubt for one moment, my reader, what the neighbors from San Rafael de Escazú saw on that day since the child, barely four years old, was found sitting on top of a huge solitary rock in the middle of the turbulent river. To top it all off, he was holding in his hands a huge apple from which he took bite after bite. But how did the child end up alone in the middle of the river? And how did he get the apple since apples were only seen at Christmas if they were in the Christmas box at all? Well, surrounded by shocked gazes, the child told them that some children dressed in blue had taken him away to play with them to the river, and when he started crying they gave him an apple. Darn those dwarfs!

Emilia Padilla García

ALBUQUERQUE (MARTÍNEZTOWN), NEW MEXICO

The Doll

There was a little old man who used to tell a story. Benito, my *primo* Benito, that was his name, who lived on the other side of the Río Puerco, around a place called El Arroyo de la Tapia. He was a musician.

One night he went to play at a dance in Salazar. He went on a donkey. The dance ended. This little old man then grabbed his violin and hit the road. There, around El Arroyo de la Tapia or thereabouts, which is across from our house, someone jumped and climbed on the donkey's rump.

Now let me tell you, that poor man didn't know what to do!

He used to talk a lot about the incident. "Who are you?" this and that, but he never got an answer, all of which caused him to spur his donkey, but that object stuck to the donkey's rump. He didn't find out who it was. He didn't, he just didn't. Don Benito simply said that he didn't know who it was.

When he got home, across from our house from where we used to live, where Lady Juanita Salas lived, do you remember where? That's where her daughter, the Lady Amada, lived. Anyway, when he got home I understand he climbed down from his donkey and hollered at them, "Catch me! I'm dying!" and he fell flat on the floor. He had fainted. The ladies then asked him, "What's wrong, Dad? What happened to you?" "The Doll," he'd answer. "The Doll." That he was carrying the doll on his back, but that was that. He was unable to speak anymore. All he could utter was "The Doll."

It wasn't until the following day that he spoke to them about The Doll that had hopped atop the donkey's rump. And the late Benito *swore* by it, that it was a doll. He was already quite old.

Manuel Pérez

BERNALILLO (EL BOSQUE), NEW MEXICO

Chaveta

There was a guy here everybody called Chaveta. Chaveta struck his mother and she cursed him when he hit her. His mother said to him, "I hope God punishes you for what you did to me."

Within a week that man was all shriveled up. Years later he was getting about in a little tiny wagon with tiny wheels. I remember that when he would come by school, I would listen for the little wagon, and it didn't matter who it was, they would grab rocks and toss them at him. God punished that man by having him go crazy. He lived in a little shack. People claim that the day he died, black smoke shot up from the house [stovepipe].

The Earth Would Part

This is the story my grandmother used to tell me. She said that she saw with her own eyes this boy who killed his mother. When he killed her, he tossed her over his shoulder to dump her in the river. When he went to do that, my grandma saw him. People came from all over, showing [them as an example] what punishment could bring you. The boy was full of worms!

Long ago people maintained that if you mistreated your mother or you answered her back and she put a curse on you, the earth would part and there you'd be until the earth would spit you back up. By the time the earth spit you back up, you'd be totally out of your mind. Back then curses were alive and well. Like now, you don't see anything like what I saw back then with my own eyes.

Mariel Romero Ocaranza

CHULA VISTA, CALIFORNIA

My Grammy

There's nothing less traditional than Tijuana, though many people think it is. I grew up and I was educated from kindergarten through high school in my beloved grungy city. I never thought that Tijuana had a lot of "culture" or "tradition," because it didn't feel like it was Mexico. To me, it was like the farthest corner of everything traditional about Mexican society, on the border with a country that wants nothing to do with Mexico. Therefore, very NOT Mexican.

Fortunately, my mother put me in a Catholic school where I was told all about the legends of my town and Baja California, and I grew to be fascinated with them. Juan Soldado, La bailarina sin cabeza, Tía Juana, Los Misioneros...

In my teens, I wondered where all this interest in mysticism came from and why I felt so comfortable with it. My mother was also comfortable with mystical, magical things, and her interest in the metaphysical and the supernatural has always given me space to breathe different and interesting airs.

The person who was an even bigger closet *bruja* than us was my yaya, Grammy. *Mi abuelita.* She didn't even know how much of a witch she was, but I think she knew, at least a little. She was a great poker player and she didn't even need to look at the cards to know what they were. She didn't need to even pick up the phone to know who it was when the line started to ring. She was a big-hearted, funny, devout Catholic woman. I suppose that's why she never allowed herself to explore "that side" of her personality further. I did not have long to get to know her well. She died, sadly, when I was in elementary school.

In middle school, I got the opportunity to learn about the Day of the Dead. I was surprised that the strict nuns at my school had contests every year for the best altar. Competition? *¡Mi mero mole!* (Right up my alley!) Every classroom would compete on the Day of the Dead. My class won first place every year.

In high school, I changed to a federal school. La Escuela Preparatoria Federal Lázaro Cárdenas. The biggest public high school in Tijuana, built right over the infamous Casino de Agua Caliente. I lost touch with all of these traditions again, focusing more on schoolwork.

My senior year, my mother married a lovely gringo and I had to move to San Diego. I felt very separated from my life in Tijuana so I decided that I would make an altar for my grandmother in October 2002, back in my house in Tijuana. Just to feel more like a *mexicana*.

In Tijuana, I went to El Mercado Hidalgo and got everything I needed. Sugar skulls, candy, *papel picado, pan de muerto*, the works. The best for my Yaya. Then I went to her house and grabbed a pair of her gloves and scarves which still smelled like her favorite perfume. That smell of violets moved my soul. I felt connected to her as I built the altar and as I breathed in her scent. I really, really believed she was going to visit the altar. "It would be an honor," I thought.

My mom was grateful to me for building it, my older sister thought it was cool but creepy, and our maid, Raquel (more like a member of our family, my *nana*), just spied on me from afar while I constructed it.

The altar lacked big important symbols like the palm-frond archway, the marigold walkway, and the cross drawn in sand on the floor, but it looked fantastic anyway. This time I didn't have an army of teenage girls helping me build it.

All covered in candles, the altar emitted a purple and gold haze. At my local Copy-Pronto I blew up a picture of my yaya when she was eighteen years old. I placed pictures of my grandpa on the altar when he was young too (he passed away even before Yaya did). I also put a little wooden violin on the altar (among other odds and ends) because she was a socialite and loved classical music. "The Blue Danube" by Strauss was her favorite.

My yaya's weakness was also on the altar—alcohol and shot glasses. She also loved sweets so that's what I put on the altar as her main meal. But the setting looked incomplete. It needed more color so I went to the corner bakery, Donas Venecia (which has been there since forever), to get some colorful pastries. I needed something that would last the night so I bought big round sugar cookies, the size of my hand, with big round colorful sprinkles on them. I loved these when I was a little girl. Yaya would like them too, I thought. I placed them on the left side of the altar, all stacked on a pretty porcelain plate.

It was the night. I lit all the candles as I looked into my yaya's eyes (in the picture, of course) and I said, "I hope you don't scare me tonight, but I really want you to enjoy what I've made for you. I miss you."

My mom and my sister came to see the altar and they congratulated me on how beautiful and sentimental the altar was. I was very proud. Then Raquel showed up and said, "You do know that if the dead visit the altar, they eat the soul of the food and then, when you eat it, it tastes like absolutely nothing. . . . Right?" I shivered.

"Sure," I answered nervously while my brain processed a million chilling thoughts.

It was 10 p.m. Yaya would be arriving in two hours. I decided to go to bed before I ran into her and fainted. I also locked up my sister's cat in the bathroom so he wouldn't jump onto the altar and ruin it. My sister left for a party and said she would be arriving late.

The next morning, I opened my eyes and stared out the window in my room. It was a nice clear, crisp autumn morning. I took my time getting up. I went to the kitchen to get a glass of water, when suddenly I noticed something very strange about the altar. The cookies!

One of the cookies was casually resting next to Yaya's picture. A foot or so away from the rest. The sprinkles. Those damn sprinkles were staring straight back at me!

I was in shock. I put the glass of water down and went to look for the cat. "He had to be the culprit!" I thought as I tried to convince myself that I was nuts. He was asleep, still locked in the bathroom.

"My sister," I thought. I ran to her room, shook her awake. "How dare you!" I shrieked at her. She was drowsy and confused. I took her to see the altar and her eyes peeled wide open.

"Did you do that when you came in last night?" I asked desperately. She squealed a little squeal, pushed me aside and said "NOOOO," as she stared at the cookie. Her eyes told me the truth. Yaya . . . had been here.

We couldn't control ourselves and we just stepped away from the altar. Later in the day, Raquel came in the house and asked me with a smirk, "So, are you going to eat the food?" I just shook my head. "No, I don't think so. Will you help me throw the food away?" "Sure," she said. I asked her, "You weren't here last night, were you?" She looked at the cookie, then back at me and said, "No, why?" She's always being funny like that, so I said, "C'mon, you didn't MOVE the cookie?" She stepped back a little, shaken. "The cookie moved?" she asked. Then we just proceeded to take the food down, quietly.

I have not built an altar since. I found the power of the supernatural overwhelming, but I think I'm ready to build another one for the next Day of the Dead. The next obvious choice, my grandpa Pepe. That will be interesting. He was a surgeon.

Luciano Sánchez

ALBUQUERQUE (LOS GRIEGOS), NEW MEXICO

Shiny Apples

My dad and many other people from Guadalupe would talk about flying sparks in the shape of a small train. But I never got to see flying sparks. Back then when I was a small boy, those strange things didn't exist. What I did discover at home, before coming to Albuquerque, were eggs right in front of our house. Yes, we had chickens, but they were all in the chicken coop.

We also found very shiny apples, very, very glass-like, and that's when there were no apples or any other fruit trees around. At least when a fruit vendor or someone like him goes, then one can believe or accept things like that.

What we always did was to burn all of that stuff in the stove. We never kept anything, that is to say, to eat. We were afraid. Just to look at that apple, without knowing where it came from, was bad business.

Andrés Sánchez Rojas

PHOENIX, ARIZONA

The Little Girl

This occurred when I was about fifteen years old. The name of the place over in Mexico was La Empacadora Maya (The Maya Cannery). There they canned all kinds of fruit, for example, melons, cucumbers, and other fruits. It was a huge cannery. We worked at that factory across from where we lived. That's where the national highway went through. Nothing else was there, only the cannery. Next to it was a ranch.

It was about noon. There were about four of us boys, all about the same age. I joined them and we started talking. And, as I say, it was in broad daylight. I came from the cannery to the ranch where the boys were because it was only a matter of crossing the highway. Anyway, we were chatting when a little girl about ten or twelve years old went by, asking for her mother.

That struck us as very strange. In that area there were only two houses near the factory, plus the ranch. Then we looked at each other. The little girl was crying, asking for her mother. We asked her where she was going, because it wasn't a normal thing, practically speaking, to see a little girl her age alone. The closest ranch was about twenty or twenty-five miles away. Then we went and stopped her and asked her who she was. The only thing she would answer, sobbing, was, "I want to see my mother." "But where do you live? Where do you come from?" But she wouldn't tell us anything. Nothing at all! All that she would say was, "I want to see my mother."

Then she got ahead of us. She continued toward the highway. She was running alongside the highway. Those of us who were asking her who she was, where do you come from, because she was just a little girl, saw that she disappeared into the distance about a half a mile away. There was a canal that crossed the highway. She was about to reach that canal. I was already on horseback. Then I said to my friends, "We must catch up with her so we can see where she's headed. There's no ranches nearby, and we must catch up with her to find out who she is or where she's headed."

Above that canal that crossed the highway, right there is where she turned the corner. I saw her when she took the turn. What a surprise that was when I turned, galloping on my horse! I don't believe she had gained much on me, but I no longer saw her and I felt a bit scared. The other boys were running but on foot. I was the first one to make the turn because I was on horseback. I stopped and was surprised because I no longer saw her. The road where she turned the corner, well, you could see it in its entirety; it went no farther.

The other guys finally caught up with me and said to me, "Well, where's the little girl?" "I don't know, I don't see her." "Well, take off after her on your horse. You'll catch up with her in just a bit." Well, I galloped about two or three miles, more or less, in the canal. I looked for her in the canal and along the edges and in the woods and I never found her.

When I was on my way back home, I don't know, but I felt like a cold sweat and I felt badly because the girl disappeared on me and because she was just a little girl. And it happened in broad daylight!

That's one of the things I wanted to tell someone because I lived through it. That's something that happened to me and, as I say, I wasn't alone. There were several of us and we were all asking ourselves, "Who was that little girl?"

Next day my friends took off in the direction the little girl came from; they went to swim at a place called San Juan Prieta. It's also like a canal, but the majority of us from the small ranches would go there to swim. It was there where they found a large cache of money. I don't know exactly how much it was, but my four friends, the ones who were with me when we were looking for the little girl, were very happy when they got home.

But many times in my lifetime I've asked myself, "Who was the little girl? Where did she come from? And why was she looking for her mother?" We asked among the rest of the ranches. As I say, there was a ranch where we saw her. And there was a ranch about twenty-five miles farther away. Who could possibly travel that distance unless they did so in a truck or car? It's not easy to walk that many miles. For a long time I would ask people where that little girl came from and I never could find out.

The Little Pigs

I wasn't alone. All of us in the family were at home. It was already late, about six o'clock in the evening, and almost getting dark. The only one who wasn't home was my father because he got home late. He was in charge of the place where we lived; he was in charge of all the workers.

We heard a noise coming from a sow and her piglets. We looked for her because you could hear the ruckus that occurs when a sow walks with her little pigs. But she wasn't walking on land. She was flying! We saw her, heard her, and she flew above us. She wasn't very high. Then she came at us from another direction. There was a ranch that faced the ocean. That's the direction from where the sow was coming, accompanied by her piglets, making all kinds of noises, but as I said, she wasn't walking. Instead, she passed us by in the sky. She was coming from the direction of that ranch that faced the ocean where a married couple lived, but the couple didn't have anything to do with those of us who lived in the area.

It wasn't very dark so you could say that it was a vision or something. And I wasn't the only one who saw the sow; rather, we all saw it. We just stood there watching! That's all we did! Who knows what it was? Something spiritual perhaps?

Eddie Torres, Jr.

BERNALILLO (EL BOSQUE), NEW MEXICO

The Man without a Head

Here where we live is called El Bosque. There's a place that used to be called La Abeyta, and my father used to tell me that this gentleman ran into this other man and something must have happened between them, because that man cut off the gentleman's head, presumably for money. And I understand that the gentleman would go without a head. That's what my father told me when I was a child.

Later, I was already a young man, about eighteen, nineteen years old. I had a girlfriend and at that time we were living in San Lorenzo. I had to go on foot. As old as I was, it seemed like I would see someone and then I would take off running from being scared. I would run from my house to my girlfriend's house because people said that a man without a head would come out. I never got to see him. People declared that he would come out here at a place called El Puente Blanco (the White Bridge), and my father declares that this man [the one without a head] from one day to the next accumulated money.

People claim that dwarfs came out and gave him bars of gold. Those were stories that went around.

Superstitions

I worked in Duke City [Albuquerque]. I was about eighteen, nineteen years old. You would hear that a woman, a young lady, would appear here at Sandía Pueblo. One time I was coming from work about one or two o'clock in the morning. It was windy and I saw—and the mind works in different ways—a paper that was tangled up in the middle of the road and it seemed like the car wasn't moving. I got home shaking. I recall that clear as day. Poor Mom! I was pale from being scared. Something appeared on the road. I went back the next day in the daytime and there was the paper stuck to a fence post.

You would hear lots of stories. My dad told me once that he found some lemons with needles stuck in them. And he believes a lot in that sort of thing. I used to get my hair cut with this woman here in Bernalillo, and she would burn it because she swore that otherwise the witches would come, sweep and gather up the hair, and use it for evil doings.

My grandma wouldn't leave dirty dishes overnight. She wouldn't go to bed until they were clean, because she said that the witches would steal the dishes at night. That's why I wash the dishes before going to bed so that the witches don't show up!

Eileen Dolores Treviño Villarreal

SAN ANTONIO, TEXAS

Fragrances

Very well, I have three stories that are very close to my heart: my mother and brother's deaths and then one about a very old flag in the city of Goliad, Texas.

To begin with, it was the month of February 1994. My mom had passed away a month before, and I was still very much in pain because of her death. I was at home one night standing inside the living room, facing the dining room. It was about nine o'clock at night. I stopped and I was looking toward a window and suddenly from up above where I was standing, a fragrance, the most beautiful thing, came to me.

Immediately I knew it was my mother. This had never happened to me before. I was standing up, and the fragrance comes at me, like so, from above, from the ceiling, and I thought: "Mom, it's you, right? Is it you? Are you all right? Are you happy?"

At that very instant I headed for the other room to tell a friend of mine who was there. "Listen, Mom is here." In a split second I returned and by then the fragrance, strong and precious, had disappeared. I know that it was my mother. The fragrance was, well, the only thing I can do is to give you an example.

In February, when the mountain laurel blooms, it has a fragrance that smells like grapes, but I don't have those kinds of trees. They're neither at my house nor in the neighborhood. That's all I can tell you. Something very pleasant, more or less like laurel. That was my mother's message to tell me, "Don't be sad. Everything is fine."

And after that, after that encounter, I began to feel a little bit more relaxed and months later, much more at ease. But I know that it was my mother and it's the first episode that she started and I already know that others will be forthcoming. I don't know when they'll be coming and don't know in what fashion, but I know that they're coming by way of the fragrance.

The second episode occurred in May of 2000. My brother had died three weeks earlier. I was at his home with his wife. His wife is from Morelia, Michoacán, and then she said to me, "You make the funeral arrangements; you take charge of all that." Fine. And I had been staying with her for a week, and the burial had taken place three days before that.

I was sitting down in my brother's office. He and I were very close. There were his fax machine and his telephone to the right of his desk, and I was sitting in his chair. His wife was sitting in front of the desk and we were talking, and suddenly here on the right where his fax machine and telephone are located, a fragrance hit me.

To give you an idea what it was like, it was like eucalyptus. My brother suffered from arthritis and while I'm talking with my sister-in-law, why, here comes the fragrance again. And I says, "My God! Here we go again." A minute later here comes the fragrance from the eucalyptus so strong that I knew that it was my brother. I then asked my sister-in-law, I said to her, "Angélica, can you smell the fragrance? Come close." She says, "No, no, no, I don't smell anything."

I then commenced crying because I knew that it was my brother and I said to her, "He's here. Pedro is here." I said to him, "Dear brother, you're here, right?" And the strong fragrance stayed like that for about ten minutes. I started talking to him. "What are you trying to tell me, dear brother? That you're okay, happy? That everything is fine where you are? That you liked the funeral we arranged in your honor, that we bid you farewell with so much honor and so much beauty?"

I cried and cried because I knew that he was present, not for his wife but for me, because she couldn't smell the fragrance. She started to cry also. I said to her, "Pedro is here." "But where, where?" "No [you don't understand], it's a fragrance." "But I don't see a thing." "No, that's because he came to see me to show me that he's fine." About ten, twelve minutes later, the fragrance disappeared.

The third episode also occurred in 2000, during the month of November. My group, called The Bejareños, I was the president at that time, was invited to the city of Goliad, Texas. They were going to have a fair of all the groups that were here in Texas: the Spaniards, the Indians, and the Mexicans. It was going to be a huge fair. As it was, I know this gentleman from the Río Grande Valley, he's a collector of antiques. Then on that day in November 2000 he came and he said to me, "Eileen, I have a flag, the Borgoña, which is very old." I said to him, "Is it original?" "Yes, it's from 1600 and the red part with the cross made of velvet, that material comes from Genoa, Italy. Come see the flag when you're through here." On my side of the family the Treviños, before they came to Spain in 1500, were in Genoa and I said to myself, "Boy! I have to go."

At five o'clock in the afternoon I headed for the prison in Goliad. There were two flags, one from María Laxilaria and another one from

Borgoña. And there were some people present, chroniclers and genealogists around us and then I touched very lightly the flag's velvet and I said to myself, "If this flag could talk, I wonder what it could tell me about my ancestors? Who made this flag? One of my grandmothers? Who carried this flag in battle?" Then I started talking with the group of people. Five minutes later, well, what do you think happened to me again? A fragrance from the Borgoña flag hit me, not the one from María Laxilaria, but the one from Borgoña came a fragrance so wonderful, the fragrance of a woman, and that one I can't give you any details because it's such a smooth fragrance, so light and so beautiful that if the color rose had a fragrance, that's what it would be. Then I was muttering to myself in a low voice, "Oh, how beautiful, if it's an ancestor!" And everyone was like, "What, what's wrong with you, what, what are you seeing, what, what are you saying?" I said to them, "I'll explain it to you a little later." This pretty and beautiful fragrance didn't last long, ten, twelve minutes, and then it began to dissipate. It was a forewarning that if it was a great-grandmother, then she came from the Treviño side of the family; she made the flag or had a hand in part of it, doing the cross or whatever. But she tried to tell me that she had received my message and she was telling me, "Yes, I'm here, I had something to do with the flag."

These are the three episodes. I have a photograph of this flag when I went to Premont, Texas, a year later that I had taken with my friends who have the flag, but I already knew that it wasn't going to do anything. It only happened once.

Teresina Ulibarrí

LAS VEGAS, NEW MEXICO

He Quit Being Mean

One time my mom was saying that they, Dad and Mom, raised this boy. My siblings and I called him Uncle Miguel. But I understand that he was horrible. He was a very terrible man. He used to come to my mother's house, he lived in Los Chupaderos. He came here every evening. I guess he was already married. And all he did was to cause mischief. He was terrible.

Then one time when he was on his way from Los Chupaderos to here, because the road bends a little—he would come on foot to help my father and my uncle—he saw a man ahead of him, but he couldn't catch up with him. By the time he got to this one place, he could no longer see the man. Upon his return home—it was already night—right there where he was

walking, he heard a horse that was breathing very hard, and it was galloping. It was about to run over him. I mean about to run over him, really run over him. He was running scared as all get-out.

All of a sudden, he fell where there's a waterfall, a spring called El Chorro. My uncle Miguel says that the man he saw fell down the Voladero [precipice] and sounded like a loud gunshot. At that very moment his [Miguel's] wife and mother-in-law opened the door to see what the shouting and all the commotion was about, and he fell forward and fainted. I don't know whether it was from being scared after what he saw or not. But from then on he turned into a good man. He quit being mean.

Supersticiones, misterios, y lo paranormal

Cuando Dios quiere, no hay puerta que se cierre.

Enrique Campos

POMONA, CALIFORNIA

Se oían unos pasos

En una población de Oaxaca, México que se llama San Pedro, estaba viviendo yo con una muchacha. Una noche de repente se despertó en la madrugada. Se puso morada y señalaba al techo pero no podía hablar. En ese momento me sentía presionado.

Agarré unos huevos como había visto que también usaba la gente pa sacar los malos espíritus. Pues fue lo que hice entre oración y cuando pudo ella hablar, dijo que había visto unas personas reflejadas en el techo de la casa. Después que me pudo platicar ella, la limpié.

Así luego comencé a oír pasos afuera de la casa como de un animal que daba vueltas por junto al muro. Yo de ningún momento tuve miedo. Nada me intimaba, pero esa energía se sentía. Y como fue una energía muy fuerte con la que estaba luchando, se oían unos pasos como de un animal (*knock, knock, knock*), todo afuera donde estaba la puerta. Como a los cinco minutos se quitaron y todo regresó a la normalidad.

Connie Chacón

PUEBLO, COLORADO

Un pajarito

Dicen que cuando se están despidiendo algunos dolientes, entra un pajarito. Eso me pasó a mí cuando recién vinimos aquí a Pueblo. Estaba enferma mi mamá y se murió.

En la mañana tenían la puerta abierta, era en el verano, y entró un pajarito. Entró ahi en el cuarto con las alitas caidas, y dijo la mamá de mi comadre Rosa,

—Este pajarito trae malas nuevas. Viene d'allá del Rito. ¡Quién sabe que le habrá pasao a mi familia!

Vino y lo pescó con sus alitas caidas y medio entumido el pajarito y lo agarró y le metió el buchito en l'agua y lo 'chó pa juera. Güeno, ya en la tarde llegaron las nuevas. Es que se había muerto mi mamá.

Cuando están agonizando su gente diuno vienen a despedirse diuno. Mi mamá se despidió de mí. Ese pajarito vino cuando mamá se murió.

Un ruido en la casa

Un tío mío que vivía cerquita donde vivíamos nosotros se casó. Recién casao estaba, y todas las noches les hacían ruido en la casa a él y a su esposa y iban a dormir allá en casa porque tenían muncho miedo. Luego pusieron ellos un papel y una pluma pa que escribieran los del ruido a ver por qué, si alguien se había muerto o qué sería, o si había un tesoro en la casa o alguna cosa. Pero no escribieron nada.

Siguieron ruidos en la casa arriba, y no supieron por qué, pero allá en casa iban a dormir ese tío mío y su mujer porque tenían miedo porque hacían muncho ruido en la casa.

Juan Bautista Chacón

PUEBLO, COLORADO

Tres chiflidos

Iba yo una vez a case 'e este señor. Éste era albolario. Jui yo ahi y le di unos centavos pa ver si era brujo. Jui a pagale, con dos primos míos. Otro día yo iba salir pal rancho, ves, porque yo estaba casao con otra señora. Iba salir pal rancho a caballo esa tarde. Tenía horas. Iba salir por la tarde. Pues me dijo el albolario,

—Te adivino una cosa.

—Bien—pero no me va a creer usté esto.

Yo estaba sentao asina mirando, como a la puerta hoy. Tenía una ventanita pacá, con cortinas, y los otros muchachos estaban sentaos ahi. El señor estaba sentao por allá en una cama, cuando di vista pa la ventana. Tenía como una cirgüela con un cordel, y me quedaba mirándola a ella. Y se abría la cirgüela y se cerraba. Se abría y se cerraba. Yo me quedé con las greñitas ya poco paradas.

Logo me dijo,

—Tú tienes miedo.

—No—le dije—. ¿Por qué?

—¡Pos tú no creyes en brujas!

— ¿Por qué voy a creyer en brujas? Nunca ha visto niuna.

Pos él era albolario, ¿ves? Y me dijo,

—Güeno, pos yo te voy adivinar una cosa.

—Güeno, está bien—le contesté.

No hacía muncho que lo había visto, pero nunca había estao en su casa yo.

—Güeno. Te voy adivinar una cosa. Mañana tú vas pa la sierra, pal rancho de tu suegro. Vas a caballo, y vas a ir poco tarde.

—Sí, sí, tarde.

—¿Y no creyes en brujas?

—No, yo no creyo en brujas.

—Y antes que salgas pa la sierra a caballo, lo vas herrar. Le vas a poner herraduras.

—Sí, es verdá. Le voy a poner herraduras.

Yo ya me puse sospecho que él estaba atinando lo que yo tenía pensao. Logo siempre cuando estaba platicando se quedaba con el ojo a la cirgüela. Tavía estaba fregando la cirgüela. Tavía estaba abriéndose y cerrándose.

—Tú estás nervioso. Yo creyo que tú tienes miedo.

—No—le dije—. ¿Por qué voy a tener miedo?

Y los otros, eran primos míos, me miraban y medio se sonreían, porque ya ellos sabían que él era albolario.

—Pos ora verás, cuando llegues a la casa esta tarde que estés poniéndole herraduras al caballo, te va pegar tres chiflidos un animal, en frente 'e tu casa.

Yo vivía en la sierra donde comenzaba el monte. Mi casa estaba en la orilla de la sierra, y abajo había pinos. ¡Munchos pinos! A la derecha, al lao, pal *west*, era ladera. Había nomás un banquito. Muy bonito banquito había.

—Ahi cerca 'e tu casa te van a pegar tres chiflidos—y tenía yo güen perro, un German shepherd. Ahi andaba.

—Sí, está bien.

—Los vas oír bien, ¿pero no vas a tener miedo?

—No—le dije—. Yo miedo por qué le voy a tener.

—¿Y vas ir pa la sierra?

—Sí, sí me voy.

Y le platiqué a la vieja cuando llegué a la casa. Ella hablaba mexicano lo mesmo que nojotros [era angla]. Le dije lo que me había dicho Teodoro, así se llamaba el albolario.

—¿Quién sabe—me dijo ella—, si te vaya hacer mal?

—No. Mal no me puede hacer, pos yo me llamo Juan. Yo no le tengo miedo a nada. Yo no le tengo miedo.

Pos dicho y hecho. Le estaba poniendo la herradura a los caballos y ya estaba pa 'cabar y pegaron tres chiflidos. ¡Bien los oyí! Tres parejitos viniendo de mi casa parriba 'e la loma, y dije yo entre mí, "Es verdá."

Güeno, yo no tenía miedo. Ya entré y la mujer ya tenía la cena pa cenar pa irme, y le dije,

—¿Oyites los chiflidos que chiflaron arriba 'e la loma?

—No, no oyí nada—pos ella estaba en la casa.

—Esos tres chiflidos que me dijo Teodoro, me chiflaron.

—No vayas. No sea que te vaya pasar algo en el camino.

—No. Me pase lo que me pase, voy.

Güeno. Cené y busqué mi cotón. Era verano pero siempre era frío, poco fresco. Puse mi cotón en los tientos y puse la maleta pa echale la comida, y eché lo que iba mandale mi vieja a mi suegra pa la sierra. Monté el caballo y me jui.

Sería como la milla, milla y media, y se me hizo pardito. Me dio Teodoro tres bancos.

—En el último te van a chiflar. En el primer banco te van a chilfar otra vez dos veces. En el segundo banco te van a chiflar tres veces. ¿Y no tienes miedo?—dijo.

—No. ¡Qué miedo!

Antes de salir yo me fajé—tenía una '38—y me la fajé, y le dije a ésta [su esposa],

—Tú te vas con mamá—porque vivía cerquita mamá, y me jui yo.

Llamé el perro y se jue conmigo. Pos dicho y hecho. Nomás llegué a este banquito, ahi están otra vez los chiflidos. ¡Cerquita, hermano! Se me pararon las greñas, pero me jui.

Dejando uno por otro, había escondido un cuarto de mula, pos yo tomaba muncho en ese tiempo. ¿Pa qué voy a decir una mentira? Ahi sí me dieron ganas de tomar un güen trago de licor. Ya cuando llegué al otro banco ya estaba oscuro. Pegaba la luz de la luna, pero era un cañón y iba pegando muncho la sombra en la esquina aquí. Ya iba yo quizás como al otro banco, como unas ocho o nueve millas de allá yo de la casa. Nomás llegué al otro banco y me pegaron otros tres chiflidos. Yo ya sabía que es lo que me había dicho el albolario. Yo dije, "Se va 'parecer algún animal." Por alguna cosa era el albolario. Yo ya llevaba la bolsa llena de cartuchos.

Güeno, dejando una por otra, pasé el lugar y me jui. Ya nomás pasé arriba, era planiao, porque iba subiendo siempre parriba 'e la sierra. Ahi era planiado y le di al caballo al trote. No. Pos ya no me pasó nada. Llegué a la casa, pero siempre me metió unos jalonazos de miedo.

Eso es too lo que recuerdo d'este señor, el albolario.

Adrián Chávez

ALBUQUERQUE (ATRISCO), NEW MEXICO

Visiones

Yo conocí este señor. Ese hombre lo podía uno ver hacer visiones. Por ejemplo, iba en su caballo él, montao, y le llegó a causar visiones a otro compañero que iba con él. Tiraba su cuarta y le dijía,

—Ya se me cayó mi cuarta. ¡Dámela!

Y se apeaba su compañero y cuando se iba a agachar, bien vido que lo iba a picar una víbora; se hacía víbora su cuarta de él. Al fin no la quiso agarrar su compañero. Tuvo que apearse Eduardo, el de las visiones, por la cuarta, y enseñale que no era víbora, que era su cuarta. Esto lo oí platicar yo. Eran vaqueros ellos los dos.

En otra vez cuando llegaron al rancho, entró el compañero de Eduardo pa dentro, y vido que se le vino encima una osa, de allí dionde estaba, onde dormía él en la camalta. Pues se le prendió él a l'osa de las orejas y andaba luchando con ella cuando ábrese Eduardo la puerta.

—¿Pero qué andas haciendo?—es que le dijo.

—Este animal. . . .

Es que traiba una almuada.

—En una d'éstas que me hagas reír, que te burles de mí, te voy a dar un balazo.

Pues se llevaban muy duro ellos los dos. Otra vez lo hizo Eduardo que se juera llenando el cuarto de agua. Antonces se subió su compañero en una silleta, y cuando ya iba a subir más alto l'agua de él se dejó ir y cayó en el suelo . . . no en l'agua.

Pues munchas d'esas tonteras pasaban. Cómo las haría Eduardo, ¡yo no sé! Ese hombre me platicaba él que de joven anduvo muncho con los circos; ahi aprendió él munchas cosas.

Samuel Córdova

ALBUQUERQUE (SAN JOSÉ), NEW MEXICO

La Nene

Había un hombre, Benito Lucero, en esos tiempos, y era violinista. Tocaba violín. Y no tenía, creo, en qué andar. Vivía en Gualupe y vino a tocar en un baile a Salazar, a pie.

Cuando iba de aquí pallá, de Salazar pa Gualupe, ahi en el Puertecito onde decían de La Nene, ahi iba don Benito con su violín abajo del sobaco. Iba pedo. En ese tiempo había licor, el primero que hubo, cuando se le apareció un *baby* en el camino, llorando, engüelto en unas garras, y lo agarró en brazos y se jue pa su casa. Cuando ya iba a la casa, ya era en la madrugada, es que le habló el baby,

—Tata. Yo tengo "llentes."

Loo se le cayó el baby y se asustó muncho. Pero no supimos qué se hizo el baby. Despareció.

La Ñeca

Platicaban del Puertecito, y yo mantengo que entemecían a la plebe con las mentiras. Muncha plebe tenía miedo que los mismos viejos hacían eso.

Una vez me despacharon a mí en la tarde, de Gualupe a Salazar, a que avisara que alguien se había muerto. No me acuerdo quién había muerto. El cuento es que era ya en la tarde.

Jui. Tenía un caballo blanco, muy güen caballo, muy mansito, muy gordo. Cuando venía de aá pacá, que tenía que pasar por el Puertecito, pero tenía que pasar el Arroyo de la Tapia primero. Ya estaba oscuro. ¡Oh, yo venía tan ancho y cantando yo! Al pasar el arroyo ese, aulló un coyote, y me espanté yo.

Y no, ni por aquí traiba yo de La Ñeca que decían que en el Puertecito le salía a uno. Me acordé. Decían que se le subió a uno en las anancas ¡Uh, quién sabe qué tanto! Pues cerré los ojos y le abrí al caballo. Ahi voy. No pasó nada.

¡Quién sabe qué será!

Había otro lugar, ya, ya cerca de la casa. Le decíanos la Joyita. El caballo iba muy alborotao, queriendo correr. Estaba oscuro, y vide venir como un hombre en el camino. Bien le vide camisa blanca y sombrero. Y aquel caballo alborotao queriendo correr. Y yo que se me levantaba hasta el cabello parriba de miedo. "¡Se me va a encajar en las anancas esa cosa!

¡Quién sabe qué será!" Aquel caballo destornudaba y aquí está queriendo correr conmigo.

Pues al fin, destornudó uno y no, era un burro, de un hombre que tenía cuatro burros pintos. Se paraban en el camino, como son tan bobos, tamién a velo a uno. Pues se ladearon par un lado del camino, y antonces sí le rompí al caballo. Diuna vez me conocieron aá en la casa que iba todo zurro.

Yolanda del Villar

SAN ANTONIO, TEXAS

Las manitas

La historia de las manitas que se pintan en la parte trasera de los carros, es una historia del dominio común entre los habitantes de San Antonio, Texas, y cuenta de un accidente sucedido hace mucho tiempo. Este accidente sucedió en una de las muchas vías ferroviarias que pasan por San Antonio.

Según la leyenda, era un autobús escolar que fue arrollado por el tren y fallecieron todos los pequeños que el autobús transportaba. A pesar de que a simple vista las vías ferroviarias se sitúan sobre el nivel de la carretera cuando las personas apagan sus coches y ponen sus vehículos en neutral, éstos son empujados misteriosamente hacia la vía ferroviaria y sólo dejan de ser empujados al encontrarse al otro lado de la vía.

La leyenda dice que son los espíritus de los niños que tratan de evitar otra tragedia, ya que cuando va a pasar el tren este fenómeno no sucede. Lo cierto es que se trata de una leyenda, ya que se han buscado archivos de accidentes ferroviarios sucedidos en tal lugar con las características del antes mencionado y no se ha encontrado nada.

Sin embargo, cuando recién emigramos de México a San Antonio éste era uno de nuestros lugares favoritos a visitar. Cada vez que algún pariente nos visitaba, la visita a los rieles era obligatoria. Hace aproximadamente catorce años que esta costumbre desapareció debido a un hecho que hasta la fecha no nos hemos podido explicar.

Mi hermano una vez se encontraba de visita en San Antonio y para no perder la costumbre fuimos a los rieles a que nos "pucharan" los niños. Sólo que en esta ocasión le pusimos talco a la parte trasera del vehículo, pues habíamos escuchado que las huellas de las manitas quedaban impresas en los coches.

Mi hija mayor tenía diez años de edad y junto con su prima de la misma edad viajaban en la parte trasera del carro quedando de frente a la parte posterior del mismo. Al llegar al lugar que ya mencioné, realizamos la maniobra tantas veces hecha con anterioridad, sólo que esta vez la experiencia fue diferente y aterradora. Al mismo tiempo que el vehículo empezó a deslizarse por la carretera, mi hija y su prima lanzaron alaridos de terror haciendo que el desconcierto reinara entre los adultos. Las pequeñas aseguraban haber visto el momento justo cuando las huellas de las manitas se imprimieron en el vidrio posterior del carro. Sin embargo, no vieron nada más.

Al llegar a casa revisamos el lugar empolvado con anterioridad y efectivamente se podían percibir pequeñas huellas sobre el talco. Éste fue el final de nuestras visitas a los rieles.

Años más tarde en un programa radial el locutor también platicó su experiencia con el lugar. Además, una cadena de televisión nacional vino a San Antonio con el propósito de grabar un reportaje sobre el tema. El locutor platicó que él y su esposa acompañaron a la reportera al lugar.

Era un domingo en la mañana y el lugar es un lugar que no tiene casas alrededor; por lo tanto es un lugar solitario y silencioso. Silencio sólo interrumpido por los curiosos que van en busca de una experiencia diferente. El locutor dice que al empezar las grabaciones se percataron que se oía mucho bullicio, pero era un bullicio de voces infantiles como cuando hay recreo en una escuela. Esto les llamó la atención debido a que era domingo. Aún así pensaron que cerca debía de haber un parque o lugar de paseo y de allí provenía el bullicio.

Intrigados por este suceso, se dieron a la tarea de manejar varias cuadras a la redonda tratando de encontrar la fuente del bullicio, pero su intento fue en vano. No había escuelas o parques cerca del lugar. Al percatarse de esto sintieron como los vellos de su piel se erizaron y Oscar, el locutor, prometió no volver a molestar la paz de los espíritus.

Pasos

Esta historia yo no la he verificado personalmente pero mi vecina... Bueno, yo tengo 10 años, no, 12 años, viviendo en la casa donde vivimos ahorita. Yo tenía como aproximadamente un año de vivir en esta casa cuando se cambió esta familia que era el señor grande, el señor mayor, su esposa, doña Leonor, y sus hijos, dos hijos solterones, cuarentones, Willie y Rudy. Doña Leonor es de descendencia creo méjicoamericana y don Willie también, y sus hijos hablan muy bien español aunque son méjicoamericanos pero ya como tercera o cuarta generación.

Cuando ellos se cambiaron ahí pues es una casa vieja, grande, y la empezaron a restaurar, y en la parte de atrás de la casa principal, en la mera esquina y en la parte de atrás, tenían, lo que nosotros llamamos garaje. Entonces los muchachos, los solterones estos, lo habilitaron como cuarto de solterón. Ellos vivían allá en la parte de atrás. No vivían con su papá y su mamá.

Pues resulta que uno de ellos, Willie, oía pasos que iban de su casa en la noche, o en la madrugada, a la puerta del garaje que ahora era el cuarto de ellos, y se paraban allí en la puerta. Entonces Willie abría la puerta pero no miraba nada. Se asomaba a ver, a ver si . . . porque aunque tiene cerca la casa, siempre uno tiene que estar más pendiente se vaya a meter alguien a robar o algo, pero miraba y no, nadie.

Intrigados por estos pasos que oían, doña Leonor se dio a la tarea de preguntar a gentes que habían vivido antes en el barrio y que sabían quién había habido antes, de que si había algo allí, que qué pasaba, que por qué se oían esos ruidos. Una vecina mía de la misma calle, vivió diez años antes en esa casa, antes de que vinieran doña Leonor y su familia. También se llama Leonor. Cuando doña Leonor se cambió fue y le preguntó a Leonor (la segunda Leonor), y entonces la segunda Leonor le dice, "No, sí nosotros también oíamos esos pasos pero no, no sabemos qué eran," pero ya le dio información a quién le podía preguntar, quién había vivido antes que ellos ahí. Doña Leonor, total, que se dio a la tarea de investigar.

Resulta que había este señor que era celosísimo y que vivía con su esposa y dos niños pequeños, el niño de 10 y la niña de 8 años. El señor celosísimo, un día en uno de esos arranques de celos, mató a la señora y entonces los niños, asustados como estaban, corrieron y se escondieron en el garaje. El señor salió, se fue tras de ellos, y los mató en el garaje. Después él se ahorcó en el garaje.

Pensamos que se atribuyen los pasitos que van, los pasos que se paran en la puerta del garaje . . . no sabemos si son los niños corriendo o si es el señor que los va persiguiendo a los niños. No se sabe. Y todavía se oyen ruidos.

A la madre la mataron en la casa y ahí en la casa no se oye nada. Los pasos son de la casa al garaje y se paran en la entrada.

Esto ocurre en la esquina de San Fernando y Calle 34, en el West Side. Este hecho ocurre desde hace más de 20 años y se siguen oyendo pasos. Bueno, últimamente ya no le he preguntado a doña Leonor cuyo marido Willie murió de cáncer y luego murió Willie, el hijo. Ahora vive el nieto con doña Leonor, pero no le he preguntado si él también ha oído esos pasos.

No les da miedo vivir allí. Allí viven. Mientras no sean fantasmas que mueven las cosas, pues pueden vivir con los fantasmas.

Filiberto Esquibel

LAS VEGAS, NEW MEXICO

¿Qué no quieres ir al funeral?

Si tú quieres que yo te diga de que hay cosas que no podemos explicar, te voy a platicar una cosa, una cosa que me pasó a mí. Tenía un carro viejo. Tenía un carro Chevy, viejo, le di un *overhaul*. Pues yo no había compuesto un carro que no comenzara. Dende un prencipio hasta el otro. Dende chiquito me crie dándole *overhaul* a gatos, *bulldozers* y maquinarias. Le di un *overhaul*. Era un '36 Chevy. No, no, no, no quería prender. Le chequié too y güeno. Teníanos en ese tiempo un funeral entre unas personas muy cerca. Yo estaba acabando de componer el carro pa prendelo. Luego dijo la mujer,

—¿Qué no quieres ir al funeral?

—Pus yo quisiera componer este carro. Lo necesito pa ir al trabajo. Curre tú.

Pues esta persona [el muerto], cierta persona, se 'nojó porque no quise ir yo al funeral. El día que lo iban a enterrar [al difunto], se enojó. Se me quedó a ver, a componer el carro. Le chequié el carbulador. Le chequié los puntos. Le chequié too. Too estaa bien. Se soponía comenzar. Gaselín. Too tenía. Le di al *starter* hasta que tomé la batería, y los '36 Chevys se les podía dar cranque. Le di cranque. ¡Nada! Ni, ni lucha hacía, y le dejé el cranque puesto al carro. Ya me dolía l'espinazo. En ese tiempo llegó tal gente pa la casa. Y llegó mi suegro adelante. Me dijo,

—¿Qué no lo has poído componer? ¿No ha prendío el carro?

—No quiere—le dije—. Le cayó hasta la batería. Ya me cansé de dale cranque. Ya me cansé. Ora lo voy a prender atrás de la troca de mi tío y le voy a pegar una jalaa a éste nomás de puro coraje.

Y en ese tiempo vinía cierta persona de allá del funeral pacá, dolientes del enterrao. Ya se le había bajao el coraje al dijunto, y pasó cerquita una mujer.

—¿Qué pasa?—dijo—. ¿Qué no puedes comenzar el carro?

—No—le dije—. No quiere comenzar.

Yo no maliciaba nada.

—¡Válgame Dios!—dijo—. Pus yo no sé cómo no comienza y eres muy güen macánico.

Y le alisó el *fender* asina [con la mano], y entró pa dentro. Siguimos platicando yo y mi suegro. Y le dije,

—Pus ya l'hecho el trae a este carro de toos moos. Ya llevo too el santo día. De toos moos y no quiere.

Le puse la llave otra vez. Nomás en cuanto se movió el ingenio y prendió el carro. Explícame tú eso.

Hubo esta cierta persona [el muerto], y no me quería, ¿ves? Tuvimos una dificultá.

Mi anillo con unas porquerías

Yo con mi esposa juimos al baile un sábado en la noche. Otro día teníanos que ir pa Alburquerque. En la noche juimos al baile. Y dijo,

—Ponte tu anillo, tu *wedding ring*.

Era media celosa. Güeno, es una cosa muy bonita, el anillo. Me lo puse y juimos al baile. Cuando volvimos del baile le dije,

—Me lo voy a quitar pa no perdelo, porque mañana tenemos que ir pa Alburquerque.

—Güeno—dijo—. Lo echas en mi cajón.

Ahi tenía mis *cufflinks* y prendedores así de la mujer, y eché mi anillo. Tenía mi nombre por dentro y lo eché en la caja. La tapé. Cerré el cajón. Era como la una de la mañana. Durmimos un rato. Luego recordamos a las muchachas de mañana pa ir pa Alburquerque a comprar *groceries* y a visitar a la tía que crió a mi esposa. Güeno, juimos y volvimos el lunes, en la madrugada. Muy de mañana nos vinimos de Alburquerque. Y tenía la idea mi esposa de que llegáanos a la casa y chequiaba el cajón de correo.

—Mira—dijo cuando íbanos entrando—. ¡Mira! Hay una carta; está una carta estampada, estampada aquí en Las Vegas.

Jue echada aquí en Las Vegas, *okay*? Poco gorda la carta. La abrí y tenía un retrato puerco de tal persona. Estaba el anillo mío de casorio adentro la carta, y lo vide. Atrás tenía mi nombre. "¿Pus qué pasa aquí?" Fui a buscalo aá dentro onde lo guardé. Ese lunes en la mañana estáanos allá en Alburquerque antes que pasara el correo. ¿Cómo puee echar esa carta el domingo, y ir el domingo aquí en Las Vegas? Tú explícame eso.

—Mira—le dije a mi esposa—. Éste es mi anillo. Ahi está la carta pegada. Ahi está la carta con la derición de aquí. Mira qué día salió. ¿Cómo puee el anillo cruzar el tiempo, a que pudiera haber echao día jueves, viernes o sábado pa que hubiera caido aquí?

No había nada en el correo el domingo cuando nos juimos. Siempre le echaba la llave cuando me iba pa alguna parte, porque la plebe estaba cerquita de l'escuela y me sacaban las cartas. Las tiraban. Muy traviesos.

—¿Tú tienes una explicación cómo pudo ir en el correo mi anillo, caminar patrás en tiempo, y venir a esa carta?

—Que si ónde lo había dejao ese anillo.

—¿Tú no has andao en un hotel?—me dijo mi esposa.

Yo no salía pa ninguna parte, pero alguien me tenía mal idea. Mi anillo estaba ahi en la carta con unas porquerías. ¿Pero cómo jue a dar ahi en el correo?

Enterraron el cajón delante de mí

Güeno. Pasó otra cosa. Y a ver cómo me lo explicas. Cuando mi madre se murió, tenía ea un anillo que había comprao. El original se le perdió. Se le cayó en el sinke, y no lo jallamos. No lo pudimos jallar. Loo después compró otro baratito. Cuando mamá se murió, yo vide que cuando cerraron el cajón, que se llevaa su anillo de casorio todo bien arreglao. Llevaa las manos hechas cruz. Ahi iba su anillo. *I made darn sure* que estaba su anillo. La enterraron. Enterraron el cajón delante de mí. Ese cajón no se abrió ajuera de mi vista. No se despareció. La enterramos. Otro día me dijo mi esposa,

—Oyes—dijo—. Pus, ¿qué no está el anillo de tu mamá aquí? ¡Cómo se parece! Tiene su nombre por dentro también.

L'anillo que se soponía llevaa mi madre, estaba en mi cajón. *That I remember. I still got the ring. I can't explain that. Maybe she wanted me to have something. I still have it.*

Puea que nunca lleguemos en la vida de nosotros a explicar qué pasó. Pero pasan las cosas. Las ha [he] visto.

Bencés Gabaldón

BERNALILLO, NEW MEXICO

Una palmazón

En otra vez un tío mío es que estaba cortando trigo. Luego había lo que es una sociedá. Es la Sociedá de Nuestro Padre Jesús. De toos modos, empezó un hombre a darse azotes con las espigas de trigo. Es que le dijieron los hermanos, "¿Pa qué estás haciendo eso, hombre?," haciéndose azotes como los Penitentes.

—¡Mira!, es que le dijo uno d'ellos—. Te va castigar mi Tata Dios por eso. Te va castigar.

Güeno. No creyó él. Con el tiempo le salió una palmazón aquí en el espinazo. Andaba buslándose d'ellos, de los Penitentes, y por eso le salió esa palmazón. Ya no vivía; estaba muriéndose.

Tuvo que entrar a la sociedá él pa que se le quitara eso que él había producido, lo que había hecho él, ¿ves? Nomás entró a la sociedá y se le quitó todo. Ya no volvió él a mover nada d'eso.

Son cosas que pasaban ésas, y no es mentira. Esas cosas pasaron. ¡Y pasan! Por eso no sirve hacer uno eso. Esa clase de negocio, mira, de querer uno buslarse de otro, no pasa. No pasa. Eso le hace mal a uno mesmo, ¿qué no?

Esto es lo que me acuerdo yo. Es como nos platicaban a nosotros munchas veces, cosas que no sabe uno ni cómo andan ni cómo caminan ni nada.

Nasario P. García

LOS RANCHOS DE ALBURQUERQUE, NEW MEXICO

Un mono

Te voy a contar lo que en papá me platicaba. Posible que él estuviera joven toavía. Yo no estaba nacido en ese tiempo. Güeno, el cuento es que en papá me platicaba que él y sus amigos iban a los bailes en Salazar. Era, en ese tiempo, muy mentao. Hacían munchos bailes en ese lugar.

Había un hombre; él tocaba el violín. Y una noche venía de Salazar. No sé si vendría en un burro o en una mula, pero no era caballo. Ahi en un lugar que le dicen El Alto de los Jaramillos, ahi venía este hombre, el músico, solo. Cuando llegó en El Alto ese es que salió uno, como un mono, y se le subió en las anancas. El hombre se asustó muncho. El cuento es que cuando llegó a la casa, que vido la luz, se desmayó.

En ese Alto de los Jaramillos, según platicaba en papá, qu' es que ahi salían munchas cosas. No eran brujas, pero como bultos y cosas asina.

Adelita Gonzales

ALBUQUERQUE, NEW MEXICO

Sonaron cadenas

Munchos creiban verdaderamente en brujerías que venían más antes. Creiban en eso. Yo nunca creí en nada d'eso; ni creibo. ¿Quién sabe? Puede que sí haiga.

Hubo una vez y mi esposo, Salvador, iba Salvador, iba y cuando pasó en frente de El Coruco sonaron cadenas. ¡Que aquel hombre llegó a en casa casi como desmayao! ¡No sé cómo le hizo! Y loo le dije,

—¿Qué, qué pasa?

Llegó y nos gritó,

—¡Vengan! Vamos conmigo a desensillar el caballo.

Ya era en la noche. Venía de a case de don Teodoro García. Y logo le dije yo,

—¿Qué, qué pasó?

—Yo no sé—dijo—. Vamos conmigo. Desensillen el caballo y cierren la puerta—les dijo a las muchachas.

Dice él que cuando pasó que sonaron cadenas ahi en El Coruco y el caballo se espantó. Y le digo,

—Yo no sé.

Puede que sí pasen esas cosas. Yo nunca tuve sustos asina.

Tú sabes doña Melesia y todos ellos, puede que ella te haiga platicao; a ella sí que se le apareció un burrito.

Yo no, oye. Yo nunca, nunca en mi vida que tengo no vide tal cosa así.

Gilberta Herguera Turner

WINCREST, TEXAS

Cantó la gallina después de asada

Santo Domingo de la Calzada es un pueblo grande de La Rioja, cuya capital es Logroño. Antes, la provincia de Logroño, cuya capital era también la ciudad de Logroño, como ahora, pertenecía a Castilla la Vieja.

Santo Domingo posee una iglesia muy peculiar, pues en su interior hay un gallinero muy bonito, con unas ricas verjas forjadas, en el que habitan un gallo y su compañera, la gallina. Ambos son blancos como la nieve. Todos los años esta pareja de aves se cambia y se introduce en el gallinero una pareja nueva. No sé lo que ocurre a la pareja antigua, y creo que no quiero ni saberlo, ni siquiera pensarlo, pues me imagino que termina en la mesa de algún lugareño.

Además del gallinero, la iglesia tiene otra peculiaridad: su campanario no está adosado a ella sino que se encuentra al otro lado de la calle.

El dicho de "Santo Domingo de la Calzada que cantó la gallina después de asada" viene de la época del medievo, hacia el siglo XII más o menos. Habitaba por aquel entonces en el lugar un gran señor feudal, y se cometió un crimen. No recuerdo bien si fue robo o asesinato. Creo que fue asesinato, y el señor ordenó a sus soldados encontrar al culpable y ahorcarlo.

Éstos encontraron a un hombre al que acusaron del crimen y sin más lo colgaron de un árbol a la salida del pueblo. Los amigos del ahorcado lo buscaron y encontraron su cadáver balanceándose en el árbol. No sabiendo qué hacer rezaron a Santo Domingo, pues estaban seguros de la inocencia de su compañero. Acabada la oración, cuál sería su sorpresa, el ahorcado resucitó y todos muy contentos se encaminaron hacia el pueblo.

Mientras esto ocurría, en la casa señorial se estaban preparando las viandas que serían servidas esa misma noche a los invitados del gran señor durante una fiesta que éste iba a dar. Estaban los cocineros preparando las gallinas asadas y todos los demás manjares que las acompañarían.

Llegó la hora de la cena y mientras los comensales estaban reunidos a su alrededor, llegaron unos criados del señor a informarle de que el pueblo estaba alborotado, pues se había visto pasear por él con sus amigos al ahorcado criminal. El señor no se lo creyó y envió a averiguar a los criados si eso era verdaderamente cierto. Al rato volvieron y, en efecto, trajeron la noticia de que verdaderamente estaba vivo, pues ellos mismos lo habían visto pasearse con sus amigos por las calles del pueblo.

El gran señor siguió creyendo que esto era cosas del vulgo y exclamó, Me creeré toda esa sarta de mentiras cuando esta gallina que está en esta fuente para ser devorada por mis invitados se levante y cante.

No había casi acabado de pronunciar tales palabras cuando la gallina se levantó y se paseó cacarequeando por toda la mesa. De ahí viene la frase, "Santo Domingo de la Calzada que cantó la gallina después de asada."

Mi amiga Raquel, natural de este pueblo, que me contó esta historia también me dijo que si el gallo canta y quiquiriquea durante la celebración de una boda es un buen augurio y es señal de que los nuevos esposos serán muy felices y vivirán muchos años juntos.

Bueno, pues debe de ser verdad, pues durante su boda el gallo cantó y cantó y quiquiriquió y quiquiriquió hasta el punto de que apenas se los pudo oír dar el sí a los novios y al cura declararlos marido y mujer. Raquel y su marido llevan felizmente casados más de treinta años. Efectivamente el canto del gallo fue un buen augurio.

César G. López

UPLAND, CALIFORNIA

La Santa Compaña

De todas las regiones de España, aquélla donde las tradiciones sobrenaturales más perduran es sin duda alguna Galicia. Quizás por su antepasado celta, o porque es una región donde las brumas y el paisaje boscoso se prestan más a ello. Lo cierto es que la mayoría de los gallegos y gallegas creen en fantasmas, fenómenos sobrenaturales y, por supuesto, en las brujas, las famosas *meigas*. No hay cuento o leyenda que no las incluya, hasta el punto de que se habla de Galicia como *terra meiga*, o tierra de brujas, o embrujada.

Quizás de todas las leyendas y tradiciones la más fuerte y persistente sea la de la Santa Compaña, o Santa Compañía. Se asegura que en los bosques o caminos de Galicia una persona puede encontrarse por la noche con la Santa Compaña. Es un grupo de espíritus o almas en pena, que están condenados a recorrer los caminos por culpas que cometieron en este mundo y que les impide disfrutar del descanso eterno. Generalmente estos espíritus forman una procesión y suelen ir vestidos con hábitos religiosos o con sábanas blancas o sudarios. Suelen ir precedidos por una persona que lleva una cruz de madera, una campana o bien un caldero con agua bendita. A veces esta persona no está muerta todavía, pero tiene que hacer esto como penitencia por algún crimen horrendo que ha cometido.

Si una persona encuentra a la Santa Compaña por un camino, lo más común es que le inviten a la procesión, lo cual significa que la persona muera en un espacio de tiempo muy corto.

La historia que narro aquí no me pasó a mí personalmente; me la contó un marinero que hacía el servicio militar conmigo en la Base Naval de Cartagena en España, que está en el Mediterráneo. No recuerdo su nombre, sólo que su apellido era Atienza, y que era un pescador profesional de Huelva. Antes de que su barco fuera estacionado en la Base de Cartagena, había estado destinado en la Base de El Ferrol, en A Coruña, Galicia.

Los hechos que narro le habían ocurrido a otro marinero, cuyo hermano se lo contó a Atienza, quien a su vez me lo contó a mí. Esta es la historia:

Una noche del mes de noviembre (que es el mes de las ánimas) la barca en la que faenaban un grupo de pescadores se perdió en medio de un temporal. La niebla era tan densa que no podían ver ninguna luz de la costa, aunque no se habían alejado mucho. Cuando ya se habían resignado a morir, entre el ruido del viento percibieron claramente el sonido de una campana y pensando que se trataba de una iglesia que conocían, pusieron rumbo hacia el lugar de donde les parecía que procedía aquel sonido. Milagrosamente la barca pasó por entre los escollos de la costa sin sufrir ningún daño, quedando varada en una pequeña playa totalmente desconocida para ellos. Allí no habían ni casas ni iglesia alguna, pero la campana seguía oyéndose débilmente hacia el interior. En este punto los marineros que estaban extenuados, decidieron que uno de ellos fuera a averiguar dónde estaba la campana y pidiera ayuda. Le tocó la suerte al hermano del amigo de Atienza. Éste se internó por entre los árboles buscando un camino, guiado siempre por el sonido de la campana. Al poco rato se encontró algo que cambió su vida para siempre. Junto a un cruce de caminos presidido por un crucero, vio una procesión de penitentes, distribuidos en dos hileras, todos cubiertos con sábanas blancas y llevando cada uno un cirio ardiendo, menos el primero que iba tocando una campana y recitando una letanía a la que todos contestaban a coro.

Muerto de miedo, el marinero se arrodilló en la tierra y les preguntó dónde estaba el pueblo más cercano. Entonces uno de los penitentes, sin hablar, le señaló un camino, y le dio el cirio que llevaba en la mano. Siguiendo estas indicaciones el marinero pudo llegar a una aldea donde le socorrieron a él y ayudaron a los otros marineros. A la mañana siguiente nadie podía comprender como la barca había podido llegar hasta aquella playa en medio de la tormenta sin estrellarse en los escollos. Era como si hubiera pasado volando sobre ellos. De tal manera que tuvieron que poner la barca sobre una carreta y llevarla por tierra hasta su pueblo, que no estaba muy lejos. Pero lo más sorprendente es que cuando el marinero que había pedido ayuda a los penitentes miró el cirio que uno de ellos le había dado, descubrió horrorizado que no era un cirio, sino el hueso de la pierna de una persona, aunque presentaba señales de haberse quemado por una punta.

La impresión que el marinero recibió fue tan fuerte, que quedó medio atontado y durante tres días estuvo sin comer, beber, ni hablar con nadie, falleciendo al cuarto. Todas las personas que iban en la barca quedaron convencidas de que los habían salvado las ánimas, y que sólo el marinero que vio a la Santa Compaña pagó con su vida la salvación de las vidas de sus compañeros.

Después del entierro del marinero, al que asistió todo el pueblo, sus compañeros depositaron en la iglesia, al pie de la Virgen del Carmen, una reproducción de su barca, como exvoto, por haberlos salvado de la tormenta, tal y como es costumbre en Galicia.

Así es como me lo contaron, y así es como lo cuento.

Benjamín "Benny" Lucero

ALBUQUERQUE, NEW MEXICO

Cosas extrañas

¡Y cosas extrañas ha [he] visto yo! Originalmente no. Muy corto tiempo hace. Puede que haga dos o tres años. Una de las cosas más hermosas que yo ha [he] visto. Hasta entre la familia pensaron que era mentira.

De aquí de Alburquerque nos juimos un día viernes pal rancho en Cabezón, yo y mi mujer. Saqué viernes del trabajo y nos juimos, porque estábanos con las ganas de matar carne. Ya hacía muncho tiempo que no habíanos matao carne. Estaba con las ganas yo de jallar un novillo grande que tenía. No lo jallé pero jallé otro, y lo encerré en el corral que tiene Eduardo Valdez ahi en la Mercé. Le dije a la mujer,

—En la mañana vamos en la troca y lo traemos.

Llegamos a casa oscuro ese viernes. Le di comida al caballo y la mujer me dio de cenar a mí. Después de que me dio de cenar, pues naturalmente me dieron ganas de ir al escusao.

Salí. Nomás en cuanto no la vide esta cosa muy extraña que te dije antes. Cuando estaba sentao en el escusao, nomás en cuanto me levanté, y voy oyendo un ruido como una música. Luego vide una cosa tan hermosa, en la forma como diun cigarro, pero cosa muy grande, como la forma diun cigarro con una cola muy larga. Los colores de la luz y la hermosura que era aquella cosa. Lo mesmo que ver tú un *helicopter* que no tenga alas, pero con la cola *muncho* más larga.

Hay un banco que le dicemos El Banco de la Cañada de la Máquina, y la Cañada del Camino. Nosotros tamién tenemos, como ustedes, una Cañada del Camino. Ése era el camino viejo, y loo hay una máquina de trigo que hubo años pasaos, que la enterró l'agua ahi, y de ahi pa delante le quedó el nombre de El Banco de la Cañada de la Máquina. Jue en ese banco onde bajó la cosa ésa.

Pero como te digo, esa cosa era en la forma de un cigarro, como un tren, en la forma de un tren. ¡Una cosa muy grande, muy bonita! Y es un banco muy alto onde bajó. Bajó hasta que aplaneó de la cañada. Al llegar al arroyo, cuando aplaneó, se le acabó la luz de la cola, y adelante hizo una llama. De ahi se despareció.

Con el mesmo ruido que hizo—yo le hablaba a mi mujer—y nomás en cuanto no la miró ella, porque ella se quedó lavando los trastes hasta que no salió y tiró l' agua.

—Ahi 'bajó una fregadera d' esas—le dije—. Una fregadera d' esas. Ésas que dicen que andan ahi en el viento.

Cuando yo truje la forma de la cosa aquí, a Alburquerque, con el mayordomo, le platiqué, y él me puso atención. Los otros dicían que yo mentía. El mayordomo me dijo,

—Ése era un UFO. Píntemela—me dijo, y yo ya le pinté la cosa asina.

En un café estábanos. Le estaba platicando. Le dije yo que estaba casi que ni la familia me creiba. La única que me cree es la mujer porque ella la vido. Porque cuando vine aquí a Alburquerque, vino mi hija a verme, y ahi estaba mi nieta. Yo platicándole a mi muchacha en español y a mi nieta en inglés. Y loo hasta ella, la muchacha, me dijo,

—Era un UFO *daddy*—me dijo—. Era un UFO.

Y loo le dice mi hija a la muchachita, a la nieta,

—*Grandpa saw a* UFO! *That's what it is*—dijo—. *It's a* UFO.

Y el mayordomo me dijo tamién. Me dijo que ésa era un UFO.

—*Okay.* Pus vamos a ver—me dijo la nieta.

Fíjate tú, hasta la chamaca dudaba,

—*Come on, grandpa! Come on, grandpa! Don't lie to us!*

Y loo le dije a mi nieta,

—Mira. Te voy a dijir una cosa hijita. El *grandpa* no va a dijir una mentira a la familia, y asina no te va a dijir a ti—le dije.

—Yo quiero que me lleven—dijo—el otro sábado pa ver si la miro.

Pos yo ha [he] visto cosas extrañas pero yo no sabía qué esto era.

—Pueda que no la mire, pero te voy a llevar.

—Mira apá. Eso está entre los dos nietos y tú—dijo mi hija, porque dijieron que iban estar yendo al Cabezón hasta que vieran una.

Pos una vez cuando andaban jugando en el patio, ahi detrás de la casa, haciéndose oscuro, cuando caminó una cosa semejante a la que vide yo pero más lejos, pal rumbo de San Ysidro. Ahi viene la cosa. Ella, la chamaca, jue la que la vido. ¡Y sí! Caminó. Venía pal lao de San Ysidro. La mesma cosa que la que había visto yo, pero *más* lejos, no tan cerquita. No oímos ruido ni nada d'eso como yo; era muy lejos. Como pal rumbo de San Ysidro. ¡Pos pronto se despareció aquella cosa! Cuando de güenas a primeras se formó otra, en la forma de un güevo. Reluciente pero pal rumbo de Cuba. Y ahi estamos con aquel azoro. La vieron ellos, los nietos. Tamién se despareció en el aigre.

Pero ésta que te dije antes despareció, cerquita, como tres cuartos de milla del Cabezón!

Si un día te enseño yo onde mero se despareció, dices tú, "No la vido lejos."

Manuel de Jesús Manzanares

PUEBLO, COLORADO

Vi el cuerpo de un hombre

Un día, creo que era hasta día domingo, estábanos yo y el vecino trabajando con los caballos en la 'cequia, limpiando la 'cequia. A mediodía vine a comer. Cuando me arrimé, nomás cuanto me senté a la mesa, estaba una puerta pal otro cuartito, vi el cuerpo de un hombre en la puerta esa. Perfectamente de aquí de los hombros pa bajo. Pero cabeza, nada. Pero no le dije nada a la vieja, porque si le digo, no se queda sola aquí en la casa.

Me jui otra vez a trabajar despés de mediodía y le dije,

—A la tardecita llevas las orquillas pa nomás cuitiamos de limpiar la 'cequia, amontonamos la alfalfa—la teníanos arrastrada.

Yo loo cuando acabamos la alfalfa le dije,

—¿Sabes qué pasó a mediodía?

—Saldrían las bestias juyendo—dijo.

—No—le dije—. Yo no sé si me notates cuando me senté yo allá en la mesa. Me levanté muy liviano.

—Sí, te noté que te levantates pallá pero no supe por qué.

Antonces le dije lo que había sucedido. En este tiempo estaba un cuñao mío en el hospital muy enfermo, y too esto me aprevino. Pues luego decían que avisaban ellos, los enfermos, que iban a morir. Dije yo, "Pus quién sabe mi compadre Antonio."

¡Y sí! El día siguiente vinieron avisarnos que mi compadre, mi cuñao, se había muerto.

La huija board

Esto jue tavía cuando estábanos con mi mamá y papá allá en el rancho del Rito del Oso. Nos descuidamos nosotros y dejamos una ternera crecer a más de seis meses sin echale fierro. Por dónde se metió esta ternera pal rancho de los vecinos—eran unos italianos—y vinieron ellos y la herraron con el fierro d'ellos. Dijo en papá,

—Pus no podemos hacer nada. La ternera ya la debiéramos de haberla llevao antes de los seis meses.

Pero en efecto que la ternera loo se les perdía a los italianos con las vacas de nosotros. Y mamá, ella era más decidida, dijo,

—No. Yo no les dejo mi ternera a estos ladrones.

—Oh—dijo papá—, déjaselas. No podemos hacer nada.

Y un día dice mamá,

—No. Yo no se las dejo—y convenció a en papá en fin y nos dijo él,

—Lleven las vacas allá pal otro rancho, pal rancho del Indito—que le dicen.

Pus juimos yo y mi hermano y llevamos las vacas pallá. Allá matamos la ternera. La matamos y la desollamos y en papá y mamá echaron la carne en el bogue y se jueron pa Aguilar a llevársela a mis agüelitos que vivían allá porque mamá no quería que se lograran la ternera los italianos. El cuero ya no me acuerdo qué hicimos con él. Por ahi lo enterramos, yo creo. Ya no me acuerdo porque matamos la ternera como robada.

Güeno, naiden supo más que mi papá, mamá, mi hermano y yo. Eran los únicos que sabíamos qué había sucedido d'esa ternera. Pus después vino el italiano que había herrao la ternera a preguntar qué se había hecho la ternera.

—Yo no sé qué se haría. Tú la herrates. Yo no sé—dijo mamá.

Naiden no supimos. Naiden supo. Nada. Al fin lograron mis agüelitos la ternera que nos robaron.

Por cuántos años después, un cuñao mío tenía una d'esas *huija boards*, que le llaman, una tablita que tenía todo el alfabeto, el sol, la luna, y las estrellas y qué. Logo como un corazoncito y éste corría pallí y pacá.

Pos una noche estaban monquiando ahi con la *huija board*. Estaban mi hermanita y un sobrinito mío, y ellos tenían que ponele las manos al corazoncito este. Por dónde ya no sé quién de los que estaban ahi, se le ocurrió preguntar que si qué se había hecho la ternera que habían herrao los italianos. Pues ya empezó el corazoncito. El maldito corazoncito ese corría pallá y loo corría pacá y ansina. Y loo empezó a deletriar. Deletrió y dice, *"Vidal and the old lady took it to Aguilar."*

Naiden de los que estaban allí, naiden sabía lo que había sucedido más que yo y mi hermano, papá y mamá. ¿Cómo supo esa diantre de *huija board*? No sé. Yo siempre era, como le dije a usté, muy incrédulo en esto. Esa vez me escamó como había deletriado la *huija board*: *"Vidal and the old lady took it to Aguilar."*

Un tropel de caballos

Una noche salimos pallá fuera yo y mi vieja cuando se oyó un tropel de caballos como que pasó un bonche 'e caballos y parecía que habían aventao la milpa. Se me abrió la boca. Y le dije a ella,

—Ya las bestias de mi compadre abrieron la puerta.

Había un caballo que abría la puerta. Le pegaba a los alambres con 'l hocico. Antonces me jui a chequiar y no jallé nada. Estaba muy oscura y agarré el farol d'estos de aceite que teníanos. Me anduve por toda la milpa parriba y nada. Ya me vine.

—No—le dije aquélla [su mujer]—, pus que coman hasta que quieran.

En la mañana nomás aclaró y me levanté a ir a correlos. Lo primero que hice jue dar vista a la puerta del cerco a ver si estaba abierta. ¡Nada! ¿Qué sería? Yo no sé. Hasta el día no puedo saber qué pudiera ser.

Las luces del carro puestas

En una ocasión habíanos llegao a casa de algún lugar. Tavía la Bernice, mi hija, estaba chiquita. La casa estaba ansí entre nosotros y mis padres. Estaba la puerta ansí pa delante. Par este lao había una ventana y acá habíanos parquiao el carro. Cuando estábanos aquí, aquélla con la niña en los brazos, y yo queriendo abrir la puerta, por fin abrí la puerta que entramos. Por la ventana vido la vieja que estaban las luces del carro puestas. Me dice,

—Pues, ¿qué dejates las luces puestas?

—No—le dije—. No las dejé—pero siempre jui y las apagué, y nunca pudimos saber qué era lo que lo hacía.

En otra ocasión juimos de aquí al campo a dar güelta a las vacas allá. Cuando llegamos, ya estaba oscureciendo y pasamos del Rito ansina parriba. Subimos parriba de un altito. De ahi alcanzaba ver yo bultos de animales. Mi esposa se quedó sentada en el carro, y yo me apié y me jui a pie. Vide a las vacas y loo caminé pallá y allá andaban los caballos tamién. Loo me arrendé pal carro.

Pus cuando venía allá lejos se prendieron las luces en el carro. Me vine yo al rumbo de las luces. Cuando ya me acerqué, cerca del carro, se apagaron. Llegué yo allá y le dije a la vieja,

—¡Tú sí que sabes bien! Cuando andaba allá lejos que no me servían las luces las prendites y cuando venía aquí cerca las apagates.

—No—me dijo—. Yo no las atoqué.

—¿Pus cómo se prendieron?

Hasta el día no sabemos nosotros qué jue lo que jue. Pero eso nos sucedió.

Consuelo Martínez

ESCONDIDO, CALIFORNIA

La mujer misteriosa en blanco

Yo recuerdo que apenas eran unos meses después de celebrar mi quinceañera, y mi abuelito Ramón estaba enfermo. Estaba tratando de recuperarse de un ataque (había sufrido varios) y estuvo postrado en cama por unos meses. Era el fin de semana del cuatro de julio, y usualmente pasábamos los días festivos en casa de mis padres en Rosarito en Baja California en México donde mi padre construyó una casa para cuando se jubilara. Mientras tanto, sus padres vivían en esa casa.

Era un sábado por la noche, el día 2 de julio, pero técnicamente era el 3 de julio ya que era la una o las dos de la mañana. Ya yo me estaba quedando dormida en una de las recámaras en el piso superior con el resto de la familia y algunos familiares que estaban de visita cuando de repente oí a mi hermanita menor y a mi prima que gritaron y salieron corriendo a sus cuartos. Ellas estaban en el pasillo del piso superior cuando vieron a una mujer delgada con pelo largo y negro en un traje blanco de mucho vuelo, casi como una bata.

En aquel entonces les preguntamos que si qué las había asustado y dijeron que estaba una mujer en el piso bajo al lado de la cama de mi abuelito. Mi abuelito tenía su cama en un cuarto bastante amplio que se podía ver desde el pasillo del piso superior.

Les dijimos a mi hermanita y a mi prima que se acostaran, que probablemente era nuestra tía que iba al cuarto de baño. Más tarde nos preguntamos que si quién sería la persona de la bata blanca. No había mujer en casa que tuviera una bata blanca, de manera que nos quedamos pensando que si quién sería la mujer.

Dos días más tarde cuando nos venimos a casa, era el día cuatro de julio, y como una hora después de haber regresado de la casa en Rosarito, repicó el teléfono. Nos avisaban que mi abuelito Ramón se había muerto.

Ahora la mujer misteriosa en blanco que visitó a mi abuelito en su cabecera apenas dos días antes de su muerte tiene todo su buen sentido.

Phoebe Martínez Struck

PUEBLO, COLORADO

Hacen ruido los muertos

Yo acerca de brujerías nunca vi nada d' eso. Ni luces ni nada d' eso que platicaban. Ni bultos. L' unico que sí creo es que le hacen ruido los muertos a uno porque eso sí pasó en mi familia. En una vez yo tampoco no creía en eso.

Una vez cuando vivíamos en el rancho estábanos en la cocina, creo que ya era en la nochi, cuando de repente se calló una bandeja, y loo dice Ernesto, mi esposo,

—Alguien nos anda haciendo ruido, trantando de decirnos algo.

—Oh—le dije—. ¿Crees tú en brujerías, tonterías d' esas? Yo no creo. Pues, estaría mal la bandeja puesta y se calló.

—No—dice él—. Alguien nos hizo ruido, vino a decirnos algo.

Otro día en la mañana una vecina se murió.

—¿Ves?—me dijo—. Te platiqué que se iba a morir alguien.

Pos, ya de ahi no se supo más d' eso hasta que nos vinimos pacá pa Pueblo. Vivíanos ahi en Avondale. En ese tiempo estaba mi mamá muy enferma, y lo que sí que estábanos acostaos. Nomás en cuanto nos habíanos acostao. Se nos espantó el sueño. No teníanos más de aquel cuarto y la cocina. Tenía un *arch door* grande derecho a la estufa. Teníanos estufa de gas, *butane gas,* y de repente se prendió la llama de la estufa, y le digo a Ernesto,

—¡Mira! Se prendió la llama de la estufa.

Ya se levantó y dice,

—Pues, ¿qué no estaba bien cerrao el gas?

¡Y no! Pos, estaba cerrao, y jue él allá a las botellas de gas. Teníanos botellas allá juera. Y no. Estaba todo bien. Güeno. Cuando entró se apagó la estufa y se volvió acostar. Cuando se acostó, se prendió la llama otra vez. Estaba la cafetera arriba de la llama, y dice mi esposo,

—Pos, ¿qué está pasando aquí?

Me dio miedo a mí. Luego dice él,

—Oh, alguien nos anda haciendo ruido (vino a decirnos algo).

—Oh—le digo—. Ya vas con tu ruido. [Risas]

Yo tenía miedo, pero al mismo tiempo no quería creer lo que vía. Ahi en eso yo no sé qué le haría que se apagó al fin la llama, pero otro día en la mañana nos avisaron que se había muerto mi mamá. Me telefoniaron. Antonces estaba ella allá en Gallup. Me telefoniaron de allá al trabajo que se había muerto. Por eso en veces me da miedo eso de ruidos.

Más antes que me casara yo con Ernesto, mi *grandma* le había dicho de ruidos a mi madre, y yo como que creía porque mi mamá nunca que yo me acuerde dijiera mentiras. Pero antes de que murió mi grandma, estaba muy enferma, y vivían ella y mi agüelo allá bajo en un lugarcito. De todos modos, era en la noche cuando sintieron ellos que alguien andaba en l' azotea. Y salió mi padrastro a ver qué pasaba. Que parecía como cuando anda un caballo allí arriba. Dando golpes. Isque le dice mi mamá, "Sal, porque se van a tirar el techo."

Salió pero no se vía nada. Loo esque le grita él de allá [de la azotea], qué ónde mero. Mi mamá con la escoba le dicía ónde mero, pero no había nada. Después, otro día, halló mi mamá de que había muerto mi grandma.

Cuando mi mamá me platicaba eso todo se me hacía como modo de mentiras, pero no. De que hacen ruido los muertos, quizás sí hacen.

Una baraña

En un tiempo vino Nestor, hermano de mi esposo, a casa ya como a las dos o tres de la mañana. Isque vinía un—estaba haciendo aigre—terremoto y le dio a él muncho miedo. Vinía una baraña [cizaña] d' esas grandotas atrás dél sin saber lo que era. Se volvió corriendo allá por la puerta del cerquito—tenían un cerquito de tabla. Entró por la puerta y la baraña se jue todo el camino.

Isque antonces no más volvió a salir en la nochi. Pero isque era una bruja, dijo él.

María A. Mongalo

RIVERSIDE, CALIFORNIA

El bebito

Decía mi papá que un señor iba manejando en ese tiempo su carreta. Dijo que venía bien asoleado y quién sabe qué cuántos kilómetros en su carreta y de repente en el camino oyó llorar un bebito. Lloraba incansablemente, muerto de hambre y de frío. Allí estaba abandonado a un lado del camino.

Entonces, según mi papá, el señor dijo, "Ése es un niño y no puedo dejarlo abandonado. Tengo que abajarme y ir a ver."

Se dice que llegó él y vio al niño y lo cargó en los brazos. "Mire," dijo el niño, "mis uñitas," y se le salieron las uñas enormes.

El hombre quedó mudo y le pegó una fiebre altísima por varios días hasta que logró poder decir lo que le había pasado.

Cesaria Montoya

LAS VEGAS, NEW MEXICO

Se murió su compadre

Mi papá nos contaba, güeno, no mi papá nomás, mi agüelita tamién, que tenía mi agüelita un tío, y se llevaban muncho uno con el otro. Siempre andaban jugando. Y isque le dicía el viejito,

—¡Mire comadre! Si usté no aprende a decirme "compadre" y un día yo me muero primero que usté, yo voy a venir y me la voy a sacudir.

No le dicía "compadre"; le dicía mi "tío." Así siguieron. Pus muérece el viejito, y oímos algo en la tardecita. Estaba la viejita sola, mi agüelita, con mi papá y con su hermanita, una tía mía. Estaban chiquitos, andaban jugando arriba la cama, y ea [la abuelita] estaa haciendo cena, cuando isque se levantó mi *daddy* de la cama.

—¡Mamá! ¡Mamá! Ahi entró mi tío.

—¿Qué tío?

Ya no me acuerdo cómo se llamaba el viejito. Eh, mi tío Antonio se llamaba.

—Pus, ¿qué es él?

—Pus yo no sé—le dijo—. Entró por ahi por la puerta y parece que se metió ahi atrás de la máquina.

Tenía una máquina de coser atrás de la puerta mi agüelita.

—Oh—le dijo—. Tú estás loco. Qué estás ahi soñando.

—No, mamá. Sí entró.

Y le dijo mi papá cómo andaba vestido, que traiba un vestido pardo, que no traiba zapatos. Nomás el calcetín. Y traiba una camisa blanca y traiba un puño de la manga desabrochao.

Pos, eh, no pasó más. Se acostaron los niños; se durmieron. Ea se quedó alistando cena pa cuando llegara quizás el viejito. Luego en eso oyó que vinía un muchacho chiflando, de una tiendita, porque antonces había esta tienda, y era el nieto del viejito que se murió que vinía chiflando. Que vinía avisale que se había muerto su compadre. Llegó y no le dicía nada el muchacho; estaa chiflando, sentao en el marco de la puerta. Le dice mi agüelita,

—¿Pus qué andas haciendo a estas horas?

—No—isque le dijo—. Vengo de allá de la tienda y llegué por aquí.

—No, no, no—le dijo—. No me mientas, no me mientas. Dime a qué vienes—, porque ea sabía que el viejito estaa enfermo.

—No. Vine avisale que se murió su compadre.

Pus no pasó más. Envolvió a los muchachitos, los levantó.

—¡Vamos!—le dijo—. Ayúdame con la niña.

"Nos juimos a l'otra banda," dicían entonces, onde estaba el viejito, y entraron onde estaa el viejito tendido. Ya lo tenían tendido en una mesa. Nomás entraron que se hincó mi agüela a rezar, isque estaa mi papá jalándola. Y ea, que se callara.

—¡Mira, mira, mira cómo está vestido!

Traiba un pantalón pardo, una camisa blanca con el puño desabrochao, y no traiba zapatos. Pus atendido ya muerto. Ya se levantó mi agüelita y se jue pa la cocina a platicar con la viejita [la esposa del viejito].

—Comadre, pueda que sea verdá.

Cuando estaa acabando de platicar, isque levantaba la mano el viejito como pa onde vivía mi agüelita.

—Pueda que sí juera avisale mi esposo esa noche que había acabao.

Será verdá o no será, no sé. Pero ¿por qué ahora no pasan cosas así? ¡Superstición! Era se me hace a mí que pura superstición.

Se había caido la copa

Tenía la cocina mi mamá, como abajo, y loo subían tres pisitos pa entrar pa la sala. Y un muchacho que criaron mi papá y mi mamá estaa sentao acá arriba del último pisito. Tenían un calentón de leña puesto asina como ora en un rincón, con copas muy bonitas. ¿Te acuerdas que había unos calentones que tenían como unas copas muy bonitas arriba? Bueno, cuando menos acordamos—y yo andaba jugando allí en el suelo en la cocina— oímos el golpe. Pasó en el cuarto. Pus el muchacho de una vez se levantó y voló pallá, y loo mi papá y mi mamá y toos juimos allá. Se había caido la copa esa del fogón y estaa tranpada muy juerte. No se podía cae sola; pus se cayó *anyway. So,* ahi se quedó en el suelo.

Conque ahi están eos, "¿Qué pasará, qué pasará, pus qué pasaría?" En eso estaban cuando llegó alguen avisar que se había muerto una prima hermana de mi mamá. Figuran que la prima vino avisar.

Tamién tenía yo una tía mía, la hermana de mi papá, una tía muy querida. Ya no me acuerdo cómo se llamaba mi tía. Ea vivía en Colorao, y isque entró un cernícaro [cernícalo]. ¿Sabe lo que es un cernícaro? Es un gavilancito, chiquito. Entró. Isque se le paró a mi tía en la cabeza. No lo espantaron; nomás se salió el gavilancito. Pero pronto llegaron avisales a mi papá y mamá que había muerto la tía allá en Colorao.

Eos dicían que era un aviso que al muerto le daba Dios permiso de que viniera hacerlos saber.

José Nataleo Montoya
LAS VEGAS, NEW MEXICO

Cayó llorando Genoveo

Cuando se muría alguien, tocaba que les avisaban de alguna manera. Yo me acuerdo tavía d'este Genoveo. Cuando murió su mamá, viviános arriba la mesa, ahi en San Pablo. Estaba la cocina y loo estaba un zaguán. Loo estaba el cuarto. Pus ahi estáanos durmiendo yo y mi agüelita, y una prima de mi esposa y una hija estaan en el zaguán. Y mi tío Estelito, él había llegao de la sierra, y estaa durmiendo en la cocina. Le pusieron la cama en la cocina. Como ora, por ejemplo, ahi la puerta esa. Asina.

En la mañana se levantó la tía esta Rafelita. Así se llamaba ea. Cuando jue a poner lumbre, vido un charco de sangre en los pies del tío, porque el tío este era compadre de la mamá de Genoveo. Pus ya jue y le dijo a mi agüelita que el hijo seguro que estuvo malo, como siempre estaba enfermo él. Pus ya se levantaron. Hasta lo recordaron a Estelito. Taa estaa durmiendo.

—Oyes. ¿Qué estuvites malo anoche?—le dijieron.

—No—les dijo—. ¿Por qué?

—Mira. Ahi taa hay sangre.

—No—les dijo—. Pus yo no me levanté. Yo ni escupí ni naa.

Al rato cayó llorando este Genoveo que su mamá había muerto. Cuando murió isque había echao un cuajarón de sangre. Eso sí me acuerdo yo velo. Yo estaa como de unos seis años, yo creo, antonces.

Rima Montoya

ALBUQUERQUE, NEW MEXICO

Casos de duendes

Por aquellos tiempos, cuando Costa Rica, salvaje y agraria, se desplegaba en extensiones de bosques, selvas, fincas y potreros donde se oía el largo trino imperturbable de los pajarillos, el borboteo de aguas claras por entre las rocas de montaña, el crujir de carretas por los caminos y el lejano cantar de las lavanderas. Es cuando los campos eran de los bueyes y la gente de la tierra, cuando se molía con piedra y no había más trigo que el maíz.

Era en esos tiempos los hombres aún conversaban con los muertos, y rogaban a los santos para que obraran milagros, cuando en las noches de tormenta sacudían los cielos "truénganos y jucilínganos" como grandes bolas de fuego que atravesaban los inmensos cielos. En tales tiempos la leyenda respiraba entre la gente y se susurraban casos de encuentros con la Llorona, la Segua, el mismo Cadejos y no podía faltar los molestos duendes, fastidiosos como piojos y pulgas.

Cuentan que a los duendes les encanta fastidiar tanto a mayores como a los niños y gozan de mover objetos de un sitio a otro, de echar porquerías en las comidas, hasta de estorbar los nidos de las gallinas, y peor que todo esto, son famosos por alejar a los niños de casa y perderlos. Lo jorobado es que se aparecen y desaparecen por capricho y más de una vez le han enredado el camino al pobre inocente. Los que los han visto dicen que llevan en la cabeza un gorro, como boina verde o azul, llevan barba y tienen las orejas grandes y puntiagudas.

Éste es el caso que le ocurrió un día a Ñor Feliciano, vecino de Río Segundo. Cuentan que salió muy de madrugada, antes de salir el sol, para coger el bus que pasaba por San Antonio a las nueve y media. Tenía harto tiempo para llegar, pues de Río Segundo a San Antonio no hay más de media hora a pie. Cuando llegó a La Ribera vio un atolladero y para no embarrialarse, se metió por entre una cerca para salir más adelante. A las diez varas salió de nuevo a la misma calle por donde iba. Siguió "volando pata" un buen rato y no llegaba a San Antonio. Muy extrañado estaba de no reconocer el camino por donde andaba, pues el buen hombre creía saber de todos esos contornos como sus manos. Siguió andando por el camino, fijado en llegar a coger el autobús. Anduvo hasta que se vio completamente desorientado. Hacia adelante, pegaba con cerca, hacia atrás se topaba con alambres. Buscaba salida para un lado y se enredaba en una chamarasca; buscaba salida para el otro y le atajaba una zanja. Desconsolado y sin poder salir de aquel enredo se sentó en un tronco a descansar. Al largo rato vislumbró donde era que estaba. ¡Había ido a parar casi llegando a San Francisco!

Rápidamente se paró para devolverse. Cuando por fin le faltaba poco para llegar a la estación, oyó el pito del autobús. Aliviado, Ñor Feliciano le silbó al que manejaba, le hizo señas, y finalmente le gritó y por nada en el mundo el condenado de la máquina quiso parar para recogerlo. El pobre alma de Dios tuvo que esperar hasta el día siguiente por culpa de los "confisgaos duendes." Ñor Feliciano afirma que ese día "no jueron otros los que se rieron de yo."

Pero como venía diciendo. No hay nada que entretiene más a los duendes que perder a los chiquillos. Allá por San Rafael de Escazú desapareció, un día de tantos, un niño de los de Saborío de cuatro años. Los padres ya no sabían por dónde buscar así que reunieron a todos los vecinos para que ayudaran a encontrar al niño perdido. "Quién sabe dónde se habrá metido," se decían unos a otros. Recorrieron los cafetales donde hoy día está Sareto y demás negocios. Algunos hasta llegaron a decir que había bajado un tigrillo de la montaña y se lo había llevado. Otros fueron hasta orillas del río pensando que quizás el niño se había desbarrancado, pero no encontraron huella.

Cuando empezó a entrar la desconfianza y el desespero, alguien oyó gritar lejos por donde el Río los Anonos. En carreras fueron a ver qué pasaba, y para alivio de todo el mundo, un joven había finalmente encontrado al chiquillo. Pero no vaya Ud. lector a dudar de lo que ese día presenciaron los vecinos de San Rafael de Escazú, pues el niño de cuatro años escasos se encontraba sentado encima de una gran piedra solitaria en medio del turbulento río. Y para colmo de asombros, sostenía en sus manos una gran manzana a la cual le iba dando mordisco tras mordisco. ¿Pero cómo fue el niño a parar a esa piedra sola en medio del río? ¿Y cómo consiguió la manzana, si la manzana sólo en Navidad y eso si alcanzaba el aguinaldo? Pos en medio de ojos asustados el chiquillo contó que unos niños vestidos de azul se lo habían llevado para jugar con él, que le llevaron hasta el río y que cuando empezó a llorar le dieron una manzana. ¡Caramba con esos duendes!

Emilia Padilla-García

ALBUQUERQUE (MARTÍNEZTOWN), NEW MEXICO

La Ñeca

Contaba un viejito, Benito, mi primo Benito, el que vivía al otro lao del Río Puerco, en el Arroyo de la Tapia que le dicen. Era músico.

Una noche jue a tocar a un baile, a Salazar. Güeno. Jue en un burro. Se acabó el baile. Agarró su violín el viejito este, y aquí viene por el camino. Por ahi en el Arroyo de la Tapia, que está delante d' en casa, ahi brincó uno y se le subió anancas del burro. Ora verás. ¡Pues aquel pobre hombre no jallaba qué hacer!

"¿Quién eres tú?" que pallá y que pacá, contaba muncho él. No, no le respondía. Pues aquí va aquel hombre embocándole al burro y aquel bulto anancas en el burro. No supo quién era; no supo. No supo. Don Benito decía que no supo quién era.

Cuando llegó a la casa, al otro lao de casa, onde vivíanos nosotros, onde vivía la señá Juanita Salas, ¿te acuerdas tú? Ahi vivía su hija, señá Amada. De todos modos, cuando llegó es que llegó y se apeó y les gritó a ellas, "¡Agárrenme! ¡Me vengo muriendo!" y cayó destendido, desmayao. Es que le preguntaban ellas, "¿Qué tiene papá? ¿Pus qué le dio?" "La Ñeca," es que decía. "La Ñeca." Que traiba la muñeca en el espinazo, pero ya no pudo hablar más. Eso era todo lo que decía.

Hasta otro día no les platicó de La Ñeca que se le había subido anancas del burro. Y lo *juraba* el dijunto Benito, que era una muñeca. Ya estaba viejito él.

Manuel Pérez

BERNALILLO (EL BOSQUE), NEW MEXICO

El Chaveta

Aquí estaba uno que le decían el Chaveta. El Chaveta le pegó a su mamá y le echó una maldición ella cuando le pegó. Su mamá le dijo, "Espero que te castigue Dios por lo que hiciste conmigo."

Ese hombre como en una semana quedó todo seco. Años más tarde andaba en un carrito chiquito con unas rueditas. Yo me acuerdo que cuando venía a la escuela escuchaba yo el carrito, y no importaba quién era, agarraba piedras y se las tiraba. Ese hombre lo castigó Dios con la loquera.

Vivía aá en una casita. El día que murió él decían que salió un humo negro de la casa.

Se rajaba la tierra

Ésta es la historia que me dijía mi abuelita. Ella misma dijía que vido este muchacho que también mató a su mamá. Cuando la mató se la echó aquí en el hombro para ir a tirala en el río. Cuando fue a tirala mi abuelita lo vido. Vinieron gentes de todos los lugares, enseñándoles como ejemplo, que lo que iba a un castigo, iba. Estaa todo lleno de gusanos el muchacho.

Más antes dijían si que tratabas mal o le respondías mal a tu madre, si te echaba una maldición, se rajaba la tierra y así estabas hasta que no te escupía la tierra bien pa juera. Ya cuando te escupía la tierra, estabas bien menso. Se veía mucho la maldición. Como ora, no se mira nada de lo que yo alcancé a ver con mis propios ojos.

Mariel Romero Ocaranza

CHULA VISTA, CALIFORNIA

Mi yaya

No hay nada menos tradicional que Tijuana, tal como piensa mucha gente. Yo fui criada y educada desde kinder hasta el penúltimo año de preparatoria en mi querida ciudad mugrosa. Yo nunca creí que Tijuana tenía mucha cultura o tradición porque no se sentía como si fuera México. Para mí, Tijuana es como un rincón alejado de todo lo que es tradicional de la sociedad mexicana, la ciudad pegada a la frontera de un país que no quiere nada que ver con México. En conclusión, es una ciudad NO muy mexicana.

Afortunadamente, mi mamá me ingresó en una escuela católica donde me contaron todas las leyendas de mi pueblo y Baja California y me fasciné con ellas. Juan Soldado, La bailarina sin cabeza, Tía Juana, Los Misioneros . . .

Durante mis años adolescentes, yo me preguntaba que si de dónde venía todo aquel interés sobre el misticismo y por qué es que me sentía tan cómoda con todo ello. Mi madre también se sentía cómoda con cosas místicas y mágicas, y su interés en lo metafísico y lo sobrenatural siempre me ha dado espacio para respirar aires diferentes e interesantes.

La persona que era más bruja aún era mi yaya, mi abuelita. Ella ni siquiera sabía lo mucho que era de bruja, pero, yo creo que sí sabía, al menos un poco. Ella era muy buena para el póker y ni siquiera tenía que ver las barajas para saber qué tenía en la mano. Ella ni siquiera tenía que contestar el teléfono para saber quién era cuando empezaba a sonar. Tenía muy buen corazón, era chistosa, y muy católica. Me supongo que por eso que nunca quiso explorar más allá ese lado de su personalidad. Yo no tuve mucho tiempo para conocerla mejor. Desgraciadamente falleció cuando yo estaba en la primaria.

En la secundaria tuve la oportunidad de aprender sobre el Día de los Muertos. Me sorprendió que las monjas tan estrictas tenían cada año un concurso para escoger el mejor altar. ¿Competencias? ¡Mi mero mole! Cada grupo competía para el Día de los Muertos. Mi salón de clase se sacaba el primer lugar todos los años.

En la preparatoria, me cambié a una escuela federal. La Escuela Preparatoria Federal Lázaro Cárdenas. La escuela más grande en Tijuana, construída encima del Casino de Agua Caliente de buena y mala fama. Yo dejé de estar en contacto con todo tipo de tradición, enfocándome más en mis estudios.

En mi último año de prepa, mi mamá se casó con un gringo encantador y me tuve que mudar a San Diego. Yo me sentí muy separada de mi vida en Tijuana de manera que decidí construir un altar para mi abuelita en octubre del año 2002, en mi casa en Tijuana. Simplemente para sentirme como una mexicana.

En Tijuana fui al Mercado Hidalgo y compré todo lo que necesitaba: calaveras de azúcar, dulces, papel picado, pan de muerto, de todo. Lo mejor para mi yaya. Luego fui a su casa y agarré un par de guantes y unas mascadas que todavía olían a su perfume favorito. El olor de violetas me conmovió el alma. Me sentí "conectada" con ella según iba construyendo el altar y según respiraba su perfume. Yo realmente creía que ella iba a visitar el altar. "Sería un honor," pensé yo. Mi mamá quedó agradecida por haberlo hecho, mi hermana mayor pensaba que estaba curado, pero miedosa, y nuestra muchacha, Raquel (más que sirvienta, un miembro de mi familia, mi nana), espiaba desde lejos mientras yo construía el altar.

Al altar le faltaban grandes e importantes símbolos como, por ejemplo, el arco de palmera, el camino de cempasúchil, y la cruz de arena dibujada en el suelo, pero no importaba, se veía fantástico. Esta vez no tenía a un ejército de muchachas adolescentes que me ayudaran. Todo cubierto de velas, el altar emanaba una luz morada y dorada. Engrandecí en el Copy-Pronto de mi colonia un retrato de mi Yaya cuando ella tenía dieciocho años. Puse retratos de mi abuelito en el altar cuando él también era joven (él murió aún antes de que muriera Yaya). También coloqué en el altar un violinillo hecho de madera, porque mi abuelita era muy social y le gustaba la música clásica. "El Danubio Azul" por Strauss era su composición favorita.

Otro punto débil de mi yaya también estaba en el altar—el licor y los caballitos. También le gustaban las cosas dulces, entonces eso fue lo que puse en el altar como su comida principal. Pero todo el arreglo se veía incompleto. Necesitaba más color así que fui a la panadería en la esquina de la calle, las Donas Venecia (que ha estado ahí desde hace años), para comprar algunos postres pintorescos. Quería algo que durara toda la noche y por eso compré galletas grandes y redondas de azúcar, del tamaño de mi mano, salpicadas con granitos grandes de azúcar y con mucho color. A mí me encantaban cuando era niña. Pensé que a yaya le gustarían también. Las puse a la izquierda del altar, todas acomodadas en un plato de porcelana.

Ya era noche. Prendí todas las velas y miré directamente en los ojos de mi yaya (en el retrato, claro) y dije,

—Ojalá que no me espantes esta noche, pero de veras quiero que goces de lo que te he hecho. Te extraño.

Mi mamá y mi hermana vinieron a ver el altar y me felicitaron de lo hermoso y sentimental que se veía. Yo me sentí muy orgullosa. Luego Raquel se presentó y dijo,

— ¿Sí sabes que si los muertos visitan el altar, se comen el alma de la comida y luego, cuando tú te la comes, no sabe absolutamente a nada, verdad?

Me dio un escalofrío.

—¡Claro que sí!—le contesté bien nerviosa mientras un millón de pensamientos espantosos atravezaron mi mente.

Eran las diez de la noche. Yaya llegaría en dos horas. Decidí acostarme antes de toparme con ella y desmayarme. También encerré al gato de mi hermana en el baño para que no brincara en el altar y lo distruyera. Mi hermana se fue a una fiesta y dijo que volvería tarde.

A la mañana siguiente, abrí los ojos y miré hacia fuera por la ventana de mi cuarto. Era una mañana otoñal, clara y fresca. Me tomé mi tiempo para levantarme. Fui a la cocina por un vaso de agua, cuando de repente noté algo muy raro en el altar. ¡Las galletas!

Una de las galletas estaba descansando tranquilamente al lado del retrato de yaya. A eso de un pie o más del resto del arreglo. Los granitos de azúcar. Esos malditos granitos me estaban mirando.

Me quedé asustadísima. Dejé el vaso de agua y me fui a buscar al gato. "¡Él tenía que ser el culpable!" Pensé mientras trataba de convencerme de que estaba loca. El gato estaba dormido, todavía encerrado en el baño.

"Debió haber sido mi hermana," dije yo. Corrí a su cuarto y la desperté. "¡Qué te pasa!" dije con miedo y coraje. Ella estaba media dormida y bastante confundida. La llevé a ver el altar y peló los ojos.

—¿Tú hiciste eso cuando llegaste en la noche?—le pregunté desesperadamente.

Dio un chillido, me empujó al lado y dijo "NOOOO" al mirar la galleta. Sus ojos me decían la verdad. Yaya . . . había estado allí.

No nos podíamos controlar y simplemente nos retiramos del altar. Más tarde durante el día, Raquel entró en la casa y me preguntó con una sonrisa, "Pues, ¿qué te vas a comer los postres?" Yo apenas moví la cabeza. "No, yo creo que no. ¿Me ayudas a tirarlos?" "Claro," me contestó. Luego le pregunté, "¿Tú estuviste aquí anoche? ¿Dónde estabas?" Ella miró la galleta, luego a mí y dijo, "No, ¿por qué?" Como siempre andaba de payasa, le dije, "No andes con bromas. Tú no fuiste la que MOVISTE la galleta, ¿verdad?" Se hizo para atrás, temblando un poco. "¿La galleta se movió?" preguntó ella. Entonces las dos calladitas nos pusimos a quitar la comida del altar.

Desde ese entonces yo no he construido otro altar. Me di cuenta que el poder de lo sobrenatural puede ser agobiante, pero creo que ya estoy lista para construir otro para el próximo Día de los Muertos. Claro, el altar para la próxima vez, será para mi abuelito Pepe. Ése sí que será interesante. Él fue cirujano.

Luciano Sánchez

ALBUQUERQUE (LOS GRIEGOS), NEW MEXICO

Manzanas relumbrosas

En papá y munchas otras gentes de Gualupe platicaban que volaban las brasas así como un trenecito. Pero yo nunca llegué a ver brasas. En ese tiempo cuando yo era muchacho no había nada cosas d'esas. Lo que llegué a jallar en casa, antes de venirnos pa Alburquerque, jueron güevos ahi adelante de la casa. Sí teníanos gallinas y todo, pero todas estaban en el gallinero.

Y tamién llegamos a jallar manzanas muy relumbrosas, bien, bien vidriosas, sin haber manzanas o árboles de fruta allá ni nada. Taavía cuando va un frutero o alguien pues antonces puede uno decir, puede uno creer que sí.

Pues no, llegamos a echar en la estufa todo eso. Nosotros nunca llegamos agarrar nada, pa comer, diremos. Teníanos miedo. Porque de ver aquella manzana ahi, sin saber diónde vino, ¡mal!

Andrés Sánchez Rojas

PHOENIX, ARIZONA

La niña

Esto sucedió cuando yo tenía quince años. El lugar allá en México se llamaba La Empacadora Maya. Allí empacaban todo tipo de frutas. Dígamos que ya sean melón, pepino, y otras frutas. Era un empacador grande. Nosotros trabajábamos en ese empaque, en frente de donde nosotros vivíamos. Allí pasaba la carretera nacional. Nada más estaba; solamente la pura empacadora. Y al lado de la empacadora estaba un rancho.

Era más o menos como mediodía. Éramos como unos cuatro chamacos de la misma edad. Yo llegué a donde estaban ellos y nos pusimos a platicar. Y como le digo, era completamente de día. Yo llegué de la empacadora al rancho de ellos porque no era nada más que cruzar la carretera. De todos modos, estábamos platicando cuando pasó una niña como de unos diez o doce años preguntando por su mamá.

A nosotros nos extrañó. En ese lugar nada más eran dos casas que había cerca de la empacadora y el rancho. Entonces nosotros nos miramos. La niña iba llorando, preguntando por su mamá. Nosotros le preguntamos a dónde iba, porque no era normal ver a una niña prácticamente de esa edad sola. El rancho más cortito estaba como unas veinte o veinticinco millas. Entonces fuimos y la paramos y le preguntamos quién era. Ella lo único que decía, "Yo quiero ver a mi mamá," llorando. "¿Pero dónde vives? ¿De dónde vienes?" pero no nos contestaba nada. ¡Nada! Nomás nos decía eso, "Yo quiero ver a mi mamá."

Entonces nos adelantó ella. Siguió rumbo a la carretera. Iba corriendo y a conforme corría la carretera. Todos nosotros los que estábamos preguntando quién eres, de dónde vienes, porque era una niña, vimos que se alejó como una media milla. Pasaba un canal que cruzaba la carretera. Ella iba llegando a ese canal. Ya yo andaba en un caballo. Luego yo les dije a mis compañeros, "Hay que alcanzarla para ver a dónde va. No hay ranchos cortitos para allá, y hay que alcanzarla para ver quién es o ver a dónde va."

Sobre ese canal que cruzaba la carretera, ella dio vuelta allí. Yo la alcancé a ver cuando dio vuelta. ¡Cuál fue mi sorpresa cuando yo di vuelta corriendo en mi caballo! Yo pienso que ella no había avanzado muncho, pero yo ya no la vi y sentí como que me entró miedo. Los otros muchachos venían corriendo pero ellos caminando. Yo fui el que di vuelta primero porque iba en el caballo. Yo me paré y me quedé asombrado porque ya no la miré. El camino donde dio la vuelta, pues, se miraba completamente; no tenía para dónde más ganar.

Ya llegaron los otros y me dicen, "¿Pues dónde está la niña?" "Yo no sé, no la veo." "Pues vete corriendo en el caballo. Y orita la vas alcanzar." Pues yo corrí como dos o tres millas, más o menos, en el canal. Yo anduve buscándola en el canal y en la orilla y en el monte, y no la encontré.

Cuando iba patrás a casa, no sé, pero me llegaba como una aigre muy helado y me sentí mal porque se me desapareció la muchacha y porque era una niña. ¡Y pasó en pleno día!

Ésa fue una de las cosas que yo tenía ganas de contarle a alguien porque yo lo viví. Fue algo que me pasó, y como le digo, no estaba solo. Fuimos varios y todos nos estábamos preguntando entre sí, "¿Quién era la niña?"

Otro día se fueron mis compañeros rumbo a donde vino la niña; se fueron a bañar a un lugar que se llama San Juan Prieta. Es como un canal también, pero la mayoría de ranchitos íbamos a bañarnos allí. Allí ellos encontraron una gran cantidad de dinero. No sé yo exactamente cuánto fue, pero mis cuatro amigos, los que estaban conmigo cuando buscábamos la niña, llegaron bien contentos a casa.

Pero toda mi vida he pensado, ¿Quién era la niña? ¿De dónde vino? ¿Y por qué andaba buscando a su mamá? Nosotros preguntamos en los demás ranchos. Como le digo, había un rancho donde la vimos a ella. Y había un rancho como veinticinco millas más lejos. ¿Quién pueda llegar caminando si no viene en camión o carro? No es fácil caminar esa cantidad de millas. Yo todo el tiempo andaba investigando de dónde salió esa niña y nunca supe quién era.

Los marranitos

No estaba yo solo. Estábamos toda la familia en casa. Ya era tarde. Eran como las seis de la tarde, y ya estaba casi escureciendo. El único que no estaba era mi papá porque llegaba tarde. Él era el encargado del lugar donde vivíamos; él era el que se encargaba de todos los trabajadores.

Nosotros escuchamos el ruido de una puerca y sus puerquitos. La buscamos porque se oía el escándalo que lleva una puerca cuando va andando con todos los animalitos. Pero no venía por la tierra. ¡Iba volando! Nosotros la miramos, la oímos, y nos pasó por arriba. No iba muy alto. Entonces aproximaba por otro rumbo donde nosotros estábamos. Había un rancho que estaba par lado del mar. De ese lado venía la puerca con esos animalitos gritando, pero, como digo, no iba caminando sino que pasó por el aigre. Venía del lado de donde vivía una pareja en ese rancho que estaba pal mar, pero la pareja no tenía relación con nadie de los que conocíamos en ese lugar.

No estaba muy noche para decir que era una visión o algo. Y no nomás la miré yo a la puerca, sino que la miramos todos y nos quedamos viendo. ¡Nada más! ¿Qué podría haber sido? ¿Algo espiritual?

Eddie Torres, Jr.

BERNALILLO (EL BOSQUE), NEW MEXICO

Hombre sin cabeza

Aquí es el bosque donde vivemos. Aquí está un lugar que le dijían La Abeyta, y me platicaba mi papá que este señor se encontró con este hombre y que quizás algo le pasó a este señor, que le cortó la cabeza ese hombre quisque por dinero. Y isque salía el señor ahi sin cabeza. Me platicaba mi papá de niño.

Más tarde yo estaba grande; tenía dieciocho, diecinueve años. Tenía una novia yo y entonces vivíanos en San Lorenzo. Tenía que andar a pie. Grande yo, se me hacía que vía a alguien y comenzaba a correr de miedo. Corría de mi casa a la casa de la novia porque decían que salía un hombre sin cabeza. Nunca me tocó ver. Dijía la gente que salía aquí onde le dijían el Puente Blanco, y mi papá dice que este hombre [el sin cabeza] de la noche a la mañana agarró dinero.

Disque eran duendes y que le salieron y le dieron unas barras de oro. Eran historias que te platicaban.

Supersticiones

Yo trabajaba en el Duke City [Albuquerque]. Yo tenía como dieciocho, diecinueve años. Dijían que salía una señora, una muchacha, aquí en el pueblo de Sandía. Yo venía como a la una o las dos de la mañana del trabajo. Estaba vientoso y vide—y la mente trabaja en diferentes *ways*—un papel que estaba enredado en el camino y parecía que no se movía el carro. Llegué a casa temblando. Me acuerdo bien, bien. ¡Pobrecita mi mamá! Blanco pálido de miedo. Algo me salió en el camino. Jui patrás el siguiente día de día y ahi estaa el papel en el poste atorado.

Te contaban munchas historias. Mi papá me llegó a contar que jalló unos limones con agujas metidas. Y cree muncho mi papá d'eso. Yo me cortaba el pelo con una señora aquí en Bernalillo y me lo quemaba porque dijía que venían y lo agarraban y lo juntaban todo el pelo las brujas pa hacer mal.

Mi abuela no dejaba los trastes de noche. No se acostaba hasta que estaban bien limpios, porque dijía ella que venían las brujas y agarraban los trastes en la noche. ¡Yo por eso antes de acostarme friego los trastes pa que no vayan a venir las brujas!

Eileen Dolores Treviño de Villarreal

SAN ANTONIO, TEXAS

Fragancias

Bueno, tengo tres cuentos que son muy a mi corazón: el fallecimiento de mi madre y el fallecimiento de mi hermano y luego con una bandera muy antigua en la ciudad de Goliad, Tejas.

Comenzando, el mes de febrero de 1994, mi mamá tenía un mes de fallecida, y yo estaba con mucho dolor todavía de su muerte. Estaba yo en mi casa una noche y yo estaba parada dentro de la sala de mis casa, al comedor. Eran como las nueves de la noche. Me paré allí y estaba viendo a una ventana y de repente, de arriba donde estoy yo parada, se me viene una fragancia, la cosa más hermosa.

Inmediatamente yo sabía que era mi madre. Esto nunca me había pasado antes. Estaba yo parada, y se me viene la fragancia, de así de arriba, del techo y pensé, "Mami, eres tú, ¿verdad? ¿Eres tú? ¿Estás bien? ¿Estás contenta?" En ese instante fui al otro cuarto a decirle a una amiga mía que estaba allí. "Oye, que aquí está mi mamá." Al segundo me regresé y ya se había terminado la fragancia, pero fuerte y preciosa. Yo sé que era mi madre. La fragancia era, bueno, lo único que te puedo dar es un ejemplo.

En febrero, cuando el laurel tiene las flores, tiene una cierta fragancia como de uvas, pero yo no tengo de esos árboles. Ni los hay en mi casa ni en la vecindad. Es lo único que te puedo decir. Algo muy suavecito, más o menos al laurel. Eso fue el mensaje de mi mamá para decirme, "Ya no estés triste. Todo está bien."

Ya después de eso, de ese encuentro, ya me comencé a sentir yo un poco más tranquila y a través de los meses con más tranquilidad. Pero yo sé que fue mi madre y es el primer episodio que comenzó y yo ya sé que vienen más a mí. No sé cuándo vienen y no sé en qué manera, pero yo sé que vienen en el modo de la fragancia.

El segundo episodio pasó en mayo del año 2000. Mi hermano había fallecido hacía tres semanas. Estaba yo en su casa de él con su esposa. Su esposa es de Morelia, Michoacán, y entonces ella me dijo,

—Haz los detalles del funeral, tú te encargas de todo eso.

—Bueno. Y había estado quedándome yo con ella por una semana, y ya tuvimos el entierro tres días anteriormente de eso.

Estaba yo sentada en el escritorio de mi hermano. Él y yo éramos muy acercados. Estaban su *fax machine* y su teléfono al lado derecho en su escritorio, y yo sentada en la silla de su escritorio. Entonces su esposa estaba al lado enfrente del escritorio, y estábamos platicando y, de repente, de aquí del lado derecho donde están su *fax-machine* y su teléfono, se me viene una fragancia.

Para decirte de cómo era, como eucalipto. Mi hermano padecía de artritis y entonces yo estoy hablando con mi cuñada y de aquí estoy que se me viene otra vez la fragancia. Y digo, "¡Ay, Dios! Ya vamos otra vez." Al minuto se me viene la fragancia del eucalipto tan fuerte que yo ya sabía que era mi hermano. Entonces, yo le pregunté a mi cuñada, le dije, "Angélica, ¿puedes oler esta fragancia? Acércate." Dice, "No, no, no huelo nada."

Luego yo comencé a llorar porque yo ya sabía que era mi hermano y le dije, "Aquí está, aquí está Pedro." Le dije, "Manito, aquí estás, ¿verdad?" Y así estuvo la fragancia por unos diez minutos, tan fuerte. Yo me puse a platicar con él. "¿Qué me quieres decir, Manito, que estás bien, contento? ¿Que todo está bien donde estás? ¿Que te gustó tu funeral que te dimos, que te mandamos con tanto honor y tan bonito?"

Yo llora y llora porque yo sabía que él estaba allí, pero no para su esposa sino para mí porque ella no olía la fragancia. Ella comenzó a llorar también. Le dije, "Aquí está Pedro." "¿Pero dónde, dónde?" "No, es una fragancia." "Pero yo no veo nada." "No, porque me vino a ver a mí para darme la señal que él estaba bien." Ya a los diez, doce minutos, se quitó la fragancia.

El tercer episodio ocurrió el mismo año del 2000 en el mes de noviembre. El grupo mío de "Los Bejareños," yo era presidenta en ese tiempo [de noviembre del 2000], nos invitaron a la ciudad de Goliad, Tejas. Iban a tener una feria de todos los grupos que estuvieron aquí en Tejas, los españoles, los indios, el mejicano. Iba a ser una feria enorme. Entonces, yo conozco un señor que es del Valle, es coleccionista de antigüedades. Entonces, ese día de noviembre de 2000 vino y me dijo, "Eileen, tengo una bandera, la bandera de Borgoña, que es muy antigua." Le dije, "¿Es original?" "Sí, es del 1600 y la parte roja de terciopelo de la cruz, ese material viene de Génova, Italia." Por el lado de mí los Treviño antes de que llegaran a España en el 1500 estuvieron en Génova y dije yo, "¡Ay! Tengo que ir a ver." "Ven a ver la bandera, ya cuando termines aquí."

A las 5 de la tarde me fui al Presidio en Goliad. Estaban dos banderas, una de María Laxilaria, y otra la de Borgoña. Y estaban unas gentes, otros cronistas, otros genealogistas, allí alrededor de nosotros y entonces yo toqué muy ligeritamente el terciopelo de la bandera y dije, "Si esta bandera podría hablar, ¿qué me diría de mis antepasados? ¿Quién hizo esta bandera? ¿Una de mis abuelas? ¿Quién cargó esta bandera en la batalla?" Entonces comencé a platicar con el grupo de la gente. A los cinco minutos, ¿pues qué crees que me pasa otra vez? Me viene una fragancia de la bandera de Borgoña, no de la María Laxilaria, pero de la de Borgoña, me viene una fragancia tan hermosa, una fragancia de mujer, y esa sí no te puedo dar detalle porque es una fragancia tan suave, tan ligera y tan hermosa que si el color rosa tuviera una fragancia, eso es lo que sería. Entonces estoy yo hacia abajo diciendo, "¡Ay qué hermoso, sí es la antepasada!" Y todos y "¿Que qué tienes, que qué estás viendo, que qué dices?" Les dije, "Ahorita les explico." No dura mucho, diez, doce minutos, esta fragancia tan bonita y tan hermosa y ya después se comenzó a quitar. Era un aviso, si era una tatarabuela, y yo sé que venía del lado de los Treviño, ella hizo esta bandera o tuvo alguna parte de la bandera, ya poniendo la cruz o lo que sea, pero ella me quiso dar a mí que ella había recibido mi mensaje y me estaba dando, "Sí, yo estoy aquí, yo tuve algo que ver con esta bandera."

Teresina Ulibarrí

LAS VEGAS, NEW MEXICO

Se le quitó lo malo

Una vez platicaba mi mamá quisque eos, papá y mamá, criaron este muchacho. Y le dijíanos nosotros mi tío Miguel. Pero isque era muy atroz. Muy atroz era el hombre. Vinía él pa cas' e mi mamá; él vivía en los Chupaderos. Todas las tardes vinía pacá él. Quizás ya estaa casao. Y él, puro hacer, puro hacer mal. Era muy atroz.

Luego una vez cuando vinía de aá pacá, isque porque hace güelta el camino asina, cuando vinía de aá pacá—se vinía a pie ayudale a mi papá y a mi tío—vido que delante dél vinía un hombre, pero no lo pudo alcanzar. Ya cuando llegó a cierto lugar, ya no vido el hombre. Cuando iba de aquí pallá, pa su casa—se jue noche—y ende mismo que iba él, isque se oyó como que iba un caballo resollando muy recio, y que galopiando, que ya lo tranpaba, y que ya lo tranpaba y que ya lo tranpaba. Y él que iba a greña a greña.

Cuando en eso que, ende cayó en el Chorro, onde cai agua de onde está un ojito le dijían el Chorro. Mi tío Miguel dice que el hombre ese que vido cayó pa bajo del Voladero y sonó como un balazo recio. En eso abrieron su mujer y su suegro la puerta, a ver qué era el grito y too eso y él cayó desmayao pa entro. No sé si de miedo, de lo que vería. Pero de ahi pallá era un hombre muy güeno. Se le quitó lo malo.

six

Handsome, with Hoofs and Tail

....

Where evil's at stake, the devil's always one step ahead of you.—Jesusita Aragón

INTRODUCTION

Any mention of the Devil brings certain images to mind. Everyone has a mental picture of him—usually in the form of a man with horns and a tail, endowed with supernatural powers, and likely to wage battle against those forces that represent good. Reputed to be an angel who lost his precious place in heaven due to his excessive pride, the Devil epitomizes evil and is generally associated with a dark and lugubrious world. His duty-bound role is to seduce "good" people into joining him and his legions of sinners.

Other names that may be invoked when speaking of the Devil are Satan and Lucifer, but for Latinos in the Southwest—and for our purposes—he is simply *El Diablo* or *diantre*. Expressions like *Él es el vivo diablo* (He's a real devil, or He's mean as hell) are common and negative in tone. The Devil is the embodiment of evil (*la cosa mala*) and is therefore to be feared and avoided.

I recall going to the Church of the Virgen de Guadalupe in my community for the catechism lessons that Mrs. Gonzales taught to children preparing for their First Holy Communion. In the lessons, we were instructed on the principles of the Catholic Church and how we should uphold them. During the lessons, in a discussion of good and evil, the Devil was mentioned as representing the antithesis of virtue and was associated with black. Virtue, in contrast, stood for good and was pure and white.

Intrigued by these opposites and what I perceived to be a contradiction because of the way our local priest dressed, I asked Mrs. Gonzales what turned out to be an inauspicious question, one that she undoubtedly found annoying. "If the Devil wears black and represents evil," I asked, "then why does the priest wear black?" Her answer, as I recall, was quick and to the point: "Just because!" Our exchange was a source of entertainment for the class and an embarrassment to me, and a satisfactory answer to my question was never forthcoming.

The foregoing episode could well be woven into a story about the Devil, with a moral underpinning perhaps characteristic of the old-timers' stories. The Devil was—and to some extent still is—a popular figure among Latinos of the Southwest who continue the tradition of story-telling. Long ago his name was used to scare children and ensure their good behavior, although in most cases the ultimate consequences of disobedience were left unspecified. But attitudes do change, as we learn from María A. Mongalo, who facetiously says, "Back then [when she was a child] people were afraid of the Devil. . . . Now it's the Devil who's afraid of us."

The stories that follow offer some different perspectives on the Devil and the people unlucky enough to run into him when evil spirits are at work. These spirits, lest we forget, represent death and are intended to inflict physical or psychological pain on those vulnerable to the Devil's wiles.

One such incident occurs in José Sánchez Rojas's story about Gabriel García, who traded his soul to the Devil so his father's murder could be avenged. Gabriel reneged on the agreement, incurring the Devil's wrath. Following a series of confrontations, Gabriel García outsmarts his adversary. The Devil's intrusion of a different sort takes place in Isabel Romero's narrative where, ironically, a squabbling couple settles their differences after the Devil comes between them.

The Devil also intervenes, but with an amusing twist, in "Evil Spirits," recounted by Jesusita Aragón. In an argument with his wife, the husband jokingly challenges the Devil to show his face, only to have him do precisely that, scaring the wits out of a now repentant husband. But the Devil is not always what it appears to be either. In "The Devil" by Linda Chávez, nuns warn their students about a dark object on the premises that is suspected of being the Devil; it turns out to be none other than a nun in her black habit.

Other stories portray the Devil as a black animal spewing fire from its eyes, a dog, a bull, and a coyote. But the most captivating presents the Devil as a debonair dancer who whirls a beautiful girl around the dance floor. While dancing, because of some unexplained indiscretion (perhaps the Devil violated his pact with the witches, his underlings), she scratches

Trading post national historic site, Ganado, Arizona. Photo by Nasario García, 2003.

his face, scarring him permanently. The young woman turned out to be a witch.

As mentioned earlier, evil spirits symbolize the Devil, and the Devil represents death. There is no better treatment of death, the grand equalizer, than Rolando Hinojosa Smith's account in "Death and Obedience," in which the Devil plays a part. This tale with folkloric tendencies, which comes from the Lower Río Grande Valley in Texas, captures the democratic essence of death and reminds us that the Devil cannot be ignored. Hinojosa Smith provides a fast-moving and quasi-humorous handling of a serious topic that will resonate throughout the southwestern United States.

Jesusita Aragón
LAS VEGAS, NEW MEXICO

Evil Spirits

I'm one who believes in evil spirits. I believe there is such a thing. Many people have had bad experiences with evil spirits. One time during Mass there was a wedding going on. And the husband said to his wife, "I'll be back in a little while to get you and Mom. I'm going to go look around,"

and he went and got drunk and forgot all about them. Late at night he showed up to pick them up.

"What time is this to be showing up to go to the dance?" said the mother.

And he started to carry on and who knows what all. Talking nonsense.

"And let the Devil take me away!" all this, that, and the other.

"Keep quiet!" said his mother. "It can come and get you."

"Let him take me."

And he went outdoors. No sooner he went outside than he came back in all disheveled and scratched up, his clothes all torn up and everything.

"Good gracious!" he said to them. "The Devil almost took me with him. You don't know how close he came."

"You asked for it," said his mother to him. [Laughter]

Juan Bautista Chacón

PUEBLO, COLORADO

He Spotted His Tiny Horns

Max Trujillo had a small band. He played at dances and organized a dance around the Hernández settlement, in a small town people called El Santo. He was having a dance when the lights started going out while the people were dancing. The lights kept going out and coming back on. Then I don't know why he went outside, probably to fetch something, a lantern or something from the house.

Then a man bumped into him, and this Max Trujillo asked him where he was headed. He (Trujillo) kept staring at this man close up and saw that he had tiny horns. Before he could invoke the sign of the cross, the man said to him, "Here I am making the rounds," and he scratched Max Trujillo's face.

José D. Chávez

BERNALILLO, NEW MEXICO

God Put the Devil on This Earth

My parents and grandparents saw this stuff about witches. Because as far as being around is concerned, they are around. Even at this very moment there's lots of them. They do so many things that they sell their soul to the Devil. That is why nowadays the Devil has taken advantage of everyone. In a way the Devil has already benefited, because the old folks used to say, "Remember that an epidemic is coming. A very bad epidemic is going to come and it's going to wreak havoc with people on this earth." And I said to myself, "What epidemic?"

Now that I'm older, I'm seeing it. I stop to see and to think. Why, there you have the epidemic with pot, cocaine, crack, and all the junk that's coming in from all directions. But look, all these things come from the Devil. God put the Devil on this earth. He put him here not so he could punish us. He's not the one to punish us. God's the one who punishes us.

Leonila "Linda" Galván de Chávez

CLAREMONT, CALIFORNIA

The Devil

People in my town used to say that the Devil would come when he wanted to scare the children who caused mischief. Back then when I was a little girl, children were afraid. That's no longer true.

I had girlfriends who would say, "The Devil appeared before our eyes whenever we were bad."

I was in a boarding school that was like an old school, and it was headed by nuns. They would say to us, "Don't go down that corridor because there's a woman there who crosses the corridor at night." Well, the person walking down the corridor wasn't a woman or the Devil. It was a nun!

Rolando Hinojosa Smith

AUSTIN, TEXAS

Death and Obedience

Don Osbaldo Benjamín Coy, a hardworking farmer, was worried, and he had a right to be. His wife, Doña Carmelina, was about to give birth to their tenth child, but it wasn't that she was in any danger. She was a big, healthy farm girl, but ten children, sighed Don Osbaldo Benjamín, was a bit much.

He'd begun to worry when the twins, numbers six and seven, had come unannounced, much like those sudden-like hurricanes that form in the Lower Río Grande Valley of Texas without so much as a by-your-leave. But come they did, as did numbers eight and nine. But ten! And no, he sighed again. It wasn't that ten was an unlucky number. The worry came from the number that, counting him and his wife, totaled twelve and that was just too uncomfortably close to thirteen; and that, as he well knew, was the unlucky number.

What to do? What to do?

A close neighbor, his compadre in fact, recommended prayer, but directly to God, he had said. "No intermediaries of any kind, compadre. Get me?" Don Osbaldo Benjamín had nodded absently, but as he crossed the cotton field, he decided prayer was worth a try.

And God came to the Valley to see Don Osbaldo Benjamín, and only him, for only he had summoned God.

But it proved to be a brief and disappointing meeting: Don Osbaldo Benjamín, suffering from a toothache the day God came calling, was not in the best of moods.

He argued with the Lord. Accused him of neglecting the poor, seeing only the rich and favoring them.

It's said that God shrugged his shoulders and disappeared in a mist of heavenly light.

The Devil, who, according to sinners and saints alike, neither sleeps nor rests, waited for Don Osbaldo Benjamín. It's no secret that Valleyites claim that it's hotter than hell itself down there, and this may be so since the Devil himself was leaning on a shady chinaberry tree as he waited for Don Osbaldo Benjamín to make his way through the cotton fields.

After a warm greeting, the Devil offered his services. He waited and waited and finally humphed out a "Well, what's it going to be? You need financial help or not?"

Reliable sources say that Don Osbaldo Benjamín turned down the Devil's generous offer: riches to the tenth child who could then do what he wanted with the money. All he wanted, said the Devil, was obedience.

Don Osbaldo Benjamín thought on this for less than a split second. "No," was the rejoinder. "You lie. You mislead. The truth is in you only because you never let it out."

The Devil, not as good a loser as God, fumed and made the temperature in the Valley rise to 115 degrees Fahrenheit as he, too, disappeared before Don Osbaldo Benjamín's astonished eyes.

But the problem remained. His wife, Doña Carmelina, carrying number ten in her arms, brought Don Osbaldo Benjamín a cool glass of limeade. She asked whom he had been talking to and he told her. Then he told her about turning down God, too.

"Was that wise?" she asked.

For his part, Don Osbaldo Benjamín shrugged his shoulders and said that the only equalizer was death for it took both the rich and the poor.

At the mention of death, Doña Carmelina crossed herself, said a silent prayer, and walked rather hurriedly inside the house.

Don Osbaldo Benjamín rolled a cigarette, lit it, and took a sip from his limeade. "Death," he thought. "The great equalizer."

They'd manage, he said to himself. They always had before. But it was the nearness to the number thirteen that bothered him.

As he placed the empty glass on the ground, a cold breeze cut through the thick branches of the chinaberry tree. Don Osbaldo Benjamín looked at the sky and stared at the hot, white sun.

"Why a cool breeze?" he wondered. He then removed his hat to wipe the sweat off his brow when the breeze whipped up again and he shuddered somewhat. "The dead of summer and a cool breeze," he marveled. As he turned toward his wife who was now feeding the chickens, there appeared a young woman dressed in white who smiled at him.

"And where did she come from?" Don Osbaldo Benjamín asked himself. He opened his mouth to say something to mask his surprise and found his mouth had gone dry.

Beautiful, he managed to think, was a poor word. She was special, somehow. She walked toward him, smiled, and pointed to a shady spot on the ground and invited him to sit.

"I'm Death," she said. "Could I help you?"

Don Osbaldo Benjamín stared at the ground and thought, "I must be going mad. And Carmelina, why can't she see this person I'm with? Goodness, I am going mad."

Death smiled and reassured him that no, he was quite sane.

"Do you," he blurted out, "do you read minds too?"

She nodded and said, "Yes. Nothing to it."

They sat in silence for a moment and Death spoke again: "I'll be number ten's guardian. All I want is obedience, but then, that's what the Devil wanted and what God demanded. Isn't that so?"

The cool breeze returned momentarily and wafted through the chinaberry tree.

"Yes," said a confused Don Osbaldo Benjamín. "But what is it you want from me, us, him?"

"Obedience."

"But, but, you're Death. You'll take him from us."

She nodded, smiled again, and said, "Of course. I come for everyone, for you, for Doña Carmelina."

"But he's only a baby, our baby."

Death then promised that she would not take number ten until after both his parents were dead. Was that fair enough? she then asked.

Don Osbaldo Benjamín hesitated and looked toward Doña Carmelina who had finished feeding the chickens. He tried to raise his arm to call to her, but found he couldn't move. Except for his breathing, everything else in him was paralyzed.

"Do we have a contract?" Death prodded.

"And he'll want for nothing? And my family?"

"Riches beyond your dreams. One proviso, though. Number ten musn't walk in the rain, ever. He's a magical child and full of electricity. Remember that."

The years passed and one by one the Coy family died. First it was Doña Carmelina, and then the twins, and then the others, finally Don Osbaldo Benjamín, until number ten, now named Juan José, remained as the sole survivor.

One autumn day, when the Valley orange blossoms gave off their sweetest aroma, Juan José, now at age fifty and fit as a well-tuned fiddle, slipped and fell near the same shady spot where Death and Don Osbaldo Benjamín had met half a century before.

Grunting a bit and struggling to get up, Juan José saw a beautiful young woman, dressed in white, who smiled at him.

"I'm rich," he said, "a bit fat perhaps, but fit, and I've a nice home. Too, I've lived a good life, I'm unmarried, and I suppose it's time for me to settle down."

Before he spoke, Death came to him and said, "Of course I'll marry you."

Dazed by her proposal, he stood by the tree and temporized. "Clouding up a bit, but it's autumn in the Valley, and you have to expect it."

At this, Death glanced skyward and saw some menacing clouds approaching from the Gulf of Mexico. She pursed her lips and said, "Get inside, you don't want to get wet, do you?"

"Why should I? All my life I've not been allowed to walk in the rain, to splash in rain puddles, to run through the weeded cotton fields or to raise my arms to the sky. Let's stay here, you and I."

Death shook her head, brought her left dainty white hand to her face, and when she removed it the beautifully perfect face had been replaced by a skull.

Juan José recoiled and headed for home, running as fast as he could.

"Too late," warned Death. "You disobeyed me. Stop."

Unable to move, Juan José looked at the specter.

With one slight movement of her bony fingers, the house disappeared in a cloud of smoke. With another slight movement, the tree disappeared, leaving Juan José at the mercy of the coming rain.

"You're Death, and I'll cheat you. For once, someone will win over Death. Yes."

Sadly, Death shook her head, and with her left hand summoned him and pointed to where the house once stood.

There, by the front door, was Don Osbaldo Benjamín. Healthy, hale, and very much alive. He was angry, too.

He asked, "Did you disobey Death?"

Juan José lied and said no.

Sadder still, Death walked to Don Osbaldo Benjamín and said, "He was a bad investment, wasn't he?"

Defiant still, Juan José strode to where his father stood and asked, "Didn't I treat you well? Didn't I make money for all the family? Why, when I was born we were poorer than church mice and twice as miserable. And what are you doing here? You're supposed to be dead. And what happened to the house?"

With this he turned to Death who, strangely enough, appeared taken aback by Juan José and his temper.

Relenting somewhat, Death raised her left hand again, and the house reappeared. Untouched.

A wide grin appeared at Juan José's mouth. "I always win, and now I don't want to get wet. Ha!"

His father walked toward Death and asked, "What are we to do?"

"Nothing," said Death. "But keep your eye on the house."

With this, Juan José entered the house before the first raindrops. The storm, a *chubasco,* as they say in the Valley, passed quickly. As soon as the rain stopped, Juan José stepped out, saw that his father had disappeared and that Death was recovering some clothes from the ground.

"Why, those look like the clothes I was just wearing."

"You won't be needing them," said Death. "Look at yourself, as naked as the day you were born."

What happened next may be too sad to relate or to contemplate, but no story in the Valley remains unfinished.

Juan José began to shrink in size, smaller, smaller, smaller, until once again he was a baby in his mother's arms.

Don Osbaldo Benjamín suddenly appeared, as did the other nine children. The house, smaller now, and quite humble, stood where it had once stood.

The day was clear, the burning sun stood over them all. The pavement, the cotton fields, everything trembled under the blistering heat.

Death appeared again, and this time Doña Carmelina saw her, as did the other children. The baby, number ten, began to cry, to kick up a fuss, but was soon hushed by his mother's lullaby.

Beautiful as ever, Death smiled for the last time and said, "It could have been a dream, couldn't it? For now, I'll say this: all of us are dead, including me, of course, but you, all of you, have your lives ahead of you. Live them well, but understand this, wherever you go, wherever you are, I'll be there. Waiting."

Valley people don't believe such stories, but they do tell them and repeat them on occasion because Death, like a good mother, is never far away.

And that, perhaps, is why Death, *La Muerte,* is feminine in this culture.

María A. Mongalo

RIVERSIDE, CALIFORNIA

The Nahua

It is said that it was the Devil, and that when it was seen on the roads, in the village streets, the people would run. They would go to bed early. There was no TV. Perhaps back then, in the silence of the night, one could hear more noises.

And you could hear the Nahua oxcart. The Nahua oxcart was by itself. There was not even a soul who could hear it, being that there were no oxen pulling it, and you could hear it running fast down the street. Back then the people were afraid of the Devil and they didn't dare look out. They were afraid. All of that was done to scare the kids. I believe even the grown-ups got scared! Now it's the Devil who's afraid of us.

That's why I say that kids grew up being good and respectful, even the adults. There were many beliefs. A small boy or girl was not apt to answer his father or mother or an uncle or a grandparent in a disrespectful way because the Devil would come and punish you. Or if you were going to get spanked and you ran, the earth would part and swallow you. Back then there was a lot of fear. Nowadays there's nothing like that.

Luis Esteban Reyes

UPLAND, CALIFORNIA

A Hunter from the Plains

This hunter from the Plains spent all his time hunting. He was a real show-off. He was always saying things like, "Nothing's going to happen to me. I'm the king, the boss, around here. I'm going to hunt 'chigüiros' [plains animals], I'm going to hunt deer, or whatever."

One time he went deer hunting, and he saw a deer. He fired five or six shots at it and it didn't fall. The deer charged him. He caught him by its horns and lifted it up, and the guy kept on stabbing it with his knife, but the deer never keeled over.

From then on the hunter doesn't recall anything, but when he came to, the people claim that he returned with his friends and they went to look for the deer and they never found it. It was hardly possible for the deer to have survived, above all with all the shots the hunter fired at him along with the stabbings he delivered with his knife.

It's as if the Devil himself were there waiting, and the deer appears at certain times of the year at the *espinadero,* a place with thickets in the Plains.

Isabel Romero

LAS VEGAS, NEW MEXICO

The Coyote Turned into the Devil

There was this man. He was single, already old. Carlos López was his name. He was a half-breed. He was half-French. He lived alone on a ranch. His mother lived with him, but she was already quite old. He used to go to dances, and his mother would stay home. Then when he was on horseback on his way to the dance he saw a coyote and took off after him. It was already getting dark, and he took off after the coyote on his horse to rope him. He crossed the highway, and there was a huge rock. When he crossed the road, there was the coyote on top of the rock [laughter], turned into the Devil.

That was the end of going to dances for Carlos López. When he reached the rock, because he jumped on top of the rock, he saw that it was a black animal. It was spewing fire from its eyes. It was black with a long tail. It was on top of the rock, and it had horns. The coyote turned into the Devil.

Fire Shot Out of Its Eyes

I was just a kid, but I heard that there was this couple, a man and a woman, who used to fight a lot. Foolishness, jealousy. Close by there was a small slope and an embankment. There were lots of boulders there, and when the wife left her house she saw an animal that came out from behind the embankment. It was black. Then she turned back and asked another woman to go with her to see the black thing that she had spotted. The woman went. The thing was black, black, with a long tail, and fire shot out of its eyes. Through its mouth. [Laughter] Now, there's more! As fire was coming out of its eyes and through its mouth, [laughter] it was a very long animal, with a long tail, and with hooves, like big feet.

As a result, the wife fainted from fright. She fainted. As gossip would have it, the husband kept repeating, "I wonder what Juanita is doing that she doesn't, that she doesn't come in?" Well, the wife had fainted. [Laughter] She fainted. He found her passed out. "What's wrong with you?"

Finally he went and started pouring water on her head until she came to. "Well, what are you doing here?" That's when she told him what she had seen. The remedy was such that they never fought again. It was an evil spirit.

Victoria J. Sánchez

OCEANSIDE, CALIFORNIA

She Was Stone Cold

This is a very brief story I heard in the 1950s in East Los Angeles. The story goes something like this: a young man attended a party and there met a very beautiful girl dressed in a long white dress. They spent time together and danced throughout the evening and into the night. While dancing, he noticed that she was stone-cold.

After the party, he offered to take her home. They walked to her home, where he left her at the entrance to the house. Sometime later, he came back to the house where he had left her because he wanted to see the beautiful girl in the white dress once again. A man claiming to be her uncle answered the door and told him the girl in question had been dead for several years. The uncle told him that she was buried at the Calvary Cemetery in East Los Angeles, but that he should not reveal the girl's name to anyone.

The young man then went to the cemetery, where he found her headstone with the date of her death.

Andrés Sánchez Rojas

PHOENIX, ARIZONA

Someone Hollered in the Distance

I remember one time my family and I were in an area cleared of trees. People would go there to the peaks and used those areas around the peaks to plant corn. The corn was already on the stalk and we were harvesting it because animals like the javelina and the raccoon ate it. They would go and eat the corn when the cornstalks started bearing corn.

My brother-in-law's father has a very clear voice when he hollers. He can be heard far away, because he's someone who hollers with a really clear voice. One morning when we were getting ready to head home from the peaks, he heard someone holler in the distance. Way over like on the side of a mountain. Then he returned the holler. He heard the holler once again, but this time he heard it closer and he answered him still again. Before he knew it, the holler was right at his feet, and they say that if he had answered this last time, it's possible that he would have been lifted into the air because the one answering was the Devil!

You Couldn't See Its Face

Pedro and I had gone hunting, and it was already about three o'clock in the morning. He said to me, "We're not going to catch anything. Let's go." Then we climbed down through this place called El Tanque de Mendoza (Mendoza's Tank). Many people go there because it's a place to go swimming. Practically anyplace at night, however beautiful it might be during the day, looks different at night. It's something *quite* different.

We climbed down and we were already on the paved road where there's a ford and the water goes through. Pedro reminded me that water is drawn from there for the village. When we reached the ford he started drinking water. Then I got thirsty so we were both drinking water at the same time. All of a sudden from up above on the road we saw someone on horseback, and Pedro says to me, "Look! I wonder who it is?" "I don't know," I said to him, "but it's headed where we're going." "Let him get close and then I'm going to ask him who he is."

We were headed toward Camalote, and it was coming from a town called Los María. But before he got to where we were, the horse had to cross the ford, but he didn't cross the ford. He continued instead where there were some rocks. That "friend" sparkled a lot. All we could do was to look at it. As I say, it didn't cross the ford. It continued straight, where the water cascaded. All you could hear was the noise coming from the horseman's spurs. We were startled and didn't know what to do, whether to run or not because, as I say, in reality we didn't know what it was. We looked at it as he came toward us. You couldn't see its face. You couldn't see a thing, only a dark object, and the clothing sparkled when the moon shined on it because that area is very shady and has many trees. Given the shadows of the trees, the moon would shine on it and it sparkled. By the time it got quite close to us, you could hear a little bell like the sound of a school bell. Suddenly it disappeared. We never found out what it was. I believe it was the Devil.

José Sánchez Rojas

PHOENIX, ARIZONA

Gabriel Spoke to the Devil

Gabriel García was twenty years old. I was younger, about twelve years old. He is my cousin. As it turned out, they killed his father, who is my mother's brother. An uncle killed Gabriel García's father, whose name was José García, and Gabriel, a little boy, was left alone, parentless, because shortly thereafter his mother died also. And Gabriel spoke to the Devil and told him that he would give him his soul but that he had to avenge his father's death. That's how Gabriel García's story starts.

He was single, later on he got married. Then one day the Devil popped out at him and said, "What happened? Didn't I say you shouldn't go inside the church?" Gabriel answered, "There was no such agreement," and Gabriel grabbed the little skull he was carrying with him—he was in a forest with lots of trees and shade—and gave it a good kick. Where it rolled to wasn't far.

Gabriel took off with a wicker basket draped over his shoulder, with his small machetes inside, to where there were some relatives near the river. The Devil catches up with him and says, "What happened? The machetes represent real life." Gabriel got angry and engaged the Devil in a series of machete blows. In the process, the Devil would grab the butt end of the machete. He didn't have a weapon, only his fingernails. The Devil wrested the two machetes from Gabriel and stuck him up on a tree, but not a very tall one, whereupon Gabriel grabbed his small sack of tobacco and in it found the Devil's tiny skull.

Gabriel had thrown it away in the forest, but it turned up there once again. Well, his wife died and he gave up going here and there. He was left alone with his daughters, but since he no longer had his wife he stayed in the countryside.

One day someone tried to kill Gabriel García. He was resting with his head up against the *parota* plant, and they kicked him and dragged him away. Where that happened is a main road used by many people.

They tried to kill him in Chiquilistlán, where the slaughter of four persons took place. Gabriel had a small machete tied to his waist and shots were fired. Two of Gabriel's brothers-in-law and a compadre were with him. Shots were pumped into Gabriel, and he in turn delivered a few machete blows to this one person's forehead. And he put his foot up against him to pull the machete [from the body]. Then the dead person keeled over. He simply keeled over and died. Gabriel, for all of the bullets they pumped into his chest, was still on his feet and headed for home. He had bullet holes in his body, all over his shirt, but not a drop of blood. There was nothing wrong with him.

I'm telling you that because I saw all of that happen. I was traveling with my uncle Isabel de Solera, one of those who died, from Agua de Xiculetán, and my two brothers-in-law. I saw it all. I was about twelve years old at the time. I took off to inform my uncle's family that they had killed him. That's something real that I saw and not something I was told.

A Black Horse

In Chiquilistlán a black horse would show up and pass through the middle of town. I don't know at the present time, because it's been thirty years since I returned. The people were obsessed by the Devil in all of those small ranches. Everyone was afraid of the Devil.

I have seen him in the shape of a dog. One day I fired a series of shots at him and not a single one penetrated. The dog took off. The Devil used to come at me any old place. One day he came at me in the shape of a bull and I fired at him with a carbine, but nothing happened to him. When I got married the second time, the Devil disappeared for good.

Ophelia Ipolita María de Gracia Sandoval de Rinaldi

BERNALILLO, NEW MEXICO

It Happened in Las Cruces

This is a story my mom used to relate. This happened in Las Cruces. Apparently there was this family that was very mean. They were from Mexico, and one of the women went crazy and then they had to take her to jail. Other family members also went crazy. They were all in jail, but before taking them to jail, they had destroyed everything, ransacked everything, and I understand they broke up the furniture and dug holes in the wall.

People said it was the Devil that had appeared, and that it was because of him that they had caused all the damage. But they were hauled off to jail and there they were crazy as all get-out. Mom said that people would go see them, but that they were there like on display. But I understand they were really crazy to the point of looking like slobbering monkeys, all of them. I understand they performed some kind of an evil. That was one of Mom's stories.

Ernesto Struck

PUEBLO, COLORADO

His Tail Protruded from between His Ankles

These musicians went around playing everywhere. One time they went to Questa, New Mexico, which is north of Taos. They went to play. Long about midnight perhaps, a very beautiful girl came in the dance. Inside the dance hall was a young man. He was an ordinary sort of guy, very friendly with everyone, and he went to ask the girl to dance. Very well. She spent some time with him. When he had her captivated, he hugged her, where-upon she looked to one side and saw his tail. It protruded from between his ankles:

All he got out of it was a scratch right in his forehead where she grabbed him and dug in her fingernails. And the scuttlebutt is that he never got rid of the scratch mark. Never!

I guess she was a witch. She invoked, as they say, the witchcraft names of yesteryear. That's it! She disappeared and took off. She turned into a kind of fireball.

Eileen Dolores Treviño Villarreal

SAN ANTONIO, TEXAS

The Devil with Chicken Feet

Years and years ago here in San Antonio, but I mean many years ago, a dance took place. A girl from here in San Antonio was asked to dance by a nice young man who was well dressed. They went out to dance and people say that this occurred in a place that no longer exists, a club called El Camaroncito. I believe it's on the West Side of the city.

The story has it that she was wearing a dress cut low in the back because it was hot. She was dancing with this nice young man, dancing up a storm, when she looked down and saw that she was suspended in the air halfway up from the floor. When she saw that she kept climbing in the air, she screamed, and he put his hand behind her back and burned her. When he came down and hit the floor, everybody noticed that he had chicken feet, and he disappeared. She was dancing with the Devil and that is why he burned the low neckline part of her back.

Adelina Valdez Chávez Baca

BERNALILLO (EL BOSQUE), NEW MEXICO

The Devil Was on the Loose

You know what womanhood was like in Guadalupe. They would tell you to dress decently. A girl wouldn't dare go out into the street half-naked. She just wouldn't. And we wouldn't go out wearing pants. People would say that the Devil was tempting us. We had to dress decently. People

would say, "There they are teasing the men." We had to wear long clothes, not like now that the girls go out in shorts with their belly buttons sticking out and all. That's something we couldn't do. Shorts were not seen and pants were not worn. And we had to go out with our shoes really shined. Back then we didn't go into the church without putting on a hat. People would say that if we did all those things in public [not be dressed decently], that we were inciting the Devil who was on the loose.

Cruzita Vigil
LAS VEGAS, NEW MEXICO

The Devil and Witches Are One and the Same

There were all kinds of stories when we moved here to Las Vegas. The Devil and witches are one and the same. An uncle of mine used to tell the story when he was working with this fellow, and this fellow had a girlfriend, quite a ways away, you see? I understand there was going to be a dance, and he said to my uncle, "I can't find a way of going to the dance," said this friend to my uncle.

"Then I'll take you," said this other man.

"But how? We don't have anything to go on."

"Never mind. I'll take you if you wish to go. I'll take you."

"Okay, the important thing for me is to go."

As soon as it got dark, this man showed up and he said to my uncle's friend, "Okay, are you ready? Climb on piggyback!" [Laughter] He took him all the way to the doorstep of the dance hall. Then the man said to him, "Whenever you're ready to leave, just whistle for me."

He danced with his girlfriend and had lots of fun. When he was ready, he whistled for the man.

"Once again, climb on me piggyback!"

Then that man took him back the way they came. [Laughter] My uncle used to say that that man indeed took his friend to the dance and brought him back. It was a curious thing.

Guapo, con pezuñas y cola

Donde pone uno los ojos, el diablo mete la cola.

—Jesusita Aragón

Jesusita Aragón

LAS VEGAS, NEW MEXICO

La cosa mala

Sí creyo en la cosa mala. Yo creyo que hay. A muncha gente le ha llegao a pasar munchas cosas con la cosa mala. En un tiempo ahi en misa había un casorio, y le dijo el marido a la mujer,

—Orita vengo por ti y por mi mamá. Voy yo a dar la güelta—y jue y se puso una parranda y no se acordó. A media noche cayó ya por ellas.

—¿Qué horas son éstas de ir al baile?—le dijo la mamá. Y empezó él a desparatiar y qué sabe qué tanto. La borrachera.

—¡Y que me lleve el diantre!—que pallá y que pacá.

—¡Cállate la boca!—le dijo su mamá—. Te puede llevar.

—Que me lleve.

Y se salió pa juera. Pues de allá entró too desgreñao y too rasguñao, la ropa rota y too.

—¡Qué bárbara!—les dijo—. Por tanto y me lleva el diablo. Ustedes ni saben.

—Pus tú querías—le dijo su mamá. [Risas]

Juan Bautista Chacón

PUEBLO, COLORADO

Le vio los cuernitos

Max Trujillo tenía una bandita. Tocaba en los bailes, y hizo baile por ahi en el poblao de Hernández, ahi en un pueblito que le dicían El Santo. Estaba haciendo baile él y logo empezaron las luces apagarse cuando estaba bailando la gente. Se apagaban y se prendían. Logo no sé a qué salió él pa juera. Iba trae alguna cosa, algún farol o algo de la casa.

Logo lo topó un señor y le preguntó Trujillo que par ónde iba. Se quedó muy cerquita mirándolo al señor y después le vio los cuernitos. Antes que le citara las cruces, le dijo el señor, "Aquí ando," y le rasguñó la cara a Max Trujillo.

José D. Chávez

BERNALILLO, NEW MEXICO

Dios puso al diablo en este mundo

Mis padres y abuelitos llegaron a ver estas cosas de brujas. Porque de que las hay, las hay. Toavía orita hay munchas. Hacen tantas cosas que venden su alma al Diablo. Por eso orita ya el diablo se aprovechó de todo el mundo. De un modo ya se aprovechó porque dijían los viejitos, "Acuérdecen que va a vinir una epidemia. Va vinir una epidemia muy mala y ésa va acabar con la gente del mundo." Y dije yo, "¿Pus qué epidemia?"

Ora que estoy viejo, lo estoy viendo. Yo que me pongo a ver y a pensar. Pus ahi está la epidemia con la marijuana, con el *cocaine,* con el *crack,* y con todo el garrero que están metiendo dondequiera. Pero mire, todas estas cosas vienen del diablo. Dios puso al Diablo en este mundo. Él lo puso no pa que nos castigue el diablo; no nos castiga el diablo. Es Dios el que nos castiga a nosotros.

Leonila "Linda" Galván de Chávez

CLAREMONT, CALIFORNIA

El diablo

Decían en mi pueblo que el diablo aparecía cuando quería asustar a los niños que hacían mal. En aquella época cuando yo era niña sí tenían miedo los niños. Ya ora no. Yo tenía amigas que decían, "Se nos apareció el diablo cuando éramos malas."

Yo estuve en un internado, que era como una escuela antigua, y dirigido por monjas. Decían ellas, "No pasen por ese corredor porque ahi anda una mujer que cruza el corredor por la noche." Pues, no era una mujer o El Diablo la que iba caminando por el corredor. ¡Era una monja!

Rolando Hinojosa Smith

AUSTIN, TEXAS

La muerte y la obediencia

Don Osbaldo Benjamín Coy, un labrador muy trabajador, estaba preocupado, y tenía todo el motivo para creerlo. Su esposa, doña Carmelina, estaba para dar a luz a su décimo hijo, pero no es que estuviera en ningún peligro. Ella era una mujerona joven saludable del campo, pero diez hijos, decía suspirando don Osbaldo Benjamín, ya era el colmo.

Él empezó a preocuparse cuando los gemelos, números seis y siete, nacieron repentinamente, como esos huracanes inesperados que se forman en el Valle del Río Grande del sur Texas como sin permiso. Pero dicho y hecho nacieron ellos como también los números ocho y nueve. ¡Pero diez! Y no, suspiró de nuevo; no es que el número diez fuera un número de mala suerte. Su preocupación le vino más del número de familia ya que contándose a él y a su esposa, llegaba a doce, y ese número le incomodaba porque se aproximaba al trece; y este número, como bien sabía, era un número de mala suerte.

¿Qué hacer? ¿Qué hacer?

Un vecino amigo, en realidad su compadre, le recomendó que rezara, pero le había dicho que directamente con Dios. "Ningún intermediario, de cualquier tipo, compadre. ¿Me entiende?" Don Osbaldo Benjamín había asentido que sí sin darse cuenta, pero al cruzar el campo de algodón, decidió que el rezo valía la pena.

Y Dios vino al Valle a ver a don Osbaldo Benjamín, y solamente a él, porque sólo él le había pedido a Dios que viniera.

Pero resultó siendo una reunión breve y desconsoladora: don Osbaldo Benjamín, que estaba con un dolor de muela el día que Dios vino a visitarlo, no estaba de buen humor.

Él discutió con el Señor. Le acusó de hacer poco caso de los pobres, viendo y favoreciendo solamente a los ricos.

Se dice que Dios se encogió de hombros y que desapareció en una neblina de luz celestial.

El Diablo, que, según los pecadores tanto como los santos, ni duerme ni descansa, esperó a don Osbaldo Benjamín. No es ningún secreto que los Vallecienses reclaman que hace más calor que en el infierno allí donde ellos viven, y tal vez sea verdad ya que el Diablo mismo estaba respaldado contra un jaboncillo mientras esperaba a que don Osbaldo Benjamín atravezara los campos de algodón.

Tras una bienvenida calurosa, el Diablo le ofreció sus servicios. Él esperó y esperó y por fin echó un soplido de "Pues, ¿qué me cuenta? ¿Usted necesita ayuda financiera o no?"

Las fuentes verdaderas comprueban que don Osbaldo Benjamín rechazó la oferta generosa del Diablo: las riquezas al décimo hijo que en cambio podría hacer lo que le diera la gana con el dinero. Lo único que quería, dijo el Diablo, era obediencia.

Don Osbaldo Benjamín pensó en esto por apenas un breve segundo. "No," fue la respuesta. "Tú mientes. Tú engañas. La verdad está dentro de ti porque nunca dejas que se escape."

El Diablo, no sabía perder como Dios, desprendió vapores e hizo que la temperatura del Valle subiera a 115 grados Fahrenheit mientras que él mismo desapareció en la presencia de aquel asombrado don Osbaldo Benjamín.

Pero el problema persistía. Su esposa, doña Carmelina con el número diez en los brazos, le trajo a don Osbaldo Benjamín un vaso de "limanada" fresca. Ella le preguntó que si con quién había estado hablando y le dijo. Luego le dijo que también había rechazado a Dios.

—¿Fue prudente eso?, le preguntó ella.

Por su parte, don Osbaldo Benjamín se encogió de hombros y dijo que el único igualador era la Muerte porque se lleva tanto al rico como al pobre.

Al mencionar la Muerte, doña Carmelina se persignó, rezó una oración en silencio, y se metió en la casa un tanto de prisa.

Don Osbaldo Benjamín hizo un cigarrillo, lo prendió, y tomó un trago de su limanada. "La muerte," pensó él. "La gran igualadora. Se las arreglarían ellos mismos," dijo para sí. "Siempre se las habían arreglado en el pasado. Pero era lo cercano del número trece que le molestaba."

Al colocar el vaso vacío en la tierra, una brisa fresquecita atravezó por los brazos tupidos del jaboncillo. Don Osbaldo Benjamín dio un vistazo hacia el cielo y miró fijamente el sol blanco y ardiente.

"¿Por qué una brisa fresquecita?" se preguntó. Luego se quitó el sombrero para limpiarse el sudor de la frente cuando la brisa se conmovió otra vez y se quedó él un poco callado. "En pleno verano y una brisa fresquecita," le maravillaba. Al voltearse hacia donde estaba su esposa que ahora estaba echándoles de comer a las gallinas, apareció una joven vestida de blanco, sonriéndose con él.

"¿Y de dónde vino ella?," se preguntó don Osbaldo Benjamín. Abrió la boca para decir algo como para disfrazar su sorpresa y se dio cuenta que tenía la boca seca.

Bella, se le ocurrió, era una palabra débil para describirla. Ella, la Muerte, de algún modo era algo especial. Ella se le acercó, se sonrió, y apuntó a un lugarcito sombreado en la tierra y lo invitó a que se sentara.

—Yo soy la Muerte—dijo ella—. ¿En qué puedo servirle?

Don Osbaldo Benjamín miró fijamente a la tierra y pensó, "Yo creo que me estoy volviendo loco. Y Carmelina, ¿por qué no puede ella ver a esta persona con quien estoy yo? Dios mío, me estoy volviendo loco."

La Muerte se sonrió y le aseguró que no, que él estaba bien sano.

—¿Usted—palabra que se le escapó—, usted puede adivinar los pensamientos de una persona?

Ella movió la cabeza y dijo,

—Sí. Es pan comido.

Se sentaron en silencio por un momento y la Muerte volvió a hablar: "Yo seré el guardián del número diez. La única cosa que quiero es obediencia, pero también es lo que el Diablo quería y lo que Dios demandaba. ¿No es cierto?"

La brisa fresquecita retornó por un breve momento y flotó por el jaboncillo.

—Sí—respondió don Osbaldo Benjamín un poco confuso—. ¿Pero qué es lo que quiere de mí, de nosotros, de él?

—Obediencia.

—Pero, pero, usted es la Muerte. Usted nos lo va a quitar.

Movió la cabeza, sonrió otra vez, y dijo,

—Claro que sí. Yo vengo por todos, por usted, por doña Carmelina.

—Pero él es apenas un bebé, nuestro bebé.

La Muerte entonces prometió que no se llevaría al número diez hasta que ya no vivieran sus padres. Luego preguntó que si eso era justo.

Don Osbaldo Benjamín miró a donde estaba Carmelina que acababa de echarles de comer a las gallinas. Trató de levantar un brazo para llamarla, pero vio que no se podía mover. Con la excepción de la respiración, todo lo demás en su cuerpo estaba paralizado.

—¿Tenemos un contrato?—preguntó La Muerte.

—¿Y a mi hijo no le faltará nada? ¿Y a mi familia?

—Más riquezas de las que se pueda imaginar. Pero con una condición. El Número Diez jamás podrá caminar en la lluvia. Él es un niño mágico, lleno de electricidad. No se le olvide.

Los años se fueron pasando y uno por uno fueron falleciendo los miembros de la familia Coy. Primero, doña Carmelina, y luego los gemelos, y después los demás, y finalmente don Osbaldo Benjamín hasta llegar al número diez, cuyo nombre ahora era Juan José, el único que quedaba vivo.

Un día de otoño, cuando el azahar del Valle producía su aroma más dulce, Juan José, ahora con cincuenta años de edad, y más sano que una manzana, se resbaló y cayó cerca del mismo sitio sombreado donde La Muerte y don Osbaldo Benjamín se habían conocido hace medio siglo.

Gruñiendo un poco y batallando para levantarse, Juan José vio a una joven muy bonita, vestida de blanco, que se sonreía con él.

"Yo soy rico," dijo él, "tal vez un poco gordo, pero más sano que una manzana, y con una casa muy bonita. También he tenido una buena vida, soy soltero, y me supongo que ya es hora de que yo me case."

Antes de pudiera hablar él vino la Muerte y le dijo,

—Por supuesto que me caso contigo.

Aturdido por su propuesta, se quedó parado él cerca del árbol y contemporizó. "Se está poniendo un poco nublado, pero es otoño en el Valle, y eso se espera."

Entonces la Muerte miró hacia el cielo y vio unas nubes amenazantes que se venían acercando desde el Golfo de México. Apretó los labios y le dijo,

—Métete dentro. No quieres mojarte, ¿verdad?

—¿Y por qué? Durante toda mi vida no he podido caminar en la lluvia, chapotear en los charcos, correr por los campos de algodón o levantar los brazos hacia el cielo. Vamos a quedarnos aquí, tú y yo.

La Muerte movió la cabeza, se puso la mano izquierda y delicada en la cara y cuando se la quitó, aquella cara de perfecta belleza había sido sustituída por una calavera.

A Juan José le dio asco esto y se fue a casa, corriendo lo más rápido que pudo.

—Ya es muy tarde—le advirtió la Muerte—. Tú me desobediste. Detente.

Sin poderse mover, Juan José dio una mirada al fantasma.

Con un pequeño gesto de sus dedos huesudos, la casa desapareció en una nube de humo. Con otro pequeño gesto, desapareció el árbol, dejando a Juan José a la misericordia de la lluvia que ya venía.

—Tú eres la Muerte, y yo me escaparé de ti. Por primera vez, alguien le ganará a la Muerte. Sí.

Con una cara triste, la Muerte dio muestras de desaprobación, y su mano izquierda lo llamó y apuntó al lugar donde estaba la casa.

Allí, cerca de la puerta delantera estaba don Osbaldo Benjamín. Más fuerte que un roble, y bien vivo. También estaba furioso.

Él preguntó,

—¿Tú desobediste a la Muerte?

Juan José mintió y dijo que no.

Aun triste, la Muerte se acercó a don Osbaldo Benjamín y le dijo,

—Fue una mala inversión, ¿verdad?

Aun con tono provocativo, Juan José se fue a donde estaba su padre y le preguntó,

—¿Qué no te traté bien yo? ¿Qué no gané dinero para toda la familia? Pues, cuando yo nací éramos más pobres que unas ratas y dos veces más miserables. ¿Y qué haces ahora? Debes estar muerto. ¿Y qué pasó con la casa?

Con esto se volteó a ver a la Muerte que, aunque parezca extraño o no, se quedó sorprendido con el temperamento de Juan José.

Aplacándose un tanto, la Muerte volvió a levantar la mano izquierda, y la casa reapareció. En perfectas condiciones.

Le vino una sonrisa grande a Juan José. "Yo siempre gano, y ahora no me quiero mojar. ¡Ha!"

Su padre se acercó a la Muerte y preguntó,

—¿Qué vamos hacer?

—Nada—dijo la Muerte—. Pero ojo con la casa.

Con esto, Juan José entró en la casa antes de que cayeran las primeras gotas de agua. La tormenta, un chubasco, como dicen en el Valle, pasó bien rápido. Tan pronto como dejó de llover, Juan José salió para fuera, vio que su padre había desaparecido y que la Muerte estaba recogiendo unas ropas de la tierra.

—Pues, esa ropa se parece a la ropa que yo llevaba hace un momento.

—Ya no las vas a necesitar—dijo la Muerte—. Mira nomás, en cueros como el día que tú naciste.

Lo que sucedió después tal vez sea demasiado de relatar o contemplar, pero no hay cuento en el Valle que no tenga fin.

Juan José empezó a menguarse, haciéndose cada vez más chiquito y chiquito, hasta llegar a ser una vez más una criatura en los brazos de su madre.

De buenas a primeras apareció don Osbaldo Benjamín como también lo hicieron los otros nueve hijos. La casa, ahora más pequeña, y bastante humilde, estaba donde había estado antes.

El día estaba claro, y el sol bochornoso por encima de todos ellos. El pavimento, los campos de algodón, todo temblaba con el calor ardiente.

La Muerte volvió a aparecer, y esta vez doña Carmelina la vio junto con sus hijos. El niño, número diez, empezó a llorar, a armar un ruido, pero pronto se apaciguó con la melodía de su madre.

Bella como siempre, la Muerte sonrió por última vez y dijo, "A lo mejor fuera un sueño, ¿verdad? Por el momento, diré esto: todos nosotros estamos muertos, inclusive yo, claro, pero ustedes, todos ustedes, todavía les quedan sus vidas. Aprovéchenlas, pero entiendan esto, a dondequiera que vayan, no importa donde estén, allí estaré yo. Esperando."

La gente del Valle no cree en ese tipo de historias, pero sí las cuentan y las repiten de vez en cuando porque la Muerte, como una buena madre, nunca está lejos.

Y es por eso, quizás, que la Muerte, es femenina en esta cultura.

María A. Mongalo
RIVERSIDE, CALIFORNIA

La Nahua

Decían que era el diablo, y que cuando se veía en los caminos, en las calles del pueblo, corría la gente. Se acostaban temprano. No había TV. Tal vez en aquellos tiempos, en el silencio de la noche, se oían más ruidos.

Y se oía la carreta nahua. La carreta nahua era la carreta sola. No había ni quién oyera, pues no había animales llevándola, y se oía que iba rápido corriendo así en la calle. En ese tiempo la gente le tenía miedo al diablo y no se atrevía a asomarse. Tenían miedo. Eso era para espantar a los niños. ¡Yo creo que hasta los grandes se espantaban también! Ahora es el diablo que nos tiene miedo a nosotros.

Por eso le digo que los niños se crecían más buenos y con más respeto, y hasta los adultos. Había muchas creencias. Un niño no era capaz de contestarle mal a un papá o a una mamá o a un tío o a un abuelito porque el diablo te iba a venir a castigar. O si te iban a pegar y corrías, se abría la tierra y te tragaba. Entonces había mucho temor. Ora no hay nada como eso.

Luis Esteban Reyes
UPLAND, CALIFORNIA

Un cazador llanero

Un cazador llanero se la pasaba cazando. Era muy fachoso. Siempre iba diciendo cosas como que, "A mí nunca me va a pasar nada. Yo soy el monarquía aquí. Voy a cazar chigüiros [animales del Llano], voy a cazar venados, o lo que sea."

Una vez se fue a cazar venado y vio al venado. Tiró cinco o seis disparos y no cayó. Se le vino de enfrente el venado. Lo cogió, lo levantó, y el tipo seguía apuñalándolo con el cuchillo y el venado nunca cayó.

Entonces el cazador ya no se acuerda de nada más, pero cuando se levantó dice la gente que él volvió con sus amigos y fueron a buscar el venado y nunca lo encontraron. Nunca hubiera sido posible de que el venado hubiera vivido sobretodo con los tiros que le pegó con el rifle y las puñaladas con el cuchillo.

Es como si fuera el mismo diablo que está allí pendiente, y aparece en ciertas épocas del año el venado en el espinadero [un lugar en el Llano].

Isabel Romero

LAS VEGAS, NEW MEXICO

Se golvió el coyote diablo

Había un hombre. Era soltero, viejo ya. Carlos López se llamaba. Era coyote él. Era mitá francés. Vivía en un rancho, solo. Pues su mamá dél estaa con él pero ya muy viejita. Y se iba al baile él. Aá se quedaba la viejita. Lego cuando iba al baile a caballo vido un coyote y le rompió. Ya escureciendo, y le rompió en el caballo con el cabresto. Cruzó el *highway*, y había una piedra muy grande. Cuando cruzó el camino, ahi estaba el coyote arriba la piedra [risas], hecho el diablo.

Cuando llegó a la piedra, que brincó a la piedra, vido que era un animal negro. Echaba lumbre por los ojos. Era negro con la cola muy larga. Estaba en piedra y tenía cuernos. Se golvió el coyote diablo. Pues ya no golvió ir al baile Carlos López.

Echaba lumbre por los ojos

Yo estaa mediano pero oía que había una gente, el hombre y la mujer, que peliaban muncho. Tonteras, celos. Y cerca había una laderita y un banquito. Había munchos peñascos allí, y cuando salió la mujer de su casa vido que era un animal que había salido. Qu'era negro. Y loo que se volvió. Isque ea llamó otra mujer, que juera con ea a ver que había visto una cosa muy fea. Fue a ver [la mujer]. Qu'era negro, prieto, con la cola muy larga, y que echaba lumbre por los ojos. Por la boca. [Risas]

Pos ora vas a ver. Cuando andaa [risas] echando lumbre por los ojos, por la boca, era un animal muy largo, con cola larga, y las pezuñas, eh, como muy patón.

Pos la mujer se desmayó del rebato. Se desmayó. Que dicía el hombre [el esposo],

—¿Pus la Juanita qué hará, qué hará que no, que no entra?

Pues se desmayó la mujer. [Risas] Se desmayó. La jalló desmayada allá.

—¿Pues qué te pasa?

Al fin jue, enpezó echale agua en la cabeza, hasta que la recordó.

—Pus, ¿qué estás haciendo aquí?

Ahi le contó ea lo que había visto. Jue tal remedio que no más golvieron a peliar. Era el espíritu malo.

Victoria J. Sánchez

OCEANSIDE, CALIFORNIA

Tenía el cuerpo bien helado

Éste es un cuentecito que yo oí durante los años 1950 en East Los Angeles. El cuento es algo así: un muchacho joven fue a una fiesta y allí conoció a una muchacha muy bonita vestida en un traje largo y blanco. Se pasaron el tiempo juntos y bailaron toda la tarde y hasta parte de la noche. Mientras andaban bailando, él se dio cuenta que ella tenía el cuerpo bien helado.

Después de la fiesta, le pidió que si la podía acompañar a su casa. Se fueron andando a su casa donde él se despidió de ella a la puerta de su domicilio. Un buen rato después, regresó él a la casa donde la había dejado porque quería ver una vez más a la muchacha hermosa vestida de blanco. Un hombre reclamando que era su tío vino a la puerta y le dijo que la muchacha por quien preguntaba había fallecido varios años atrás. El tío le dijo que ella estaba sepultada en el Cementerio Calvario en East Los Angeles, pero que no le diera el nombre de la muchacha a nadie.

Entonces el muchacho se fue al cementerio donde halló su lápida con la fecha de fallecimiento.

Andrés Sánchez Rojas

PHOENIX, ARIZONA

Alguien gritó a lo lejos

Me acuerdo una vez estábamos yo y mi familia en un desmonte. La gente iba a los cerros allá y usaba esas partes de los cerros para sembrar maíz. Ya estaba el maíz listo y lo estábamos guardando porque los animales se lo comen, como el jabalí, el mapache. Iban y se comían el maíz cuando estaba jiloteando.

El papá de mi cuñado tiene una voz muy clara para alzar su grito. Se oye lejos, pues es una persona que grita muy clarito. Una mañana cuando ya nos íbamos a ir para la casa de los cerros, él oyó que alguien gritó a lo lejos. Por allá como en una falda se oyó. Entonces le contestó él. Volvió a oír el grito, pero esta vez lo oyó más cortito y le volvió a contestar el próximo grito. Sin darse cuenta lo tenía (el grito) en los pies, y dicen que si él hubiera contestado el grito esta última vez, posiblemente lo hubiera levantado en el aire, porque el que estaba contestando era el diablo.

No se le miraba su cara

Fuimos de cacería yo y Pedro, y ya eran como las tres de la mañana. Me dijo él, "No vamos hallar nada. Vámonos." Entonces bajamos por un lugar que se llama El Tanque de Mendoza. A éste va mucha gente allí porque es un lugar donde se bañan. Prácticamente en la noche cualquier lugar por muy bonito que sea en el día, en la noche se ve diferente. Es algo *muy* diferente.

Bajamos y ya estábamos en la carretera pavimentada donde hace un vado para que l'agua pueda pasar. Pedro me acordó que de ese lugar acarrean agua para el pueblo. Cuando ya bajamos al vado él comenzó a tomar agua. Entonces me dio sé a mí y comenzamos a tomar agua juntos. De repente sobre la carretera venía una persona en un caballo, y me dice Pedro, "¡Mira! ¿Quién será?" "No sé," le dije, "pero va pallá donde vamos nosotros." "Orita déjalo que se arrime y le voy a preguntar quién es."

Nosotros íbamos rumbo al Camalote, y esta persona venía de un pueblo que se llama Los María. Pero antes de que llegara a donde estábamos nosotros, el caballo tenía que pasar por el vado, pero no pasó por el vado sino que continuó derecho rumbo entre las piedras. El amigo ese brillaba mucho. Nomás nos quedamos viéndolo. Como le digo, él no pasó por el vado. Él continuó derecho, sobre donde caía l'agua. Nomás se oía el ruido de las espuelas del hombre de a caballo. Nos quedamos viendo así y no hallábamos qué hacer, si correr, porque le digo, en realidá no sabíamos qué era. Lo miramos donde venía. No se le miraba su cara. No se le miraba nada, nada más de negro, y su ropa brillaba cuando la luna le pegaba porque ese lugar es muy sombrío y tiene muchos árboles. En ratos con la sombra de los árboles le pegaba la luna y él brillaba. Cuando ya se acercó bastante a nosotros, se le oía como una campanita así como el sonido de la campana de una escuela. Pronto desapreció. No supimos qué era. Yo creo que era el diablo.

José Sánchez Rojas

PHOENIX, ARIZONA

Gabriel le habló al diablo

Gabriel García tenía veinte años, y yo más chico, como de doce años. Él es mi primo. Resulta que a él le mataron a su papá, que viene siendo hermano de mi mamá. Un tío mató al papá de Gabriel García, que se llamaba José García, y Gabriel, chamaco, quedó solo, sin papá, porque poco después se murió su mamá también. Gabriel le habló al diablo y le dijo que le daba el alma pero que lo tenía que vengar a su papá. Así empieza la historia de Gabriel García.

Él estaba solo, no casado. Después se casó con su esposa, y luego un día le salió el diablo y le dijo, "¿Qué pasó? ¿Qué no te dije que no deberías entrar a la iglesia?" Gabriel dice, "No, que no tenemos ningún compromiso," y agarró la cabecita que traiba Gabriel allí—estaba él en un monte de árboles y siembra—y le dio una buena patada. Pues para donde cayó, no estaba muy lejos.

Ya se vino Gabriel con una canasta a la espalda con los machetitos, llegando ya a donde estaba una parentela junto al río. Lo alcanza el diablo y le dice, "¿Qué pasó? Ésa es la vida real, porque yo vi los machetes." Gabriel se enojó y agarró al diablo a machetazos. Resulta que el diablo le agarraba el machete al pie de la cacha. Él no estaba peleando con nada, solamente con las uñas. Le quitó los dos machetes a Gabriel y lo encajó arriba de un árbol, pero alto, y va Gabriel y agarra su costalito de tabaco y encontró la cabecita del diablo.

Él la había tirado al monte y resultó allí otra vez. Pues, murió su señora y él terminó andando para arriba y para abajo. Se quedó con sus hijas, pero como ya no tenía a su señora se quedaba en el campo.

Un día lo quisieron matar a Gabriel García. Estaba él en una raíz de parota acostado por la cabecera y le dieron una patada y lo sacaron. Allí eso es un camino real donde pasa mucha gente.

Lo quisieron matar en Chiquilistlán, donde hubo una matazón de cuarto personas. Traiba un machetito por aquí en la cintura Gabriel y se agarraron a balazos. Andaban dos cuñados de Gabriel y un compadre con él. Entonces le dieron balazos a Gabriel y él le dio machetazos en la frente a esta persona. Y le dio una patada para que se le saliera, que se le saliera el machete. Entonces el finado cayó. Pues el finado cayó y se murió. A Gabriel por todos los balazos que le dieron en el pecho, todavía iba caminando ya pa irse a casa. Balazos a cuerpo todo los tenía en la camisa acumulados, pero limpiecito de sangre. No tenía nada.

Ésa es una cosa que le cuento porque yo vide todo eso. Yo venía con mi tío Isabel de Solera, uno de los muertos, de Agua de Xiculetán, y mis dos cuñados. Lo vide yo. Yo estaba como de doce años entonces. Yo me fui avisarle a su familia de mi tío que lo habían matado. Eso es una vida real que yo vide y no me contaron.

Un caballo negro

En Chiquilistlán aparecía un caballo negro que pasaba por el medio del pueblo. Ahorita no sé, porque hace treinta años que no he regresado. El pueblo estaba posesiado por el diablo en todas esas rancherías. Todos le tenían miedo al diablo.

Yo lo he visto en forma de perro y un día le tiré unos balazos y ninguno le entró. El perro se fue. En dondequiera me salía el diablo. Un día se me vino en forma de un toro y le di con una carabina, pero no le pasó nada. Cuando me volví a casar la segunda vez, se desapareció el diablo.

Ophelia Ipolita María de Gracia Sandoval de Rinaldi

BERNALILLO, NEW MEXICO

Pasó en Las Cruces

Esto era una historia que mi mamá contaba. Esto pasó en Las Cruces. Aparentemente había esta familia que era muy mala. Era de México, y que una de las mujeres se volvió loca y loo tuvieron de llevarla a la cárcel. Otros miembros de la familias tamién ellos se volvieron locos. Los tenían ahi todos en la cárcel, pero antes de llevarlos a la cárcel, habían destruido todo—que habían tirado todo, y que quebraron los muebles, que habían hecho pozos en la pared.

Dicían que era el diablo que se les había aparecido y que por eso habían hecho todo ese daño. Pero los llevaron a la cárcel y ahi los tenían bien locos. Mi mamá dicía que gente iba a verlos, pero quizás los tenían ahi como *display*. Pero que estaban bien locos que hasta parecían changos y babosos todos. Quisque habían hecho algún mal. Eso fue una historia de mi mamá.

Ernesto Struck

PUEBLO, COLORADO

Le salía la cola por los talones

Unos músicos andaban tocando ondequiera. Una vez jueron pallá en Questa, que está al norte de Taos. Jueron a tocar. Como ya a medianoche, quizás, entró una muchacha muy bonita al baile. Dentro de la sala estaba un muchacho. Él era muy corriente, muy gente con todos, y se jue a sacala a bailar. Güeno. Se pasó el tiempo con él. Loo que ya la agarró él, la abrazó, y le vido ella por un lao la cola. Le salía la cola por los talones.

Él todo lo que sacó jue un rasguño aquí en la frente donde lo agarró ella y le metió las uñas. Y se dice que nunca se le borró el rasguño. ¡Nunca se le borró!

Era bruja quizás ella. Reclamó los nombres, como dicen, de antes. Pos ya. Se desapareció y se jue ella. Se hizo como una bola de lumbre.

Eileen Dolores Treviño Villarreal

SAN ANTONIO, TEXAS

El diablo con los pies de gallina

Hace muchos, muchos años, aquí en San Antonio, pero muchos años, se llevó a cabo un baile. Una muchacha, de aquí de San Antonio, la sacó a bailar un joven muy simpático, bien trajeado. Salieron a bailar y dicen que ocurrió esto en un lugar que ya no existe, en un club que se llamaba El Camaroncito. Creo que está al lado oeste de la ciudad.

La historia es de que ella andaba con un vestido descotado de la parte de atrás porque hacía calor. Ella estaba bailando con este joven simpático, baila y baila, cuando vio para abajo ella que ya había subido en el aire casi a medio del salón. Cuando vio que estaba subiendo gritó y le puso él la mano detrás de la espalda y la quemó. Cuando se cayó, toda la gente notó que él tenía los pies de gallina y desapareció. Estaba bailando con el diablo ella y por eso es que la quemó en el escote.

Adelina Valdez Chávez Baca

BERNALILLO (EL BOSQUE), NEW MEXICO

El diablo andaba suelto

Tú sabes cómo estaba allá en Guadalupe el *womanhood*. Te dijían que te vistieras decente. No salía una muchacha media en pelota pa la calle. No salía. Y no salíamos con pantalones. Dijían que el diablo estaba tentándonos. Que nos vistiéranos decentemente. Dijían, "Ahi andan provocando a los hombres." Teníanos que usar ropa alta, no como hora que salen [las muchachas] en *shorts* con el ombligo afuera y todo. Eso nosotras no podíanos hacer. Los *shorts* no se veían y pantalones no usaban las mujeres. Y teníanos que ir con los zapatos bien shainiaditos. Antonces no entrábanos a la iglesia sin poneros sombreros. Dijían que esque porque si hacíanos esas cosas [vestirse mal] en público estábanos provocando al diablo que andaba suelto.

Cruzita Vigil

LAS VEGAS, NEW MEXICO

Eso de diablos y de brujas es la misma

Aquí había cuentos cuando nos mudamos pacá pa Las Vegas. Eso de diablos y de brujas es la misma. Dicía un tío mío que él estaa trabajando con un compañero, y este compañero tenía una novia, poco lejos, ¿ve? Isque iba haber baile y le dijo él,

—Yo no jallo cómo ir al baile—el amigo este, a un tío mío.

—'Tonces—le dijo lotro hombre—yo te llevo al baile.

—¿Pero cómo? Pus si no tenemos naa en qué.

—No. Yo te llevo, si tú te atreves ir. Yo te llevo.

—Güeno, el cuento es ir a ver a mi novia.

Nomás se hizo escuro llegó el amigo y le dijo,

—Güeno, pus, ¿ya estás listo? ¡Súbete en mí! [Risas]

Lo llevó hasta la puerta de la sala. Loo, le dijo el hombre ese,

—Cuando ya te quieras ir, nomás me chiflas.

'Tuvo bailando con la novia y todo eso. Cuando ya él quería irse le chifló.

—¡Súbete en mí otra vez!

Lo llevó el hombre ese por onde antes estaban otra vez. [Risas] Dicía mi tío que sí lo llevó a su amigo y lo trujo. Taa curiosa la cosa.

seven

Enchanted Places and Buried Treasures

···

There's no evil deed worse than greed.

INTRODUCTION

In the preface I offered a synopsis of my maternal grandmother's grip-ping story about a man whose thirst for gold led him to an ill-fated ven-ture into prohibited territory and then into insanity. Many years later, when I was exposed to the classics in Spanish literature, I was struck with what Juan Ruiz (1283?–1351?), the Arcipresta de Hita, had to say about money in his classical work *El libro de buen amor* (*The Book of Good Love*). His scathing indictment of individuals with an avaricious appetite for money is brought to light when he says that money makes the mute talk and the lame walk.

Humans' propensity for coveting money has not changed over the past seven centuries, as we shall see in the ensuing stories. Francisco Argüelles, in "He Buried Large Amounts of Money," tells us about a man who amassed enormous wealth and then, because of his undying greed, pre-ferred to take his money with him to the grave.

While money tempts and in many cases corrupts people in diverse and peculiar ways, its allure is constant in at least one way; namely, the desire to "strike it rich" overnight and thus turn a dream into reality. The Spaniards' search for the Seven Cities of Gold or the treasures of El Dorado in New Mexico during the sixteenth century is no different than the search for treasure today, almost five centuries later, as people play the lottery or try their luck at local casinos, hoping to become instant millionaires.

I recall my paternal grandfather's passing in 1972 at age one hundred. He had moved to the Río Puerco Valley northwest of Albuquerque around 1880, where he homesteaded and lived practically all his life. Once word spread of his death, it did not take long for treasure hunters to ran-

Old wood stove, typical in Hispanic homes of New Mexico in the early twentieth century. Photo by Nasario García, 2001.

sack his ranch home, left locked but unoccupied. People evidently had heard of the lantern that would mysteriously light up in the kitchen in my grandfather's absence (see Preface) and interpreted this to signal that there was money in the crawl space beneath the wooden floor (*entarime*). The floors were ripped up and holes were dug throughout the kitchen, but the treasure seekers never found anything.

My father, who had a way with words, incorporated an old adage in his expressions of distress over the destruction the treasure seekers had caused: *Pa que veigan sinvergüenzas, "No todo lo que reluce es oro"* (Let that be a lesson to you scoundrels, "For all that glitters is not gold"). Such is the case in Eliel Germán Soriano's tale regarding the shadow that hovered near the site where treasure was presumed to be buried, though none was ever discovered.

Union Depot, romanesque revival style, 1889–1890, Pueblo, Colorado. Photo by Nasario García.

The antithesis of what occurred in Soriano's narrative and at my grandfather's home, where no caches of money were found, happened to Linda Chávez and her family in Mexico. In "The Cursed Chimney," she talks about lights that would come on by themselves in the kitchen, a mystery intensified by the appearance of a walking figure. After the grandmother died, treasure was discovered under the chimney (part of Southwestern Latino lore is that corner chimneys have been known to contain treasures underneath), and the curse that plagued the home for years suddenly lifted.

A story with a different slant that unfolds in Costa Rica is Rima Montoya's "Escazú's White Peak." The two unlikely characters are a Spanish gypsy and an Indian hermit from the New World. Both are single mothers with an abiding love for their sons, whose lives revolve around wealth and happiness. For one son, these are found in dreamland, El Encanto (The Enchantment); for the other, wealth lies in gambling dens. Both mothers and sons live in a land of enchantment, where dreams are born and legends are kept alive.

Both buried treasures and places of enchantment conjure up striking images that run the gamut from glittering pots of money to places that pique the imagination because of their air of mystery. The specter of finding gold nuggets, shiny silver coins, and jewelry in a country home where lights illumine an abandoned dwelling lulls people into dreams of riches that are never fulfilled.

Francisco Argüelles

OCEANSIDE, CALIFORNIA

He Buried Large Amounts of Money

When I was about ten years old, I took one of my first trips to Mexico with my family. We went to a home in San Luis Potosí. Before we got there, my mother told me that if we saw or heard anything, not to be scared. She said that she and her brothers and sisters grew up with unexplainable things going on, but my grandmother claimed that whoever was causing those noises at night had always been there and that they were harmless.

We would hear dishes rattling in the cupboards, faucets turning on and off by themselves, doors opening and closing, and footsteps and other noises. Because my mother had talked to me about the noises, I wasn't scared or freaked out.

My grandmother told my mother, aunts, and uncles that the man who owned the land where their houses were built was into the occult, and she thought he might be the one behind the noises.

The same man owned a great deal of land in that town, San Luis Potosí. He was a really wealthy man! He said that when he died he would rather be buried with his money than to let anyone have it. So he buried large amounts of money in some of the land that he owned.

Some people said that if someone dug up the money, that person would die. There were really poor people living on the land and they approached the new owners about digging it up if they could split the money.

The person who actually dug up the money *did* die days later. But the family that now owned the land became wealthy overnight. They went from a little shack to building a big home and a clothing and shoe store. To this day that home and the store are still there on the same street only a few buildings from where my mother grew up.

Samuel Córdova

ALBUQUERQUE (SAN JOSÉ), NEW MEXICO

An Enchanted Place

I believe you knew where I lived. My *primo* Teodoro García was the last owner of that property there in Guadalupe. And people used to talk about El Puertecito, which is south of Guadalupe, where La Mesita is located. People said that it was an enchanted place. They claimed that two goats would climb down from the top of that mesa in the morning to drink water in a small spring down below.

Well, one day my compadre Teófilo and I were herding the goats—we were little—and I said to him, "Let's go see if those goats are up there. There's a way up on the other side of the mesa."

We climbed up. There wasn't any sign of anything. We didn't see anything. And the goats were never seen again, either. I think it was all lies.

And that came from the old-timers. Liars! I think they were nothing more than lazy, shiftless loafers. And that's where they made up all of that stuff.

Leonila "Linda" Galván de Chávez

CLAREMONT, CALIFORNIA

The Cursed Chimney

My house—it was an old house, quite old in fact—had corridors and a patio in the center, and the rooms were all around the patio. In between the rooms and the patio, there was like a porch. Then at night ever since I had the power of reason, I didn't like to go to bed.

Oh my, was I afraid! The kitchen doors would be left open, and in the kitchen there was a huge fireplace that could be seen from what we called a living room. My grandma would have me knit so I could entertain myself, as there was nothing else to do. Then all of a sudden the kitchen would light up like lightning. It's as vivid as if it were today, and I said to my grandma, "Grandma, something was left on in the kitchen."

"Don't pay any attention to it," she'd say to me. "You're just seeing things. Start praying."

I started praying and suddenly I heard and saw a person in between the rooms, and my grandma muttering. "Quit bothering us. There's no such person. You're only imagining things that your friends tell you about."

"The woman in black. There it comes. Can't you hear it?" Then I'd go to bed.

We had a small dog. We called him Chiquito, meaning small. He would get scared and get under the blankets with me. And I would see the woman come close to the edge of the bed. "Listen, grandma. Here it [the woman] is close to me!" I thought I was the only one who had seen her, but my cousins had also seen her.

As time went on, one of my uncles told me that "thing" really did exist. It wasn't a ghost because several persons in the family saw her. It was one of my grandma's sisters, Isabel. I never found out what the mystery was, because the family never tried to find out what might be there.

According to the scuttlebutt, when grandma died the house was sold. When it was sold, the fireplace was torn down, and toward the back of the chimney they found an earthen jar full of gold coins. Word has it that grandma refused to say anything because she thought that there was a curse on the chimney and for that reason you weren't supposed to tamper with it.

After that experience, I was never again afraid of ghosts.

Rima Montoya

ALBUQUERQUE, NEW MEXICO

Escazú's White Peak

Around the same time that the gypsy Casilda Montoya found refuge in the mountains of Escazú, the story of María Zárate, who went to live amid the crevices of the Escazú peaks, was making the rounds throughout the provinces of Costa Rica. María Zárate arrived in Escazú around the year 1823. They say she was an Indian who lived alone with her son, whom she loved above all else. Her ambitious son wished only to be rich and asked his mother to help him obtain his desire.

One day, María "Ña" Zárate heard that in the foot hills of Pico Blanco, the highest peak of the Escazú range, there was a cave filled with gold, precious stones, and many other treasures. She found the cave that led to El Encanto, a dreamland where all the inhabitants lived happily for centuries, enjoying perfect health and riches of all kinds, but from which no one could leave for long lest they quickly grow old and die. Ña Zárate obtained gold for her son on the condition that she stay on to live in El Encanto and help its other inhabitants.

Her son became wealthy and powerful, while she was forced to live under the spell of death if ever she left the cave for long. But Ña Zárate visited the neighboring towns of Escazú and Santa Ana, bestowing good fortune on the people who befriended her. She was famed as a curandera, and people from far and wide came to her looking for healing.

The story of Ña Zárate is well known throughout Costa Rica, and some of the old campesinos have seen her wandering through the fields at the foot of Pico Blanco. Others even witnessed her approaching the cave opening that leads to El Encanto, but they turn away, well aware of the curse that overcomes anyone who takes any of its gold.

The story of Casilda Montoya, on the other hand, is familiar only to some of her family members, and even then much mystery remains about her origins. Sometime in the early 1800s, Casilda, a Spanish gypsy, landed on the shores of Costa Rica with the rest of her circus companions and settled in the grasslands known today as La Sábana, at the edge of San José. Some time after her arrival, she fell in love with the man who would father her son and with whom she ran away one night, leaving the circus in hopes of a better life. Soon after she became pregnant, her companion abandoned her and the unborn child. Casilda returned to the village of Escazú, where she went to live high in the mountains, close to Pico Blanco, around the same time that Ña Zárate and her son moved into the region. Casilda's son, Jesús, carried his mother's maiden name, and like the son of any gypsy, he made a good living in horse trading, not to mention from his skill at gambling. Nothing is known of Casilda's life after that except that she, a foreigner, stayed to live in the cool mountains of Escazú.

Perhaps some connection exists between these two single mothers in their struggle for survival and love for their sons. The town of Escazú is still a legendary place filled with mysterious events. While some campesinos claim that Ña Zárate still wanders the gardens of Pico Blanco, others, such as Francisco Montoya and his daughter, have seen a young woman of self-assured gait walking down the garden path of their 200-year-old adobe home in Escazú and disappear before their eyes at the front door. Could Casilda be revisiting family? Who knows? Are the young gypsy and the Indian woman one and the same? The mysteries of Escazú adorn the village walls, pass through the smoky homes of women making tortillas, and settle in the fields as men plow with oxen the lands of their ancestors. Yes, people, mysteriously drawn by these mysteries, still flock to Escazú.

Eliel Germán Soriano

POMONA, CALIFORNIA

A Shadow More Than Anything Else

Personal stories regarding the supernatural that one hears as a child always contain an element of uneasiness. People would always talk about dwarfs, treasures, vampires, extraordinary sorts of things. I didn't have grandparents, but my parents would tell me stories.

This personal story of my dad has to do with a ghost that really. . . . One day my dad went to a cultivated piece of land that was his principal responsibility. He was young and had a horse with him whose name was Bur. He was in a calm mood just like any other day when he went to visit the field; it looked like any common ordinary day.

But that day turned out to be really incredible. According to him, this is what happened. As he got there, it was already getting dark, and he says, "I'm going back to my village," when suddenly he noticed that there was a tree in the distance. And in that tree he could see something very dark, which was an illusion. You couldn't see what it was. A shadow more than anything else, and he got a little scared.

Then he said, "I wonder who it is? I'm going to find out for myself," and he came closer to that object, but scared witless, when suddenly he noticed that that shadow was also moving toward him. As it was, he got even more frightened because of what he saw. He saw the shadow flying above the ground. Because he didn't believe in any of that stuff, he said to himself, "It can't be a man."

Then he saw how that shadow was coming closer and closer and he felt even more fear, and he said, "I'm leaving. I can't take this anymore." He was about to leave, but he felt uneasy. "No, I'm going to see, because my parents told me once that whenever I saw something like this it meant a buried treasure."

Now curiosity about the treasure got hold of him. He said, "And it doesn't matter if it's something supernatural. I'm going. I'm willing to do whatever the shadow asks."

Interested in the treasure, he decided to go with that unknown ghost. Up until that moment he was scared, but he said, "I'm going. I'm going with the ghost." He was so afraid that even thinking of the decision made him tremble—and he was usually very indecisive. But it could mean money. The ghost stood still at a distance. So, it was a very scary moment. After standing for a moment he saw that the shadow was moving away. Dad says he thought the experience was a very supernatural one because he had never seen anything like it.

Then he saw the ghost moving away. It was like it came from those mountains, but they're small and known in my village as "small breasts." The idea, according to him, is that the ghosts like the one that came at him are born there. He regretted everything later, and that he didn't converse with the ghost. There really must have been a buried treasure, even though my dad didn't believe in that stuff.

Lugares encantados
y tesoros

··

No hay peor malicia, que la codicia.

Francisco Argüelles

OCEANSIDE, CALIFORNIA

Enterró grandes cantidades de dinero

Cuando yo tenía diez años, hice uno de mis primeros viajes a México con mi familia. Fuimos a una casa en San Luis Potosí. Antes de que llegáramos allí, mi mamá me dijo que si veíamos o escuchábamos cualquier cosa que no nos espantáramos. Dijo que ella y sus hermanos se habían criado con ruidos sin poder explicarse por qué ocurrían, pero mi abuelita reclamaba que la persona que venía provocando esos ruidos de noche siempre había estado allí y que no eran peligrosos.

Oíamos los trastes temblar en el trastero, los grifos que se abrían y cerraban, las puertas abriéndose y cerrándose, y pasos y otros ruidos. Siendo que mi mamá me había hablado de los ruidos, yo no tenía miedo ni estaba espantado.

Mi abuelita les dijo a mi mamá y a mis tíos y tías que el hombre que era dueño de la propiedad donde habían sido construídas sus casas estaba involucrado en lo oculto y ella creía que a lo mejor fuera él la causa de los ruidos.

El mismo hombre era dueño de muchas propiedades en ese pueblo, San Luis Potosí. Él era un ricachón. Él decía que cuando muriera que mejor que lo enterraran con su dinero que no dejárselo a otros. Así que él enterró grandes cantidades de dinero en varias partes de sus terrenos.

Algunas personas dijeron que si alguien desenterraba el dinero, esa persona moriría. Había algunas gentes retepobres que vivían en los terrenos y hablaron con los nuevos propietarios tocante al dinero con tal que pudieran dividirlo si lo hallaban.

La persona que en realidad desenterró el dinero *sí* murió unos días después. Pero la familia que ahora era dueña de los terrenos se hicieron ricos de un día para otro. Se mudaron de una choza a un caserón que se construyeron además de haber edificado una tienda de ropa y de zapatos. Hasta la fecha esa casa y la tienda todavía están en la misma calle a unos cuantos edificios de donde se crió mi mamá.

Samuel Córdova

ALBUQUERQUE (SAN JOSÉ), NEW MEXICO

Un lugar encantado

Yo pienso que tú conocites onde yo viví. En primo Teodoro García jue el último dueño d' ese lugar ahi en Gualupe. Y platicaban que pacá bajo onde está la Mesita que le dicen, del Puertecito. Decían que estaba un lugar encantado. Decían que venían dos cabras de arriba d' esa mesa en la mañana, a beber agua en un ojito que está ahi abajo.

Pues un día andábanos con las cabras yo y mi compadre Teófilo. Estábanos chamacos, y le dije,

—Amos a ver si están esas cabras aá arriba. Por aá aquel lao de la mesa hay subida.

Subimos. No había seña ninguna de nada. No vimos nada. Y nunca se volvieron a ver las cabras tampoco. Pienso que eran mentiras.

Y eso venían de los hombres antiguos. ¡Embusteros! Yo pienso que eran resolaneros, borregueros. Y ahi componían todo eso.

Leonila "Linda" Galván de Chávez

CLAREMONT, CALIFORNIA

Maldecida la chiminea

Mi casa—era una casa vieja, bastante vieja—tenía los corredores y un patio en el medio, y los cuartos quedaban alrededor del patio. Entre los cuartos y el patio, había una especie de porche. Entonces en la noche desde que yo tenía uso de razón, no me gustaba acostarme.

¡Ay, tenía miedo! En la cocina dejaban las puertas abiertas, y en la cocina había una chiminea enorme que se revisaba desde lo que llamábamos "la sala." Mi abuelita me ponía a tejer para entretenerme, pues no había más que hacer. Entonces de repente se iluminaba la cocina como un relámpago. Lo tengo tan al presente como si fuera hoy, y le dije a mi abuelita, "Abuelita, algo quedó prendido en la cocina." "No hagas caso," me decía. "Estás viendo visiones. Ponte a rezar." Me puse a rezar y de repente oyí y vide una persona entre los cuartos, y mi abuelita conque, "No estés molestando. No hay tal persona. Tú estás viendo imágenes que te dicen los muchachos." "La mujer de negro. Allí viene. ¿Qué no la oyes?" Y me acostaba.

Teníamos un perrito chiquito. Le llamábamos el Chiquito. Él se asustaba y se metía abajo de las cobijas conmigo. Y vía yo que la mujer se arrimaba hasta la orilla de mi cama. "Oye, abuelita. Aquí está [la mujer] junto a mí!" Yo creía que yo era la única que la había visto pero, pero también los primos la habían visto.

Después cuando pasó el tiempo, uno de mis tíos me dijo que esa "cosa" en realidad sí existía. No era un fantasma porque varias personas de la familia la vieron. Era una hermana de mi abuela, Isabel. Nunca supe qué misterio había, porque la familia nunca tocó lo que había allí.

Según dicen, cuando murió mi abuelita vendieron la casa. Cuando la vendieron, destruyeron la chiminea, y en el fondo de la chiminea encontraron una vasija llena de monedas de oro. Dicen que la abuela nunca quiso decir nada porque pensó que estaba maldecida la chiminea y por eso no se debía tocar.

Después de esa esperencia, se me quitó el miedo de fantasmas.

Rima Montoya

ALBUQUERQUE, NEW MEXICO

El Pico Blanco de Escazú

Por allá durante la misma época en que la gitana, Casilda Montoya, halló refugio en las montañas de Escazú, la historia de María Zárate, que decidió vivir entre las grietas de los cerros de Escazú, empezó a resonar a través de las provincias de Costa Rica. María Zárate puso pie en Escazú a eso del año 1823. Se dice que era una india que vivía sola con su hijo, a quien quería de todo corazón. Su hijo ambicioso quería ser rico y le pidió a su mamá que le ayudara a conseguir su deseo.

Un día Ña Zárate oyó que al pie de Pico Blanco, el pico más alto de la zona de Escazú, existía una cueva llena de oro, piedras preciosas y muchos otros tesoros. Ella encontró la cueva que iba a dar con El Encanto, un mundo de ensueños donde todos los habitantes vivían contentísimos por siglos y siglos, gozando de buena salud y de todo tipo de riquezas, pero de donde nadie podía escaparse por un largo tiempo por el temor de hacerse viejos pronto y fallecer. Ña Zárate consiguió oro para su hijo bajo la condición de que ella se quedara a vivir en El Encanto para ayudarles a los otros habitantes.

Su hijo se hizo rico y poderoso, mientras que ella fue obligada a vivir bajo la amenaza de muerte si algún día abandonara la cueva por un largo tiempo. Sin embargo, Ña Zárate sí visitaba los pueblos vecinos de Escazú y Santa Ana, ortorgándoles una buena fortuna a las gentes quienes se hicieron amigos de ella. Ella tenía fama como curandera y la gente por todos los alrededores venía a ella buscando una cura.

La historia de Ña Zárate se conoce bien por todas partes de Costa Rica, y algunos de los campesinos viejos la han visto recorriendo los campos al pie de Pico Blanco. Otros hasta observaron su caída sobre la entrada de la caverna que va a dar con El Encanto, pero son rechazados, bien conscientes del maleficio que le puede sobrevenir a cualquier persona que tome parte del oro.

Por otro lado, la historia de Casilda Montoya se conoce sólo entre algunos de sus gentes, pero aún persiste mucho misterio tocante a sus orígenes. Allá por los años de 1800, Casilda, una gitana española, desembarcó en la costa de Costa Rica con el resto de sus compañeros del circo y se establecieron en los prados en las orillas de San José que hoy día se conocen como La Sábana. Poco después de su llegada, se enamoró del hombre que llegaría a ser el padre de su hijo, y con quien se escapó una noche, abandonando el circo con la esperanza de una mejor vida. Resultó en cinta y poco después su compañero la abandonó a ella y a su hijo que estaba por nacer. Casilda regresó al pueblo de Escazú a donde se fue a vivir en las alturas de las montañas cerca de Pico Blanco más o menos durante la misma época en que Ña Zárate y su hijo se trasladaron a la región. El hijo de Casilda, Jesús, usaba el apellido de su madre y, como cualquier hijo de un gitano, se ganaba una buena vida vendiendo caballos, además de su habilidad en el juego. No se sabe nada de la vida de Casilda después de eso excepto que ella, una forastera, se quedó a vivir en las montañas refrescantes de Escazú.

Tal vez exista una conexión entre estas dos madres, su empeño por una mejor vida, y el amor para con sus hijos. El pueblo de Escazú todavía sigue siendo un lugar legendario repleto de acontecimientos misteriosos. Aunque algunos campesinos mantienen que Ña Zárate aún sigue recorriendo los jardines de Pico Blanco, otros, como por ejemplo Francisco Montoya y su hija, han visto a una muchacha joven con un paso bien seguro caminando por la senda del jardín en su casa de 200 años en Escazú hecha de adobe igual que viéndola desaparecer ante sus ojos en la puerta delantera de la casa. ¿Será que Casilda andará visitando a su familia de nuevo? ¿Quién sabe? ¿Será que la gitana y la india son la misma persona? Los misterios de Escazú adornan los muros del pueblo, penetran los hogares humeantes de las mujeres haciendo tortillas, y se acomodan en los campos donde los hombres van arando con los bueyes las tierras de sus antepasados. Sí, la gente, misteriosamente atraída por estos misterios, aún viene en tropel a Escazú.

Eliel Germán Soriano

POMONA, CALIFORNIA

Una sombra más que nada

Las historias personales de lo sobrenatural cuando uno es niño siempre tienen inquietudes. Siempre hablaba la gente de duendes, tesoros, vampiros, las cosas extraordinarias. Yo no tenía abuelos, pero mis padres me contaban historias.

Esta historia personal de mi papá se trata de un fantasma que realmente. . . . Un día mi papá fue a un campo de sembrarillo que era de él principal para ver. Él era joven y iba con una bestia que se llamaba Bur. Iba tranquilo como todos los días que iba a visitar al campo, y parecía un día común y corriente.

Pero resultó realmente increíble ese día porque dice que pasó esto—que llegando allí, ya estaba oscureciendo, y dice, "Ya me voy para mi pueblo," cuando que se dio cuenta que a lo lejos estaba un árbol, y en ese árbol podía mirar como una persona que solamente era la ilusión de que era muy negra. No podías ver qué era. Una sombra más que nada, y le entró un poco de miedo.

Entonces dijo, "¿Quién pueda ser? Yo me voy a sacar de esa inquietud," y se va acercándose hacia ese objeto, pero con mucho miedo, cuando él se dio cuenta que aquella sombra también venía hacia él. Él al darse cuenta de eso, pues se asombró más por lo que vio. Vio la sombra que volaba sobre la tierra, porque él no creía en nada de eso. Dijo, "Uno [hombre] no puede ser."

Entonces vio esa sombra como venía más y más hacia él y presintió aún más miedo y dijo, "Yo ya me voy. No puedo más." Ya se iba, pero se le vino otra vez la inquietud. "No, yo voy a ver, porque una vez mis padres me contaron que cuando vea eso, significa un tesoro. Ora me entró la inquietud del tesoro. Y no importa si sigue algo sobrenatural. Yo voy. Yo estoy disponible a lo que me pida."

Interesado por el tesoro, se decidió a ir con aquel fantasma que era desconocido. Hasta ese momento iba con miedo pero dijo, "Yo voy. Yo voy ir con él," pero del gran miedo como que le hizo hasta temblar—y era muy indeciso—y de la decisión que podía ser dinero. Se quedó parado allí distante aquel fantasma. Entonces fue un momento muy temoroso. Por aquel tesoro más que nada hubo mucho miedo, pero realmente después de estar parado un momento vio que se iba alejando esa sombra y realmente dice mi papá que le pareció una experiencia muy sobrenatural porque antes nunca había visto algo así.

Luego vido que se alejaba el fantasma. Era como de esas montañas, pero pequeñas y conocidas en mi pueblo como "tetenes." Según cree él, allí se crían los fantasmas como la que se dirigió hacia él. Arrepentido de todo, y porque no conversó con el fantasma, realmente era un tesoro, aunque mi papá no creía en eso.

Eight

The Powerful Evil Eye
....
*Pity the poor soul who comes to inflict the
evil eye on my dear son.*

INTRODUCTION

Belief in the evil eye (*mal [de] ojo*) reaches nearly all corners of the
world. It exists under different names and incorporates varying perspectives depending on the country, as is clear in Portugal, in the Basque
country in Spain, and in Latin America, especially Mexico. Because of
Mexico's proximity to the United States, the influence of the evil eye continues to be felt throughout the U.S. Southwest.

Latinos in the Southwest who have preserved the evil eye legacy—
above all in New Mexico, Colorado, and Texas—are a small though signif-
icant piece in a larger and more complex global puzzle in the annals of the
evil eye and the supernatural.

Over the years I have interviewed dozens of people, some of whom
were reluctant to discuss the *mal ojo,* shrugging it off as mere superstition,
while others were more forthcoming on the topic. For those who wished
to discuss their experiences with the evil eye, especially if they had been
directly affected, talking served as a kind of psychological cleansing.

This chapter provides a snapshot view of what the evil eye is, what it
means to the common folk, its inherent beliefs and implications, and how
it should be treated. The stories are also representative of the diversity that
exists in the Southwest. But lest we get ahead of ourselves, let us first
examine a few characteristics that may help us understand the nature and
consequences of the evil eye culture.

First, what do Latinos mean by the evil eye, and who or what is
affected? Part of what people say may depend on their own experiences
or the conception they have of the evil eye phenomenon. A common
belief is that the individual, or victim, most apt to be afflicted with the
evil eye is an infant or a small child, although an animal or a plant can

also be affected. Supposedly there are persons who possess the power to cast the evil eye but do so unknowingly, without any evil intent. In that sense one could argue that the terminology "evil eye" is somewhat of a misnomer.

A typical evil eye scenario follows. A child is born to a young couple in a small community. It is their first child and the first grandchild for the mother's parents, who customarily would reside nearby, perhaps next door to their daughter, or even in the same household. News of the newborn travels fast, and soon after the mother's traditional forty days of recuperation, relatives and friends come to offer congratulations to the parents and grandparents.

During the visitations women, not so much men, admire the baby excessively, pinching the baby's cheek, casting piercing looks into its eyes, or caressing it in various ways, all of which can have dire consequences for the child unless precautionary measures are taken. Oftentimes women will, of their own accord, wet their forefinger and make the sign of the cross on the baby's forehead, uttering a short prayer in the process. This act presumably prevents inflicting the child with the evil eye.

In other cases the grandmother would suggest half jokingly to her visiting comadres or friends something like, *"No le vaya hacer ojo a mi nieto(a). Escúpale la cara"* (Don't you dare cast the evil eye on my grandson/grand-daughter. Spit in his/her face). This ritual usually was done with water, holy water if available, followed by making the sign of the cross on the child's forehead using the forefinger and thumb to form a cross.

The *venado de ojo,* deer's eye, a legume seed, is commonly used in Mexico and parts of the Southwest to protect against the evil eye. My mother used a copper bracelet or a coral necklace with my baby sisters for the same purpose, a practice that goes back to Roman times.

Invoking religion was not only the most effective way to prevent the evil eye, but it was also required as part of treating its effects. If a child was plagued with nausea, high fever, discomfort (which some people attribute to constipation), and incessant crying following an encounter with visitors, the evil eye was suspected. If it was not known who had cast the evil eye, the child's family had two options. If the child was deemed seriously ill but not in danger of dying, a folk healer (*curandera*) in the community—one usually existed—was summoned. If, on the other hand, it was determined that death was imminent, then a Juan or Juana was sought immediately, before the next Friday elapsed. Otherwise, the child was doomed. In their hurry to ensure the baby's safety and chances for a full recovery, parents often bypassed the step of seeking out the folk healer and went directly to a Juan or Juana.

The names Juan or Juana were—and to an extent still are—considered magical in Latino communities. Others like Juan Bautista, Juan José, and Juan de Dios were also viewed as imbued with special powers. The role that a Juan or a Juana played varied little and was rather perfunctory. A good example appears in Juan Bautista Chacón's story, "A Very Sick Little Girl," in which water is transferred from the mouth of the Juan to the sick child. Other times it suffices for water to be spat on the child's face. In both cases, the sign of the cross is administered. Though this practice is simple, the results are remarkable because the child invariably is cured.

But under more normal circumstances—such as when an infant is moody and unwilling to nurse, for example—what function does the folk healer play and how much different is it from the role of a Juan? A folk healer is a general practitioner and a specialist rolled into one. She may be able to treat and cure numerous ailments, the evil eye among them, but the latter might well be her specialty. (Incidentally, folk healers in northern New Mexico and southern Colorado communities traditionally have been women, whereas in other places such as the Lower Río Grande Valley, men like Niño Fidencio are renowned.)

When called upon, the folk healer's first order of business is to inquire about the child's symptoms. If vomiting, crying, and discomfort are mentioned, she goes through a process of "examination and verification." The manner in which the diagnosis is made may vary from one folk healer to another, but generally one raw egg—sometimes two—is cracked and poured into a cup or saucer and placed underneath the head of the bed. If a human eye appears in the yolk (some say the white of the egg), it is solid proof that the child has been inflicted with the evil eye. Lucinda Atencio and Linda Chávez offer tangible evidence to that effect in their respective stories.

The techniques folk healers employ for lifting the evil eye may also differ. Some may be akin to the "Juan" approach of transmitting water to the child's mouth, at the same time invoking religion through prayer or applying the sign of the cross or both. The end result, regardless of the method used, is that the evil eye is lifted and the health of the child is restored. In Lucinda Atencio's "The Evil Eye," we see how a healer and a Juan, in separate but parallel roles, strive for the same goal: to cure the infant.

In other cases, as in Edumenio Lovato's two accounts, if the person suspected of inflicting the evil eye is known, a kind of courtesy call by the "inflictor" is all that is required to cure the child. And according to María Teresa Márquez from El Paso, pulling and snapping the skin over her spine cured her indigestion, which was attributed not to the evil eye, but to

Cleveland roller mill, built toward the end of the nineteeth century. Cleveland, New Mexico. Photo by Nasario García, 1989.

swallowing chewing gum. Indigestion could also be caused, as we were told in my own family, by drinking water and eating the inside of bread fresh from the oven (*del horno*).

María Teresa Márquez's story and those of the other informants come from New Mexico, Colorado, California, and Texas, this last state with a strong influence from Mexico, as witnessed in Eliseo "Cheo" Torres's personal account of his bout with the evil eye. Yet there is a commonality among the cases, both geographic and in substance, that links all narrators from all four states into a single coherent group and a unified purpose.

Lucinda Atencio

BERNALILLO, NEW MEXICO

Bring Me an Egg

These women brought a very sick child to me here once. And as soon as the mother walked in—she was a bit anemic—she told me that she had brought the child to see what the matter was with him, because he was very sick. I said to her, "The problem with this child is that it's constipated. He's suffering from the evil eye."

"How do you know?" she said to me.

"If you didn't know I was knowledgeable about these things, why did you bring the child to me?" I snapped at her because I got angry at how she said it.

"I didn't mean it that way."

"Look! I'll prove to you that this child's got the evil eye. Put him down on that table."

She did just that. He was very small. And the mother's even a relative of. . . . Then I said to her, "Prop him up with a pillow. Bring me an egg. Then crack it and separate the yolk from the white and put it in a saucer. Now put the saucer with the yolk at the head of the bed."

She went and did as I said. I was alone. Mela, my sister, had taken off. Right away the eye appeared. The eye appears when a child has the evil eye. The eye appeared on the egg yolk. Then I said to her, "Do you believe me now?"

"Yes," she answered. "I had never seen anything like this before."

"That's why one shouldn't doubt something unless you know what you're talking about. But take him so someone named John or Jane can spit on him. That will get rid of the evil eye. Take him and have him treated for constipation. He's constipated and suffering from fright."

So she took the little boy. He was treated and he recovered. They thought that everything I had said was mere happenstance. But a child, whenever it suffers from the evil eye, an eyelid droops. It does! That's how one knows who's got the evil eye, because they have a droopy eye.

Like me. I believe I've got the evil eye. I believe I do, too. Who knows who cast a spell on this droopy eye of mine! [Laughter]

Juan Bautista Chacón

PUEBLO, COLORADO

A Very Sick Little Girl

One time this little girl was very sick. She was a baby. I can't recall how many months old she could have been, and they took me over there with her people. The little girl's grandmother was a folk healer. This man took me over to her house. Then the woman, the little old lady, the folk healer, showed me what to do. The little girl was still small, and quite ill. They wrapped her up in a blanket and they told me to hold her in my arms.

Then I gave her water from my mouth to hers. When she was drinking water from my mouth, I sprinkled a little salt on her head. By the time I did that, that I gave her water and sprinkled salt, then I caressed her myself. I was told to walk her and rock her and the little girl fell asleep.

She didn't even feel the fever. When she fell asleep, they came and put her to bed. Next day she woke up well and sound.

Leonila "Linda" Galván de Chávez

CLAREMONT, CALIFORNIA

The Evil Eye

Well, it's a very curious thing because one day about a year after my baby was born he was very ill. Then the woman who was working for me at home, since she was the one who took care of my children, says to me, "That child's got the evil eye. He's got a horrible fever."

She was a little Indian woman and she insisted that the child had the evil eye. "No," I said to her. "How can he have the evil eye? What's all that stuff about the evil eye?" And she says to me, "You'll see."

Then she prepared whatever things she needed. The town doctor told me to let her do whatever she needed to do externally, and so she started. I brought her eggs just as she requested. She didn't call them *huevos*, she called them *blanquillos* [the former in Mexican jargon means testicles]. After I brought her the two eggs, she began to massage the little boy from head to toe in the shape of a cross.

The child fell asleep and she told me that he had the evil eye. She placed the cup with the eggs in it under the pillow. "In the morning you'll see how he's got the evil eye." Well, next day two eyes appeared in the eggs. I couldn't believe it. "Look," she said to me. "There's the two eyes of the person who inflicted the evil eye on your child!"

Celia López

SANTA FE, NEW MEXICO

"Glancing"

In my hometown of San Juan, Argentina, what is commonly called the evil eye we refer to it as "glancing." Not only do the folk healers cure the evil eye, but there are also other persons who do nothing else but cure glancing. In San Juan people believe that glancing comes about through evil doings of one or more persons inflicted on another (regardless of age, including babies) when the glancing is strongly fixed. That deed, for example, is not necessarily done on purpose if it involves a small child; it suffices for the child to be admired or loved with the whole attention fixed on him. It is common in San Juan to say when one takes a child to a party to be careful because he can be "glanced at," since many people will be looking at him. That is why, among other things, many parents pin a red ribbon to the baby's clothing because it is said that red drives the evil eye away. It is also common for people to hang a red ribbon on the rearview mirror of their cars as a helpful sign against evil that other people may be trying to inflict.

My mother, Celia Camporro, used to cure "glancing" and she became famous in the neighborhood among people who knew us. She never looked upon herself as a folk healer; rather, merely as a person who treated glancing and indigestion. In general those whom she treated more than anyone else were children, especially babies. The parents would bring babies to our house so she could cure them. At times they didn't bring the babies, but just by giving the name to my mother it sufficed for my mother to cure them. At times they only called her and gave her the name over the phone. It was very common that once my mother heard the name she would start yawning without stopping, which was an indication that the baby had been "glanced at." It was also common for adults to go to my mother for her to heal them from glancing. The symptoms people felt were a very strong headache. I remember that as an adult whenever I got a headache I would ask my mother to treat me for "glancing" and most of the time my headache would go away.

I believe the manner in which my mother treated glancing she learned from my grandmother, who was a Spaniard. The process consists of filling a deep plate with water, with a large spoonful of oil to one side. My mother would make the sign of the cross and begin with a very special prayer that she murmured (never aloud); in that prayer she would utter the name of the person she was treating. While she said the prayer, she would wet her thumb in the oil, and sprinkle it three times in the plate's water so that three drops of oil fell and they had to form a triangle because it represents the Holy Trinity. This process is repeated three times, tossing the water and replacing it each time with new water.

Based on what people believe, if the person was "glanced," the oil drops got larger upon falling in the water, some to the point of disappearing completely. If glancing became evident, then my mother would immediately begin yawning and wouldn't stop for several minutes. The yawning represents the escape of negative energy that provokes glancing. If the oil didn't mix with the water, it's because there was no glancing present. Of course we know that oil and water never mix—for me it was always a mystery how the oil drops could disintegrate in the water. I saw it happen many times. If the glancing happened to be very serious, my mother would then treat the person or baby for several consecutive days or several times a day.

According to traditional belief, when the glancing is very serious, it is recommended that three people conduct treatment at the same time without each one knowing that the others are also doing the treatment. The prayer that is recited during treatment can only be learned twice a year: on Good Friday and on Christmas Day (because they represent the death and birth of Jesus). To this day glancing is treated the same way in my family; one of my sisters does it and in this way the tradition that my mother learned from her ancestors is being maintained. She not only treats people for glancing, she also teaches other persons on designated days how to do it.

Edumenio "Ed" Lovato

ALBUQUERQUE (LOS GRIEGOS), NEW MEXICO

This Baby's Sick!

Another thing you also saw a lot of, over in San Luis, was the evil eye. I saw it. I saw it so many times I can hardly believe my eyes.

I had a little niece. JoAnn was her name. She was small. They left her there at home, and a cousin of mine, Fabiola was her name, who lived very close by, came over to visit. She started to play with my niece. My little niece was pretty. She now works in a bank. She was very pretty when she was small, and my cousin went to play with her. After she played with her, she then took off. She went home.

Well, as soon as my cousin Fabiola left, the little girl JoAnn started acting strange. I was there with her. Only my little sister Reina, Silvia, another cousin of mine, and I were there and, man, we couldn't hold her down, keep her in our arms. I tried to hold her tight, but she twisted and turned as if she had fallen. Crying! Suffering! And then we tried to give her something to eat. No such luck! Crying, with her eyes closed. Crying, twisting all around.

"Menio!" said Sylvia. "What are we going to do? This baby's sick!"

We had with us my other little sister Reina. I sent her to go after her cousin Fabe, Fabiola. I didn't think that it was the evil eye. I didn't believe too much in that sort of thing, but I was at a loss as to what to do.

"Go after her," I said. "Tell her I said to get over here."

She went and called her and brought her over. As soon as Fabiola walked in the door, she stared at the baby. She smiled. She stopped crying. Fabe picked her up in her arms and kissed her. She made a small sign of the cross on her forehead, and the baby fell asleep in her arms. She put her to bed, and she slept all afternoon. The baby slept all afternoon.

That's all the treatment she needed, but do you know that when she was being held before calling Fabiola, who had cast the evil eye on her or whatever it was, why, I couldn't hold JoAnn in my arms. Why, I would grab her and the baby would just slip from my arms. She would twist and turn every which way. She was in pain or whatever, and the worst part about it was that she couldn't talk. She was too little to talk, to say what was wrong with her.

Crying, Crying, Crying

One other time, something also happened to a nephew of mine. My sister who lived in Bernalillo went to see us over there in San Luis. There was a Mass. We went to Mass, and there in Mass, when we left the church, my sister was carrying the baby in her arms, and a sister-in-law of hers got close to her and looked at the baby, see? "Wow! What a beautiful baby!" So she says to her:, "Here, let me have him!" And she grabbed him and started playing with him.

The Mass being over, they climbed in the horse wagon, and everybody went home. My little sister came home, and no sooner had she walked in the door, that child started crying, crying, and crying. And no, the same thing! The same contortions that I saw in my niece I saw in this little baby boy. She just couldn't hold onto him! And my sister says to her husband, "Why, I don't know what's wrong with this child. Something's bothering him."

Then he says to her, "Look here. If you don't go after your sister. . . . Your sister has cast the evil eye on my son. Why don't you go get her?"

She went. Her sister was already at home. She brought her back. The same thing! As soon as she walked in the door, she hugged the baby, kissed it, and made a small sign of the cross on its forehead. Since she was nursing a child, she breast-fed the baby. He also fell asleep, he slept all day.

Twice I saw the evil eye. And I used to hear about the evil eye this, the evil eye that, but I never believed in it. I've never believed in witches and all of that stuff. Never! Nobody can possess that kind of power to dominate a person like that. I don't think so.

Manuel de Jesús Manzanares

PUEBLO, COLORADO

The Evil Eye

As far as the evil eye is concerned, the only thing I remember is what my mom used to tell me regarding my little brother who was a twin. I was a twin. We were twin brothers. My mom used to say that she believed that they had inflicted the evil eye on my little brother because these people had been at our house and they asked Dad why didn't he give one of us to them. My dad was already very ill at the time. Dad refused.

These people spent lots of time playing with the child, my little brother. After they left, my little brother became ill, vomiting, and with diarrhea. It hit him bad because he died soon thereafter. Mom believed that he died from the evil eye.

That's what I remember concerning the evil eye. But as for me personally, nothing, only what my mother told me with regard to my little brother—my little twin brother.

I heard tell that if you gave the child water with your mouth and put him in bed for a short while, that the evil eye would go away.

María Teresa Márquez

ALBUQUERQUE, NEW MEXICO

Indigestion

One day I woke up with severe stomach cramps that forced me to stay in bed. I was about ten years old. My mother called the local folk healer in the barrio to come see what was wrong with me and how I could be cured.

The folk healer asked my mother to undress me down to my chones, my long underwear. The folk healer then asked for lard and rubbed my very skinny body with it. I was nothing but skin and bones by then. The lard, which

275

came out of a large blue can, a brand popular with the neighborhood mothers, had a very strong smell.

The folk healer then had me turn on my stomach and proceeded to pull and snap my skin up and down my spine. It was especially painful when she pulled my skin behind my knees. She gave me a good jerk to remove *el empacho,* the indigestion, which she determined was my illness.

Despite my howls and cries of pain, the folk healer did not stop pulling my skin until she was sure that she had gotten rid of the indigestion.

She did admonish me not to chew or swallow any more gum or to go to bed with chewing gum in my mouth because that's what had caused my stomach problems. The next day I was fine.

Lugardita Anita Montoya
BERNALILLO, NEW MEXICO

He Died from the Evil Eye

I remember that if a small child was very attractive, that people liked very much, you had to make a tiny sign of the cross with saliva on its forehead so that the child would not get the spell, so that he did not get sick. If the parents thought that he had been inflicted with the evil eye, they took him to the person they thought had inflicted the evil eye. The person then had to get a swallow of water and transfer a little bit of it to the child's mouth.

I recall that my sister lost a very beautiful child. That beautiful child looked like a porcelain doll. He was beautiful! Well, one day she got up and found the child dead in the little high bed. I believe it was that syndrome, as it's called, child [Sudden Infant Death] syndrome. But the family claimed that he died from the evil eye. We never did find out.

Patricia Sánchez
VISTA, CALIFORNIA

The Story from Oaxaca

There was one time when I left my little boy all alone in bed sleeping at home in Oaxaca, and I went to church. When I returned my child was crying. He woke up crying over and over again and he wouldn't stop. I took him to the doctor and the doctor had him under his care for three days, and nothing doing. He just wouldn't get well. He practically died on me.

Then this woman stopped by and she said to me, "How come you have your child under the doctor's care? That's not a matter for the doctor. Take him away from the doctor. I'm going to get him well."

The woman massaged him and performed a cleansing with an egg and herbs and she cured my child. She saved him for me. That's all there is to my child's story.

Eddie Torres, Jr.
BERNALILLO (EL BOSQUE), NEW MEXICO

The Man Had Inflicted the Evil Eye

I don't say that it isn't true, but I don't believe that a person can cast the evil eye on another person, and many people my own age and younger don't believe it either. It's okay if you believe, but I don't think a person can give you the evil eye just by looking at you, just because I perform caressing gestures and then you get sick. Perhaps it's true.

My father had this man come from Albuquerque. He was a friend of my father's. I remember real, real well that the man had inflicted the evil eye on my youngest sister, the smallest one, and Dad went and called this gentleman and he came and spit on her [took water in his mouth and spit in her face]. I just don't know. They put something in their mouth and spit to remove the evil eye, and Dad says that as soon as that man did that, my little sister quit crying. I don't know about that, but I was just a kid. I've never seen anything like that myself.

Eliseo "Cheo" Torres

ALBUQUERQUE, NEW MEXICO

I Am Healed by Doña María

Whenever my mother felt that any illness we had was beyond her own curative abilities, she called upon Doña María, who was the expert traditional doctor of our neighborhood. Doña María had a cure for everything from headaches, diarrhea, and stomachaches to jealousies, anger, and rage, to hexes on husbands, wives, lovers, or enemies.

Once, when I was very young, I had a fever that was out of control. My mother's *mal de ojo* ritual and her herbal medicines did not seem to work. Therefore, Doña María was summoned to my house to administer her cures. First, of course, she wanted to diagnose the illness for herself.

I can recall Doña María asking my mother what she had done to treat my illness. My mother answered that she had given me the mal de ojo treatment—she gave me *manzanilla*, or chamomile [tea]. I remember that the manzanilla had a sweet odor but a bitter taste.

My mother explained to Doña María the mal de ojo treatment she had given me. I remembered that she had taken an egg and massaged my body from head to toe with that egg as the first step in the treatment. As I lay on my back my mother made the sign of the cross (or *crucitas*, little crosses) over every major joint in my body while reciting the Apostle's Creed three times. Afterwards, my mother broke the egg into a glass of water and placed the glass under the bed.

Doña María asked my mother to show her the glass. I could see that the egg white had risen to the surface, while the yolk had sunk to the bottom. Doña María, excited, told my mother that the white had become solid, and that the white was also oval-shaped and had assumed the shape of an eye. Doña María told us that "of course this means that Cheo is indeed suffering from a case of *ojo*."

Doña María then told my mother that she had followed all of the proper procedures, and that there was just one more thing to be done.

"I want you to take the egg outside and bury it in your backyard tomorrow morning, and be sure to dig [bury] it deep enough so that the dog doesn't dig it up," Doña María told my mother.

Then, after prescribing another medicinal herb that was stronger than manzanilla, Doña María left. My mother immediately summoned my aunts and directed them to find the herb called "borage" (or *borraja*). Within an hour one of my aunts brought some borraja to my house. My aunt explained that borraja was given to the Spanish by the Moors as *Abou-Rach,* "the father of sweat" (the name, of course, is in Arabic).

Abou-Rach indeed lived up to its name. Within minutes after I had taken a cup of borraja my body started sweating profusely and I began to cool off significantly. I also began to urinate, further purging my body of fluids, and I began to feel much better.

As I recovered, my mother explained that this borraja tea had been used by her own mother to keep the body cool as a summer drink, and that she also used it as a cure for the fever associated with measles. My grandmother would also give it to my grandfather to treat bladder infections.

The morning after I had taken borraja, I woke up with a hearty appetite—my first in days. I felt weak still, but much better. As I finished my breakfast (my favorite, *huevos rancheros*), I asked my mother to tell me more about mal de ojo. What was it? Why was I afflicted by it?

My mother explained that the mal de ojo ritual actually came from Spain to Mexico and that the Spaniards had borrowed this ritual from the Moors, who had been in Spain for several hundred years and introduced many of their traditions to the Spanish—who in turn, of course, brought them to Mexico. My mother reminded me that I was a beautiful baby, and suffered from several mal de ojo ailments, and that people would admire me and would not touch me, and therefore projected negative vibes into my body.

This, then, was the crux of the matter and the definition of mal de ojo: I had been *admired* by adults, who had quite unintentionally made me ill with their admiration. Somehow, it was imperative that after admiring a child for its beauty, an adult must also *touch* the child in order to avert the ill effects of mal de ojo.

Evil eye, then, is not quite what many people think that it is—an intentional projection of ill will toward another. Rather, it is an unintentional projection of negative vibes through quite another intention altogether—the person who causes it does not mean harm, but rather *admires* the person who comes to suffer from the ill effects of this person's regard.

"People do not *mean* to make you ill by admiring you, Cheo," my mother reassured me. "But by failing to touch you to neutralize the negative vibes from excessive admiration, they do make you ill, not realizing that they have subjected you to dangerous admiration."

My mother added that although I was twelve years old and no longer a baby, someone was still admiring me. She hadn't cured me, she said, but Doña María had been able to, by prescribing a more powerful herbal remedy, the borraja.

Eileen Dolores Treviño Villarreal

SAN ANTONIO, TEXAS

The White Part of the Egg Cooks

Mom was very much involved in those traditions of the evil eye. As soon as they heal you with an egg, they "sweep" you with the egg. They use the egg to cure the evil eye, but it has to be a fresh egg. Then they rub the egg over your body, they touch your entire body with the egg, then they make crosses and they keep saying prayers. They take a glass of water, and after they finish rubbing you with the egg, they crack it and put it inside the glass of water and place it underneath the bed, at the head of the bed, and by morning when the egg is cooked it indicates that you have been cured. The white part of the egg is what cooks; it goes from being clear to white. The water that is used is lukewarm.

It is said that the evil eye is cast by a person who has a lot of electricity in his eyesight. Then if you look at a baby boy or a baby girl and you say, "My, what beautiful eyes [hair, boy or girl]!" You have to go touch him, because if you don't touch him you don't fulfill that desire. People say that's where the evil eye comes from, from that person. If he touches him and removes the desire, the baby won't get sick. The same thing is true with objects, let's say, whatever kind, earrings, or whatever. If you don't touch them they'll break. There are powerful persons and others not so powerful. A powerful person is capable of casting the evil eye.

Adelina Valdez Chávez Baca

BERNALILLO (EL BOSQUE), NEW MEXICO

The Evil Eye

Well, there were times when a child was sick or had a stomachache, and people would say that someone had cast the evil eye on him. People would then look for a Juanita or a Juan to give the child water, spit on him [on his face] and to make the sign of the cross. And do you know that I saw many cases where the child got well? The fever would go away. I liked scientific discovery a lot, and I admired all that. I would say to myself, "How were a Juan and a Juanita able to cure the evil eye?"

I saw some kids who were burning up from a fever one minute and a short while later they were out playing. I don't know if it's like they say. Nowadays they contract a virus and get a high fever, or when they cut teeth, and then you give them an aspirin and the fever is gone. Well I don't know if it was the same thing or not. It's still a question in my mind.

I remember going with my sister to eat ice cream at the Hellers' house there in Cabezón. She was already a little grown up. I was little. When she got home she was so sick that they went to look for someone to spit on her face and she got well. I recall that situation in my home, but I don't know if the fever passed or not. I was too little to notice if Juanita was successful, because in the Guadalupe community there was a Juanita who spit on her and made the sign of the cross on her forehead. I say that she's the one who cured her. I don't have any reason to say that it isn't true.

El poderoso mal de ojo

Mal haya quien venga hacerle ojo a mi 'jito.

Lucinda Atencio

BERNALILLO, NEW MEXICO

Traeme un güevo

Me trujieron estas mujeres un muchito aquí muy malo. Y nomás entró la mamá—era media, media tísica—me dijo que había traido al muchito a ver qué tenía, que estaba muy malo. Le dije,

—Este muchito lo que tiene es que está empachao. Tiene ojo.

—¿Cómo sabe?—me dijo.

—Pus si no sabías que yo sé curar, ¿pa qué me lo trujites?—le dije porque me dio coraje con ella porque me dijo asina.

—No, dijo.

—¡Mira! Te pruebo que este muchito tiene ojo. Acuéstalo ahi en la mesa.

Lo acostó. Estaba medianito. Y ella es hasta parienta de la ... Loo le dije,

—Ponle una almuada. Trae un güevo. Lo partes y lo echas en un platito—y lo echó en un platito—. Se lo pones ahi en la cabecera.

Jue y hizo lo que yo le mandé. Estaba sola yo. Se había ido la Mela, mi hermana. Pues loo se pintó el ojo en la yema. Se pinta el ojo cuando tienen ojo. Se pintó en el güevo. Y le dije,

—¿Crees ora?

—Sí—dijo—. Yo no había visto nunca asina.

—Pus no pone uno duda cuando no sabe. Pero llévalo que lo escupa un Juan o una Juana. Con eso se le quita. Llévalo que lo curen por empacho. Está empachao y solevao.

Pus llevó al muchito. Lo curaron y sanó. Pensaron que era chanza lo que yo les había dicho, porque una criatura cuando tiene ojo, se la cae un ojo. Se le cae. Y ahi sabe uno los que tienen ojo, que tienen el ojo caido.

Como yo, yo creo que tengo ojo. Yo creo que yo también. ¡Quién sabe quién me haría ojo en este ojo! [Risas].

Juan Bautista Chacón

PUEBLO, COLORADO

Una muchita muy enferma

Una vez estaba una muchita muy enferma. Era *baby*. Ya yo no me acuerdo cuántos años podía tener, y me llevaron ahí con esta gente. La mamá de la mamá de la muchita era médica de mujeres. Me llevó este hombre allá pa la casa dél Logo la mujer, la viejita, esta médica, me dijo cómo hiciera. Estaba mediana la muchita tavía, y muy enfermita. La envolvieron en una manta y me dijieron que la 'garrara en brazos.

Logo le di agua por la boca mía. Cuando estaba bebiendo con la boca mía, le eché poquita sal en la cabeza. Ya cuando hice eso, que le di agua y l' eché sal, antonces la 'caricié yo mesmo. Me dijieron que la paseara y que la meneara y la muchita se quedó dormida. Ni sintió la calentura. Cuando ya se durmió, vinieron y la 'costaron. Otro día amaneció güena y sana.

Leonila "Linda" Galván de Chávez

CLAREMONT, CALIFORNIA

El mal de ojo

Pues era muy curioso porque un día como al año que nació mi niño estaba bien malito. Entonces la señora que trabajaba en mi casa, como ella era la que me cuidaba las criaturas, me dice, "Ese niño tiene mal de ojo. Tiene un calenturón terrible."

Era indita ella y me decía que el niño tenía mal de ojo. "No," le dije. "¿Cómo va tener mal de ojo? ¿Qué es eso de mal ojo?" Y me dice, "Pues vas a ver."

Entonces ella preparó esas cosas que tenía que preparar. El doctor del pueblo que teníamos ahi me dijo que la dejara que hiciera las cosas todo por fuera, y empezó ella con sus cosas. Le traje los huevos como ella me pidió. No les llamaba huevos; les llamaba blanquillos. Entonces que le traje dos huevos después de eso empezó a sobar al niño de pies a cabeza en forma de cruz.

El niño se quedó dormido y me dijo ella que el niño tenía mal de ojo. Le puso la tacita con el huevo debajo de la almuada. "Ya ves que en la mañana sabemos si tiene mal de ojo." Pues al día siguiente en los huevos aparecieron unos ojos. No lo podía creer yo. "¡Mira!" dijo. "Ahi están los ojos de la persona que le hizo el mal de ojo a tu niño."

Celia López

SANTA FE, NEW MEXICO

La "ojeadura"

En mi pueblo de San Juan en la Argentina al comúnmente llamado "mal de ojo" le llamamos "ojeadura." No sólo las curanderas curan el mal de ojo; también otras personas que no curan otras cosas sino sólo la "ojeadura." En San Juan existe la creencia de que la "ojeadura" es producto del mal hecho por una o varias personas a otra persona (de cualquier edad, incluso bebés) cuando se las mira muy fijamente. Ese mal no es necesariamente hecho a propósito si se trata de un niño pequeño, por ejemplo; basta que un bebé sea muy admirado o querido para que toda la atención esté puesta en él. Es común decir en San Juan cuando uno lleva un niño a una fiesta que hay que tener cuidado porque lo pueden "ojear," ya que mucha gente lo mirará. Por eso, entre otras cosas, muchos padres ponen a sus bebés una cinta roja prendida en la ropa porque se dice que ese color ahuyenta el mal de ojo. También es común que gente en sus coches cuelgue una cinta roja junto al espejo retrovisor del coche, como señal de ayuda contra el "mal" que otra gente quiera ocasionar.

Mi madre (Celia Camporro) curaba la "ojeadura" y se convirtió en una persona famosa en el barrio y entre la gente que nos conocía. Ella nunca se consideró a sí misma una curandera; sino simplemente una persona que curaba la "ojeadura" y el "empacho." En general a los que más curaba era a los niños, especialmente bebés. Los padres traían bebés a nuestra casa para que ella los curara. A veces no traían los bebés pero solo dándole el nombre a mi madre, era suficiente para que ella los curara. A veces sólo llamaban por teléfono a mi madre y le daban el nombre. Era muy común que en cuanto mi madre escuchaba el nombre ella comenzara a bostezar sin parar, lo cual era una señal de que el bebé estaba "ojeado." También era común que personas adultas fueran a mi mamá para que les curara la ojeadura. El síntoma que esta gente sentía era un dolor de cabeza muy fuerte. Yo recuerdo que, inclusive ya siendo adulta, cuando a mí me daban dolores de cabeza le pedía a mi mamá que me curara la "ojeadura" y la mayoría de las veces el dolor se me iba.

La forma de curar la ojeadura que mi madre tenía creo que la aprendió de mi abuela, quien era española. El procedimiento consiste en llenar un plato hondo de agua y tener al lado una cuchara grande llena de aceite. Mi

madre se persignaba y comenzaba una oración especial que decía murmurando (nunca en voz alta); en esa oración mencionaba el nombre de la persona que estaba curando. Mientras decía la oración mojaba su dedo pulgar
(o dedo gordo) en el aceite y lo salpicaba en el agua del plato tres veces
para que cayeran tres gotas de aceite; tenían que caer en forma de triángulo, porque este triángulo representa a la Santísima Trinidad.

Este procedimiento se hace tres veces tirando el agua del plato cada vez
y poniendo agua nueva. Según la creencia, si la persona estaba "ojeada" las
gotas de aceite al caer en el agua se agrandaban, algunas de ellas casi hasta
desaparecer. Si había ojeadura mi madre comenzaba a bostezar inmediatamente y no paraba por varios minutos. El bostezo viene a representar la
salida de la energía negativa que provoca la "ojeadura." Si las gotas no se
mezclaban con el aceite es que no había ojeadura. Por supuesto que sabemos que el agua y el aceite nunca se mezclan; para mí siempre fue un misterio el que las gotas desaparecieran en el agua. Yo lo ví muchas veces. Si la
ojeadura era muy grande, mi madre curaba a la persona o bebé varios días
seguidos o varias veces al día.

Según la creencia es recomendable que, si la ojeadura es muy grande,
haya tres personas que curen al mismo tiempo pero sin que cada una de
ellas sepa que las otras están curando. La oración que se dice durante la
curación sólo puede aprenderse durante dos días del año: el Viernes Santo
y el día de Navidad (porque representan la muerte y el nacimiento de
Jesús). Hoy todavía en mi familia se cura la "ojeadura" de esta manera; una
de mis hermanas lo hace y así está manteniendo la tradición que mi madre
aprendió de sus antepasados. Ella no sólo cura la "ojeadura" sino que también en los días señalados enseña a otras personas a hacerlo.

Edumenio "Ed" Lovato

ALBUQUERQUE (LOS GRIEGOS), NEW MEXICO

¡Esta criatura está mala!

Otra cosa que tamién se vía muncho aá en San Luis era ojo. Yo lo vi. Yo lo
vi tantas veces que no puedo creelo.

Yo tenía una sobrinita. Se llamaba JoAnn. Estaba mediana. La dejaron
aá en casa, y vino una prima mía, Fabiola era su nombre, que vivía cerquita
vino a visitar. Se puso a jugar con mi sobrina. Mi sobrinita era bonita. Trabaja en un banco ora. Ella era muy bonita cuando estaba chiquita, y jue a
jugar la prima con ella. Después de jugar con ella, se jue. Se jue pa su casa.

Pus, tan pronto como se jue mi prima Fabiola, esa chamaquita, JoAnn,
comenzó a portarse mal. Yo estaba ahi con ella. No estábanos más de yo,

mi hermanita Reina, y la Silvia, otra prima, y vas a ver tú, no la podíanos detener a la sobrina en los brazos, hombre. La quería tener así juerte en los brazos y se torcía y como que se había caido. ¡Llorando! ¡Sufriendo! Y loo le queríanos dar algo pa comer. ¡Nada! Llorando, con los ojos cerraos. Llorando, torciéndose.

—¡Menio!—dijo Silvia—. ¿Qué vamos hacer? Esta criatura está mala.

Teníanos a la otra hermanita, la Reina, con nosotros. La despaché a llamar a su prima, Fabe, Fabiola. Yo no creí de que era ojo. Yo no creiba muncho en eso, pero no sabía cómo hacer.

—¡Despáchala!—dije—. Llámala que la llamé.

Jue y la llamó y la trujo. Nomás entró en la puerta la prima Fabiola, y se quedó viéndola a la *baby*. ¡Se rió! Dejó de llorar. La agarró en brazos Fabe y la besó. Le hizó una crucita en la frente, y se quedó dormida en sus brazos. La acostó en la cama, y toa la tarde durmió. Toa la tarde durmió la *baby*.

No tuvo más cura, pero sabes que cuando estaba en los brazos antes de llamala a la que le había hecho el ojo [Fabiola], o lo que juera, pus nomás no podía detenela a JoAnn en los brazos. Si yo tamién la agarraba así y se me salía de los brazos. Se torcía pa ondequiera. Tenía dolor o lo que juera, y loo pus lo más malo es que no hablaba. Estaba muy mediana toavía pa hablar, pa dijir qué era lo que tenía.

Llore, y llore, y llore

En otra vez, algo pasó tamién con un sobrino mío. Mi hermana que vivía en Bernalillo jue pallá pa San Luis a vernos. Había misa. Juimos a misa, y aá en misa, cuando salimos, traiba mi hermanita su *baby* en sus brazos, y se arrimó una cuñada d' ella y lo vido, ¿ves? "¡Bah! ¡Qué niño tan lindo!" es que le dice. "¡Préstamelo pacá!" y lo agarró y se puso a jugar con él.

Se acabó la misa, se subieron en el carro, y todos se jueron pa sus casas. Mi hermanita se vino pa en casa, y no acabó de entrar que esa criatura estaba llore, y llore, y llore. Y no, ¡lo mesmo! Tamién los mesmos movimientos que en la sobrinita, vi en este muchito. ¡Nomás no lo podía detener! Y le dice ella a su esposo,

—Pus, no sé este muchichito qué tiene. Está sufriendo de algo.

Y luego dice él,

—Mira tú. Si no vas por tu hermana . . . tu hermana le hizo ojo a mi hijito. ¿Por qué no vas y la traes?

Ella jue. Ya su hermana estaba en casa. La trujo. ¡Tamién! Nomás entró, lo abrazó, lo besó, y le hizo una cruz. Como que ella estaba criando, le dio, le puso a *breast feed* al chamaco. Se quedó dormido tamién; too el día durmió.

Dos veces lo vi el mal ojo. Y yo oía que el ojo pacá, el ojo pallá, pero yo nunca creiba. Yo nunca ha [he] creido en brujos y too eso. ¡Nunca! Naide puede mandar ese poder pa dominar una persona así. Yo no creo.

Manuel de Jesús Manzanares

PUEBLO, COLORADO

El mal ojo

Tocante al mal ojo, l'único que me acuerdo era lo que me platicaba mi mamá de mi hermanito que era cuate. Yo era cuate. Éranos dos. Mi hermanito decía mamá que ella creiba que le habían hecho ojo porque había estao una gente y le habían dicho a en papá que si por qué no les daba a uno de nosotros. Mi papá estaba muy enfermo ya. Dijo en papá que no.

Esta gente estuvieron jugando muncho con el niño, mi hermanito. Después se jueron y se enfermó de gómitos y diarrea y le pegó malamente porque pronto murió. Decía mi mamá que creiba que de mal ojo había muerto.

Eso es lo que me acuerdo yo tocante a eso de hacer mal ojo. Pero yo referente a mí, nada, nada más que lo que me platicó mamá tocante a mi hermanito—mi cuatecito.

Oí platicar de que si le daban agua con la boca al niño y lo colocaban un rato en la cama, que se le quitaba el ojo.

María Teresa Márquez

ALBUQUERQUE, NEW MEXICO

El empacho

Un día amanecí con unos calambres bárbaros en el estómago que me hicieron que me quedara acostada en la cama. Yo tenía como diez años. Mi mamá llamó a la curandera del barrio para que viniera a ver qué tenía yo y para ver cómo me podía curar.

La curandera le pidió a mi mamá que me desvistiera y que me dejara puestos solamente mis "chones" [calzones]. La curandera entonces pidió manteca y me la untó por todo el cuerpo flaquito. Para ese entonces yo no era más que puros huesos. La manteca, que venía de un bote azul grande, cuya marca era popular con las mamás de la vecindad, tenía un olor muy fuerte.

La curandera entonces me dijo que me acostara boca abajo y me "jalaba" la piel por toda la espina dorsal. Me dolía particularmente cuando me jalaba la piel detrás de las rodillas. Me dio una buena sacudida para remudar el empacho, que es de lo que sufría, según ella.

A pesar de mis gritos y lloridos a causa del dolor, la curandera no dejó de jalarme la piel hasta que no estuvo segura de que ya no estaba empachada.

Sí me aconsejó que no volviera a mascar chicle o que me lo tragara o que me acostara en la cama con chicle en la boca porque de allí habían venido mis problemas del estómago. Al día siguiente ya estaba bien.

Lugardita Anita Montoya
BERNALILLO, NEW MEXICO

Se había muerto de ojo

Me acuerdo que cuando un chiquito que era muy atractivo, que le gustaba a alguna gente mucho, tenía uno que hacerle una crucita con saliva en la frente pa que no se le hiciera el maleficio a esa criatura, pa que no se enfermara. Si los padres creían que le habían hecho ojo, lo traiban pa la persona que pensaban que le había hecho ojo. Tenía que agarrar agua en la boca y darle al chiquito con su boca poquita agua en su boquita del niño.

Yo me acuerdo que a mi hermana se le murió un niño muy lindo. Parecía una muñeca de porcelana ese niño lindo. ¡Lindo era! Pus un día se levantó ella y lo hallaron muerto en la cama altita. Yo creo que era eso de *syndrome,* que le dicen, el *child syndrome.* Pero reclamaban que ese niño se había muerto de ojo. Nunca supimos.

Patricia Sánchez
VISTA, CALIFORNIA

La historia de Oaxaca

Había una vez que dejé a mi niño solito en la cama dormido en la casa en Oaxaca, y me fui a la iglesia. Cuando volví mi niño estaba llorando. Amaneció llorando y devolvía y no se calmaba de llorar. Lo llevé al médico, y el doctor lo tuvo tres días y nada que no se aliviaba mi niño. Ya casi lo tenía muerto.

Luego llegó una señora y me dijo,

—¿Pa qué tiene a su hijo con el doctor? No es pal doctor eso—y le hizo la bruja—. Sáquenlo del doctor. Yo lo voy a curar.

La señora lo sobó y le hizo limpia con huevo y hierbas y lo curó y mi niño se salvó. Fue toda la historia que tuvimos con mi hijo.

Mi hijo, que ahora tiene diez años de edad, tenía cuatro años cuando le pasó todo eso.

Eddie Torres, Jr.

BERNALILLO (EL BOSQUE), NEW MEXICO

El hombre le había hecho ojo

Yo no digo que no es verdá, pero no creo que una persona le puede hacer ojo a otro, y muncha gente de la edá mía, más jovenes, no creen tampoco. Está güeno si puedes creer, pero no creo que una persona te puede hacer ojo nomás por verte, porque te hago cariños y comienzas a estar enfermo. Puede que sí sea verdá.

Mi papá hizo a este hombre que viniera de Alburquerque. Era amigo de mi papá. Me acuerdo bien, bien, y mi hermana menor, la más niña, que el hombre le había hecho ojo, y fue y llamó papá al señor este y vino y la escupió. No sé. Se echaban algo en la boca y escupían pa quitarle el ojo, y papá dice que nomás le hizo eso el hombre ese y paró de llorar la niña. No sé, pero yo esaba muy niño. A mí no me ha tocado ver nada asina.

Eliseo "Cheo" Torres

ALBUQUERQUE, NEW MEXICO

Curado por doña María

Siempre que mi madre se daba cuenta de cualquier enfermedad que teníamos—que estuviese más allá de sus habilidades curativas—acudía a doña María, quien era la doctora tradicional experta en el barrio. Doña María tenía una cura para todo: desde dolores de cabeza, diarrea y dolencias del estómago; hasta cosas para los celos, el enfado, la cólera, y maldiciones sobre maridos, esposas, amantes o enemigos.

Una vez, cuando era niño, padecí una fiebre muy alta que prácticamente se salió de control de las prácticas curativas familiares. Parecía que no funcionaban los medicamentos herbarios y el ritual del mal de ojo de mi madre. Así que mandaron llamar a doña María para que fuera a mi casa y me diera sus curas. Por supuesto, ella misma quiso primero diagnosticar la enfermedad.

Recuerdo a doña María preguntándole a mi madre lo que había hecho para tratar mi enfermedad, mi madre respondió que me había dado el tratamiento del mal de ojo—ella me dio té de manzanilla, recuerdo que tenía un olor dulce, pero un sabor amargo.

Después de que mi madre le explicó a doña María el tratamiento que me había dado del mal de ojo, recuerdo que tomó un huevo y le dio masaje a todo mi cuerpo de pies a cabeza con ese huevo, como primer paso en el tratamiento. Mientras yacía boca arriba, mi madre hizo la señal de la cruz (o crucitas, crucecitas) sobre cada articulación importante en mi cuerpo mientras rezaba el Credo tres veces. Después, mi madre rompió el huevo en un vaso de agua y lo puso abajo de la cama.

Doña María le pidió a mi madre que le mostrara el vaso. Pude ver que la clara de huevo se había elevado a la altura de la superficie, mientras que la yema se había hundido hasta el fondo. Exaltada, doña María le dijo a mi madre que la clara se había solidificado y que tenía forma ovalada: había tomado la forma de un ojo. Doña María nos dijo que "por supuesto esto significaba que en realidad yo estaba siendo víctima de un caso de mal de ojo."

Entonces doña María le dijo a mi madre que ella había seguido todos los procedimientos correctos y que eso era simplemente un paso más de los que se necesitaban llevar a cabo.

"Quiero que saque el huevo y lo entierre en su patio trasero mañana por la mañana, y asegúrese de enterrarlo profundamente para que el perro no lo pueda desenterrar," le dijo doña María a mi madre.

En seguida, después de prescribir otra hierba medicinal que era más fuerte que la manzanilla, se fue doña María. Inmediatamente mi madre mandó llamar a mis tías y les ordenó encontrar la hierba llamada "borraja." En una hora, mis tías estaban de regreso con la hierba. Mi tía nos explicó que los moros le daban la borraja a los españoles como Abou-Rach, "el padre del sudor" (el nombre, por supuesto, está en árabe).

Abou-Rach ciertamente le hacía honor a su nombre. Pocos minutos después de haber tomado una taza de borraja, mi cuerpo empezó a sudar abundantemente y mi cuerpo comenzó a enfriarse considerablemente. También comencé a orinar, reacción de mi cuerpo para purgarse de fluidos, y comencé a sentirme mucho mejor.

Mientras me recuperaba, mi madre aclaró que este té de borraja había sido usado por su madre para mantener el cuerpo fresco como una bebida veraniega, y que también la había usado como cura para la fiebre que provocaba el sarampión, mi abuela también se lo daba a mi abuelo para tratar infecciones de la vejiga.

A la mañana siguiente de que tomé la borraja, me desperté con buen apetito, mis primeros días. Todavía me sentía débil, pero mucho mejor, cuando me terminé mi desayuno (mi favorito: huevos rancheros), le pregunté a mi madre que me contara más sobre el mal de ojo. ¿Qué era? ¿Por qué me había dado a mí?

Mi madre me explicó que el ritual del mal de ojo en realidad proviene de España y que a su vez los españoles lo tomaron de los moros, quienes ocuparon España durante varios siglos, transmitiendo muchas de sus tradiciones a los españoles, quienes a su vez, por supuesto, las trajeron a México. Mi madre me recordó que yo era un bebé hermoso, que sufrí de varios problemas del mal de ojo porque se admiraban conmigo y no me tocaban, y por consiguiente proyectaban vibraciones negativas a mi cuerpo.

Esto, entonces, era el meollo del asunto y la definición del mal de ojo: les causaba admiración a los adultos, quienes sin intención me habían provocado la enfermedad con esta admiración. De alguna forma, era imprescindible que después de admirar a un niño por su belleza, un adulto además debía tocar al niño para evitar los efectos de la enfermedad del mal de ojo.

El mal de ojo, entonces, no es lo que muchas personas creen que es—una proyección intencional de una enfermedad hacia otra persona—más bien, es una proyección no intencionada de vibraciones negativas a través de otra intención totalmente diferente—la persona que la causa no tiene la intención de hacer algún daño, más bien al contrario, le causa admiración la persona que llega a padecer de los efectos de la enfermedad a causa de esta persona.

"Las personas no quisieron que te enfermaras al admirarte, Cheo," me reconfortó mi madre. "Pero al no tocarte para neutralizar las vibraciones negativas causadas por una admiración excesiva, te provocaban la enfermedad sin darse cuenta que te dejaban expuesto a la admiración peligrosa."

Mi madre agregó que aunque tenía doce años de edad y ya no era un bebé, había personas que todavía admiraban mi belleza de entonces. Ella no me había curado, me dijo, pero doña María había sido capaz de hacerlo mediante la prescripción de un remedio herbario más poderoso, la borraja.

Eileen Dolores Treviño Villarreal

SAN ANTONIO, TEXAS

Lo blanco del huevo se cuece

Mi mamá estaba muy involucrada en las tradiciones estas del mal de ojo. Luego que te curan con un huevo, te barren con el huevo. Toman el huevo para curarte del mal de ojo, pero tiene que ser un huevo fresco. Entonces te barren con el huevo, te tocan con el huevo por el cuerpo, y luego te hacen cruces y andan diciendo rezos. Toman un vaso de agua, y ya después que te barren con el huevo, quiebran el huevo adentro del vaso de agua y lo ponen debajo de la cama, debajo de tu cabecera, y ya para la mañana que el huevo está cocido es que te han curado. Lo blanco del huevo es lo que se cuece, pasa de transparente a blanco. El agua que se usa está templada.

Dicen que el mal de ojo lo pone una persona que tiene vista con mucha electricidad. Entonces tú miras a un niño o a un niña y dices, "¡Ay, qué hermosos ojos, o qué hermoso pelo, qué hermoso niño o niña!" Luego tú lo tienes que ir a tocar porque si no lo tocas te quedas con ese deseo. Dicen que de ahí viene el mal de ojo de esa persona. Si lo toca y se le quita el deseo, ya no se enferma el niño. También con artículos, bueno, lo que sea, aretes, lo que sea. Si no los tocan se quiebran. Hay personas fuertes y otras no. Una persona fuerte pondría un mal de ojo.

Adelina Valdez Chávez Baca

BERNALILLO (EL BOSQUE), NEW MEXICO

El mal ojo

Pus a veces estaba un niño enfermo o malo del estógamo y dijían que le habían hecho ojo. Entonces buscaban una Juanita o un Juan que le dieran agua y lo escupieran y le hicieran una cruz. ¿Y sabes que yo vide muchas situaciones en que descansaban los niños? Se les quitaba la calentura. A mí me gusta mucho el *scientific discovery* y me admiraba todo eso y yo dijía, "¿Por qué un Juan y una Juana curaban ojo?"

Yo llegué a ver unos niños que estaban jirviendo en calentura un minuto y al ratito andaban jugando. Yo no sé si será cómo dicen hora. Hora les da un *virus* y les da muncha fiebre o cuando les salen los dientes y loo les das una espirina y se les quita. Pus yo no sé si sería la mesma cosa o no. Todavía tengo como cuestión en la cabeza.

Mi hermanita me acuerdo una vez fuimos a comer *ice cream* a casa de los Heller ahi en Cabezón. Ya estaba grandecita ella. Yo estaba chica. Cuando llegó a la casa llegó tan mala que jueron a buscar quién la escupiera y descansó. Esa situación me acuerdo yo era en mi casa, pero yo no sé si se le había pasado la calentura. Yo estaba muy chiquita pa darme cuenta si de veras trabajó esta Juanita, porque había una Juanita en la comunidá de Guadlupe que la escupió y le hizo una cruz en la frente. Yo digo que ella la curó. No tengo razón pa dijir que no.

Nine

The Wailing Woman's Agony

Don't go near the ditch because the Wailing Woman likes kids.—Rita Leyba Last

INTRODUCTION

La Llorona, the Wailing Woman, is one of the most popular and well-known figures in folklore among Latinos of the American Southwest, in particular those of Mexican descent. Even today, as interest in traditional stories of our ancestors wanes throughout hamlets or urban neighborhoods, La Llorona, through some magic, seems to retain widespread appeal.

As I lecture across New Mexico and the surrounding states regarding witchcraft and the supernatural, any mention of the Wailing Woman evokes a strong reaction, even among young children and adolescents. They may not be intimately familiar with the details regarding this roving woman of the night, who searches for the children she allegedly drowned or repents of some other mysterious transgression, but at least they have heard of her.

This is no small thing at a time when our young people are overwhelmed with an array of electronic games and gadgets. Yet, however far young people may be removed from the world of traditional storytelling, the Wailing Woman appears to be one notable exception. During the past several years she has piqued the interest of various segments of the population. Teachers in local schools, the staffs of public libraries, and storytellers in community centers or on the radio have been drawn in as part of an emerging cultural awareness, not just among Latinos but across the population as a whole.

When talking about La Llorona or any personage akin to her in other cultures, we can go back a long way—including to Greek mythology, Aztec folklore, or La Malinche, the Indian who became Hernán Cortés's mistress during the Spaniards' invasion of Mexico. Each case offers both similarities and differences that can apply to La Llorona's plight. In fact, some observers see modern-day cases of mothers in the United States who drown their children as no different from the multitude of versions of La Llorona lore that exist throughout the Southwest.

If a thousand stories were to be told about La Llorona, there would no doubt be just as many variations offered by the raconteurs, some versions with striking similarities, others with remarkable differences, and still others presenting new viewpoints and interpretations. That is La Llorona, fluid and mystical in appeal as her popularity grows and her legend is kept alive.

There is no concrete description of this woman, nor is it prudent to attempt to portray her in any definitive way. Clad at times in white, she appears as a beautiful young woman. Other times she has been described as tall and thin, perhaps wearing a black *tápalo,* a shawl popular in New Mexico, to disguise her ugly or skeletal face—her punishment for having murdered her children. Her mournful cries—"Oh, my children!" (*¡Ay mis hijos!/¡Oh hijos míos!*)—are legendary in many parts of the Southwest and beyond. According to Marcos C. Durán, her lament is a cry for forgiveness. She has also been said to shed silent "tears of blood" in her suffering as she wanders about by night.

La Llorona has been labeled everything from a ghost to an old hag, a murderer, an adulteress, and a bogeywoman. Some adults have invoked her name in much the same way as they have the *agüelo,* her counterpart, the bogeyman, to scare children into obedience with stories of this sad figure who roams the countryside, wandering along rivers and arroyos and scaring both children and adults (mostly men).

She is also likely to have appeared in the inner city along a primary canal (*acequia madre*), a drainage ditch (*renaje*), or a cement water channel. Wherever she appears and whatever her situation, she tends to be viewed as nameless (apart from her sobriquet of La Llorona) and pathetic, tormented by supernatural forces beyond her control. Still, Jesusita Aragón, the renowned midwife from Las Vegas, in a rare display of empathy, not only gives her a name, Chigüila, but also maintains that she does not intend any harm.

In a departure from such a serious tone, a little levity is sometimes added. Juan Bautista Chacón's "La Llorona" is a good example. In it an old man drapes a white bedsheet over his head and attempts to frighten the children of the community. We also learn from Salomón Lovato that pretending to be someone you are not can backfire if suspicions are aroused—and if a kid is a deadeye with a slingshot.

Now and again the mystery surrounding La Llorona is somewhat anti-

Portrayal of La Llorona. Costume is one hundred years old. Photo by Nasario García, 1997.

climactic, such as when she is found to be neither a witch nor a ghostly apparition, but a vixen searching for her lost cubs. The cries of the vixen resemble those of a woman in distress. Or the crying woman may be nothing more than two tree branches rubbing against each other on a windy night.

No discussion of La Llorona would be complete without mentioning death, a leitmotiv that always accompanies her tale. "*Agonizar*" in Spanish means to be dying, and so one could say that La Llorona's laments signify a perpetual state of dying, *agonizando* in retribution for her transgressions. As Marcos C. Durán suggests, maybe God has implored her "to bid goodbye to the world by telling her to ask for forgiveness by crying." Thus it is her spirit that wanders while she atones for her sins, as though in Purga-

Rawlins House, 1899 or 1902, Las Vegas, New Mexico. The Harvey Girls (waitresses at the local Harvey House) resided on the second floor in 1902. Photo by Nasario García, 2000.

tory, yearning for the peace that probably will forever elude her. That is part of La Llorona's legacy. After all, what would La Llorona be without crying?

Jesusita Aragón

LAS VEGAS, NEW MEXICO

There Comes Chigüila

I don't know anything about the Wailing Woman. Perhaps there was such a thing. Right here in this alley, dressed in white, you hear a woman cry far off in the distance. She walks about crying. She doesn't harm anyone, but she roams around crying. My grandparents used to say that she cried for her son. When the king ordered all the children to be beheaded, because he wanted to see if they would behead the Baby Jesus, the Wailing Woman is reputed to have said, "Rather than to see my son beheaded, I'd rather drown him." And she tossed him into the river and drowned him. That's why she cries, but she doesn't do anyone any harm.

One night when I was outside getting some fresh air—for thirteen years I took care of seven male patients belonging to the state here in this house. After I tended to my evening chores, washing dishes and all, I went outside to the porch to get some fresh air. My son was sitting outside and talking with me, when all of a sudden I hear this crying and crying. And there was this poor woman they called Chigüila, an unflattering name (possibly meaning locust). She used to drink a lot. My son said to me, "There comes Chigüila, Tita."

"Really? Poor thing, poor thing," because she lived so down and out.

"No. It's not her," he said. "Look! It's a white ghost."

And he stood up and saw the Güila.

"It's no Güila," I said to him. "It's the Wailing Woman. She's harmless."

No. She didn't flee. Who knows how far she went, crying? Then she disappeared. She let out like a holler. Like a moaning sound. That's all.

I wasn't afraid, because my grandfather whenever he heard the cry he would say, "There goes the Wailing Woman grieving."

Juan Bautista Chacón

PUEBLO, COLORADO

The Wailing Woman

I did hear something about the Wailing Woman. Okay, once upon a time, many years ago when I was young, there were rumblings about the Wailing Woman.

Alongside the road there was a cemetery, and that's where she passed by, because El Rito is made up of two small plazas. It's called the Cañón de las Placitas. To the north is the Cañón del Rito and to the south La Placita. And those people from the villages would go by on that road where the cemetery is located. Then at a certain hour, as people were going by, they would hear the Wailing Woman.

And one time some boys came out—they were actually already grown men, and they said, "Well, what's going on with the Wailing Woman?"

And they would see ghosts. They would see a white ghost that passed by on the road next to the cemetery, and at that hour people wouldn't dare be out because they were afraid.

These older boys went over to see what was happening that day at the same time, and here goes the Wailing Woman. They got close, two or three of them, and they took off after the Wailing Woman. On the road where she was running, she dropped the bedsheet that she was wearing.

Well, it wasn't the Wailing Woman! It was someone else, somebody more astute than they. It was a man, and they caught him. He was even an acquaintance of theirs. He did it just to give them a hard time and to keep them from going by the cemetery. That's all.

Marcos C. Durán

PUEBLO, COLORADO

It Was a Vixen

Back then when I was a child, the story went around that the Wailing Woman would show up at the village square and that she was a tall woman. But it turned out to be a lie because, as you know, there's an animal that's called a vixen, and these female foxes, as I understand it, would pass through the village, but I wasn't born back then. My father had taken over the ranch that's ours now—it was like a wooded area, and it was called El Rancho. There were lots of animals, such as coyotes and vixens and that sort of thing, you see?

So, as the population increased, the animals migrated more toward the mountains. Coyotes already were around but they were becoming scarce. As for the vixens, they stayed back because they were very good at eating chickens. Lots of them!

Then later on, on this one occasion, I was already a married man—I got married in Santa Cruz, New Mexico, to my wife who was a schoolteacher—and the same thing. One of those wailing women went by. And you know how we people are, claiming the Wailing Woman this and the Wailing Woman that, and the fact that tonight we'll catch her and all that sort of stuff, but many were just fooling themselves.

And do you know what it was? It was a vixen, an animal. There were vixens, many of them, and that's what it was, a vixen, because vixens all of a sudden cry like a child, like a woman. That's one thing I can tell you, that it was not the Wailing Woman.

But people claimed that she was a woman dressed in black, and that she was a tall woman who cried out at night, who perhaps had lost a loved one or whom God was imploring to bid goodbye to the world by telling her to ask for forgiveness by crying.

But it was nothing but lies. It was a vixen. Why, I myself realized that it was a vixen, and this is the only story I can relate to you regarding the Wailing Woman.

Joe E. García

PRESCOTT, ARIZONA

She Cried Tears of Blood

Many years ago when I was a little boy, my parents and the rest of the family were living on a ranch about thirty miles from Prescott, Arizona. The ranch had a name, but I forgot it already. At that time I had an older brother, one older sister, and a younger sister.

What I'm about to tell you happened on a weekend, as far as I can remember. I believe it was a weekend or some other holiday, because other kids and their parents were visiting us. Anyway, there was lots of food. That I'll never forget, because when you're a kid you love to eat, especially sweet stuff such as *bizcochitos* and *sopa*.

Anyhow, it was late in the day and it was already getting dark when we were told a story about the Witch/Wailing Woman. The person who told us the story was an old lady, probably not as old as we thought, because when you're a kid you think everyone is old. In any case, here's the story.

The Witch/Wailing Woman was one person, you see, but whenever she went looking for her little kids, she would turn into two people. She cried like the Wailing Woman, but the dark shadow was that of a hunch-backed woman who looked like a witch and moved slowly between the trees in the woods near the ranch.

We were also told that she cried tears of blood because she had killed her children. So, as the old lady was telling us the story, all of a sudden we heard a very loud and sad crying sound in the woods.

The lament got louder and louder. All of us kids were scared to death. It was a scary sound, like she was in a lot of pain. She moaned and moaned, but we never did see the Witch/Wailing Woman's face, only her shadow. I don't know about the other kids, but I did not go into the woods for a very long time after that.

Even the woman who was telling us the story got scared. Those are my memories about the Witch/Wailing Woman. We were told other stories, but that one has stuck with me until now.

Adelita Gonzales

ALBUQUERQUE, NEW MEXICO

The Wailing Woman

And do you remember what the Wailing Woman was? It was a little she-fox, a vixen. As for me, look, they used to say that it was the Wailing Woman, and it wasn't.

One time my father-in-law, Antonio Gonzales, was there. We were sitting around. It was already dark. My husband wasn't home. I don't know where he was. It was summertime. And people used to say that the Wailing Woman would cry. Very well, then. There was my father Antonio, I remember. He was sitting on a chair outside. About that time, he heard the little vixen. Then he said, "Girls," to me and to his daughters. "Come! Come here! Listen! Listen! The Wailing Woman is crying!"

Right away we grabbed ahold of him. And he laughed, "Look, listen!" It was crying just like a woman. Just like a woman.

Then he said, "Do you know what that is? That's the Wailing Woman, and people say they don't know what it is. But I know what it is. It's a little vixen that's lost her cubs," he said. "She can't find them."

Many times people would say, "Oh, it's the spirits that are running loose." Not so! Once a person's dead, he doesn't return, he doesn't return. They used to say that the dead would come back to life. Look, there's my husband [he's dead]. They ask me if I'm scared of him. A dead person doesn't scare me. You know whom I'm afraid of? The living! Not the dead.

Mauricio Hernández

OCEANSIDE, CALIFORNIA

Oh, My Dear Children!

As a little kid I remember my grandmother telling us the story of La Llorona (the Wailing Woman). She told us that when she was about twelve years old she was walking by the railroad tracks and she saw this beautiful tall lady with long black hair dressed in white. But when she took a closer look, she noticed that the lady wasn't walking but floating in the air—her feet off the ground—and then when she rounded the corner of this building, my grandmother heard the lady cry, "*¡Ay, mis hijos!*" (Oh, my children!).

Grandma then ran back to her house, and to this day all the grandkids enjoy her story about La Llorona.

Rita Leyba Last

BERNALILLO, NEW MEXICO

I Saw This with My Own Eyes

I don't believe in witches. I don't believe in those things, but I saw this with my own eyes. One night when I was fifteen years old we went to a dance here in Bernalillo, and we got home about three o'clock in the morning. We were living in El Llanito. The outhouses were in the corral, far from the house. My father went in the house, and Mom and I went to the corral to go to the outhouse before going to bed, and she says to me, "Look at that light, how it's bouncing! It's a ball of fire," and we looked toward the west.

I looked. It was a ball of fire that was jumping up and down. It would hit the ground and then jump up and hit the ground and then it would jump again, and Mom says to me, "Look, my dear daughter. That's witchery or something."

"Mom, I'm looking, but I don't believe it."

"Well, I wonder what it is?" she said to me.

"I don't know, Mom, but I don't believe it."

"Hurry up! We better head home because I don't know what that thing might be. It's an evil spirit."

That's one thing I saw myself, but I don't know, I don't know what it was. One of my brothers drowned in the ditch at the age of three, and we never again heard stories about the Wailing Woman.

Salomón "Sal" Lovato

ALBUQUERQUE, NEW MEXICO

Smack in the Middle of the Forehead

There was a woman over in San Luis. They referred to her as the Wailing Woman. Well, we kids were real brats, but I wasn't afraid. Like I say, we were smart-alecks. We were raised having everything, not like other poor kids.

We were messing around, and I had made. . . . Over in San Luis there weren't any rifles. We had slings. Do you know what a sling is? Slingshots.

There were slingshots with a fork, a Y-shaped stick, and then there were slings like what we used. You see, you'd put the rock inside the leather strap. That's where you'd load it with a rock, fold the leather, swing it around, and then you let go of it. You could kill someone.

One time this woman came out to scare us. I remember. I was very small. And, what was the lady's name? I don't recall. But, anyway, there were a lot of kids around, and we were carrying those slings with us and we fired at her. She never scared us again. Someone smacked her right in the middle of the forehead!

Manuel de Jesús Manzanares

PUEBLO, COLORADO

She Had on Like a Black Slip

This happened when I still lived in El Rito del Oso. Right next to our place there was a place that was abandoned. There was a small mountain pass, and there was a neighbor who claimed that right there in that mountain pass the Wailing Woman would come out, especially on Fridays at midnight. He claimed that whenever the Wailing Woman flew, that she had on like a black slip.

I guess I was always very doubtful about matters pertaining to witches, but I was a kid, and every time it got a little dark and I went by that small mountain pass I was a little scared that the Wailing Woman would jump out at me.

As time went on, I grew a little. I got braver. A cousin of mine lived farther down from us, more toward the east from the mountain pass, and I got it into my head that I was going to go to my cousin's house and that I was going to stay until close to midnight so as to go by the pass at midnight, on a Friday, to see the Wailing Woman.

By then I thought that I was already a man. I wasn't afraid. I was about sixteen years old, more or less. I didn't tell anyone what I had in mind. I took off. I was on horseback. I took off through the small mountain pass. I went past it. Nothing! Then I said to myself, "Perhaps it's not time." I turned back and went through the pass one more time, to see if the Wailing Woman would cry, but nothing. I never heard it. I never heard anything. So I told my father: "There's no such thing as the Wailing Woman, Dad. Those are nothing but stories that Don Bonifacio has conjured up."

May he rest in peace, he's already dead. Fine, as a result I never again paid any attention to the Wailing Woman. And that's the end of the story.

María Teresa Márquez

ALBUQUERQUE, NEW MEXICO

The Storyteller

El Barrio del Diablo, one of the meanest and roughest parts of El Paso, did not have paved streets or sidewalks. The streets at night were dark and unsafe.

Crime, drugs, and murder were not uncommon. The police, when they dared to enter the neighborhood, did so at their own risk. Most of the time the police were not friendly.

My street, Spruce Street, was unpaved, and when it rained it was filled with ruts and large puddles of water that became wading pools for the street kids. There were no streetlights.

After sunset, most mothers kept their children indoors. However, in the summertime there was one activity that the mothers considered safe. They knew Julianita, the Spruce Street storyteller. She lived with her sister and brother and was the housekeeper while they worked outside the home. Their home was a very modest adobe dwelling with a front yard filled with wild plants.

The mothers trusted Julianita to send their children home at the appropriate time. She would gather the Spruce Street children around her after dinner, after she had fed her family and taken care of the dishes.

We would sit in front of her house, on the dirt since there were no sidewalks. Julianita would ask what we wanted to hear. Storytelling was her only form of entertainment aside from her housework. On Sundays she would go to church with her sister while their brother recovered from a weekend of drinking.

Julianita was short, a little chubby, and wore clothes that were threadbare and came down to her ankles. Because she did not work outside the home, she wore worn-out and patched clothes. She always wore a large apron with big pockets that she used to carry things in.

Julianita was also an herbalist. She knew how to cure simple illnesses with *yerbas*.

She was a good storyteller. One of the favorite stories among us kids was La Llorona. No matter how many times we heard the stories, we would always ask for it. Stories about El Diablo and brujas who turned into owls at night were also favorites.

My house was at the very end of the unpaved, rutted street. Spruce Street T-boned a paved ditch that separated Mexico from the United States. The ditch carried runoff water from the city streets. All sorts of things could be seen floating, especially after heavy rains. The water was usually loaded with contaminants that glowed in rainbow colors.

Beyond the street was what we used to call La Isla de Córdova, a farming community that belonged to Mexico. Once the sun set, Spruce Street and La Isla de Córdova were dark, dark, dark.

Many families in the neighborhood farmed and used the water from *la acequia*, the ditch that ran on the margins of the streets. La acequia on Spruce Street was at the end of the street, which meant that when I went home after dark, after Julianita finished recounting La Llorona, I had to cross la acequia.

I always ran home as fast I could to avoid getting caught by La Llorona. I knew that she would rise from the flowing waters and catch me and pull me into the cold ditch water if I wasn't careful. What made my flight from La Llorona even scarier was that the front yard of my house had a long, heavy gate with a large bolt used to secure it. I had to reach through a crack in the gate to unlock it and then push as hard as I could to open the heavy gate. I would slip through and run the length of the long yard to my house, which was usually dark. We did not have electricity and would borrow electricity from our neighbors by crossing an electrical wire over the fence between the houses.

My greatest fear was that I would fall and La Llorona would catch me. After catching my breath, I would be grateful that once again I had escaped the clutches of La Llorona.

The next evening I would be out with the rest of the Spruce Street kids waiting for Julianita to come out and tell us more scary stories.

Damiano Romero

LOS RANCHOS DE ALBURQUERQUE, NEW MEXICO

It Was a Tree Branch

Well, I don't believe there was such a thing as the Wailing Woman, but many people claimed that it was the Wailing Woman. I used to spend a lot of time in the countryside, and one night there was a cry. It sounded like the cry of a lion; it resembled a bobcat's cry. It bothered me all night long.

By morning it disappeared. By that time when the crying ceased, a cousin of mine went to where the crying was coming from, to see what it was, and it was a tree branch pressing against another. It was like a cross, a fork, one branch on top of the other. Whenever the wind blew, one branch moved one way and the other one in the opposite direction, and that's where the creaking was coming from. It sounded just like a woman wailing.

Many times I believe that's what people heard. The wind would be blowing, and these branches stuck against each other, and there you had the crying, the moaning.

Isabel Romero

LAS VEGAS, NEW MEXICO

A Cunning Old Hag

And regarding the Wailing Woman, there was this place I was familiar with. There was a small river and a poplar grove. Then, many times back in the olden days, people used teams of mules or horse wagons. There were no automobiles or anything like now. And there was a forest.

Well, there in that forest is where the Wailing Woman came out. Now, the Wailing Woman was a widow. She was already old. She would hide in between the shrubs, and whenever someone went by who was carrying food, she would moan, "Ayyyy!" She wept. People would then toss the food to her and she'd dash off. There she was. And of course the Wailing Woman got the better end of the deal.

Then finally there was a man, my Uncle Abel. He was terrible! He was very mischievous and he went and camped in a place close by. Then one morning he got up early. He was an early riser, quite a guy. He was going after the horses when the Wailing Woman popped out, and he, of course, was not afraid. He went and took a peek. Wham, wham! Three blows. "Ouch, my little brother! Don't, don't, don't hit me."

It was the Wailing Woman, known to people as a cunning old hag. Whenever she came out, people would toss food at her. She had it made. That time when my uncle struck her, "Oh, my little brother! Don't hit me. I'm Julana."

"This is so that you don't pull this crap again." And so he beat the dickens out of her. He beat her up with a rope or a whip. He gave her either a good beating or a good flogging. That was the end of the Wailing Woman!

Ophelia Ipolita María de Gracia Sandoval de Rinaldi

BERNALILLO, NEW MEXICO

The Monsters

Well, it was the story about the bogeyman. "Don't go to the ditch. Don't go near the ditch because the bogeyman is there." Well, we didn't go. Back in those days we were very obedient. We were scared. We were not to enter certain places because the bogeyman was there. He supposedly would come out when it got dark.

Later on I heard that it was the Wailing Woman. "Don't go near the ditch at night." We were told that the Wailing Woman was a lady who strolled along the ditch looking for her children, but if she found other kids she would take them with her.

That's the same thing I would tell my children, because we had the ditch right next to our house. At times they didn't understand too much about the Wailing Woman, but they did understand about monsters. Afterwards it was all about, "Don't go near the ditch because there's monsters," not about the Wailing Woman.

Eileen Dolores Treviño Villarreal

SAN ANTONIO, TEXAS

The Wailing Woman

San Antonio has its Wailing Woman, too. A woman drowned her three children in the San Pedro Creek, in the middle of San Antonio, many, many years ago. Later she would cry, and many people have said, that is, certain people, many years ago, when speaking about the same Wailing Woman, that they could see her crying at night, at midnight, crying at the San Pedro Creek. She would be crying for her children she had drowned. No one knows why she drowned her kids.

Alfredo Ulibarrí

LAS VEGAS, NEW MEXICO

The Wailing Woman

Back then at night in El Cañón, when I was coming back from seeing my wife, before we got married. Because she lived far from where I lived, I'd go see her on horseback. And when I was on my way back, all of El Cañón cried just like foxes. They cry like a small child, and people claimed that it was the Wailing Woman. Those foxes do indeed cry like a wailing woman, for sure.

But you get scared. You always get startled. You get goose bumps. No sooner said than done, I would dig my spurs into my horse and head home. By the time I got home at night, there were times when I would put the horse, saddle and all in the corral, because I got scared. I was alone, alone. I was scared shitless!

But the foxes do cry like a small child. That's why people say that it was wailing women. I believe they were foxes, because I saw them.

La agonía de La Llorona

No vayan a la cequia porque a La Llorona le gustan los niños. —Rita Leyba Last

Jesusita Aragón

LAS VEGAS, NEW MEXICO

Ahi viene la Chigüila

Yo de La Llorona no sé. Pueda que sí hubiera. En este callejón aquí al lado, vestida de blanco, se oye llorar muy lejos, es que La Llorona. Ella anda llorando. No le hace mal a naide, pero anda llorando. Dijían mis agüelitos que lloraba por su hijo. Cuando el rey ordenó que degollaran a todos los niños, porque quería ver si degollaban al Niño Dios, La Llorona es que dijo, "De ver a m' hijo degollao, mejor lo hogo." Y l'ochó en el río y lo hogó. Eso es lo que ella llora, pero no le hace mal a naide.

Una noche cuando estaba yo en el fresco, porque yo cuidé siete hombres pacientes del estao por trece años aquí en mi casa, y loo cuando yo vi mi negocio en la noche de lavar trastes y todo, me salí pal portal al fresco. Estaba m' hijo sentao aá juera platicando conmigo, cuando oigo llorar y llorar. Y había una pobre que le dijían la Chigüila, por mal nombre (quizás una chicharra). Bebía muncho. Me dijo él,

—Ahi viene la Chigüila, Tita.

—¿De veras? Pobrecita, pobrecita—porque vivía tal y mal.

—No. No es—dijo—. ¡Mira! Es un bulto blanco.

Y se paró él y vido la Güila.

—No Güila—le dije—. Es La Llorona. No te hace nada.

No. No juyó. Hasta quién sabe hasta ónde iría llorando. Y loo se desaparece. Daba como un grito. Como un grito nomás. Era todo.

A mí no me daba miedo porque mi agüelito cuando se oía el grito, dijía,

—Ahi anda La Llorona penando.

Juan Bautista Chacón

PUEBLO, COLORADO

La Llorona

Yo oí algo de La Llorona. Güeno, en un tiempo, ya hace munchos años, estaba un joven, y andaba con la bulla de La Llorona.

En el camino estaba un camposanto, y por ahi pasaba, porque El Rito son dos placitas. Le dicen el Cañón de las Placitas. Pal norte es el Cañón del Rito y pa bajo le dicen la Placita. Y los de las placitas pasaban por ahi por ese camino por onde está este camposanto. Luego a cierta hora, ahi cuando iba pasando gente, es que salía La Llorona.

En un tiempo salieron muchachos, pos hombres ya, y dijieron,

—¿Pos qué pasa con La Llorona?

Y vían bultos. Vían un bulto blanco que pasaba la calle del camposanto, y la gente en esa hora no podía caminar porque tenían miedo.

Estos muchachos grandes jueron a ver qué pasaba ese día a la misma hora, y aquí va La Llorona. Ellos se arrimaron, eran dos o tres, y le rompieron y arrancó La Llorona. Ahi en el camino onde iba, se le calló la sábana que llevaba puesta. Pues no era La Llorona. Era otro, otro más astuto que ellos. Era otro hombre, y ahi lo pescaron. Era conocido d'ellos mismos. Nomás pa 'celes el tormento de no dejarlos pasar por el camposanto. Era todo.

Marcos C. Durán

PUEBLO, COLORADO

Era una zorra

En ese tiempo que yo era niño, andaban con el cuento que les llegaba La Llorona a la placita y que era una mujer larga. Pero salió a ser mentira porque usté sabe que hay un animal que le dicen la zorra, y las zorras pasaban por la placita asegún entiendo cuando yo, pos tavía ni nacido era en esos tiempos yo. Había 'garrao en papá ese rancho que tenemos, y era como monte, era como un monte, y le dicían El Rancho. Había munchos animales, lo que era coyotes y zorras y todo eso, ¿ves?

De modo es que ya cuando se jue poblando el lugar, pos los animales ya se jueron más a la sierra y ya coyotes, pos sí había, pero ya estaban acabándose. Y las zorras, ésas sí se quedaban porque son muy buenas pa las gallinas. ¡Munchas!

Luego después, en una ocasión, tamién ya hombre yo casao—yo me casé en Santa Cruz, Nuevo México con mi señora, era mestra ella—y tamién pasó una de esas lloronas. Y usté sabe cómo semos la gente, pues que pasó La Llorona y que La Llorona pallá y que esta noche sí la 'garramos y todo y pallá y todo pacá, pero munchos se engañaron.

¿Y sabe usté lo que era? Era una zorra; era un animal. Había zorras, munchas, y eso era lo que era, una zorra, porque las zorras redepente lloran como un niño, como una mujer. Ésa es una de las cuestiones que yo puedo dicirle, que no era La Llorona.

Pero la gente dicía que era una mujer vestida de negro, y que era una mujer larga, y que de noche iba a llorar, y que quizás se le había muerto alguien o quizás Dios la estaba despachando a que se despidiera del mundo, pidiendo perdón llorando.

Pero eran mentiras. Era una zorra. Ya porque hasta yo mesmo me di cuenta que era una zorra, y éste es el único cuento que puedo dicirle de La Llorona.

Joe E. García

PRESCOTT, ARIZONA

Lloraba lágrimas de sangre

Hace munchos años cuando yo era niño mis padres y la demás familia vivíanos en un rancho como treinta millas de Prescott en Arizona. El rancho tenía nombre, pero ya se me olvidó. En aquellos años tenía yo un hermano mayor, una hermana mayor, y una hermanita menor.

Lo que te voy a contar pasó un fin de semana, según lo que yo recuerdo. Creyo que era un fin de semana o un día de fiesta, porque había otra plebecita y sus padres ahi en casa visitándonos. Pero de toos modos, había muncha comida. Eso no se me olvida, porque cuando uno está chiquito te gusta comer, especialmente cosas dulces como bizcochitos y sopa.

De too modos, ya era tarde y se estaba haciendo oscuro cuando nos contaron la historia de la bruja, La Llorona. La persona que nos dijo la historia era una mujer vieja, quizás no tan vieja como pensábanos porque cuando eres un chamaco piensas que toos son viejos. En too caso, aquí te va la historia.

La bruja, es decir, La Llorona era una sola persona, ves, pero cuando salía a buscar a sus niños, se volvía dos personas. Lloraba como La Llorona, pero la sombra oscura era diuna mujer jorobada como una bruja, y se movía despacito entre los árboles del bosque que estaba cerca del rancho.

Tamién nos dijieron que es que lloraba lágrimas de sangre porque había matao a sus hijitos. De toos modos, cuando la vieja nos estaba contando la historia, de redepente oyimos un llorido muy alto y triste en el bosque.

El llorido se puso más y más alto. Toda la plebe estábanos muy espantada. Era un llorido muy feo, como que la bruja, La Llorona tenía un dolor bruto. Lloraba y lloraba, pero nunca le vimos la cara, solamente la sombra. Yo no sé los otros muchachos, pero después d'eso yo no me acerqué al bosque por muncho tiempo.

Hasta la misma mujer que nos estaba contando la historia se espantó. Ésos son mi recuerdos de La bruja, La Llorona. Nos contaban otras historias, pero ésa hasta hoy día se me queda en mi cabeza.

Adelita Gonzales

ALBUQUERQUE, NEW MEXICO

La Llorona

¿Y sabes lo que era La Llorona? Era una zorrita, una zorra. Yo, mira, decían que era La Llorona, y no era La Llorona.

Una vez estaba mi suegro, Antonio Gonzales. Estábanos sentaos. Ya era oscuro. Mi esposo no estaba ahi. No sé ónde estaba. Estaba en el verano. Y decían que lloraba La Llorona. Güeno, estaba mi papá Antonio, yo me acuerdo. Estaba sentao en una silleta ahi juera. En eso oyó llorar la zorrita. Loo dijo,

—¡Muchachas!—a mí y a sus hijitas—. ¡Venir! ¡Vengan pacá! ¡Escuchen! ¡Escuchen! Está llorando La Llorona.

Diuna vez nos agarramos con él. Y él se rió,

—¡Miren y escuchen!

Estaba llorando lo mismo que una mujer. La misma cosa que una mujer lloraba. Loo dice,

—¿Saben lo que es eso? Ésa es La Llorona, y dicen que no saben qué es, pero yo sí sé qué es. Es una zorrita que perdió sus hijitos—dijo—. No los jalla.

Munchas veces decían, "¡Oh que son las ánimas que andan por ahi!" ¡No! Si ya del que se muere no güelve, no güelve. Pues decían que aparecen muertos. Ahi está mi esposo [está muerto], mira. Dicen que si no me da miedo a mí. No me da miedo con un muerto. ¿Sabes a quién le tengo miedo? ¡A los vivos! A los muertos no.

Mauricio Hernández

OCEANSIDE, CALIFORNIA

¡Ay, mis hijos!

Cuando yo era niño me acuerdo que mi abuelita nos contaba la historia de La Llorona. Nos contó que cuando ella tenía como diez años iba andando cerca de la línea del ferrocarril y vido esta muchacha alta y hermosa con el cabello negro, vestida de blanco. Pero cuando se arrimó a verla más cerca se dio cuenta que la mujer no iba andando sino que iba flotando en el aire—sin los pies en la tierra—y cuando dobló la esquina de este edificio mi abuelita oyó a la mujer que lloraba, "¡Ay, hijos míos!"

Entonces mi abuelita salió corriendo a casa, y hasta la fecha todos los nietos gozan de su historia sobre La Llorona.

Rita Leyba Last

BERNALILLO, NEW MEXICO

Esto lo vi con mis ojos

Yo no creo en brujas. Yo no creo en esas cosas, pero esto lo vi con mis ojos. Una noche cuando yo tenía quince años fuimos a un baile aquí en Bernalillo, y llegamos a la casa como a las tres de la mañana. Vivíamos en El Llanito. Los privados, los escusaos, estaban en el corral, lejos de la casa. Mi papá entró a la casa, y mi mamá y yo fuimos andando para el corral a ir al escusao antes de acostarnos, y me dice mi mamá,

—¡Mira esa luz como va brincando! Es una bola de lumbre—y vimos pal rumbo del oeste.

Yo vi. Era una bola de lumbre que iba brincando. Pegaba al suelo y loo brincaba y pegaba al suelo y loo brincaba, y me dijo mi mamá,

—Mira, mi 'jita. Eso es una brujería o algo.

—Mamá, estoy viendo, pero no creo.

—¿Pues qué puede ser?—me dijía.

—No sé mamá, pero yo no creo.

—¡Apúrate mi 'jita! Mejor vámonos pa la casa porque yo no sé qué será eso. Es una cosa mala.

Eso sí vi yo, pero yo no sé, yo no sé qué sería. Uno de mis hermanos se ahogó de la edad de tres años en la cequia y nunca volvimos a oír la historia de La Llorona.

Salomón "Sal" Lovato

ALBUQUERQUE, NEW MEXICO

En la mera frente

Estaba una señora ahi en San Luis. Le decían La Llorona. Pus éranos muy terribles nosotros, pero yo no tenía miedo. Como digo, teníanos una poca de educación. Nos criamos muy sobrantes de todo, no como otra plebecita, pobrecita.

Y estábanos monquiando y había hecho yo. . . . Aá no había rifles. Había hondas. ¿Sabes lo que es una honda? Jondas. Había jondas con la horqueta y había hondas d' esas de las que nosotros usábanos. Ves, la honda era de vaqueta, le echabas la piedra ahi, se doblaba la vaqueta, le dabas güelta y la tirabas. Podías matar a cualquiera.

Una vez salió esta señora a meternos miedo a nosotros. Me acuerdo, chiquito yo. Y, "¿cómo se llamaba la señora esa?" No me acuerdo. Pero, de todos modos, había munchos chamacos y tráibanos de esas hondas y le tiramos. No volvió más a meternos miedo. ¡Alguien le dio en la mera frente!

Manuel de Jesús Manzanares

PUEBLO, COLORADO

Llevaba como naguas negras

Esto era tavía cuando vivía yo en El Rito del Oso. Ahi en seguida del lugar de nosotros había un lugar abandonao. Estaba un puertecito, y había un vecino que reclamaba de que ahi en ese puertecito salía La Llorona, especialmente los viernes a la medianoche. Decía él que cuando volaba La Llorona, que llevaba como naguas negras.

Yo quizás siempre jui muy incrédulo en estos negocios de brujos, pero estaba mediano y siempre cuando me tocaba pasar así poco nochecito por el puertecito, iba con poco miedo de que juera a salir La Llorona.

Pasado tiempo, yo ya crecí poco más. Ya me di ánimo. Un primo hermano vivía más abajo, más al oriente de ahi del puertecito, y se me metió en la cabeza de que yo iba ir pa case mi primo y me iba a estar hasta cerca de la medianoche pa venir y pasar ahi a la medianoche, día viernes, pa ver La Llorona.

Antonces se me hacía que ya era hombre yo. No tenía miedo. Tenía yo como dieciséis años, más o menos. No le dije a naide porque ése era mi mente. Me vine. Yo andaba a caballo. Me vine por ahi el puertecito. Pasé.

¡Nada! Loo dije, "No, pus tal vez no es la hora." Me devolví y pasé patrás otra vez, a pasar de güelta a ver si lloraba, pero no. Nunca la oí. Nunca oí yo nada. Ya le dije a en papá,

—No hay nada de Llorona apá. Esos son cuentos de don Bonifacio.

Dios lo tenga en paz; ya es muerto. Güeno, pues ya no puse yo más atención de La Llorona. Y ahi se acabó el cuento.

María Teresa Márquez

ALBUQUERQUE, NEW MEXICO

La cuentista

El Barrio del Diablo, una de las áreas más malas y violentas de El Paso, no tenía calles pavimentadas o aceras. Las calles de noche estaban oscuras y eran peligrosas. La ola de crímenes, drogas, y muertes era común. La policía, cuando se atrevía a entrar en el barrio, lo hacía por su propia cuenta y riesgo. La mayor parte del tiempo la policía no era muy amistosa.

Mi calle, la Calle Spruce, no estaba pavimentada y cuando llovía se llenada de baches y charcos grandes donde metían los pies en el agua los chamacos que vivían en esa calle. Por la noche no había luces en las calles.

Después de la puesta del sol, casi todas las mamás hacían que sus niños se quedaran en casa. Sin embargo, en el verano había una actividad que las madres no consideraban peligrosa. Ellas conocía a Julianita, la cuentista de la Calle Spruce. Vivía con su hermana y su hermano y era el ama de casa mientras ellos trabajaban fuera de la casa. Su casa era una casa muy humilde de adobe con una yarda al frente llena de flores silvestres.

Las mamás confiaban en que Julianita despachara a los niños a casa a una buena hora. Ella juntaba a los niños de la Calle Spruce y los ponía alrededor de ella después de la cena tras haberle dado de comer a su familia y de lavar los platos.

Nos sentábamos delante de su casa, en la tierra ya que no había aceras. Julianita nos preguntaba que si qué queríamos oír. El contar cuentos era su único entretenimiento fuera del trabajo de casa. Los domingos iba a misa con su hermana mientras su hermano se recuperaba de sus borracheras de fin de semana.

Julianita era bajita, un poco gordita, y usaba ropa vieja que le llegaba hasta los tobillos. Siendo que no trabajaba fuera de la casa, por eso es que usaba ropa vieja y remendada. Siempre llevaba puesto un delantal grande con unas bolsotas en las que llevaba sus cosas.

Julianita también era arbolaria. Ella sabía curar enfermedades ordinarias con yerbas.

Ella era una buena cuentista. Uno de los cuentos favoritos de los niños era La Llorona. No importa las veces que escucháramos los cuentos, siempre pedíamos La Llorona. Los cuentos acerca del diablo y las brujas que se volvían tecolotes por la noche, también era nuestros favoritos.

Mi casa estaba a fines de la calle sin pavimento y llena de baches. La Calle Spruce pegaba con una acequia de cemento que separaba a México de los Estados Unidos. Por la acequia corría agua que se desparramaba de las calles de la ciudad. Se podía ver todo tipo de garrero flotando en el agua especialmente después de las tormentas. El agua normalmente iba llena de contaminantes que brillaban en diferentes colores como un arco iris.

Más allá de la calle se encontraba lo que solíamos llamar La Isla de Córdova, una comunidad de agricultura que pertenecía a México. Una vez que se ponía el sol, la Calle Spruce y La Isla de Córdova se volvían bien, bien, bien oscuras.

Muchas familias en la vecindad cultivaban la tierra y usaban el agua de la acequia que corría al margen de las calles. La acequia en la Calle Spruce estaba a fines de la calle, lo cual quiere decir que cuando yo me iba a casa después de oscurecerse, después de que Julianita había narrado lo de La Llorona, yo tenía que cruzar la acequia.

Yo siempre corría a toda prisa para que no me pescara La Llorona. Yo sabía que ella podía saltar de las aguas corrientes, pescarme y arrastrarme al agua fría de la acequia si no tenía cuidado. Lo que hacía que mi escape de La Llorona resultara todavía más espantoso era que la yarda delante de mi casa tenía una puerta larga y pesada con un cerrojo para seguridad del hogar. Yo tenía que meter la mano por una abertura en la puerta para abrir el cerrojo y luego empujar con todas las fuerzas posibles para poder abrir aquella puertota. Me metía y corría la larga distancia de la yarda a mi casa que usualmente estaba oscura. No teníamos electricidad y se la pedíamos a nuestros vecinos cruzando un alambre eléctrico por encima del cerco que separaba ambas casas.

El peor temor que tenía yo era caerme y que me pescara La Llorona. Después de recobrarme la respiración, me sentía agradecida una vez más por haberme escapado de los agarrones de La Llorona.

Damiano Romero

LOS RANCHOS DE ALBURQUERQUE

Era un brazo de árbol

La Llorona, pues yo no creibo que había tal cosa, pero munchos dijían que era La Llorona. Yo estaba muncho en los campos, y una noche estaba un llorido. Parecía como llorido de un león; parecía como llorido de un gato [montés], y toa la noche molestó.

Ya en la madrugada se quitó. Pues a esas horas cuando se quitó el llorido, un primo hermano jue pallá pa onde estaba el llorido a ver, y era un brazo de árbol atrincao a otro asina. Como hizo cruz, atrincao. Cuando hacía viento, movía este brazo pacá y aquel pal otro lao, y ahi estaba el rechinaido. Lloraba lo mismo que una llorona.

Yo creo que eso sería lo que oía la gente munchas veces. Estaba haciendo viento, y estos palos se pegaban, y ahi estaba el llorido, llorido.

Isabel Romero

LAS VEGAS, NEW MEXICO

Una vieja camaldolera

Y eso de La Llorona, había un lugar que lo conocí. Había un río mediano y una alameda. Luego, munchas veces ahi en aqueos años, la gente usaba tiros de mulas o tiros de caballos en los carros. No había automoviles, naa como ora. Y había un bosque.

Pues ahi en tal bosque salía La Llorona. Güeno, pues, La Llorona era viuda. Vieja ya. Y ésa se enbocaa entre las jaras, y cuando iba pasando alguien que llevaa comida, "¡Ayyyy!" Lloraba. Pus le tiraba la comida y arrancaan a juir. Ahi estaa La Llorona. Y luego, pues, güeno, pus La Llorona se clavaa.

Luego al fin una vez había un hombre, mi tío Abel. ¡Bárbaro! Era muy atroz él y campó en un lugar ahi. Loo se levantó muy en la madrugada él. Era muy madrugador, muy hombrote. Iba por los caballos allí, cuando salió La Llorona, y él, pus, no tenía miedo. Se jue y se asomó. ¡Palo, palo! Tres azotes. "¡Ay!, nito. No me, no me, no me pegues."

Pus era La Llorona, una vieja, camaldolera, como dijían. Pus salía, y le tiraban la comida. Ea se clavaba. Ahi cuando le pegó mi tío, "¡Ay!, nito. No me pegues. Soy Julana."

"Pus pa que no güelvas." Y le pegó una suriguanga. Le dio con un cabresto o con un chicote. Le pegó una azotería o le pegó una turra. Ahi se acabó La Llorona.

Ophelia Ipolita María de Gracia Sandoval de Rinaldi

BERNALILLO, NEW MEXICO

Los monstruos

Bueno, era la historia del Coco. "No vayan pa la cequia. No se vayan a la cequia porque ahi está el Coco." Pues no íbanos. En esos días éranos muy obedecientes. Teníanos miedo. Y que no entráranos a cierto lugar porque ahi estaba el Coco. Salía en la noche cuando estaba muy oscuro.

Después oí que era La Llorona. "Que no vayan a la cequia aá en la noche." Nos contaban que La Llorona era una [mujer] que andaba en las orillas de la 'cequia buscando a sus hijitos y si hallaba niños ahi se los llevaba.

Eso tamién le contaba yo a mis hijitos, porque nosotros teníanos la cequia en seguida de la casa. Ellos a veces que no entendían muncho de La Llorona, pero sí entendían de los monstruos. Ya después era que "no se vayan a la cequia porque hay munchos monstruos," no de La Llorona.

Eileen Dolores Treviño Villarreal

SAN ANTONIO, TEXAS

La Llorona

También San Antonio tiene Llorona. Una mujer ahogó a sus tres hijos en el San Pedro Creek, en el centro de San Antonio, hace muchos, muchos años. Ya después lloraba ella, y han dicho muchos, bueno ciertas gentes, hace años, hablando de la misma Llorona, que la veían llorando en la noches, a la medianoche, llorando en el San Pedro Creek. Llorando por los niños que había ahogado ella. No se sabe por qué ahogó a los niños.

Alfredo Ulibarrí

LAS VEGAS, NEW MEXICO

La Llorona

En ese tiempo ahi hasta de noche en el Cañón, cuando iba de ver a mi esposa, antes de casarnos, porque ea vivía lejos de onde vivía yo, iba a caballo a vela. Y cuando iba, too el Cañón lloraba como lloran las zorras. Lloran como un muchito chiquito, y dijían qu'era La Llorona. Las zorras esas sí lloran como una llorona, ciertamente.

Pero te espantas. Siempre te espantas. Se te enchira el cuero. Pus le apretaba al caballo y me iba. En la noche que llegaa aá, había veces que metía el caballo contoy silla al corral, porque me daba miedo—pus solo, solo. ¡Y un zurrón! Pero las zorras lloran como un muchito chiquito. Por eso dicen que son las lloronas. Yo creo qu'eran las zorras, porque yo las llegué a ver.

Glossary

This glossary is aimed primarily at helping the Spanish speaker who is not familiar with the Spanish dialect of northern New Mexico and southern Colorado, although the pronunciation and orthography of many of the terms from these two regions may well exist in other parts of the southwestern United States. The existence of archaisms such as *mesmo* (mismo), *dijites* (dijiste*)*, *cuasi* (casi), or *truje* (traje) takes us back several hundred years in northern New Mexico, whereas in states like California and Texas, this linguistic phenomenon is much more recent in comparison. The principal reason is because of the immigration of Spanish speakers to the Southwest from Latin American countries such as Argentina, Nicaragua, and Colombia, and especially Mexico. But so-called Mexicanisms (*trastes=platos*) imported from Mexico, including those derived from Náhuatl (*chíquete=chicle*), and local Anglicisms (*bogue=buggy*), coupled with an array of additional pronunciations (*muría=moría, siñor=señor*) contribute to the Spanish dialect of northern New Mexico and southern Colorado.

Regional Word	Standard Spanish Word	Translation
A		
abajarme	bajarme	to get down (from a wagon)
a case 'e	en casa de	at so and so's house
a en papá	a papá	(for) dad
aá	allá	there; over there
abajan	bajan	they come or go down
abajo	bajo	I come or go down
abandonao	abandonado	abandoned
abujas	agujas	needles
acabao	acabado	finished
acidente	accidente	accident
acostao/a	acostado/a	(he/she) is lying down; (he/she has) gone to bed; (he/she is) in bed

Regional Word	Standard Spanish Word	Translation
acuérdesen	acuérdense	remember
agarrábanos	agarrábamos	we grabbed; earned
agüelita	abuelita	grandma
agüelitos	abuelitos	grandparents
ahi	ahí	there
aigre	aire	air; wind
ajuera	afuera	outdoors
ajueros	agujeros	holes
albolario	arbolario	herb healer
alborotao	alborotado	excited, worked up
Alburquerque	Albuquerque	(modern spelling)
alguen	alguien	someone
almuada	almohada	pillow
amaraa	amarrada	tied up
amás	además	besides; in addition to
anancas	en ancas	on the rump (of a horse)
andaa	andaba	he/she/you walked, ran around
andaan	andaban	they/you walked, ran around
andao	andado	walked; run around
ánsar	ansara	goose
ansí	así	thus; in that way
ansina	así	thus; in that way
antonces	entonces	then
apá	papá	dad; father
apagates	apagaste	you turned off
apié	apeé	to dismount; to get down
aplaneó	llegó	he reached (the ravine)
aqueos	aquellos	those (things, matters)
arbularios	arbolarios	herb healers
arrancaan	arrancaban	they took off running
arrastraan	arrastraban	they/you dragged; excelled
arreglao	arreglado	arranged; repaired, fixed
arrendé (me)	volví (me)	I turned back
asegún	según	according to
asina	así	thus; in that way
asustaa	asustada	scared, frightened
atoqué	toqué	I touched
atrás	detrás	behind

Regional Word	Standard Spanish Word	Translation
atrincao	atrincado	up against (something)
automoviles	automóviles	automobiles
aventao	aventado	excelled; farted
avisale	avisarle	to inform him/her/you; to notify him/her/you
avisales	avisarles	to inform them/you; to notify them/you
ayudale	ayudarle	to help him/her/you
azotería	paliza	a beating

B

bajábanos	bajábamos	we climbed down
bajao	bajado	climbed down
baliaron	balearon	they/you shot (at), wounded
balió	baleó	he/she/you shot (at), wounded
bajo	abajo	underneath
baquiaba	baqueaba (retrocedía)	to back up
bogue	"buggy"	buggy
bonche	montón	bunch; bundle
borrachada	borrachera	drunkenness
buscalo	buscarlo	to look for him/it
buslándose	burlándose	making fun of
buslarse	burlarse	to make fun of someone

C

cabresto	cabestro	rope
caidas	caídas	falls; fallen
caido	caído	fallen
cajete	tina	tin tub; bathtub; vat
cajón	ataúd	coffin
calentón	fogón	wood stove
camalta	cama	bed
campaban	acampaban	they/you camped
campiando	acampando	camping
carbulador	carburador	carburetor
'caricié	acaricié	I caressed
casao	casado	married
casorio	boda	wedding

Regional Word	Standard Spanish Word	Translation
cequia	acequia	ditch
cerrao(s)	cerrado(s)	closed; shut
chamacos	muchachos	boys
chequiaba	revisaba	he/she/you checked
chequiar (chequear)	revisar	to check
chequié	revisé	I checked
'chó	echó	he/she/you put it (outside)
cirgüela	ciruela	plum
clas	clase	class; kind; type
clavaa	clavaba; clavada	he/she/you nailed; nail-studded
colgao	colgado	hung up
Colorao	Colorado	Colorado
componer	arreglar	to fix
comprale	comprarle	to buy from/for him/her/you
compralo	comprarlo	to buy it
comunidá	comunidad	community
contale	contarle	to tell him/her/you
contoy	con todo y	together with; with everything
coraje	furia	anger
corajudo	de genio vivo	ill-tempered
correlos	correrlos	to chase, run them off
cosechao	cosechado	harvested
'costaron	acostaron	they/you went to bed; put to bed
cranque	manivela	crank (car)
craquiaba(n)	daban palmadas	he/she clapped; they/you clapped
creelo	creerlo	to believe it
creiba(n)	creía(n)	I/he/she/you believed; they/you believed
creibo	creo	I believe
creyer	creer	to believe
creyes	crees	you believe
creyo	creo	I believe
criatura	niño(a); bebé	child; baby
cuasi	casi	almost

Regional Word	Standard Spanish Word	Translation
cuidáanos	cuidábamos	we took care of
cuidao	cuidado	care; careful
cuitiamos	dejamos; paramos	we quit
cuñao	cuñado	brother-in-law
curalo	curarlo	to cure him
curre	corre	run; scoot

D

d'ella	de ella	hers; from her
d'ellos	de ellos	theirs; from them
d'en	de en	from
d'en casa	de en casa	from home
d'esa	de esa	of that; from that
d'eso	de eso	of that; from that
d'éstas	de estas	of these
d'estos	de estos	of these
d'este	de este	of this
dale	darle	to give to him/her/you
de a case	de la casa de	from his/her house
debíanos	debíamos	we owed; we ought to
decíanos	decíamos	we said; would say; used to say
deciles	decirles	to tell them/you
degollao	degollado	slaughtered
dejao	dejado	allowed; left
dejates	dejaste	you left (behind)
dél	de él	his
deletriao	deletreado	spelled (out)
deletriar	deletrear	to spell (out)
deletrió	deletreó	he/she/you spelled (out)
dende	desde	since
derición	dirección	direction; address (home)
desabrochao	desabrochado	unbuttoned; unzipped
desgreñao	desgreñado	disheveled
deshojalo	deshojarlo	to shuck (corn)
desmayao	desmayado	fainted
desparatiar	desparpajar	to spoil; to prattle
desparece	desaparece	he/she disappears; you disappear

Regional Word	Standard Spanish Word	Translation
desparecieron	desaparecieron	they/you disappeared
despareció	desapareció	he/she/you disappeared
desparezco	desaparezco	I disappear
destendido	extendido	spread out; stretched out
destornudaba	estornudaba	he/she/you sneezed; would sneeze
destornudó	estornudó	he/she/you sneezed
detenela	detenerla	to hold her back; to detain her
diantre	diablo	devil
dicemos	decimos	we say
dicía	decía	he/she/you said, used to say
dicían	decían	they/you said, used to say
dicirle	decirle	to tell him/her/you
dificultá	dificultad	difficulty
dijemos	decimos	we say
dijían	decían	they/you said, used to say
dijíanos	decíamos	we said, used to say
dijiera	dijera	(for him/her/you) to say
dijieron	dijeron	he/she/you said
dijir	decir	to say
dijunto	difunto	corpse; dead person
dionde	de donde	from where
disparatiando	disparatando	talking nonsense; acting foolishly
dispensa	despensa	pantry; storage shed
disque	dizque; se dice que	apparently; supposedly; it is said
diun	de un	of a(n)
diuna	de una	of a(n)
diuno	de uno	belonging to oneself
doblaos	doblados	folded
durmido	dormido	asleep
durmimos	dormimos	we sleep

E

ea	ella	she
echale	echarle	to put, toss in
echao	echado	tossed in

Regional Word	Standard Spanish Word	Translation
edá	edad	age; period
embolaos	borrachos	drunks
embrujao	embrujado	bewitched
empachao	empachado	suffering from indigestion (baby)
enbocaa	embocaba	pushed ahead
enchira	hincha	he/she/it swells up
enfermalo	enfermarlo	to get him/it sick
enfermedá	enfermedad	illness
engüelto	envuelto	wrapped up
enpelotaba	desnudaba	he/she/you undressed; stripped
enpezó	empezó	he/she/you started
enseñale	enseñarle	to show him/her/you
entemecían	intimidaban	they intimidated
enteresao	interesado	interested
enterrao	enterrado	buried
entrábanos	entrábamos	we entered; used to enter
entráranos	entráramos	for us (to enter)
entro	dentro	inside
entumido	entumecido	numb
envenenao	envenenado	poisoned
eos	ellos	they
escamó (me)	espantó (me)	he/she/it scared me
escuro	oscuro	dark
escusao	escusado	outhouse
espantaos	espantados	scared
esperencia	experiencia	experience
espirina	aspirina	aspirin
esque	dizque; se dice que	apparently; supposedly; it is said
estaa	estaba	he/she/it was; you were
estáanos	estábamos	we were
estábanos	estábamos	we were
estao	estado	state; been
estrellido	temblor	tremor
estuvites	estuviste	you were

Regional Word	Standard Spanish Word	Translation
F		
fiero/a	feo/a	ugly
fierro	hierro	iron; branding iron
friego	lavo	I wash (dishes)
G		
galopiando	galopando	galloping
ganao	ganado	cattle; livestock
garramos	agarramos	we grabbed, seized
garrao	agarrado	grabbed; seized
garrar	agarrar	to grab, seize
garrara	agarrara	(for you) to grab, seize
gaselín	gasolina	gasoline
golpiao/a	golpeado/a	beaten up
golvieron	volvieron	they/you returned
golvió	volvió	he/she/you returned
gómitos	vómitos	vomits; vomitings
greso/a	grueso/a	thick
Gualupe	Guadalupe	Guadalupe
güelta	vuelta	turn; return
güelve	vuelve	he/she/you returns
güen	buen	good
güeno/a	bueno/a	good
güero(s)	huero(s); rubio(s)	blond
güevo	huevo	egg; testicle; ball
güevón	perezoso	lazy
H		
ha	he	I have (*haber*)
habelas	haberlas	to have them
habíanos	habíamos	we had
hablale	hablarle	to speak to him/her/you
haiga	haya	there is (*haber*)
hallao	hallado	found
herrao	herrado	shod (horse); branded (cow)
herrates	herraste	you shoed; you branded
hicites	hiciste	you did; you made
hinchinchó	hinchó	it swelled, puffed up
hogo	ahogo	I drown

Regional Word	Standard Spanish Word	Translation
hogó	ahogó	he/she/you drowned

I

íbanos	íbamos	we went, used to go
ingenio	motor	motor (car/truck)
ispiaba	espiaba	I/he/she/you spied (on)
isque	dizque; se dice que	apparently; supposedly; it is said

J

jalaa	halaba	he/she/you pulled, towed, used to pull, tow
jalándola	halándola	pulling it, towing it
jallaba	hallaba	he/she/you found; discovered
jallaban	hallaban	they/you found; discovered
jallamos	hallamos	we found; discovered
jallar	hallar	to find; discover
jallé	hallé	I found; discovered
jerró	erró	he/she/you missed (target)
jirviendo	hirviendo	boiling
jita	hijita	dear daughter
jogón	fógon	stove (wood); heater
jondas	hondas	slings
jue	fue	he/she/you/it went
juera	fuera	(for him/her/you) to go
juera	afuera	outside
jueron	fueron	they/you went
juerte	fuerte	strong
jui	fui	I went
juía	huía	he/she/you fled; escaped, would escape
juimos	huimos	we fled
juir	huir	to flee; to escape
juntra	junto a	near; close to
juyendo	huyendo	fleeing; escaping
juygan	huyan	(for them/you) to flee
juyó	huyó	he/she/you fled; escaped

Regional Word	Standard Spanish Word	Translation
L		
l'agarraba	lo/a agarraba	he/she/you grabbed, caught it
l'agua	el agua	water
'l anillo	el anillo	ring
'l asilo	el asilo	asylum
l'eché	lo eché	I poured it
l'escuela	la escuela	school
'l espinazo	el espinazo	backbone; spine
l'hecho	lo hecho	what is done
l'hizo	lo hizo	he/she/you made it
'l hocico	el hocico	the snout; mouth
l'ochó	lo echó	he/she/you poured it
l'osa	la osa	bear
l'único	lo único	the only thing
l'zotea	la azotea	roof
lao	lado	side
lazao	lazado	roped; lassoed
lego	luego	then; afterwards; later (on)
leido	leído	read
levantates	levantaste	you lifted; got up
limpiale	limpiarle	to clean (car)
llamaa	llamaba	his/her name was
llamala	llamarla	to call her
llegáanos	llegábamos	we arrived, would arrive
llegao	llegado	arrived
llentes	dientes	teeth
llevaa	llevaba	he/she/you carried; took away; wore; led
llevalos	llevarlos	to take them
llevao	llevado	carried; taken
logo	luego	then
loo	luego	then
loquera	locura	craziness
lotro/a	el/la otro/a	the other
M		
'marré	amarré	I tied; secured
m'hijo/a	mi hijo/a	my daughter/son

Regional Word	*Standard Spanish Word*	*Translation*
macánico	mecánico	mechanic
malificia	maleficio	spell; enchantment
mamao	mamado	nursed; fed
mandale	mandarle	to send to him/her/you
matao	matado	killed; slaughtered
médico	arbolario	herbalist
menso	tonto; estúpido	dumb; stupid
mentao	de mucha fama	well known
mercé	merced	land grant
mesmo/a	mismo/a	same
mestro/a	maestro/a	teacher
mitá	mitad	half
mono	muñeco/a; fantasma	doll; ghost
monquiando	traveseando	being naughty, mischievous
montaja	montaje	assembly; montage
montao	montado	mounted
moos	modos	manners; ways
muchichito/a	muchachito/a	little boy/girl
muchito/a	muchachito/a	little boy/girl
muncho/a	mucho/a	a lot
muría	moría	he/she/you/it died, would die
murirse	morirse	to die
muvimiento	movimiento	movement

N

naa	nada	nothing
nagua	enagua	skirt; underskirt
naide	nadie	nobody
naiden	nadie	nobody
nito	hermanito; niñito	little brother; my good (dear) boy
niuna	ni una	not a one
nochi	noche	night
nojó	enojó	he/she/you got mad
nomás	solamente; nada más	only; nothing more
notates	notaste	you noticed
nuevas	notícias	news

Regional Word	Standard Spanish Word	Translation
Ñ / N		
ñeca	muñeca	doll
nojotros	nosotros	we
O		
obedecientes	obedientes	obedient
oido	oído	heard
olvidao	olvidado	forgotten
onde	donde	where
ónde	dónde	where
ondequiera	dondequiera	wherever
oportunidá	oportunidad	chance; opportunity
ora	ahora	now
oyer	oír	to hear
oyí	oí	I heard
oyimos	oímos	we heard
oyindo	oyendo	hearing
oyites	oíste	you heard
P		
pa	para	for
pa 'celes	para hacerles	to make for them
pacá	para acá	over here
pa cas' e	para casa de	headed for (mother's) house
pader	pared	wall
pagale	pagarle	to pay him/her/you
pal	para el	for the
pallá	para allá	over there
pa qué	para qué	why
par	para	for
parao/a	parado/a	stopped; standing up
parecer	aparecer	to appear
pardito	un poco gris	a little gray
parquiao	aparcado; estacionado	parked
parriba	para arriba	up there
pasao/a	pasado/a	past
pasiador	vagabundo	vagrant; bum
pasiándose	paseándose	visiting

Regional Word	Standard Spanish Word	Translation
patrás	para atrás	backwards; toward the back
pedo	borracho	drunk
peliaban	peleaban	they/you fought
peliar	pelear	to fight
pensábanos	pensábamos	we thought, used to think
pensao	pensado	thought
perdelo	perderlo	to lose him/her/it
pesao	pesado	heavy; boring; difficult
planiao	planeado	planned
platicao	platicado	talked
plebe	muchachos	boys
plebecita	muchachos	boys; kids
poblao	poblado	populated
poído	podido	able to; could
ponele	ponerle	to wear it; to place it
poníanos	poníamos	we put, used to put
porche	portal	porch; entrance hall
pos	pues	well
posesiado	poseído	possessed
prejuzgosa	prejuzgada	prejudgmental
prencipio	principio	beginning
prendelo/a	prenderlo/a	to start (the car)
prendío	prendido	turned on; lighted; started (the car)
prendites	prendiste	you turned on; lit; started (the car)
probe	pobre	poor
puee	puede	he/she/you can, are able to
pus	pues	well

Q

quebraa	quebrada	break (special favor)
qu'es que	dizque; se dice que	apparently; supposedly; it is said
qu'era	que era	that was
queríanos	queríamos	we wanted
Questa	Cuesta	Cuesta
quisque	dizque; se dice que	apparently; supposedly; it is said

Regional Word	Standard Spanish Word	Translation
R		
Rafelita	Rafaelita	Raphaela (diminutive)
rasguñao	rasguñado	scratched
rechinaido	rechinando	squeaking
redepente	de repente	all of a sudden; suddenly
renaje	drenaje	drainage ditch
robao	robado	robbed; stolen
rodiaba	rodeaba	circled; surrounded
S		
sacala	sacarla	to remove her/it
salíanos	salíamos	we would go out, leave
sei	sí	yes
seigas	seas	to be (impossible)
sembrarillo	sembrío	sown land
semos	somos	we are
sentao	sentado	seated
shainiaditos	con buen brillo	really shined
siguimos	seguimos	we follow; followed
silleta	silla	chair
sinke	lavabo	sink
sintía	sentía	he/she/you felt
sociedá	sociedad	society
solevao	solevado	slight case of fright
sopa	capirotada	bread pudding with raisins and cheese
soponía	suponía	supposed
subíanos	subíamos	we climbed, used to climb
suriguanga	friega	beating
T		
taa	todavía	yet; still
tamién	también	also
tan	bien	really (crazy)
tapao/a	tapado/a	covered; dense; stupid
tavía	todavía	yet; still
telefón	teléfono	telephone
telefoniaron	telefonearon	they/you telephoned

Regional Word	*Standard Spanish Word*	*Translation*
tenela	tenerla	to have her/it
teníanos	teníamos	we had, used to have
tercer	tercera	third
terremote	terrón	clump of earth
tirala	tirarla	to toss it
toavía	todavía	yet; still
tomao	tomado; borracho	drunk
tonces	entonces	then
tonteras	tonterías	foolishness; stupidity
too/a	todo/a	all
toos	todos	everyone
traiba	traía	he/she/you brought, used to bring
tráibanos	traíamos	we brought, used to bring
traido	traído	brought
traila	traerla	to bring it
tranpada	trampada	packed
trastes	platos	dishes
tresquilar	trasquilar	to shear
tresquilando	trasquilando	shearing
triques	tretas	tricks
troca	camioneta	truck
troquero	camionero	truck driver
truje	traje	I brought
trujiera	trajera	(for you) to bring
trujieron	trajeron	they/you brought
trujites	trujiste	you brought
trujo	trajo	he/she/you brought
turra	zurra	flogging, whipping
tuvo	estuvo	was

U

usaa	usaba	he/she/you used
usábanos	usábamos	we used
usté	usted	you

V

| veigas | veas | (for you) to see |

Regional Word	Standard Spanish Word	Translation
veigo	veo	I see
velo/a	verlo/a	to see him/her/it
verdá	verdad	truth
vía	veía	he/she/you saw, would see
vían	veían	they/you saw, would see
vide	vi	I saw
vido	vio	he/she/you saw
vieja	esposa	wife (term of endearment)
vientoso	ventoso	windy
vinía	venía	he/she/you came, used to come
vinir	venir	to come
vistía	vestía	would dress; used to dress
vites	viste	you saw
vivemos	vivimos	we live; lived
voltiábanos	volteábamos	we turned, used to turn

W X Y Z

zurrón	mucha mierda	lots of shit

Informants

BIOGRAPHICAL DATA

The information provided here aims only to give the reader a brief look at the informants' backgrounds; it is by no means intended to serve in lieu of an all-inclusive summary of the interview or information provided through correspondence.

Jesusita Aragón

Born March 26, 1908, Las Vegas, New Mexico. Interviewed for an hour on April 11, 1994, in Las Vegas. Passed away in 2005. Perhaps the most renowned midwife in the state's history; she delivered thousands of babies in her lifetime. She will always be remembered for her altruistic nature.

Francisco Argüelles

Born October 4, 1978, in La Jolla, California; currently lives in Oceanside, California. His stories show a duality in that they take place in both Mexico and the United States. Written in English, they were submitted for inclusion in the present collection on October 29, 2005.

Lucinda Atencio

Born in Cañón, New Mexico, Sandoval County, July 14, 1894; passed away in Albuquerque on November 24, 1978. A folk healer whose knowledge of medicinal herbs as well as Latino folklore of northern New Mexico was incalculable. Two separate interviews: one on August 19, 1977, and the second on March 30, 1978. Total time of interviews about two hours.

Enrique Campos

Born August 27, 1981, in Dewa (Degua), Mexico. Interviewed on October 17, 2005, in Pomona, California. Interview, specifically on witchcraft and the supernatural, lasted about twenty minutes.

Connie Chacón

Born in Ojo Caliente, New Mexico, on May 7, 1908. Married Juan Bautista Chacón in Santa Fe, New Mexico, in 1946. Moved to Pueblo,

Colorado, in 1952. Interview held on October 6, 1983, was less than an hour. It focused on short stories.

Juan Bautista Chacón

Born September 9, 1912, in El Rito, New Mexico. Moved with his wife to Pueblo, Colorado, in 1952. In his interview of October 6, 1983, he spoke chiefly about witchcraft although other topics were discussed. Interview lasted about forty-five minutes.

Adrián Chávez

Born December 15, 1913, in Armijo, southwest Albuquerque, and moved to Guadalupe in the Río Puerco Valley with his stepparents in 1926 and remained there until 1941. A musician with a penchant for humor. Resided in the Armijo area until his death in December 2006. Interview of August 16, 1977, over an hour.

José D. Chávez

Born April 9, 1921, in Cuba, New Mexico. Moved to Bernalillo circa 1930. Worked as a young boy for the WPA to help support his family. Profound and philosophical thinker. March 16, 2000, interview, covering an array of topics, lasted about an hour and a half.

Samuel Córdova

Born March 17, 1895, in Guadalupe, New Mexico, and died September 4, 1979, in Albuquerque. Wonderful storyteller whose poetic descriptions were seductive. Was philosophical in his outlook on life. A veritable gentleman whose words spoke volumes. Interviewed on August 17, 1977, for an hour.

Yolanda del Villar

Born August 29, 1961, in Nava, Coahuila, Mexico. At present she resides in San Antonio, Texas. Interview in Spanish on the supernatural was held at the University of Texas at San Antonio on September 8, 2005.

Marcos C. Durán

Born in 1899 (day and month unknown) in Los Pinos, New Mexico, close to the Colorado border and died in Pueblo, Colorado, on February 27, 1984. Interview of February 26, 1980, consisted of folklore in general, including witchcraft stories. Interview lasted about an hour and a half.

Sofia L. Durán

Born November 15, 1901, in Conejos (?), Colorado. Married Marcos C. Durán. Interview of March 7, 1980, consisted of folklore in general. It about one hour and fifteen minutes. She died in Pueblo, Colorado, where she had lived for many years, which is also where the interview took place.

Filiberto Esquibel

Born August 7, 1928, in Cañada del Medio, New Mexico. Interviewed April 18, 1994, in Las Vegas, New Mexico, for an hour and a half. Well-known musician throughout the state and versatile raconteur. He spoke on a variety of topics, from music, education, and politics to cultural traditions.

Juvenal Fuentes

Born May 3, 1968, in Tonatico, state of Mexico. Migrated to the United States in 1987. Resides in Oceanside, California. His story, written in Spanish, was submitted October 30, 2005. He taped ghost stories for radio broadcasting while he lived in Mexico.

Bencés Gabaldón

Born May 12, 1894, in San Luis, New Mexico. A longtime resident of Bernalillo, north of Albuquerque, where he died on March 12, 1994. A devout Catholic, he sang *alabados* (religious hymns) with a passion. Drove his old truck until near the end of his life. Interview of December 29, 1981, lasted about an hour. Covered an array of topics regarding Latino culture.

Leonila "Linda" Galván de Chávez

Born October 4, 1925, in Monterrey, Nuevo León, Mexico. She came to the United States in 1955. Currently resides in Claremont, California. The interview, conducted on October 16, 2005, lasted less than an hour. She talked about buried treasure, the Devil, and the evil eye.

Joe E. Garcia

Born March 14, 1936, in Prescott, Arizona. He is a Korean War veteran and worked as a power-company lineman. After leaving the Air Force, he worked in California, New Mexico, and Alaska, constructing power lines. His story was sent to me via regular mail on November 8, 2005.

Nasario P. García
Born September 10, 1912, the year New Mexico became a state, in Guadalupe (Rincón del Cochino), New Mexico; passed away March 9, 2001, in Los Ranchos de Alburquerque. A veritable encyclopedia regarding rural life, with a beautiful command of colonial Spanish. Several interviews over a twenty-five-year period, starting on October 18, 1979, totaled five to seven hours.

Teodorita García-Ruelas
Born January 5, 1908, in Guadalupe, New Mexico, where she lived until marrying Felipe Ruelas in late 1930s in Albuquerque's Martíneztown. Quite well versed on her birthplace and family way of life. She died in Albuquerque. Interview conducted March 27, 1980, lasted slightly over an hour.

Carmelita Gómez
Born May 12, 1909, in Aguilar, New Mexico. Interviewed May 2, 1994, in Las Vegas, New Mexico, for about a half hour. Good sense of humor; liked to tell family stories, among them those related to witchcraft.

Adelita Gonzales
Born June 11, 1909, Guadalupe, New Mexico, and died in Albuquerque on February 20, 1990. Self-taught in reading and arithmetic, which enabled her to become post-mistress. Renowned *rezadora* (prayer leader); knowledgeable about various facets of Latino culture. Interview of August 16, 1977, lasted nearly two hours.

Reynaldo Gonzales
Born April 13, 1914, in Los Juertes, New Mexico. Principal information shared in interview, which lasted about an hour, pertained to ranching and farming, witchcraft stories, and corrupt politicians in Las Vegas, where he made his home since 1946 until he passed away in April 2003.

Gilberta Herguera Turner
Born on November 4, 1942, in San Pedro de Gaíllos in the Segovia province of Spain. Married Kenneth, a career airman in the U.S. Air Force. She's pursuing a master's degree in Spanish, University of Texas at San Antonio. Resident of Wincrest, Texas, where interview took place on October 6, 2005.

Mauricio Hernández

Born February 14, 1983, in Mexico City. Currently a resident of Oceanside, California; he has been in California nine years. Devoted to honoring his ancestors on Día de los Muertos (Day of the Dead). His brief story for this book was written in English and submitted October 30, 2005.

Rolando Hinojosa Smith

Born on January 21, 1929, in Mercedes, Texas. Pioneer in Chicano literature and renowned for his fictional works portraying life in the Lower Río Grande Valley of Texas, from people's language, customs, and happiness to social and racial strife. Has garnered numerous literary accolades. Adept at writing in either English or Spanish. A giant in the canons of Chicano literature. Story received via regular mail on November 19, 2005.

Rita Leyba Last

Born September 28, 1932, in Bernalillo (El Llanito), New Mexico. Married to William Last. She and her husband currently live in Bernalillo, home for most of her life, but she lived in rural New Mexico when she started school. Interview of August 6, 2000, lasted an hour and a half.

Celia López

Born in San Juan, Argentina, on November 19, 1959. She was awarded a doctorate in history from the University of Sevilla, Spain. Married to Tom E. Chávez, a historian, she is an associate professor in the Honors Program at the University of New Mexico. Stories sent via e-mail on February 5, 2006.

César G. López

Born January 7, 1939, in Cartagena, Spain. Came to this country many years ago. Received his doctorate from the University of Southern California. Currently professor of Spanish at Scripps College in Claremont, California. His story on the *meigas* (*brujas*), popular in Galicia, Spain, was submitted via e-mail in Spanish on January 9, 2006.

Edumenio "Ed" Lovato

Born February 12, 1913, in San Luis, New Mexico, in the Río Puerco Valley. An avid reader and a "pack rat" whose treasure trove included riddles, stories, folk sayings, and ballads on New Mexican folklore, which he was willing to share. Interview of July 30, 1985, lasted one and a half hours.

Salomon "Sal" Lovato

Born in San Luis, New Mexico, on April 4, 1915. Allegiance to his birthplace and strong defender of ranchers' rights against alleged government injustices. Tremendous reservoir of information on his region. Interview lasted about three and a half hours; took place on October 10, 1979, in Albuquerque.

Tomás Lozano

Born in Granollers, Spain, on March 10, 1967, but has been a New Mexico resident for a number of years. He is a folklorist and professional musician who links New Mexico's Latino music with Spain via Mexico. His stories in this collection were submitted in Spanish via e-mail on December 16, 2005.

Benjamín "Benny" Lucero

Born June 29, 1924, in Cabezón, New Mexico. Married Egripina (Pina) Lovato in 1945. Moved to Albuquerque in early 1950s; returned to Cabezón after retirement, where he is buried. Died on April 7, 2004. Interview of December 29, 1981, contains invaluable information on rural life.

Manuel de Jesús Manzanares

Born on January 1, 1912, in El Rito del Oso, Colorado, in Huérfano County. Moved to Pueblo, Colorado, in 1947. Shared various kinds of stories, including witchcraft lore. Interview of October 5, 1983, centered on folklore and lasted around an hour and fifteen minutes.

María Teresa Márquez

Born in El Paso, Texas (date and month not known). At present a librarian at the University of New Mexico's Center for Southwest Research; specializes in Chicana/Chicano literature. Has published numerous articles in that area. Holds master's degrees in library science and public administration. Her stories for this book were submitted in English in November 2005.

Consuelo Martínez

Born September 23, 1978, in Santa Ana, California. She has ties to Baja California, where her parents own a home. At the present time she makes her home in Escondido, California. Her handwritten story was donated on October 30, 2005.

Phoebe Martínez Struck

Born April 4, 1919, in Taos, New Mexico. Married Ernesto Struck. Both she and her husband moved to Pueblo, Colorado, in 1952, where the interview took place on October 13, 1983; it lasted about thirty minutes. She shared stories and riddles.

María A. Mongalo

Born September 10, 1961, in Granada, Nicaragua. Came to the United States circa 1981. At present time lives in Riverside, California. Interview took place at Scripps College, Claremont, California, on October 17, 2005. Topics dealt exclusively with witchcraft tales heard from family members.

Cesaria Montoya

Born February 5, 1929, in San Pablo, New Mexico. Interviewed April 4, 1994, in Las Vegas for an hour and a half. Spoke about a variety of topics ranging from politics, education, religion, fiestas, and games to superstitions and the supernatural. Has clever sense of humor. Still resides in Las Vegas.

Filimón Montoya

Born June 30, 1915, in Cañón de Fernández, Taos County. In an interview slightly over an hour, taped on May 23, 1994, in Las Vegas, he spoke of disappearance of religious customs, lack of respect among youth toward elders, games, and traditional holidays among Latinos, plus stories of sorcery and ghosts, and corruption in politics. Has passed on since interview.

José Nataleo Montoya

Born July 3, 1929, in San Pablo, New Mexico. Interviewed May 23, 1994, in Las Vegas. Spoke for an hour and a half about ranch life in general as well as religious ceremonies, popular holidays, education, politics, and, of course, ghosts and the supernatural.

Lugardita Anita Montoya

Born April 6, 1924, in Old Town Albuquerque. Married Sabino Montoya on December 16, 1940, in Bernalillo, New Mexico, where her parents moved when she was very young. Shared her way of life in traditional Latino culture. Interview of December 15, 2000, lasted more than an hour.

Rima Montoya
Born November 15, 1969, in Seville, Spain, but has also lived in Costa Rica, her father's birthplace. A freelance writer, she has lived in New Mexico for several years and currently resides in Albuquerque. Her story for this book was submitted in English via e-mail in December 2005.

Rudy Montoya
Born March 12, 1927, in Albuquerque, New Mexico. Comes from a political family in Sandoval County. His cousin Joe Montoya was a U.S. senator for many years. Straightforward in his discussion of several topics related to his culture; the August 22, 2000, interview lasted about an hour.

Emilia Padilla García
Born in Pecos, New Mexico, on July 24, circa 1885, and died in Albuquerque on August 26, 1972. An orphan after her father died in a coal cart accident, she married Teodoro José García in 1898 at age thirteen. She was interviewed along with her husband in 1968; both died in 1972 in Martíneztown in Albuquerque.

Manuel Pérez
Born April 4, 1932, in Bernalillo, New Mexico. Has lived there all his life. His paternal grandfather came to New Mexico from Spain as a sheepherder. Interesting family background. Knows his hometown well. Interview of May 15, 2000, lasted less than an hour.

Luis Esteban Reyes
Born October 29, 1966, in Bogotá, Colombia. Came to the United States about ten years ago as a student. An engineer, he is married to a dentist. Interviewed October 17, 2005, in Upland, California; his countryside stories relate to witchcraft in Colombia. Interview lasted about thirty minutes.

Damiano Romero
Born June 4, 1916, in Casa Salazar, New Mexico; died in Albuquerque on February 22, 1984. Interview of August 18, 1977, lasted about an hour and a half; was provocative and philosophical. Spoke of Christmas, sports, religion, superstitions, folklore, and government's intrusion in rancher's way of life.

Isabel Romero

Born November 5, 1896, in Sabinoso, New Mexico. In interview of April 8, 1994, in Las Vegas, lasting a little over an hour, he spoke of being a cowboy on the famous Bell Ranch, a sheepherder, and a goatherd. Stories about his grandfather's buffalo-hunting ventures. Tales of ghosts added to the luster.

Mariel Romero Ocaranza

Born April 8, 1985, in Chula Vista, California. Grew up in Tijuana, Mexico. Came to the United States in 2003. In Tijuana she heard the legends of Baja California, including Tía Juana and Juan Soldado. At present a student at San Diego State University. Her story in English was sent via e-mail on November 29, 2005.

Luciano Sánchez

Born July 12, 1910, in Guadalupe, New Mexico. Moved to Los Griegos in Albuquerque in 1943. Recalled the camaraderie and respect among rural people. Story of multiple family deaths during influenza of 1918 is moving. December 29, 1977, interview in Los Griegos lasted less than an hour.

Patricia Sánchez

Born June 1, 1974, in Oaxaca, Mexico. Has lived in the United States six years. Currently resides in Vista, California. Handwrittten story in Spanish was submitted for this collection on October 30, 2005.

Victoria J. Sánchez

Born August 1, 1933, in McNary, Arizona. At present she and her husband Jess reside in Oceanside, California. Her story in English, submitted November 6, 2005, takes place in East Los Angeles in the 1950s.

Andrés Sánchez Rojas

Born November 11, 1962, in Tecomán, Mexico, in the state of Colima. At present time lives in Phoenix, Arizona. Interview lasted about forty-five minutes; was conducted in Peoria, a Phoenix suburb. The discussion focused on topics linked to personal encounters with supernatural phenomena.

José Sánchez Rojas
Born March 19, 1949, in Lázaro Cárdenas in the state of Michoacán, Mexico. Now lives in Phoenix, Arizona. Interviewed in Peoria, a suburb of Phoenix. Interview lasted about half an hour; it addressed topics of the supernatural based especially on personal experiences.

Ophelia Ipolita María de Gracia Sandoval de Rinaldi
Born March 26, 1933, in Las Cruces, New Mexico. Family moved to Bernalillo, New Mexico, in 1945. Mother and grandmother, she earned a bachelor's degree from the University of New Mexico. Intimately acquainted with Bernalillo. May 5, 2001, interview lasted about an hour.

Eliel Germán Soriano
Born December 18, 1987, in Tlacotepec, Mexico, in the state of Puebla. Interview took place in Pomona, California, October 17, 2005. It lasted around twenty minutes.

Ernesto Struck
Born in Ranchos de Taos, New Mexico, on January 9, 1918. Moved to Pueblo, Colorado, in 1952. Retired from Disabled American Veterans circa 1974. Interviewed in Pueblo on October 13, 1983. Spoke of folklore, short stories in particular. Interview lasted about a half hour.

Eddie Torres, Jr.
Born October 1, 1941, in Bernalillo, New Mexico. Married Viola Mora. Very active in community affairs. Retired from the Albuquerque Fire Department. Currently lives in El Bosque in Bernalillo. Interview on a number of subjects was about an hour long.

Eliseo "Cheo" Torres
Born June 14, 1945, in Poteet, Texas, but grew up in the Corpus Christi area of Texas. Greatly influenced by El Niño Fidencio of Espinazo, Mexico, which has resulted in a life-long study of and devotion to *curanderismo*. At the time this work was completed, he was vice president of student affairs at the University of New Mexico. His story in Spanish and English was sent via e-mail.

Eileen Dolores Treviño Villarreal

Born November 1, 1948, in San Antonio, Texas, where she continues to make her residence. Interview, which lasted about forty minutes, took place at the University of Texas at San Antonio on September 8, 2005. The specific topic was stories of the supernatural.

Alfredo Ulibarrí

Born February 14, 1923, in Las Vegas, New Mexico. Principal features of interview, held April 11, 1994, were superstitions and ghostly apparitions, education, politics, and family customs. Interview lasted just under an hour. He and his wife Teresina still reside in Las Vegas.

Teresina Ulibarrí

Born August 14, 1926, in Lagunita, New Mexico, was interviewed in Las Vegas on April 13, 1994, for about an hour. Spoke of her experiences as a farm girl, which also included political gatherings, games children played, dances and fights, religious practices, and witchcraft.

Adelina Valdez Chávez Baca

Born October 24, 1933, in Guadalupe (Ojo del Padre), New Mexico. At one time branded calves on her family ranch. Knowledgeable about farm-ranch life, including folklore and stories. At present resides in Bernalillo. Interview lasted around an hour.

Cruzita Vigil

Born in Corazón, New Mexico, on August 24, 1901. Interview, which lasted around two hours, was conducted on January 28, 1994, in Las Vegas. Her information on folk healing (including the evil eye), popular holidays, religious practices, family traditions, and superstitions was revealing.

Photographs

Unless stated otherwise, all photographs are courtesy of the informants, the informants' families, or the author.

Page xxiii, Movie set for *The Hired Hand,* constructed in Cabezón, New Mexico.

Page xxiv, Mission San Luis Rey de Francia.

Page 5, Nuestra Señora de los Dolores Church.

Page 5, Castañeda Hotel, Las Vegas, New Mexico.

Page 6, La Morada de Nuestra Señora de Dolores del Alto de Abiquiú, Abiquiú, New Mexico.

Page 10, Shaffer Hotel, Mountainair, New Mexico.

Page 10, Catholic church in Montezuma, New Mexico (north of Las Vegas).

Page 11, Sangre de Cristo Catholic Church, San Luis, Colorado.

Page 13, José D. Chávez, Bernalillo, New Mexico, March 16, 2000. Photo by Nasario García.

Page 22, Bencés Gabaldón, Bernalillo, New Mexico, August 25, 1989. Photo by Isabel A., Rodríguez; with permission.

Page 23, Nasario P. García, Los Ranchos de Alburquerque, July 15, 1980. Photo by Isabel A. Rodríguez; with permission.

Page 24, Teodorita García-Ruelas, Los Ranchos de Alburquerque, October 19, 1980. Photo by Isabel A. Rodríguez; with permission.

Page 26, Filimón Montoya, Las Vegas, New Mexico, May 30, 1994. Photo by Nasario García.

Page 27, Damiano Romero, Los Ranchos de Alburquerque, October 19, 1980. Photo by Isabel A. Rodríguez; with permission.

Page 28, Isabel Romero, Las Vegas, New Mexico, April 8, 1994. Photo by Nasario García.

Page 31, Eileen Dolores Treviño Villarreal, San Antonio, Texas, 2005. Photo courtesy of informant.

Page 32, Alfredo Ulibarrí, San Miguel del Vado Fiestas, Río Pecos Valley, New Mexico,1993. Photo by Nedra Westwater; with permission.

Page 53, Cowboy boots worn by New Mexico ranchers and wranglers. Photo by Nasario García, 2001.

Page 54, New Mexico rancher's saddle, saddle blanket, bridles, and ropes. Photo by Nasario García, 2001.

Page 59, Tomás Lozano, Ripoll, Spain, 2003. Photo courtesy of informant.

Page 60, Benjamín "Benny" Lucero, Albuquerque, New Mexico, December 29, 1981. Photo by Isabel A. Rodríguez; with permission.

Page 64, José Nataleo Montoya, San Miguel del Vado Fiestas, Río Pecos Valley, New Mexico, 1993. Photo by Nedra Westwater; with permission.

Page 65, Ophelia Ipolita María de Gracia Sandoval de Rinaldi, Bernalillo, New Mexico, 1996. Photo courtesy of informant.

Page 82, Stone home in southeastern rural New Mexico.

Page 82, The Plaza Hotel, Las Vegas, New Mexico.

Page 83, Spanish Mission, Old San Antonio, Texas.

Page 89, Reynaldo Gonzales, Las Vegas, New Mexico, August 20, 2000. Photo by Nasario García.

Page 90, Edumenio "Ed" Lovato, Albuquerque (Los Griegos), New Mexico, 1990. Photo by Nasario García.

Page 109, One-room schoolhouse, Red Wing, Colorado.

Page 110, Lucinda Atencio, Bernalillo, New Mexico, circa 1975. Photo courtesy Nasario García.

Page 112, Leonila "Linda" Galván de Chávez, Claremont, California, 2005. Photo courtesy of informant.

Page 114, Celia López, Santa Fe, New Mexico, 2000. Photo courtesy of informant.

Page 116, Salomón "Sal" Lovato, Albuquerque, New Mexico, July 9, 1980. Photo by Isabel A. Rodríguez; with permission.

Page 118, Cesaria Montoya, Las Vegas, New Mexico, April 4, 1994. Photo by Nasario García.

Page 118, Rudy Montoya, Bernalillo, New Mexico, August 22, 2000. Photo by Nasario García.

Page 120, Eddie Torres, Jr., Bernalillo, New Mexico, March 16, 2000. Photo by Nasario García.

Page 134, The Benigno Romero House, Las Vegas, New Mexico.

Page 134, Farmers' tools common among Hispanics of New Mexico and southern Colorado.

Page 139, Adrián and Vicentita Chávez, Albuquerque (Atrisco), New Mexico, June 22, 1980. Photo by Isabel A. Rodríguez; with permission.

Page 144, Filiberto Esquibel, San Miguel del Vado Fiestas, Río Pecos Valley, New Mexico, 1993. Photo by Nedra Westwater; with permission.

Page 148, Adelita Gonzales, Albuquerque, New Mexico, June 15, 1980. Photo by Isabel A. Rodríguez; with permission.

Page 149, Gilberta Herguera Turner, Wiesbaden, Germany, circa 1996. Photo courtesy of informant.

Page 151, César G. López, Claremont, California, 2006. Photo courtesy of informant.

Page 164, Rima Montoya, Escazú, Costa Rica, 2003. Photo courtesy of informant.

Page 166, Emilia Padilla García and her children, Guadalupe (Rincón del Cochino), New Mexico, circa 1910. Photo courtesy of Nasario García.

Page 167, Manuel Pérez, Bernalillo, New Mexico, 2000. Photo by Nasario García.

Page 168, Mariel Romero Ocaranza, Chula Vista, California, 2006. Photo courtesy of informant.

Page 171, Luciano Sánchez, Albuquerque (Los Griegos), New Mexico, October 12, 1980. Photo by Isabel A. Rodríguez; with permission.

Page 178, Teresina Ulibarrí, San Miguel del Vado Fiestas, Río Pecos Valley, New Mexico, 1993. Photo by Nedra Westwater; with permission.

Page 221, Trading post national historic site, Ganado, Arizona.

Page 222, Jesusita Aragón, Las Vegas, New Mexico, April 11, 1994. Photo by Nasario García.

Page 224, Rolando Hinojosa Smith, Austin, Texas, 2005. Photo by Marsha Miller, with permission.

Page 231, Victoria J. Sánchez, Oceanside, California, 2004. Photo courtesy of informant.

Page 235, Adelina Valdez Chávez Baca, Bernalillo, New Mexico, March 3, 2000. Photo by Nasario García.

Page 236, Cruzita Vigil, Las Vegas, New Mexico, October 8, 1994. Photo by Nasario García.

Page 253, Old wood stove, typical in Hispanic homes of New Mexico in early twentieth century.

Page 254, Union Depot, Pueblo, Colorado, July 1993. Photo by Nasario García.

Page 269, Cleveland roller mill, Cleveland, New Mexico.

Page 275, María Teresa Márquez, Albuquerque, New Mexico, 2005. Photo courtesy of informant.

Page 276, Lugardita Anita Montoya, Bernalillo, New Mexico, December 15, 2000. Photo by Nasario García.

Page 278, Eliseo "Cheo" Torres, Albuquerque, New Mexico, 2005. Photo by Greg Johnston, with permission.

Page 295, Portrayal of La Llorona. Costume is probably one hundred years old.

Page 296, Rawlins House, 1899 or 1902, Las Vegas, New Mexico.

Page 301, Rita Leyba Last, Bernalillo, New Mexico, 1999. Photo courtesy of informant.

Jacket photo of Nasario García by Linda I. Carfagno

Suggested Reading

Arrington Wolcott, Jann. *Brujo: Seduced by Evil.* Albuquerque: Route 66 Publishing, Ltd., 1995.

C. de Baca, Elba. *Customs and Traditions.* Booklets I, II & III. Las Vegas, NM: Self-published, n.d.

Campa, Arthur L. *Hispanic Culture in the Southwest.* Norman: University of Oklahoma Press, 1979.

———. *Treasure of the Sangre de Cristos: Tales and Traditions of the Spanish Southwest.* Norman: University of Oklahoma Press, 1963.

Espinosa, Aurelio M. *Cuentos populares españoles.* Tomo I. Stanford: Stanford University Publications, 1923; reprint, New York: AMS Press, Inc., 1967.

Espinosa, Gilberto. *Heroes, Hexes and Haunted Halls.* Albuquerque: Calvin Horn Publisher, Inc., 1972.

Espinosa, José Manuel. *Spanish Folk-Tales from New Mexico.* New York: The American Folklore Society, 1937; reprint, New York: Kraus Reprint Co., 1976.

García, Nasario. *Abuelitos: Stories of the Río Puerco Valley.* Albuquerque: University of New Mexico Press, 1992.

———. *Brujas, bultos, y brasas: Tales of Witchcraft and the Supernatural.* Santa Fe, NM: Western Edge Press, 1999.

———. *Recuerdos de los viejitos: Tales of the Río Puerco.* Albuquerque: University of New Mexico Press, 1987.

———. *Tata: A Voice from the Río Puerco.* Albuquerque: University of New Mexico Press, 1994.

Gardner, Dore. Kay F. Turner, essay. *Niño Fidencio: A Heart Thrown Open.* Santa Fe: Museum of New Mexico Press, 1992.

Heisley, Michael. *An Annotated Bibliography of Chicano Folklore from the Southwestern United States.* Los Angeles: Center for the Study of Comparative Folklore and Mythology, University of California at Los Angeles, 1977.

Jackson, Robert. *Witchcraft and the Occult.* Edison, NJ: Chartwell Books, 1995.

Jameson, R. D., ed. Stanley L. Robe. *Hispanic Legends from New Mexico.* Los Angeles: University of California Press, 1980.

————, ed. Stanley L. Robe. *Hispanic Folktales from New Mexico.* Los Angeles: University of California Press, 1977.

Kutz, Jack. *Mysteries and Miracles of New Mexico.* 2d ed. Corrales, NM: Rhombus Publishing Co., 1990.

Mendoza, Vicente T. *El romance español y el corrido mexicano.* Mexico: Imprenta Universitaria, 1939.

Rael, Juan B. *Cuentos españoles de Colorado y Nuevo México (Spanish Folk Tales from Colorado and New Mexico).* 2d ed. revised, Vols. I and II. Santa Fe: Museum of New Mexico Press, 1977; 1st ed., Stanford University Press, date unknown.

Schlosser, S. E. Retold. *Spooky Southwest: Tales of Hauntings, Strange Happenings, and Other Local Lore.* Guilford, CT: The Globe Pequot Press, 2004.

Simmons, Marc. *Witchcraft in the Southwest: Spanish and Indian Supernaturalism on the Río Grande.* Flagstaff, AZ: Northland Press, 1974.

Sneed, F. Dean. *Ghosts of Trinidad and Las Animas County.* Pueblo, CO: Shusters' Printing, 2002.

Torres, Eliseo "Cheo," and Timothy L. Sawyer, Jr. *Curandero: A Life in Mexican Folk Healing.* Albuquerque: University of New Mexico Press, 2005.

West, John O. *Mexican-American Folklore.* Little Rock, AR: August House Publishers, 1988.

Index

Page numbers for images are indicated by italics.

Índice